The Road to Peterloo

The Road to Peterloo

'A real tour de force'

Carole Bromley

Jacqueline Everett

A CIP catalogue record for this book is available from the British Library.

eBook also available on Amazon

ISBN 978-0-9932772-1-4 (Paperback)

Book layout and cover design by Clare Brayshaw

Prepared and printed by:

York Publishing Services Ltd
64 Hallfield Road
Layerthorpe
York YO31 7ZQ

Tel: 01904 431213

Website: www.yps-publishing.co.uk

Dedication

For Trevor, Anna and Alice
and
Sophia, Aaron and Alex,
and
Thomas Cooper, their great-great-great-great-great
grandfather

About the author

Born in Lancashire, brought up in Stockport, then Cheshire, Jacqueline Everett now lives in Yorkshire.

The Road to Peterloo is the second book in a planned series of interlinked novels stretching from the Napoleonic Wars onwards, exploring historical events through the lives of ordinary people. Her first book, *The Road to Waterloo* is available as an eBook or in paperback through Amazon and can also be ordered through independent booksellers.

jacquelineeverett.co.uk

About the book

This book is the second in a series featuring Thomas Cowper and his fellow soldiers. It can be read on its own, or in conjunction with the first book, *The Road to Waterloo*.

Like the first book, *The Road to Peterloo* was inspired by family history, and in particular, grew from the discovery that my great-great-great grandfather's regiment, after serving as part of the army of occupation in France, was billeted in the heart of London during the years 1819 to 1820, at the height of various scares about imminent revolution. My ancestor was billeted in the parish of St Clement Danes, somewhere between two nearby, but very different public houses favoured by reformers, The Crown and Anchor and The White Lion Tavern.

This national campaign for reform, and the authorities' response to it, lead up to the book's most significant event, the massacre on August 16th 1819 in Manchester of peaceful pro–democracy demonstrators, better known to history as Peterloo.

My story is fiction, but a good number of the events are not. In order to help readers differentiate between my fictional characters and historical characters I mention, I have briefly identified the historical figures in the notes at the end of the book.

Contents

Part Two

1

Risen From The Dead

March 1816, Pas-de-Calais, France

Thomas Cowper wasn't dead. But he might as well have been. He closed his eyes, but he could still taste the stink of swollen horse-flesh, the pall of burning bodies, and see the face of the French officer as Thomas's sabre cleaved through his skull.

He swept away the raindrops streaming down his cheeks and looked back along their ragged lines, men and horses scarcely alive in this bone-bitter spring. He counted the columns winding across the low hills and open plains. The world he had once known had changed forever since that day. How would any of them find their way now without a war to fight? Alive and yet not alive. What would the future hold for them? He straightened his cape and hunched his aching shoulders tighter, trying not to remember the gaps where once so many old friends had ridden.

He wound his fingers through Fearless's bedraggled mane; at least she had survived, but he still longed for the easy familiarity of the men he had lived with for so many years. And then, of course, there was Grace, who wasn't dead but who might as well be.

Thomas hadn't stopped writing letters to Grace. He'd merely stopped posting them. So every day, as he drilled his men and endeavoured to keep the great survivor, Private man Littlethorpe, out of trouble, he found himself imagining her new life, strutting across the stage, young men and old alike her admirers ... brooding over her last, all too brief, letter: *I was so relieved to hear you are safe, Thomas... and that the great war is over at last ... I have had an offer from the gentleman manager of a London theatre that I now feel free to accept.*

Sometimes Thomas thought he'd rather be in mortal danger and still have a sweetheart. It was foolish he knew, but in a year where there was much talk of Noah and the Great Flood, this one-sided correspondence kept him from drowning.

And still it rained: cornfields flattened, tracks turned into fast-running streams, main roads into bogs, village ponds into lakes, their own horses in as poor a condition as he'd ever seen them. And this less than a year after the Peace, when the French still viewed the army of occupation with ill-concealed hostility. To have to find food for English soldiers and horses when farmers themselves were going hungry was held to be the final insult to their nation.

Men had taken to going out in company, never walking alone, always looking behind them. What with Littlethorpe's ill-temper at any imagined injury their reluctant hosts might offer and Thomas's misery over surviving at all, not to mention the rest of them, Thomas reckoned their lines must have looked far from triumphant as they trudged through those first autumn mists to Normandy. But, at last, they had been allocated their appointed place in the British zone of occupation, though he imagined they would be no more welcome in the Pas-de-Calais than they had been in Paris or Normandy.

'Serjeant Cowper.'

He turned in his saddle and saw Littlethorpe trotting towards him, pulling to a halt as he drew level. Littlethorpe leant forward so only Thomas might hear.

'Serjeant Fallowfield's … not bloody dead after all.'

Thomas felt his face redden. The last time he'd seen Fallowfield, in Brussels, his wounds were declared undoubtedly mortal. He'd been telling himself over and over again, these last months, that no news was good news, that Fallowfield's death would not have merited anything other than a note in the paymaster's ledger. In a more rational frame of mind, he knew that this was nonsense and any news about Fallowfield would have spread through the ranks as quickly as the fires after Salamanca.

'Expected back with us in the next hour or two.'

Thomas leant closer to Littlethorpe. 'You know this for certain?'

Littlethorpe put his finger to his lips and patted his sabretache.

'Just delivered the letter to Captain Haywood, Serjeant. Gave him a bit of a shock and all. He let the cat right out of the bag.' Thomas nodded. Haywood was not known for his discretion. 'I thought you should know,' Littlethorpe said.

Fallowfield had survived. Good men had died but he still lived. Was there no justice in this world? From Littlethorpe's expression it was clear that Thomas was not the only man in the Regiment to have wished Fallowfield dead. Fallowfield's drinking had got worse before Waterloo and his face had deepened to the colour of curdled blood, 'a fiery beacon from Hell,' as the Methodist Ashby had put it, 'which should warn us all about the perils of drink.'

'So he is … fully recovered?'

Thomas tried to keep his voice steady. Over the years Littlethorpe had learnt to read Thomas's face like a book. Thomas wondered if not knowing his letters gave Littlethorpe an advantage in deciphering everything else. Littlethorpe, his self- appointed 'cousin' from neighbouring Nottinghamshire, was widely considered to be a rogue of the first order, but Thomas knew another side to the man. He understood Littlethorpe's pain in his desperate curses and threats when his Maria and all the other women followers were sent back from France to Portugal; his maniacal slashing at trees when he'd heard his beloved Dog had been killed by a Polish lancer. Thomas recognised another lost soul when he saw one, grateful for Littlethorpe's fierce loyalty, which had kept them both from madness ever since. Not that either of them spoke its name.

'Recovered enough to pick a fight.'

'So why would that be, then?' Thomas found himself saying.

'Well, think about it.'

Thomas distractedly noted that Littlethorpe never addressed him as his rank required, except when in company.

Littlethorpe bent closer to Thomas. 'So how did Fallowfield get shot when he was supposed to be minding those Netherlanders at the rear? They were all bloody terrified of him and the crapauds never got that far, did they?'

Thomas shook his head. 'Maybe he was just … careless, turned his back on them for a minute.'

Littlethorpe laughed. 'Na. Not him. Say what you will about him, he was never careless.'

'Unlucky then?'

Littlethorpe snorted. 'More like lucky whoever it was didn't make a better job of it.'

'Littlethorpe.'

Littlethorpe unexpectedly reverted to an unusually humble self. 'Just thought you'd want to know, Serjeant. S'ony what everybody's been saying. That he must have been set upon by one of our own.'

Thomas shook his head. 'That's surely just gossip.'

Littlethorpe leant across further and whispered, 'Except someone round here really doesn't like Serjeant Fallowfield.'

Thomas heart jumped. 'It hardly follows that this ... someone shot him.'

Littlethorpe shrugged his shoulders. 'Maybe not. Only Serjeant Fallowfield knows for sure. And if it's one of ours, then I expect the Serjeant might have an idea as to who it is, eh?'

'Then Serjeant Fallowfield should report the offender to his senior officer. Though it would be his word against another's, and I doubt that any of our officers would make any decision merely based on his word. Unless, of course, the other soldier was known to be of poor character.'

But Littlethorpe wasn't going to let the matter drop.

'Must have been somebody who went to the rear ... who can pick a man off even with one of our bloody useless carbines.'

Thomas raised his hands to his mouth and blew some warmth into them. 'You know, or suspect, who this ... someone is, then?'

Littlethorpe looked at Thomas as if to say he only intended to tell Thomas as much as he thought wise, as though he was once again threading his way across the quicksands of the Tormes, testing every step before him with his great stick.

'Men babble about things they don't mean to, when they're asleep ... when they're upset.' Littlethorpe stopped, as though to check his way was clear.

Thomas remembered that night when they had bivouacked with Haywood in the forest on their way to rejoin the Regiment. As Haywood's cover serjeant, he and Littlethorpe had taken it in turns to keep watch round the campfire, both sleeping fitfully, reliving Waterloo in their dreams. He wondered what Littlethorpe might have heard.

'And what might this particular man have been upset about?'

'Well, the talk is that we lost a Netherlander drummer boy, who was being minded by our dear Serjeant Fallowfield. Found dead on his knees shot in the back. I reckon that someone decided to stop Fallowfield from doing any more damage to our friends, who might, or might not, have been planning to run away.'

Thomas set his jaw. Who would be believed, if it came to it? A newly promoted serjeant, or a seasoned veteran, a lynchpin of the regiment for close on fifteen years? Then again, it was much more likely Fallowfield would find another way to take his revenge.

'You didn't see who…?'

'Course I didn't.' Littlethorpe paused. 'I was with you.'

'You were?'

'When we weren't arse-up fighting the bloody crapauds.'

'At the roll call?'

'Littlethorpe paused again. 'After the roll call. Remember, we were together the entire time, Serjeant.'

'So we were.' Thomas gripped the reins and turned Fearless's head away and cantered to the front of the column, though Fearless was slow to respond, seemingly as unwilling to exert herself as the rest of them. Fallowfield back in the Regiment, alive and well. And no doubt bent on retribution.

2

A Changed Man?

March 1816, Pas-de-Calais, France

They had paused at the crossroads, adjusted the girths on their horses and were now waiting on the brow of the hill, where the road divided. Thomas looked around him. It reminded him of the rolling hills and open skies of the South Downs with its great white cliffs that plunged into the sea; where the Regiment had spent so many years patrolling, expecting the French invasion which, in the end, never came.

Fallowfield did not come alone from the east. He was accompanied by Royal Horse Artillery men who burst through the morning light with a great clatter of horses and gun limbers. They put on such a show it was as if the 36th Dragoons were the enemy that the artillerymen planned to impress to the death.

It had finally stopped raining but in the general hubbub it had taken some minutes for even Thomas, never mind the men, to realise that Fallowfield was back in their midst. Thomas heard their surprise rumbling slowly through the ranks as Fallowfield came towards them, smiling, his face relaxed, hands slipping the reins as though he was just out for a ride. Surely this was not the same man they had lived with for the last ten years? As Fallowfield moved forward to pay his compliments to Captain Haywood, Thomas sensed an uneasy question snake its way back along the ranks. Perhaps they had misjudged the man? Perhaps he'd been chastened, as they all had, by the slaughter at Waterloo?

Thomas tried to resist the thought. He scrutinised Fallowfield's face, the signs of heavy drinking almost gone; his nose no longer Ashby's 'fiery beacon from hell', his greying hair giving him a distinguished appearance. The big man seemed amiable and at ease, exuding his old recruiting serjeant charm.

~

Serjeant Jack Fallowfield eyed the figure half-hidden by Haywood's bulk. If it isn't bloody Cowper. Likely trying to work out how I survived. Well, it wasn't on account of those herbs of yours. Na. God was on my side that day. And from henceforth. So, if you're thinking it's only Jack Fallowfield returning to see justice done, you're much mistaken. It's God you've got to worry about, now. You can't shoot a man in the back and expect the Almighty to turn a blind eye.

Fallowfield patted his sabretache, which held the Bible the Scottish minister had given him, and the lead ball they'd dug out of his shoulder blade, to remind him. Though he wasn't likely to forget. Not for a minute. Cowper would have to pay, of course, one day, when the time was ready for the vengeance of the Lord.

Can't see Freer. Now he'll need watching. Bloody radical. Or Webster. Probably still playing the invalid on his family's estate. No backbone, the so-called upper classes. Ah, Haywood has returned my greeting. Call that a smile? I'll be watching you too, sir. Jack's back. As if I'd never been away.

Fallowfield heard his companion, Captain Rowlandson, whisper, 'Good-hearted fellow, Haywood. First met him when he was a young lieutenant in the Peninsula.'

Fallowfield turned to Rowlandson. The captain had taken Fallowfield under his wing from the moment he'd joined Rowlandson's Bible classes. Fallowfield smiled back.

That's all Jack Fallowfield needed … a couple of good-hearted fellows to twist round his little finger and persuade he was as well-intentioned as themselves.

Fallowfield bowed and retired to his former place in the ranks, the men clearing a path before him. Fallowfield hadn't been so pleased with himself for quite some time.

~

Thomas didn't feel reassured. Although Fallowfield hadn't looked like a man intent on taking his revenge, Thomas couldn't help but notice his eyes. They were as penetrating as they'd ever been, able to cut deep into a man's soul. No; behind the bonhomie, the Fallowfield he knew only too well, hadn't disappeared. He was back to his old tricks, charming the people that mattered, whether new recruits whose bounty money would find its way into his pockets, or senior officers he intended to make use of.

Thomas turned to study Captain Haywood's remarkably unlined face. 'Bloody baby face,' Fallowfield used to call him, in his cups. Thomas noted unhappily that Haywood looked gratified, even if surprised, by Fallowfield's respectful greeting. Haywood was as good-natured an officer as Thomas had ever served under, and it was not his way to think ill of any fellow, until proven beyond doubt.

Thomas suddenly felt his elbow jogged. It was Littlethorpe, who had found their old companion, Byrne, bringing up the rear with the newly arrived artillery soldiers.

Thomas couldn't believe it. 'We thought we'd lost you.' Byrne grasped Thomas's hand with the muscular grip of the expert cricketer he was, grinning, his dark hair flopping over his eyes.

'Well, it's been a bit of a business, one way and another. Got cut about early on. Bleeding all over, but nothing too bad and then poor Ashby gets sliced across the face … left eye half hanging out. So I get him to the back as sharp as I can. Then it all goes black. And, damn me, Ashby loses his eye, but then is as right as rain. But while he gets pensioned off, I keep going down with fever after fever, like a wet afternoon.'

Thomas shook his hand again. 'We've missed you.'

'Not like we've missed old arse face, though.' Littlethorpe said, borrowing Bonnie Murphy's favourite phrase for Fallowfield. 'Byrne says, he's now after finding God. It beggars belief, don't it, but Byrne'll tell you.'

Thomas hesitated, though if anyone knew what Fallowfield had been up to while recovering in Brussels, it would surely be Byrne.

Byrne grinned again, keen to repeat the tale he'd already told Littlethorpe.

'They reckon he was on his deathbed when he saw the light.'

Thomas couldn't resist stating the obvious. 'But he's not dead.'

Byrne carried on, clearly determined not to have his story deflected in the telling. 'But then, when he didn't die, I suppose it might have seemed like bad luck to change his mind.'

Byrne, growing up a Catholic, on one of the great Protestant estates in Ireland, before the family took fright and moved back to England, was regarded as only second to Captain Webster in his grasp of doctrinal differences.

Thomas was still disbelieving. 'You mean the nuns persuaded him he should repent, commend his soul to God and then he would be saved?'

Byrne shook his head, dismissing the possibility of Catholicism capturing Fallowfield's immortal soul.

'Na. You wouldn't catch Fallowfield taking any notice of foreigners, especially not women. It wasn't the nuns of the Sacred Heart who got to him. It was a Scottish minister, you know, one of those that let you off your sins if you find God's grace.' Byrne's voice rose higher. 'And then you're one of the Elect. Like you've been chosen.'

Thomas once again heard his grieving mother sobbing that Michael had been God's Chosen One. Michael, the brother she'd accused him of killing.

Thomas tugged his thoughts back to Fallowfield. 'You're quite sure?'

Byrne nodded. 'Almost worth joining their ranks, isn't it? Though,' Byrne laughed, 'I'm not sure I reckon that much to any God that's got Fallowfield on the muster roll. Better off sticking to cricket.'

Thomas smiled. 'That's no change then.'

Byrne shrugged his shoulders. 'As if God had anything to do with that mess, eh?'

Thomas sighed. What with his mother's obsessions about God and Beelzebub, he'd had his fill of most shades of religion.

Littlethorpe jabbed his finger in Byrne's direction. 'You've told the Serjeant what else Fallowfield's after finding and all?'

Byrne frowned. 'Give me a chance.' He turned to Thomas. 'It's Boy. They say he's after finding Boy.'

Surely not? Thomas thought. True, Boy had been there. With the Netherlanders. He was a witness. But the argument Fallowfield had was with Thomas, not a mute seven-year old. Then again, Fallowfield was always thorough about disposing of the evidence. Thank God he'd sent Boy away to Brussels with Bonnie Murphy.

3

Crossing The Dunes

March 1816, Neufchâtel-Hardelot,
Pas-de-Calais, France

Beyond the forest, the old farmhouse stood like a beacon on the top of the cliffs, surrounded by crumbling fortifications. It had been used for years by the French army as a lookout post, and now the house and its stables were to be home for Haywood and thirty of his men. The soldiers quickly began to make themselves at home.

Suddenly there was a shout. Littlethorpe had spotted signs of fresh pig dung.

'Possibly wild boar,' Haywood wondered aloud. 'We don't want one of those spooking the horses. Best check, eh, Serjeant Cowper.'

Littlethorpe knew about pigs. And what was a wild boar other than a very large, undoubtedly ill-tempered pig.

'So what do you think, Littlethorpe? Wild boar?' Thomas asked.

Littlethorpe looked at the dung and the tracks and shook his head. 'Just farmyard ones, I'd say. Escaped, most like. Not that they'll be any sweeter tempered.'

It took them nigh on three hours to capture the two runaway pigs, prompting Littlethorpe to declare, as they fastened them at last into a couple of pigsties, 'No bloody wonder the French didn't bother to run after them. But just wait, eh, till they're properly fattened up.'

It was time for stable duties. Thomas enjoyed looking after the horses, the daily rhythm of mucking out, watering, feeding and grooming. Tonight too, it was a chance to give Fearless a decent straw bed out of the wind and rain, where he could untangle her mane and tail and groom her coat till it glistened.

Thomas stayed behind that evening until he was satisfied he had done as much as he could. He rested his head against the mare's neck. Without her steadiness under fire, he might have been killed several times in the last ten years.

'Well, my Fearless,' he said. 'We have survived. Now it's my turn to look after you.'

He patted her haunches with a last good night and left the darkness to the restless murmur of hooves and the familiar sounds of the horses settling themselves down to sleep.

~

A child's crying. Thomas dismounts and makes his way towards the noise … a small boy, in a pool of blood, between his dying mother's legs. The boy screams and runs off through the dead. Thomas begins to run too, shouting, 'I won't hurt you' and now the child is suddenly running towards him but pursued by a company of cavalry at full gallop. Thomas screams at them to halt but they keep on and on …

Thomas woke up, suffocating, sweating, in the ice-cold room he shared with his fellow serjeants. He had to get out of there. He pulled on his stable dress, taking care to strap on his sabre.

~

13

He headed away from the farm over the hill towards the sea but, even under a moonlit sky, it was a foolhardy enterprise. He scrambled slowly downwards over rough paths towards the low cliffs protecting the beach. He stopped and breathed as deeply as he could in the biting air, remembering another cliff top, ten years ago, his head spinning to the throb of the waves, the jangling chorus of birds mocking all his puny efforts to seek forgiveness. But then, above the clamour, Will Freer's voice scolding him as he pulled him back from the edge. He wished Freer were here now. He would know how to keep Boy safe. Freer would know what to do about Fallowfield. Freer always knew what to do.

Thomas picked his way closer to the shore and the vast hillocks of sand guarding the beach. He'd obviously missed the path, so there was no alternative but to cross them, if he wanted to reach the sea.

~

Anchoring himself with his sabre, he stabbed it into the slopes, slowly pulling himself up. He'd forgotten how hard it was to climb over shifting sand. As he reached the summit overlooking what felt like a great emptiness, he sat down to tip out his overflowing boots and the little avalanches tumbled into heaps. Thomas ran his fingers through them, excavating below the dune's surface to dig into its inner core as cold as death itself.

He heard a noise, turned and saw Will Freer standing there, laughing, shouting at him, daring him, and they both started to roll down the slopes of the sand dunes like madmen. But when he got to the bottom, and stood up to brush the sand from his trousers, and turned to look behind him, there was nothing there. Just the memory of himself and Freer racing across the open sands, abandoning Byrne's cricket match in favour of swimming out to the rocks, Thomas easily out-running the lame Freer to the sea and then Freer out-swimming him to the rocks. They had been happy. In the midst of war, they had been happy.

Thomas edged closer to the shore, picking over his memories. He remembered learning to swim, how Freer had persuaded him into the old horse ponds in Blatchington, how he had pummelled and bent him into shape so he could float, how Freer had saved him from sinking when he began to panic; he remembered the sheer pleasure of floating on his back, gazing at the sky.

He let out a great howl, remembering those already lost, his mother, her dead babies, his brother Michael and the roll call of men he'd served with for so many years. 'And you're supposed to be a soldier,' the voices mocked. Still trembling, he forced himself to stand up and go on, until he heard the steady beat of waves folding onto the shore, until he found himself gradually soothed and calmed by their rhythms. After all, Boy was well away from here in Bonnie's care and Bonnie Murphy was as formidable as an entire troop of cavalry.

~

He glanced at the sky. It was time to go back. He turned away from the sea, walking into the dawn as it sliced open the darkness, red-raw and orange, its brilliance vanishing under a sulky white sky. Thomas paused to breathe new life into his hands, and noticed a few flakes gently skirmishing. He hurried up the hill, head down, and arrived back only just ahead of the main body of snow. Their farmhouse was corralled inside an old castle, once built to repel the English; but now the English were billeted in its ruins, equally determined to quell the French, should any successor to the Tyrant try to follow in his footsteps.

As for Fallowfield? What would Freer say? 'Watch your back and be ready to fight the damn bastard,' he'd tell him. He and Freer had done it before, and who was to say they couldn't do it again? When Freer was here. Thomas began to feel his spirits revive. He would be ready. As long as Freer was by his side. As long as Boy was out of Fallowfield's way.

4

You're Safe Now

March 1816, Waterloo, The Low Countries

Boy woke up sobbing. She was slipping away out of reach, disappearing down a long tunnel and, however hard he ran after her, she kept on running. He blew his nose. Neither Ashby nor Bonnie seemed to have heard him. He wished Thomas were there. If Thomas heard him crying he'd hold him tight, whispering 'you're safe now', over and over again, till he finally fell asleep. And whenever Thomas held him, it was like his mother was still alive, laughing and blowing kisses into his ear.

Boy didn't mind treating Bonnie like his mother ... most of the time. But he didn't want to forget his other mother. He got out of bed and tipped his worn boots upside down, and counted out the money he'd put away. He'd almost enough now. Almost enough to pay his way.

Ashby had written the address in his book next to the map that Freer had drawn for him, but Boy had also remembered what Freer had said. 'About a hundred and fifty miles due west in a château near a town called Désvres, in northern France.' Freer was leaving any day now, to rejoin the regiment. To Désvres, where Thomas was.

You have to be good at remembering things, if you don't talk. He loved words, but not how they fix things, not how they make things too sure of themselves, when nothing is like that. Without words no one would try to make you explain things, to make you say things you don't want to. If you don't talk, people don't bother asking you what happened, what you think and how you feel. No one tries to make you say things you can't ever say.

Thomas understood. He called Thomas, Thomas. In his head. But if he spoke words aloud then he'd have to call him Serjeant Cowper, like everybody else.

Best say nothing. Best keep your own counsel, Ashby says. So he did.

5

The Château

The 36th was to move inland, a day's ride away, some of them to an abandoned château, the rest scattered across the local villages. Haywood, as usual, preferred to find his own lodgings, so Thomas was not surprised when Haywood announced that, after they'd accompanied the Regiment to the château, they and a small number of their men were to make their way back to their own billet.

'Subject, of course, to Acting Lieutenant-Colonel Bridges's approval,' he'd added hastily.

The roads were sticky and heavy underfoot, though the occasional pathways through the woodland of oak and beech offered better-drained routes over their chalky outcrops. By the time they'd made their first stop, the light drizzle of the morning had retreated, leaving a pale sky on the horizon, with darker clouds hovering above but not, Thomas thought, promising snow. The château itself, its three-storey central block flanked by two side wings and its steeply pitched roofs, was one of the grandest houses Thomas had seen, even though it had been standing empty and neglected for some years now.

It was Littlethorpe who first saw Freer, riding behind Captain Webster into the grounds. Two more of their own back from the dead, though Webster still had a cadaverous look, haunted almost, with a white-rimmed scar extending from his chin to his cheek. Haywood greeted Webster with due formality but with a warmth in his greeting which Thomas couldn't help but notice.

Thomas had initially hung back behind Haywood, restraining himself from rushing up to welcome his old friend. But Haywood soon moved away, having spotted another officer, an artillery captain, who also seemed to be waiting for the baggage wagons to arrive.

Thomas was shocked at what he saw. Freer, always scrawny, was painfully thin. He'd aged a decade in less than a year. But, lying trapped under your horse for a whole night, expecting to die, was bound to change any man. Yes, Waterloo had changed them all. Thomas hoped his face would not betray him. He moved nearer and Freer smiled back, even if it was only a shadow of his former grin.

'About bloody time and all,' Thomas found himself saying in sheer relief as he slapped Freer's back. To think he'd nearly lost Freer as well. He shuddered to imagine what would have happened if Bonnie Murphy and Louise Freer hadn't braved the scavengers that night to find their husbands.

Freer ran his hands through his mop of red hair. 'Can't get rid of me, can you, eh.'

Thomas joshed back, 'So, what are you doing here, of all places?'

'God knows, but whatever we're supposed to be doing, Wellington expects us to be here for some time. Could be up to five years, they reckon.'

'I meant, what are you doing at Headquarters? You've not gone and got a staff officer's job, have you?'

'Hardly.' Freer smiled. 'No, Louise is going to teach at the regimental school.'

Thomas was puzzled. 'Since when did the Regiment have a school?'

'Since we were at peace. At the depot. And now it's moving out here. So she'll be teaching the little ones in the day and the serjeant school master will teach the men in the evenings.'

Thomas tried to imagine Littlethorpe trading his night's drinking for a chance to learn to read and write.

'That's where the future lies,' Freer said.

Freer, the great optimist, the proud possessor of the banned *Rights of Man*, had not been entirely crushed then. Thomas, though often not agreeing with him, was relieved to see that Freer's convictions had not been extinguished in spite of his weary exterior.

'You never know, they might even be persuaded to let us have the vote one day,' Freer whispered. 'Look, I'll show you round.'

Thomas automatically slowed his pace to accommodate Freer's, whose limp was more pronounced than ever after his injuries. As Freer struggled over the uneven ground, Thomas could have sworn he saw a shadow fall across his face, the lines around his mouth already etched more deeply, his red hair beginning to lose its colour.

'Where are Louise and Billy?' Thomas asked.

Freer brushed his hair, as unruly as ever, back from his face.

'Following in the wagons along with that artillery captain's daughter.' Freer pointed to the officer now talking to Haywood.

~

Louise Freer sat back and almost smiled. Nearly there. The baggage wagons had been following the outliers of an artillery regiment from Brussels for the last hundred and fifty or so miles. Not safe in a coach, they said. Too many of Boney's soldiers still on the loose. But away from Waterloo at last. Alive. Just. Will's leg would never be the same again. As for Will himself … well, hadn't they all changed? But the months Will had spent completing Webster's plans for the Regimental Memorial had given them both some time to recover. It had also given her the chance to renew her acquaintance with Captain Charles Webster; to remember him collecting his parcels of art supplies from her father's receiving house, giving her his paintings in lieu of payment. She pursed her lips. Sometimes she wondered what might have happened if her father had not been a publican…

Still Webster was as courteous as ever to Will and herself, though there was such a warmth of feeling between the two men, she sometimes felt excluded and half-wished Webster would find himself a wife. But Webster looked destined to be a lifelong bachelor, now more concerned about the state of souls than soldiering.

Mind, her Will had always been more interested in the Battle for Progress than he was in soldiering. 'Tyranny must be defeated, in whatever form.' Well, Will Freer was an honest, free-thinking man, who would always find a cause to fight.

He'd even persuaded Captain Webster that schoolmistresses rather than schoolmasters, and Louise, in particular would be ideally suited to teach small children. Webster had also promised to find her an assistant, who would teach plain sewing to the girls.

Louise had been thinking a good deal about this since they'd been joined by young Joanna Rowlandson and her aunt. Louise contemplated the fair-haired girl with striking blue eyes, who was happily amusing her Billy, as she had been doing for most of the journey. After all, it wasn't as though she was a gentleman officer's daughter. Artillery officers rose by aptitude and merit alone, not by purchase.

Their daughters couldn't afford to be quite so fussy.

~

Freer led Thomas in the direction of the outbuildings, where the schoolrooms were now set up. Relieved to be out of earshot of any listeners, Thomas could wait no longer.

'So what news?'

'Murphy's Bonnie has wed again.'

'What?'

'To Ashby, of all people.'

Thomas thought he must have misheard. 'Ashby? Are you quite sure you mean Ashby, the Methodist, won't touch a drop of drink, let us pray Ashby?'

Freer laughed. 'When I first got his letter, I had to read it at least twice. A peculiar match, if there ever was one, what with Ashby being so pious and Bonnie liking her tipple and as loud as ever. She had her eye on his pension, I imagine.'

'Well, she'd have used up the money I gave her for Boy and it's not as though a soldier's widow can live on fresh air.'

Nor their wives for that matter, Thomas almost added. He could still feel the angry wrench of his hair when Bonnie had scraped it into a regulation queue, all those years ago, when she'd accused him and Freer of denying Dermot Murphy his share of their bounty money.

As long as she and Ashby were looking after Boy, Thomas thought, he shouldn't worry. 'So, where are they now?'

'At Waterloo.'

'At Waterloo?'

'She came back from Brussels when the tourists started to arrive. Then dragged Ashby along as well.'

23

Thomas was sure he'd misheard. 'Tourists? To the battlefield?'

Freer pushed his hair back from his face again. 'They pay the guides well. Even more for first-hand accounts.'

'Then Bonnie has no intention of coming back to the Regiment?'

Freer shook his head. 'Why would she?' Freer paused. 'Though the place isn't really the same without her effing at Murphy and blinding at everyone else, is it?'

'And Ashby?' Thomas liked Ashby.

Freer smiled. 'Still as steady as they come and doing as well as a man can with one eye.'

'And Boy?'

'He was selling souvenirs … cockades and cap badges, that kind of thing, helping Bonnie make a living.'

Thomas's heart missed a couple of beats. 'Was?'

Freer raised his hands. 'Sorry, I didn't mean to … No, he's fit and well. You'll see for yourself soon enough. He'll be arriving with Louise in the next hour or so.'

'Here. But I told him he had to stay with Bonnie.'

'He was desperate to come and see you.'

'But he was safe.'

'He hated it.'

Thomas started to pace about. 'We'll have to hide him somewhere. Before they get here. I need to find Littlethorpe. To get Boy out of the way.'

'Why, Cowper? Why?' Freer gripped his arm. 'What the hell's going on?'

Thomas hesitated. How could he possibly explain? 'Later. I'll explain later. When we've found somewhere to hide him.'

'But where?'

'You and Louise. You must have somewhere …?'

'We've a cottage in the village, but …'

'Perfect. Now let's find Littlethorpe.'

Thomas headed back to the main courtyard, Freer trailing after him.

'All right, all right, but just tell me what the hell's going on, will you?'

Thomas stopped dead. Fallowfield and the rest of the troop were riding through the château gates. Freer followed his gaze. 'That's not bloody Fallowfield I can see, is it? Talk about rising from the dead.' Freer grimaced. 'He's not been up to his old tricks again, has he?'

Thomas bit his lip. 'Let's just get Boy out of his way.'

~

Joanna Rowlandson bounced young Billy Freer on her lap and wondered yet again about the boy who never said anything. He looked about seven or eight, but Mrs Freer would talk to him without ever seeming to expect an answer. Mrs Freer was a plain-speaking woman and over the last week Joanna had come to admire her determination to make the most of her new career as the schoolmistress in the regimental school.

But Joanna's mind was really on other things. She wondered whether her father was fully recovered and whether his guns had really saved countless lives. Joanna had last seen him over a year ago, shortly before he'd left for the Low Countries. He would send for her, he'd promised, once they'd stopped Boney in his tracks. And now they had, he'd written to say he was to be stationed in the Pas-de-Calais, and if she and Aunt Rowley could manage to join him, she would enjoy the company of the other officers' families. Joanna smiled. She knew he indulged her. Aunt Rowley was always reminding her of that, but it was hard living in her mother's shadow. She had so much to live up to.

'You are very like her,' he would say, gently tapping her knee; but who else did he have to indulge and who else did she have to look up to? She was so looking forward to seeing him and all the tales he would have to tell about defeating Boney. She could hardly wait. His letters had been rather dull, full of Bible meetings and other boring things, as if he thought a young girl wouldn't want to hear about Waterloo. Sometimes, though, he'd treated her like a boy who was keen to understand how things worked. He'd once taught her about the trajectory of cannon shot, as if it were something that she might need to know. She didn't mind, though. She just wished she could be as clever as he was, show him she'd been worthy of his lessons. One day she would teach geometry too.

But now she wondered what he would think of her agreeing to help Mrs Freer at the school. She suspected enjoying the company of a mere troop sergeant-major's wife was not what he'd meant. She hadn't even dared mention it to Aunt Rowley.

Suddenly the wagon juddered to a halt. Joanna hugged Billy, who'd begun to cry, whilst the young boy clung to Louise, who remained as calm as ever, whilst Aunt Rowley snapped her fan shut, ready to do battle.

There was a hubbub directly outside their wagon. 'Mrs Freer,' someone shouted.

'Littlethorpe?' Louise looked out of the wagon. 'Is all well?' The soldier shook his head. 'Serjeant Cowper's sent me.' He dismounted and moved closer to Louise, whispering in her ear. The boy was to go with him. Joanna noticed Louise waver as she handed him over. But the boy smiled and seemed eager to go with the soldier, waving to them, as he was swung securely into place.

Louise leant over and spoke quietly to Joanna. 'Please, Miss Rowlandson, I should be very grateful if neither you, nor your aunt, tell anyone else that the boy was travelling with us.'

'But what about all the soldiers?'

'They will soon be dispersed far and wide and will think no more of the matter, I'm sure.'

'Is the boy in some kind of trouble?'

'No, but it was a mistake to bring him.'

Joanna was puzzled. 'A mistake?'

Louise frowned and clearly was going to say no more on the subject. Joanna held Billy close, her chin lightly touching his warm head covered in ginger down, and wondered: what kind of place was she was coming to?

In the silence, the last half-mile or so seemed to Joanna to stretch endlessly before them. She smiled nervously across at Louise and was rewarded by a smile. Louise leant forward. 'I'm looking forward to our time together working in the school. You're good with Billy and I expect you'll be just as good with all the other little children.' Louise held out her arms. Joanna passed Billy to her, half-asleep, and Louise cradled him on her shoulder as they bumped along the last yards of their journey.

~

Boy liked Littlethorpe. He'd been a friend of Dermot's too. And he'd been just as sad as Littlethorpe when both Dog and Dermot had been killed by the lancers.

Boy liked it when the men gave him a ride on their horses. He wasn't frightened. He used to help them muck them out. And when they'd been down in Weymouth, Thomas had allowed him to ride Fearless holding the reins, with Thomas sitting behind him. Not that he wanted to be a cavalryman or even a drummer boy. Not if it meant strangers scratching up your bones out of the earth hardly a year later, looking for souvenirs.

~

Littlethorpe tightened his grip. The lad was as skinny as a lath. Cowper'd never forgive him if Boy came to any harm. Soft as anything when he used to play with Dog. Not like most his age. And now with bloody Fallowfield on the hunt for him, the lad's walking straight back into the lion's den. Littlethorpe could only guess at what had happened at Waterloo but, whatever did happen, Boy seemed to be in the firing line as well now. And with Fallowfield licking everybody's arse since he got back, how the hell is Cowper going to keep the lad out of harm's way?

~

Thomas heard the low rumble of the wagons first before they saw them enter the driveway. He and Freer looked at each other.

'No sign of Littlethorpe,' Thomas muttered.

Freer smiled. 'Well, that's a relief.'

'But he might have missed them altogether,' Thomas fretted.

Freer turned to face Thomas. 'I gave him very clear instructions and you, of all people, know that Littlethorpe is as good at navigating woods, as he is rivers.'

Thomas heard the reproach in Freer's voice. 'You're right, of course,' but his eyes stayed fixed upon the advancing wagons, hoping that Littlethorpe had got there in time.

~

Will Freer watched Thomas staring at the baggage train. He couldn't have been happier to see Cowper but the man always did worry enough for the entire regiment and today he was practically twitching. What the hell was going on?

~

Joanna hung back, letting Louise and Billy get down from the wagon first, straight into the arms of her husband, but then her father appeared, looking much older than she remembered him. He had always made light of his injuries, writing to say that she and Aunt Rowley were not to worry, and that the nuns were taking excellent care of him. But Aunt Rowley, too, seemed concerned and fussed more than usual around her brother. He was in the company of a young cavalry captain, a sturdy fellow with light brown curls and a pleasant face, who offered to take her bag. They now seemed to be surrounded by soldiers. Another cavalry man, a serjeant, who seemed to be on good terms with her father, also came up perhaps to assist with the luggage, whilst yet another cavalry sergeant was helping Mrs Freer with Billy. Everywhere there was noise and commotion.

It was only when she turned round to look at her father once more that she realised that one of the cavalry sergeants, the older one with the grey eyes and rather large nose, was standing still and smiling, as though expecting some kind of invitation to conversation. Indeed, her father turned to her and said, 'My dear, this is Serjeant Fallowfield, one of the fine fellows who attended the Bible classes we organised while convalescing in the convent.'

Joanna's spirits fell further. She was worried about her father's new-found religious fervour. She had also been advised by a senior officer's wife that Wellington himself

29

frowned on such things as Bible classes that cut across the ranks. Then again, her father had risen through the ranks, and she began to wonder if he felt more at home with a serjeant than with a fellow captain.

Formalities with Serjeant Fallowfield over with, her father turned sharply on his heel and insisted on escorting her and Aunt Rowley to introduce them to the young captain still waiting in the courtyard. The curly-haired captain was attended by the other cavalry serjeant, the one with the brown eyes, who was hopping restlessly from foot to foot. Troop Serjeant-Major Freer had stopped to talk to him. She heard him say. 'You must visit us as soon as you can. We're in the cottage with the double attic windows on the road to the church.'

'Better than that,' Mrs Freer added loudly, you can help us with our luggage down the driveway.'

Joanna's father hurried her towards the captain, still guarding her bag.

'Captain Haywood, may I introduce you to my sister and my daughter. 'You'll remember I spoke of them often when we were in the Peninsula.'

Her father now turned to Joanna. 'This is Captain Haywood, an old friend of mine.' Captain Haywood bowed. 'Miss Rowlandson, Miss Rowlandson, I am delighted to make your acquaintance. Your father did indeed tell me a great deal about you both.'

Joanna smiled. So was this the type of company her father hoped she would keep?

~

Thomas was no longer worrying quite so much about Boy. Freer had managed to whisper that he and Littlethorpe had ridden safely away back to their cottage. No, Thomas was worried about Freer. Even building up his boot again had not compensated fully for the shortness of his injured leg. And he looked worn out. Thomas glanced at Freer and Louise, arm in arm next to him, Freer leaning on Louise, and offered to take Billy from Freer's other arm. Young Billy, or William Thomas, as he had been christened, was not happy to be passed to him. Like Boy, kicking and screaming, when he'd first found him.

'So tell me, Thomas,' Louise turned to him as they walked. 'What's all this business with Boy about?'

Thomas looked at Billy instead. 'It's a long story.'

Louise frowned. 'You mean you don't want to tell me,' she scolded.

Freer intervened. 'Maybe some things are best not explained.'

Louise protested. 'How has it come to this, Will?'

Freer sighed. 'Let's just accept, for now, that Boy is in danger and we must find a way to protect him. For the time being.'

Thomas tried to change the subject. 'And has he been well on the journey?'

'As well as you can be if you don't choose to speak,' Louise retorted.

Thomas swallowed his surprise. Louise had always been a woman who spoke her mind, but this sharpness in her manner was new.

Freer shrugged his shoulders. 'Maybe, silence is easier for him. Perhaps in time.' Freer trailed off. It's what they'd all been saying for the last four years. And now wasn't the time to tell them that Boy had once found his voice.

They'd reached the end of the drive. 'Till tomorrow then, Cowper?'

'Regimental duties permitting.'

' Just tell Haywood that you're needed here. So, at the cottage then, first thing?'

Thomas smiled. Of course, the amiable Haywood was almost certain to let him come. 'Till tomorrow.'

~

Night was beginning to fall as Haywood and Thomas trotted up the narrow lane overhung with trees. As they rode past a rusty-looking stream and spring close by some ruins. Something about the ruins troubled Thomas, reminded him of … no, it couldn't be. Must be just a trick of memory. But as they neared the farmhouse Thomas couldn't contain his curiosity any longer and asked Haywood if he knew what the ruins had once been.

'An old leper hospital, Captain Webster says.'

It was as Thomas feared. 'And the stream?'

Haywood laughed. 'It's supposed to have healing powers. According to Captain Webster.'

Thomas swallowed hard. After years of trying to get Burton Lazarus's Black Friars and their hospital out of his dreams, they'd followed him all the way here.

6

The Gates Of Hell

March 1816, Désvres, Pas-de-Calais, France

He could hear his mother's voice quite plainly, its rising tones warning him that soon she would be sobbing and tugging at his sleeve, pulling him away from the procession of Black Friars, that only she could see, heading from the hospital towards their cottage. So convinced was she that they were coming, she would describe their habits and the sound of the lepers' bells, wrenching at his sleeve even harder to pull him out of their path, his back pressed hard against their cottage wall.

As they approached the ruins, he, too, could see ghosts: Quilley killed by the firing squad Fallowfield had ordered Thomas to join; Sparrow ambushed, following Fallowfield's treachery; Tranter, whom he'd failed to save from drowning off the Goodwins. He heard his sister Hannah crying in the apple loft, felt his brother Michael fall away to the ground, saw the bottom of the ladder, his mother holding the dying Michael in her arms.

But as the procession got nearer, Thomas saw the living too: Fallowfield instructing them on their carbine drill; Fallowfield turning his back, mocking Thomas's resolve; Fallowfield rising from the dead like Christ. The Friars stopped, turned to face him, threw off their hoods and raised their arms and Thomas found himself tumbling, spinning and falling straight down to Hell.

7

Keeping Safe

March 1816, Désvres, Pas-de-Calais, France

Freer's cottage, with its double attic windows setting it apart from its neighbours, looked directly on to the road leading out of the château towards the crossroads. This was the first chance he'd had to go and see Boy and tell him Fallowfield had survived. Thomas tried to calm his thoughts and rehearse what he could possibly say, but the words just stuck in his head. He decided to wander round the village for a while, give himself more time to think. He turned up the track to the church, a squat building surrounded by high-banked walls. The pathway led on to a number of more substantial houses, built on the forest edge, opposite an overgrown path leading to a back entrance to the château.

Making his way back towards the Freers' cottage, he noticed to his surprise a tiny cabaret in the downstairs rooms of one of its neighbours. But doubtless he and Freer would not be welcome. By this time, Thomas was almost in front of Freer's house. Its door opened straight on to the road, but Thomas could see that there was a long back garden with a privy at the end of it. Rather like the cottage back in Burton Lazarus, but without the apple loft to its side.

~

Boy was playing with baby Billy when Thomas arrived, but immediately ran over to him and hugged him. Thomas began to quiz him.

'You were back at Waterloo with Bonnie and Ashby?'

Boy nodded.

'They don't mind you being here?'

Boy shook his head.

Thomas tried to probe further. 'Have you fallen out with them?'

Boy shook his head again.

'Are Bonnie and Ashby looking after you all right?'

Boy nodded.

'But you didn't like being back there?'

Boy wiped the back of his hand across his eyes and nodded again.

Thomas ran his fingers through Boy's hair and sighed. 'I understand. But Serjeant Fallowfield,' Thomas hesitated, 'has recovered from his injuries.' That was as far as Thomas got. Boy leapt up and ran off into a corner, tucking his legs underneath him, his arms crossed against his body. Thomas walked over, knelt down and put his arm round him. 'He has just returned to the Regiment. So we must find a way to get you back to Bonnie and Ashby.'

Boy shook his head violently, got up and went to hug Louise. Louise shrugged her shoulders. 'Boy wants to stay here to learn to read and write.' Boy now hugged Thomas. And to see you, of course.'

Boy hugged Thomas even tighter.

'I know I don't want you to go either, but I just want you to be safe.'

Thomas looked at Louise, then back to Boy. 'I see.' He smiled with as much confidence as he could muster. 'So we shall have to find a way of doing that, won't we?'

But how exactly to do that was quite another matter.

~

Jack Fallowfield knew he would have to bide his time. He'd been billeted in a hamlet on the other side of the forest, but close enough to the château to be employed in taking messages back and forth between the officers scattered across the villages. Soon there'd no secrets safe from him … including where Boy was. Disappeared, according to everybody he asked. Still, if he were patient enough he would eventually worm the information out of somebody. He took out his Bible, his fingers brushing against the lead ball in his sabretache. He found the already well-thumbed page with its verse, counselling forbearance. *'Vengeance is mine, saith the Lord.'* God was testing him. Like Job. All he had to do was wait until it became clear what He wanted him to do next.

8

A Strange Request

March 1816, Désvres, Pas-de-Calais, France

Joanna Rowlandson surveyed her very own classroom. Once a tack room, it had now been equipped with pine benches and tables. It was very plain, but it was hers, hers alone to do with as she wished. It needs pictures on the walls, she thought, and flowers … and children. They were to start school tomorrow, so today was all hers to enjoy.

She'd spent the last few days getting settled in the rather bare farmhouse that was now their home. Not that she felt at home there. Aunt Rowley was in charge of the house and was averse to flowers and such fripperies, as she put it, and her father was in charge of everything else. He had been finally persuaded to let her help Mrs Freer by his old friend, Captain Haywood, who'd vouched for Mrs Freer's bravery in saving her husband's life at Waterloo and her general good sense. Her father now being satisfied with the propriety of the arrangements, Joanna couldn't wait to take up her new position.

There was a knock on the door. It was Mrs Freer.

Joanna was surprised to see a flush on her cheeks and her arm round the boy who did not speak, and that she was followed in by the cavalry serjeant who'd been with Captain Haywood when they'd first arrived.

'Miss Rowlandson, may I introduce Serjeant Cowper, who fought alongside my husband at Waterloo.'

Serjeant Cowper bowed solemnly. 'I'm sorry to hear from Mrs Freer that your father was seriously injured on that day, though thankfully now fully recovered.'

'He and his men were manning the guns against the French cavalry charges.' That was all her father had ever been prepared to tell her.

'You should be proud of them all, Miss Rowlandson. Ney's forces came at us hard, time and time again. It was a wonder that anyone survived, French or English.'

Joanna thought it kind of the Serjeant to praise the artillery. 'Everyone takes us for granted, until we're not there,' her father had once said.

Louise continued the formalities. 'Serjeant Cowper, this is Miss Rowlandson, our assistant schoolmistress.'

'I'm to help Mrs Freer in the mornings,'said Joanna. 'And,' looking at Louise, 'I'm hoping to take my own class in the afternoons.'

Louise smiled. 'That is why we've come to talk to you, but first … Do you remember that I asked you and your aunt to tell nobody about the young boy being here?'

'Of course, and I have said nothing to anybody.'

'Well, Miss Rowlandson, Serjeant Cowper and I need your help again, but we do not wish to put you in a difficult position.'

'In what way?'

'You would not able to tell anyone what you were helping us with, not even your father or aunt.'

Something that she couldn't discuss with her father or aunt? Something that was just between her and Mrs Freer. Joanna rather liked the idea.

Louise continued. 'I understand I am asking a great deal of you.'

Joanna took a deep breath. 'But we would not be doing anything wrong?'

'Believe me, we are doing nothing wrong. We are only trying to prevent this young boy here from coming to any harm.'

'Then, in that case, I will agree to help you and tell nobody.'

Louise smiled. 'Thank you, Miss Rowlandson. Then I'll wait over here whilst Serjeant Cowper explains everything to you.'

Mrs Freer sat down on one of the benches at the back of the room.

Joanna suddenly felt the responsibility of a raw recruit facing up to their first battle.

Serjeant Cowper came closer and perched the young boy on the edge of a desk.

'What we're asking is if you can teach this young lad here his letters and numbers, but on his own and not in a class.'

'Not in a class?'

'He can't mix with any of the other children.'

'Not at all?'

Serjeant Cowper's expression was even more grave. 'Definitely not. He is lodging with the Freer family and nobody will be allowed to visit him there excepting myself, Troop Serjeant-Major and Mrs Freer, and possibly Private man Littlethorpe, who you have met already.'

'I understand.' She turned to the boy, 'I'm sorry we were never really introduced, were we? Will you talk to me, tell me your name, how old you are?'

But as she rather expected, the boy just smiled, then looked up at Serjeant Cowper.

Serjeant Cowper paused, then said, 'About seven or eight, we think, and he's called Boy.'

'Just Boy?'

Serjeant Cowper hesitated again. 'Boy is Spanish. His mother died when we were lifting a siege in a fortress town called Badajoz. After a terrible loss of life on all sides, I'm ashamed to say, some of our soldiers ran wild and took their revenge upon the civilian population.'

Joanna couldn't believe what she was hearing. 'Even the women and children?'

'Especially them.' The serjeant reached out and gently touched the boy's arm. 'But, then, amongst the carnage, I found Boy alive, but mute. Nobody knew what he was called, so we didn't feel it right to give him a name that was not his, so ever since, everybody's always called him Boy.'

He patted Boy on the knee, who took his hand and squeezed it. Joanna could see how much Boy loved this rather awkward, shy fellow.

'But, Serjeant Cowper, if he's Spanish, how can I teach him?'

'Oh, he understands English very well. Don't you?'

Boy nodded.

Joanna's thoughts were now racing. 'So he's not always mute?'

'Oh no. He never speaks, Miss Rowlandson.'

'But then, how am I to teach him?

'Oh, he's a very clever lad. And brave too.'

Joanna could hear the pride in the serjeant's voice, but failed to see how Boy's bravery would help her teach him his letters. She wasn't even sure where to start, but then Boy grinned at her and she knew she had to try; for his sake and for Serjeant's Cowper's, whose devotion to Boy seemed to be no less than Boy's devotion to him.

9

Swords Into Ploughshares

March 1816, Désvres, Pas-de-Calais, France

The army's postal services were considerably more efficient than they had been in the Peninsula, so it hadn't taken long for Ashby to reply. Thomas, though, found himself hesitating for a good few minutes before prising open its seal. Would they now want to take Boy back?

March 16th, 1816, Waterloo,

Dear Cowper,

I am alarmed to hear of Fallowfield's return to the Regiment and the possible consequences for Boy, on account of this grudge you say he bears him. It seems to be in Fallowfield's nature to visit suffering upon others.

Thomas put the letter down for a moment. Though he and Freer had told no one about Fallowfield's involvement in the death of Sparrow, Ashby was an observant man who missed little. Thomas picked the letter up once more.

So I urge you to talk to Boy again about whether he would be willing to come back to us as soon you can arrange it. Of course, the horrors of returning here affected us all, and,

42

now, it seems, none more so than Boy, though, strangely enough, Bonnie seems to have found some comfort in the telling of how she carried Murphy off the battlefield on her back, even if it were to no avail.

I must tell you, though, that, as there is so little work to be had back home, we are planning to stay here for at least another year, after which the number of visitors must surely drop. Once we have saved up enough money to buy a couple of looms, I will be able to set up independently as a weaver, perhaps in the cotton and linen districts away from the Midlands, where there is still much trouble and hanging of protesters. With my pension we should all be able to make a good enough living. So, if you can reassure Boy that we will not stay here forever, we would welcome him back. Also, in spite of Murphy's efforts to train him as a drummer boy, Boy has never shown any inclination to join the army, so there would appear to be little future in staying attached to the Regiment. So, we must all do whatever is best for him.

The passage of time has afforded me many moments for reflection and heartfelt prayers that our swords will one day be turned into ploughshares. It has certainly made me more determined to preach Peace not War.

I now find myself drawn even closer to those who pray to God and give thanks for the mercy he has shown to those of us who have survived. My faith has been sorely tested but now drives me onwards to live a fully Christian life.

I hope all of you are now well enough. Freer and Captain Webster took a beating that day, and it has been a hard year since. The constant rain has kept the memories of that dismal night as fresh as if it were yesterday.

Yours truly,

Samuel Ashby

PS. Bonnie has asked me to tell you that she spent wisely all the money you gave her for Boy and you will be able to see how much he has grown on account of this, in spite of these hard times.

~

One evening, the following week, Freer was in a serious mood. He'd heard that Haywood's Troop Serjeant-Major Grey wanted to retire as soon as he could persuade the Pension Board his Waterloo wounds meant his fighting days were over. With only half a dozen of these posts in the whole regiment, this would be the closest any rank-and-file-man could get to becoming an officer. Freer was emphatic. 'It'll be your last chance, because if Fallowfield is promoted above you …Well, I don't have to tell you, do I?'

Freer tapped his pipe against the stone hearth. He'd only just taken up smoking a pipe. It was, he said, on account of Waterloo. It was as much as he was willing to say about how he'd spent that night preparing to die, but was now, Thomas reckoned, finding it almost as hard preparing to live. Thomas looked at his old friend, calming himself with the gentle tap-tap shedding his pipe's ash, before refilling it to nurse its flame, cupping his hand around the bowl.

Thomas bit his lip. So, all Fallowfield had to do now was to become his Troop Serjeant-Major and then he could do what he liked with him. There would be no escape.

Freer straightened his back and sucked vigorously on his pipe. 'But we can't let that happen, can we.' After all, you've as good a chance as any.'

But the more Freer urged him on, the more Thomas realised the difficulties. Fallowfield was one of the Regiment's most senior serjeants, with many years service, and would consider the position his by right, whilst Thomas worried he'd be more concerned about his men's well-being or the state of their horses than maintaining discipline. In spite of his earlier determination not to retreat, something still held Thomas back. Was he was just scared of crossing Fallowfield yet again?

But then Thomas saw the strain on Freer's face. The last thing he wanted to do was to add to Freer's worries. It wasn't Freer's job to save him from himself. He would have to take Fallowfield on, regardless of … the other matter. He owed it to Freer … and the Regiment. Thomas leaned forward and rested his hand briefly on Freer's arm. 'You're right, but there's something you should know.'

~

Jack Fallowfield sat down on a log inside the rough shelter he'd made to keep out the rain. He had his first batch of letters to inspect, complete with fresh sealing wax and any other paraphernalia he might need. He had a good memory for handwriting and quickly picked out the letters he planned to open. Someone must know where that bloody brat had disappeared to.

Well, there was a thing. Fallowfield leant back in his shelter to contemplate the news. Troop Serjeant-Major Grey was petitioning to leave. *Worn out*, he'd written to the Pension Board. 'Aren't we all bloody worn out?' Jack Fallowfield spat out. Still, this was the very opportunity he was waiting for. All he had to do now was to find a way of getting closer to Haywood. And why the hell Cowper should remain Haywood's cover serjeant, now that Haywood was a captain rather than a mere lieutenant was an injustice in itself. After all, he, Jack, was the senior sergeant in the whole bloody regiment. He should be Haywood's cover sergeant not bloody Cowper.

10

Pimlico

April 1816, The Riding School, Pimlico, London

So far, so good. That was the first part of his and Freer's plan achieved, Thomas said to himself. He and Freer and twenty others had been sent to Pimlico for a month's training. They were to be transformed from light dragoons into lancers, the ultimate shock troops in a cavalry charge, now being introduced into the British ranks.

Pimlico riding school and barracks were squashed between a brewery and Royal parklands and only a short distance from the river. But their plans for pleasant riverside strolls were quickly abandoned when Thomas and Freer came upon a huge newly built brick prison, towering over a maze of wharves and timber yards. It was as if God himself had built it in readiness for Judgment Day.

Freer was indignant. 'As if we didn't already know that's what our betters think we deserve. Not decent houses, but a new prison.'

Thomas muttered his agreement, but his mind was set on the task in hand, for if he didn't show himself to be more than proficient he might as well give up all hopes of being promoted to Troop Serjeant-Major. So Thomas battled his lack of enthusiasm for the new weapons with a clear understanding that this was where his future lay, and that

47

unless he performed as well with a lance as he had with his sabre, then he might have no future at all. The lances were ten feet long and half a stone or more in weight, with lethal steel tips. It was hardly surprising Littlethorpe's poor Dog had stood no chance of avoiding the thrust of a well-trained Polish lancer. But Thomas still longed to be wielding his sabre. 'Reserved for close combat purposes only,' their instructor announced.

Had it always been this hard? He remembered the first time he'd been at the mercy of the drill serjeants, who'd taught the recruits their sword drill, and of Fallowfield, who'd taught them how to fire their carbines. Yes, it had always been this hard.

Thomas looked across the parade ground at Fallowfield. The big man's face was set, and he seemed determined as a man could be to master the skills needed to control the lance, to push himself ahead, to stand out in the crowd, to become the Regiment's next troop serjeant-major.

Seeing Fallowfield strain to master the art of killing at a distance reminded Thomas yet again why he was there. He would have to forget his aching neck and arm muscles and out-shine Fallowfield. After all, only one of them could be the next troop serjeant-major. As if aware of Thomas's gaze, Fallowfield turned and nodded, as if to acknowledge that, indeed, a new campaign in their war had begun.

So the days stretched ahead with muscles and heads aching with the sheer tedium of the drills, their borrowed horses less forgiving than their usual mounts and the drill sergeant never less than threatening. Did they not know how the lancers had almost won the battle of Waterloo? Did they not know what fearsome reputation foreign regiments of lancers had? Did they not want to join this glorious brotherhood on the front line?

After the first week Freer was not having any more of it. 'Someone should tell that man we've no need to be told how deadly lancers are, or that we nearly lost the battle of Waterloo, on account of them; and, if the man doesn't shut up about the glorious exploits of the French and the Polish, well …' Freer trailed off.

Freer was in a bad mood. Whilst Thomas agreed with his sentiments, he was puzzled. Why was the usually good-natured Freer so upset by the drill sergeant's hectoring tones? After all, it was standard practice to belittle your men in drill exercises, though he had to admit that he'd never seen Freer do that with any new recruits he had occasion to drill.

They were sitting quietly in The Gun Tavern, just down the road from the barracks. A low building with a grand upstairs bay window, but its adjoining premises leaning just a little too far into the street, its landlord was not too proud to make his living from the local soldiers. Littlethorpe and Byrne and most of the other men had taken themselves off to a nearby cock-fight. As for Fallowfield, he was more likely to be found in a chapel than drinking in a tavern.

Freer noisily sucked the end of his clay pipe as if to prevent himself from saying another word on the matter.

'Freer,' Thomas leant forward. 'I agree. The man's a fool but he does know how to handle those damn lances.'

Freer put down his pipe. 'What I find irritating is the praise he heaps upon the French and Poles, as though we should be grateful.'

Thomas studied Freer's expression, which had become fixed, his eyes staring into the distance. Freer suddenly stirred himself.

'Has he no idea what it's like to be on the wrong end of a lance, to see your captain, who you're supposed to be protecting, knocked clean off his horse and you can't do a bloody thing about it because the soldier who did it is half a field away.' Freer bit his lip, stuck his pipe back in his mouth, and sucked even harder.

Thomas didn't know whether to say anything else. He didn't want to push Freer any further back into the memories of that day. But Freer seemed to want to talk.

'And then he felled Libby and me. More or less at the same time. Same lancer, I expect. They all look alike in those stupid uniforms. It was a blessing I was hardly conscious, what with Libby's whole weight trapping me under her.'

Freer trailed off again and bit on his pipe. 'Probably saved my life, being stuck under Libby. No glory attached to spearing a man who looks dead already.'

Thomas gazed at his tankard, trying to avoid Freer's eyes, which were beginning to fill with tears.

'But then, with my Louise finding me as quick as she did, I suppose I'm a lucky man.'

'Any one of us who lived through that day was lucky.' Thomas tried to steady his voice, as he recalled how he too had been saved.

'I remember being chased to hell and back by a Polish lancer, flying back up the hill, Haywood holding on to my stirrup, like a sack of oats. How Fearless pulled us both up that hill I shall never know, but she got us both up to the ridge.'

'She's a good horse, Fearless. Like Libby.' Freer wiped away a tear.

Thomas knew he should be braver, and speak the truth like Louise had urged him to that first time they met.

'I've never been so bloody scared in my life, and if it hadn't been for the infantry square pulling us inside, that lancer would have got us both. No doubt about it. Saved us both. Good men the lot of 'em. First line bayonets fixed, third line taking over from second line muskets, scaring the horses, shooting the riders, round after round. Not sure I said it at the time, but neither Haywood nor I would be here without them holding that square.'

Freer raised his tankard. 'So let's drink to the unlucky ones, eh.'

Thomas raised his. 'Only you and me left now of the 1805 Leicester recruits.' Both men took a long draught.

Freer thought for a moment and nodded. 'Yes. That's right enough. Only us left.'

Thomas raised his tankard again. 'Every time we march out in columns, I can see where the others used to ride.'

He didn't add that what he really saw was the lads themselves back in their given places, much as they had been eleven years ago. It wasn't that he chose to see them, but, like his mother before him, he suffered visions, saw things that were as real as day to him but that nobody else could see. But it didn't do to tell folks that. That was his mother's problem. That's why people thought her mad. Telling people was never a good idea. At least he'd learned that much from his mother.

Besides, Thomas had been told on good authority that he'd already demonstrated the highest level of competence with a lance that the drill sergeant had observed in a newly trained man for quite some time. He'd almost felt reassured about his future prospects. So no need to ruin them by admitting he saw ghosts.

~

Unbelievably, they had a free afternoon. The riding school had been their home for the last three weeks, come rain and even snow, and exploring beyond The Gun unappealing after their long days. Freer reckoned they'd have time to visit the famous King's Arms Tavern instead, as he'd heard that there was much debate to be had about politics there. Thomas felt in need of distraction, as he'd just heard that the drill sergeant had also remarked that Serjeant Fallowfield was outstanding in his skill with a lance. Thomas felt his prospects of promotion begin to slip out of reach. For Fallowfield was also behaving most affably, most obligingly. Those who knew him of old, doubted this could be kept up for long but Thomas told himself that Fallowfield's pose as a pleasant and reasonable man would be maintained at least until he'd secured the position of troop serjeant-major. So both Freer and Thomas agreed that Boy was probably safe for the time being. But if Fallowfield got that promotion, there would be no stopping him.

But when Freer, Littlethorpe, Byrne and Thomas finally dipped across the threshold of The King's Arms they were greeted not by the noise of debate but by boisterous singing. Memories of their last camp fire before Quatre Bras began to overwhelm Thomas, but Freer tugged at his sleeve. 'Let's sit down and join in.' Byrne and Littlethorpe quickly followed.

Littlethorpe was half-way through singing 'The Lincolnshire Farmer' when two men in working clothes strode up to him, the younger one placing his hand on Littlethorpe's shoulder.

'I'd recognise that bloody voice anywhere.'

Littlethorpe tried and failed to smile. 'Jonathan bloody Burgess.'

Burgess's voice was bitter. 'Went for a soldier, did you?'

Littlethorpe shrugged his shoulders. 'They were recruiting in Leicester... just after...'

Burgess stood back and placed his fists on his hips, looking Littlethorpe straight in the eye. 'Lucky you.'

'Some of us weren't so lucky,' the older man added, running his hands over scars on both his forearms.

Littlethorpe had once admitted to Thomas he'd only just evaded capture for his part in a machine-breaking raid in his native Nottinghamshire.

The younger man jabbed his finger into Littlethorpe's face. 'But that's Richard Littlethorpe for you. You never were the most loyal of Captain Ludd's followers.'

Littlethorpe stood up and stiffened his shoulders. 'I never was one of his followers, in the first place. I was just … helping out.'

Burgess placed his hand heavily on Littlethorpe's shoulder. 'And now you're just helping out these fellows here. So we can expect you all to come back any day now, to clap us back in gaol.'

Littlethorpe shouted, 'Just because I never swore any bloody oaths doesn't mean I betrayed you. Not then. Not now.'

Burgess was not going to let it go. 'People were hanged.'

Littlethorpe pulled Burgess's hand away from his shoulder. 'Not on my account, they weren't.'

Byrne was edging closer to Littlethorpe. Thomas looked across at Freer. Could they drag Littlethorpe away before a fight broke out?

The older man grunted, 'And those food riots? Women and children starving. I suppose your friends here had nothing to do with putting them down neither.'

Freer rose to his feet and raised his hands to try and calm the older man.

'In Nottingham? We heard about them. A dreadful business, but not something we've been guilty of. Then or now. We've just been two years in the Peninsula and a year or more in the Netherlands and France fighting Boney. We're no friends of Tyrants, you can be sure of that.'

'Aye, so why do you think they've sent you back now? Eh? Not for our benefit, that's for sure.'

'But we're still in France. Like I said, to keep the peace, to stop the war breaking out all over again.'

The older man spat on the floor. 'Huh. So this is the peace, is it? It's a damn sight worse than the war.'

Burgess stopped jabbing his finger in Littlethorpe's face and turned to Freer. 'Worse I'd say... keeping out cheap wheat and fixing the top bloody price of home-grown corn'.

The older man added, 'And what with a bad harvest last year and the weather we're having right now ...'

The younger man interrupted, 'But what does anybody care. The landowners have got their money and the rest of 'em have got their machines to keep them warm.'

Freer lightly touched Burgess's arm. 'And you'd say Parliament is on their side ... not ours?' he asked quietly.

The younger man moved away from Littlethorpe and sat down heavily. 'Course it bloody is.'

Freer took his seat again. 'You're a long way from home, my friends?'

The older man wiped his brow. 'There's been a lot of talk about men in London, like Major Cartwright being on our side. So we've come to hear what he's got to say. He'll be speaking soon at a meeting in front of Westminster Hall.'

'Though what even he can do about it ...' the younger one added.

Freer smiled. 'Major Cartwright, the famous Major Cartwright who has worked tirelessly for the cause?'

Burgess looked up, surprised. 'You're a supporter?'

Freer lowered his voice. 'And of Thomas Paine and William Cobbett.'

Burgess rose from his seat and slapped Freer on the back. Freer smiled broadly. 'Then shall we all go together?'

Littlethorpe found his voice again. 'Let's drink to that. And to all the good men of the shire of Nottingham.'

'And the women, too, as I recall, eh Richard Littlethorpe.' Burgess said, and roared with laughter.

Thomas saw Littlethorpe's face drop. Burgess was not to know that in 1814 Littlethorpe had been forced, like so many others, to abandon his pregnant sweetheart in France, before being marched home to his mother country.

~

Littlethorpe and his Nottinghamshire friends, after many songs and much beer, were on good terms once again, and had been first away back into Palace Yard, Byrne bringing up their rear, with Thomas and Freer some way behind, as they made their way through the crowds outside Westminster Hall.

'Leastways, the Bourbons haven't called on us to put down any food riots,' Thomas muttered to Freer.

'Don't speak too soon.'

'I heard it from Haywood that Wellington has already refused all requests.'

'Well, that's bound to be right then, isn't it?'

Thomas reddened at Freer's quiet sarcasm, deployed whenever Thomas repeated one of Captain Haywood's untested opnions. 'I'm sure he's right though. Wellington's got too much good sense to get us involved in any of that.'

Ever since they'd narrowly missed the Reading food riots in 1815, it was something Thomas prayed he would never have to deal with. It had been a relief to leave England behind, even if it was to face the prospect of fighting Napoleon.

'So what's this Major Cartwright going to talk about?' Thomas whispered to Freer.

'Petitions, I expect.'

'Petitions?'

'The only course of action left for those of us with no vote,' Freer whispered back, sounding a bit more like his old self. 'Maybe about the likes of us getting proper representation in Parliament. That's what Cartwright wants. Annual parliaments, secret ballots, and votes for all men.'

'And women?' Thomas repeated the retort Louise had made to Freer, when she'd first met them in her father's pub in Romford, all those years ago.

'And for women too,' Freer said with a smile, 'but even those of us who agree they should have the vote hardly dare mention it in case nobody takes the proposal to give men the vote seriously.'

Although he often asked himself how an ordinary man would go about choosing a member of Parliament, Thomas was sure that women would be no more or less capable. 'You don't really believe that, do you?' he asked.

Freer shook his head. ' Well it's more a question of first things first. After all, if we men, who fought for our country, can't be trusted with the vote, what hope is there for women?'

Before Thomas could reply, Major Cartwright mounted the speakers' platform. He appeared to be a distinguished elderly gentleman in plain simple dress, and was treated with great respect by his fellow speakers. Although Thomas couldn't make out much of what he said, his voice rang out with great vigour and passion.

'What's he saying now?' Thomas kept whispering, hoping that Freer, having a greater understanding of the matter, could make more sense of it.

But Freer too was struggling to hear, though he repeated the Major's words as best he could. 'Something about we've inherited a threefold legislative system and therefore a government of all by all … but there's … a grand counteracting mischief , oh … and that's why the … house has not got a constitutional representation …'

At this point the crowd began to shout, joining in his condemnation of this grand counteracting mischief. It was impossible to hear more and Freer gestured to Thomas to follow him out of Palace Yard. Thomas turned to leave but with that sixth sense a soldier develops when on guard duty in enemy territory, he had a feeling that they were being watched, sensed in that great crowd of people, that someone was spying on them. But Freer now grabbed his arm. 'See, it's not just me who thinks it should be a government of all by all. Some of our so-called betters condemn the grand counteracting mischief as well.'

Thomas wasn't following any of this now. 'What counteracting mischief?'

Freer snorted. 'Like landed interests, the merchants and manufacturers, who don't want to pay a fair price for a man's labour. Anyone with money used to counter the common good. All those who can, and do hold governments to ransom. I mean, look at London … grand houses in squares for those who have money and stinking rookeries where everyone else is forced to live. And they say they're worried about a revolution. So they should be.'

'I never thought I'd ever hear you taking up your cudgels again.' Thomas clapped Freer on the back. 'I've missed that, Will Freer.'

Freer nodded. 'It's what war can do to a man. It destroys hope.'

Freer straightened his back. 'Let's walk up to Horse Guards, see what our betters are up to and then try and get some fresh air in St James's Park. We'll all be bloody choking to death soon. We're quite close now. Remember.'

How could he not remember? It was where he'd last met Grace.

~

Jack Fallowfield had been warned about The King's Arms. 'Keep away,' they'd said, 'if you don't want to get mixed up with those Reformers.' So when he'd heard that Freer and Cowper were going there, he'd set off in pursuit. It'd been a long time since he'd first tried to persuade Captain Dickenson that Freer had an unpatriotic admiration for that bloody *Rights of Man*. Well, Dickenson was dead, but now the chickens were coming home to roost. Freer was falling into his old ways and where Freer led, Cowper was never far behind. Killing two birds with one stone. He liked that. Remove Freer's power as a Troop Sergeant-Major to protect Cowper and both of them would be at his mercy.

He'd followed them as far as New Palace Yard, where one of those reformers was urging the kind of revolution France had fallen prey to. He stopped long enough to see them head up Whitehall towards Horse Guards, then slowly followed. His mind was made up. After all, surely the Home Department would remember he'd been useful to them before: in Nottingham, and on the south coast, watching out for the Irish, mutineers and Paine sympathisers?

Fallowfield stopped outside Dorset House. He cleared his throat, ready to explain to the Home Department officials why Troop Serjeant-Major Freer and possibly, no, definitely, Serjeant Cowper were worthy of the closest attention. His close attention.

Men of Freer's rank were not required to come back to London to undergo this training. So Freer must have volunteered to come because he'd heard that London was on the brink of revolution. Not to fight against it but to join it.

11

To Each Man A Medal

May 1816, Azincourt, Pas-de-Calais, France

As the rainy spring turned into a rainy summer, it was during a short break in this unremitting wetness that the 36th Dragoons unexpectedly found themselves enjoying their one day in the sun. It was Haywood who'd brought the news. 'But keep it under your hats,' he'd advised Freer and Thomas, who'd both smiled at Haywood's inability to keep any secret to himself for longer than a day, or, more precisely, since he'd dined with Captain Webster the previous evening.

'Not only is every soldier who was in the Waterloo campaign to receive a medal, with each man's name inscribed on it.' Haywood was quite pink, 'but I'm informed that this is the first time in British military history that this has happened and,' Haywood paused to breathe, 'they are to be awarded on the famous field of Agincourt, where the longbows of the English yeomanry won the day against superior French forces. Yet not every regiment, even in the Pas-de-Calais, is to be honoured on that field. We shall be among the few … the very few.'

Thomas had scarcely heard what else Haywood had to say other than to gather they would receive their precise marching orders in the next few days, but these would include getting their men up to review drill standard as soon as possible.

Thomas glanced at Freer and saw his well-disguised grimace. 'The men may need more than a few days to regain battle readiness, but we shall do our best, sir,' said Freer.

'Good, good. Thought I should give you fair warning.'

'What fair warning?' Thomas grumbled that evening. The few weeks they thought they had to rehearse their drills had turned out to be a few days.

'Who knows if even the horses'll remember what to do?' Freer was looking less cheerful by the minute.

Thomas shrugged his shoulders. 'As for the men…'

The Regiment had been on short rations most of the winter, and even with the coming of spring the replenishment of supplies looked doubtful. Tempers were short and Thomas realised that he was not the only one to have sleepwalked through the winter. Would they…would he, be found to be unworthy?

~

The field of Agincourt seemed rather small, not unlike Mont St Jean but rather less hilly, with ridges and slopes not so well-defined. Nobody seemed to know where the victorious longbow men had stood on that day, but Thomas had the feeling that this scarcely mattered. He wondered about Waterloo, whether that battle too would be remembered so well. He could see that the officers were much more excited about being on the field of Agincourt than the men, and couldn't avoid hearing how they talked about having sons to whom they would give their medals. Thomas suddenly found himself making a vow to hand on his medal to his own first-born son. When he had one. Things will be better, he told himself. Surely, after all these years of fighting they would be rewarded with something more than a medal? Loyal soldiers, sailors and, yes, everyone of good will, and their children too, deserved more than living on the stinking streets of London or eking out an existence on someone else's land. There must be change. If only he could believe it would happen within his lifetime. But then, what was the use of day-dreaming about sons if he hadn't even a wife? The reality of his unmarried state pulled him up short just in time, moments before the manoeuvres began.

It started and ended well, with the men in their dress uniforms, glinting in the early morning frost, manoeuvring neatly. So no-one had forgotten how to put on a good show after all. The slackness of drills and manoeuvres over the winter had been just that, a reluctance to push themselves more than they had to.

Thomas glanced around him. From where he was placed he could see Fallowfield, as upright as the proverbial ramrod. Thomas remembered the first time he'd seen him and the rest of the recruiting party back in Leicester. What a show they'd put on too. What visions of glory. Thomas pondered on the man's character. Over the years, he'd gradually come to understand more about Fallowfield's notions of being a good soldier. It meant being totally committed to whatever war he was waging at the time, and being contemptuous of any man or officer who showed the slightest sign of weakness. His only goal was to win. At any cost. Thomas examined his unforgiving features closer. How could an ordinary soldier, one full of doubts like Thomas, hope to defeat him?

Thomas's thoughts refused to settle even when Acting Lieutenant-Colonel Bridges began to declaim into the wind.

'I consider this day to be the happiest of my life ... to distribute to you those honorary badges of distinction which our gracious prince has been pleased to present each of us with …'

Our gracious prince indeed. Thomas recalled the last occasion he'd seen the Prince Regent, at Hounslow on the Regiment's return from France in 1814. Had this gracious prince now really taken such an interest in the ordinary soldier that he'd commanded that every last one of them should receive a medal, even the dead? Surely not. He'd heard said the man was a wastrel, and more of a fornicator than the common soldier, a fool who spent every penny on luxuries and fopperies, whilst his people starved and rioted for food. No, Thomas was not persuaded.

Bridges, though, was by now singing all their praises '… transmitted to posterity as a reward gained to commemorate British valour ...'

Were they really so brave? Did they have any other choice that day than to fight? Thomas gagged as he tasted again the smell of punctured intestines, eyes weeping with the acrid smoke, the sounds of the dying men and horses drowning out all others. It was all he could do to sit bolt upright on Fearless and trust she was not reliving the same vision of hell that reappeared in his dreams night after night.

'I could have wished our gallant lieutenant-colonel were present…'

Thomas's thoughts turned to their respected commander, Pennington, who'd miraculously survived terrible wounds, but was still convalescing on his family estate.

'… admiring posterity will with gratitude exclaim, he too fought at that great battle on the Plains of Waterloo.'

As the band struck up 'God Save the King', Freer bent forward and whispered, 'I recollect it being rather hilly myself. Do you think he was even there?'

Thomas grimaced at the memory of his own frantic scramble up the hill, Haywood desperately hanging on to his stirrup. 'Must have kept his eyes shut most of the time … like the rest of us.'

And as they led the men into cheers three times three for the King, Thomas gave thanks it was not the Regent they were asking God to save, or for whom they cheered so lustily. His loyalty still lay with the old King. He remembered his dead friends, his brother Michael and his mother. All gone. But that was how it was. The dead are dead forever. Though already well acquainted with Hell, he wasn't sure any more about Heaven.

12

Bluebells

May 1816, Désvres, Pas-de-Calais, France

It was an unusually dry day. Thomas was cutting through the woods to the château and heard the chattering of small children through a hazy blue mist of late flowering bluebells. He glimpsed Louise Freer and Miss Rowlandson handing out slates.

He stopped to watch: Louise very much in charge, Miss Rowlandson bending over her pupils, her fair hair glinting in the shafts of sun. Louise noticed him and beckoned him to come closer. He dismounted, leading Fearless carefully down the muddy path, tying her to a tree before she had chance to trample the flowers.

Louise had baby Billy with her; the baby was being minded by a child who seemed not much older. 'It's such a beautiful day, it seemed wrong to stay in the schoolroom.'

Miss Rowlandson called out, 'Good morning, Serjeant.'

Thomas bowed in her direction. 'Good morning, Miss Rowlandson.'

He ought to take his leave of the school party right now, but he was reluctant to go. He tried not to stare, but why hadn't he let himself notice this before? How pretty Miss Rowlandson was. Quite as lovely as Grace had been at almost the same age. Seventeen or eighteen at most. Blushing, he bent down to scoop little Billy into his arms, and carried him off to pat and finger and tug Fearless's mane.

'You must look after William Thomas more often, Serjeant,' Louise teased, when he brought Billy back to his young minder as they were all packing up. He handed half a dozen or so bluebells to Louise. 'A few for the schoolroom. They don't last long once they're picked.'

Miss Rowlandson smiled as Louise handed her the flowers to hold, 'Oh, they smell wonderful.'

Thomas smiled back. 'My grandmother used to pick them for medicinal purposes.'

Miss Rowlandson cocked her head slightly. 'Medicinal?'

Thomas smiled again. 'My grandmother collected all kinds of herbs to treat a great number of ailments. I even brought some with me.'

'And do these herbs grow in France also?'

'I imagine they do. In fact,' Thomas struggled to cast off a deep-seated wariness of the rusty stream near the old farmhouse, 'There's a spring near to where I'm billeted. It's called the healing spring. I must find out if this refers to its plants as well as to its waters.'

As they neared the school Thomas tapped his sabretache. 'Miss Rowlandson, I must take my leave. But before I go, I must ask you directly: how is your young charge doing?'

'Very well. He's doing very well.'

Miss Rowlandson twisted a lock of hair that had fallen out from under her bonnet. 'I should very much like to see some of your healing herbs. Perhaps you could bring some in to show my class?'

'As soon as I find some, I'll be sure to let you know.'

'Thank you.' Miss Rowlandson began to shepherd her charges back into the classroom, then stopped and turned briefly. 'Perhaps we may meet at the cricket match before then?' Thomas smiled and bowed. She wanted to see him again. Then he caught sight of Louise's stern face and wondered what he had done to merit her disapproval.

13

The Match

May 1816, Désvres, Pas-de-Calais, France

Thomas had been worried about the men all winter. Without a war to fight, but with hardships still to endure, morale continued to weaken. The thrice-weekly winter drills and exercises had been scarcely enough to maintain their sense of themselves as a fighting force and Thomas was dreading the summer, with their exercise fields again under the plough.

He'd first suggested putting on a match to Byrne some time ago, not long after they'd first arrived and seen the back lawns of the château.

'But not a proper match. Not after the Goodwins.' Byrne had stuttered to a halt.

'I know none of us had the stomach for one after Tranter.' Thomas had paused. 'But we've been through a lot worse since.'

Byrne hadn't seemed convinced 'But not killed on my account. You don't forget something like that.'

Thomas had felt just as guilty as Byrne over Tranter, but he'd forced himself to smile. 'It's not such a bad way to go, eh, with a barrel of beer in your sights.'

Byrne had eventually grinned back. 'Silly sod. Best bowler we had and all.'

Thomas once again saw Tranter disappearing under the waves pounding the edge of the sandbanks, the cricketers scarcely able to save themselves from the sea overwhelming the notorious Goodwins, never mind the drunken Tranter, clutching his keg of beer.

Thomas had just about managed to turn his thoughts back to the matter in hand, the poor morale of the men.

'We're sorely in need of more occupation.'

'Apart from getting drunk every night?'

Thomas had grinned, pleased to see some of Byrne's spark returning. 'Apart from that.' He'd thought for a moment. 'I suppose we should ask Haywood.'

'Might be better if we just did it.'

Thomas had shaken his head. 'We can't organise a cricket match in the middle of the château lawns without someone's permission, can we?'

Byrne had hesitated. 'If you don't mind being treated like fighting cocks.'

'Fighting cocks?'

'The officers will only be interested as long as they can place bets, just as if we were fighting cocks.'

Byrne had earned his patron in Essex vast amounts of money against those willing to gamble on the toss of Byrne's ball. Byrne, in his cups, swore it was more of a burden than defending his country against Boney.

Byrne had stared into the middle distance. 'But what we're really lacking is some decent opposition.'

'You're not thinking of playing the French.'

'If only we could. No, it's those artillery fellows I've got my eye on. Just because their guns are bigger than our guns.'

Byrne had been smiling by then. 'Anyway, if we don't get permission to use the lawns we'll just have to find another pitch.' Byrne had paused. 'We'll need a field with short grass that sheep have been let loose on. So you get me a pitch and I'll find you a team. Then we'll see how the artillery boys measure up under fire.'

'And in the meantime?'

Byrne had thrust two fingers towards the sky. 'We'll have to wait for this bloody weather to lift first.'

~

Thomas was relieved to find the day cool but with no hint of rain, for once. He saw that the artillery lads with their supporters were making their way on to the back lawns past the scrubby area where Littlethorpe and Byrne had set up a couple of frames, and where the two pigs they had spirited away from the abandoned farm house on the coast were roasting over the flames.

Byrne had enlisted enough wives and daughters of the other ranks as well as officers' servants to set up a part-marquee, part-tent, where tables had been dragged out from the château. Plates and all the other necessities had already been laid out, with a separate tent and awning provided for the officers and their families. Small children contrived to get in their mothers' way by hanging onto their pinafores or playing ball games under their feet.

As for the match, Byrne was definitely in charge. Having persuaded Haywood it would not befit any officers to play and suffer the indignity of possible defeat, Thomas was the cavalry team's nominal captain, though Byrne, as their opening bowler, would in fact be responsible for both tactics and strategy. He'd already taken advantage of the fact that the château was the 36th's headquarters and had paced out exactly where the most lumpy terrain lay. This, he declared, was where he would aim to pitch and generally discomfit the batsmen. The artillerymen, strengthened with a few of the 15th Hussars on their way back to the coast, would try to do likewise, but without the advantage of having studied the terrain with Byrne's professional eye. Byrne regarded this task as equivalent to a battle with the French.

'But rules have to be observed, unlike in war,' he declared, when one of their number suggested they should get the artillerymen drunker than they might already be, by lacing their beer with the local brandy.

~

Thomas had adopted the long-dead Sparrow's technique of refusing to be drawn to play balls that would give the fielders an easy catch. This, he had observed, tended to encourage the bowlers to become reckless. Suddenly his surroundings disappeared for a brief moment and he swallowed hard as he saw Sparrow, as large as life, once again on that fateful day on the Goodwins. Then he was back again on the field at Désvres. A natural fielder, Thomas had been persuaded by Byrne that he now had sufficient battle experience to hold his nerve under fire as an opening batsman. Thomas adjusted his feet and hands as Byrne had so often rehearsed with him and gripped the bat. He was ready to hold his ground. He smiled. Even Josh Tranter hadn't been able to dislodge Sparrow from his perch.

As frustrated as Tranter had been, the artillery lads began to show their irritation. It was as if their years of experience of firing round shot on to hostile ground had been made to count for nothing in some way they couldn't fathom. The balls started to come faster and wilder than before. It was merely a question of steadiness under fire, Thomas kept telling himself, achieving a healthy twenty-three runs before being caught out to the great disappointment of his fellows. But, after a final pairing of Littlethorpe and Freer with

Littlethorpe hitting far and wide, they left the crease with more runs than the artillerymen could match. So, as Byrne selected his terrain and took full advantage, bowling balls that twisted, span and bounced awkwardly, the artillery lads and the 15th Hussars got even more annoyed, hitting out wildly and missing more often than not.

The match ended with them reluctantly conceding defeat, just as the pigs were being cut down to be carved and served with ale and chunks of bread. The officers and their ladies had acquired rather more elegant trimmings to go with the best of the pork, whilst under Freer's watchful eye the rest of the meat was shared out fairly amongst the men.

The evening promised to stay dry, and there was so much jollity that Captain Rowlandson and his sister came over to congratulate them, accompanied by Miss Rowlandson, and in the euphoria of victory Thomas addressed her directly.

'Miss Rowlandson, I hope you enjoyed the game?'

'Indeed I did, Serjeant Cowper. I particularly admired the way in which you stood your ground in such a steady fashion.'

Thomas blushed. 'I tried to copy the manner in which a dear friend of ours, a Private Sparrow, used to play. He was a very fine friend. Killed in the Peninsula …' Thomas trailed off. 'Forgive me, Miss Rowlandson. I must apologise. I really shouldn't be talking about such matters on a day like this.'

'Quite so.' Captain Rowlandson's sister interrupted and took the opportunity to steer her niece towards the officers spilling out from their tent.

Now if I were a troop serjeant-major, Thomas thought, the aunt wouldn't have rushed Miss Rowlandson away without, at least, an apology. But then Miss Rowlandson turned and looked back. Thomas smiled and bowed low, just as he'd seen those in polite society do. She smiled, then seemed to realise that a proper lady would not have done that, so turned round, picked up her skirts and followed her father and aunt towards the other tent.

Thomas turned back to the joshing and merriment of his fellow team members and felt a little skip in this heart, a little lightening of the gloom. Thomas kept his eyes steadily upon Miss Rowlandson. He was beginning to feel more confident that she liked him too. But how would he ever know for sure if he couldn't see her again? Louise Freer had already warned him against visiting Miss Rowlandson alone when she was teaching Boy his letters. 'To protect her reputation,' Louise had said. So he would have to think of another way.

But then he saw Fallowfield make his way confidently across the field to approach Miss Rowlandson's father and speak directly to both her and the fierce aunt. He saw Fallowfield's face assume that expression he was so familiar with, the smile that said, 'Now I've got you.'

~

As soon as they'd reached the tent, Joanna Rowlandson felt the full force of her aunt's disapproval. 'As I have said before, Joanna, I do not expect to find you engaging in extended conversations with other ranks.'

'Or, at least with those I have not introduced you to,' added her father. When she protested, as she usually did when her aunt reprimanded her, her father immediately took the side of his sister. 'Your aunt's quite right. Now you are a young lady, you must behave like one, not like a child.'

Although Joanna knew some of her father's ill-temper was due to the thrashing they had received at the hands of the cavalry team, she felt cast down. He had never before been quite so critical of her behaviour.

~

Jack Fallowfield smiled when he saw Cowper's gaze rest for rather too long upon Miss Rowlandson, long enough for Rowlandson and his sister to give him short shrift and move Miss Rowlandson swiftly away. Fallowfield unfolded his arms and strolled over to the Captain, his redoubtable sister, and his slip of a daughter. He was bored with biding his time, waiting for his chance to twist gullible officers around his little finger, waiting to secure what was his by right: the troop serjeant-major's post.

It shouldn't take too much trouble to keep the girl out of Cowper's way. Like the recruiting sergeant he still was at heart, all he had to do was make the girl, the captain and the aunt feel that they were at the very centre of Jack Fallowfield's concerns and attentions. Besides, given their shared Bible classes in the convent and the captain's apparent good terms with Haywood, it certainly wouldn't harm his position if he made himself even more agreeable to the Rowlandson family.

'Captain Rowlandson, Miss Rowlandson.' Fallowfield turned to the daughter. 'And Miss Rowlandson.'

Captain Rowlandson smiled broadly. 'Fallowfield, my good fellow.' Fallowfield bowed. 'Miss Rowlandson, as you will remember, your father and I are already acquainted.'

Miss Rowlandson, looked past him to somewhere over his shoulder. 'Ah yes, the Bible classes.' She paused, glancing at her father. 'My father makes much of them.'

Judging by her expression, he guessed she didn't approve. He would have to try another way. Appeal to a sense of fair play, perhaps?

'A great pity that your gallant artillery boys were beaten today as they put up a tremendous fight. But you should know our Corporal Byrne is not really an amateur. He used to play for various gentlemen who gambled their fortunes on his skills. Surely not something you, or your father, would approve of.' And inclining his head towards the aunt. 'Nor you, of course, Miss Rowlandson.'

But the girl was not to be so easily won over. 'Still, he wasn't the only person playing on his side and we must be gracious in defeat.'

'Spoken with such a generous spirit, Miss Rowlandson. Indeed we must be gracious, win or lose. I remember when the Regiment was in Egypt we secured a great victory, but our commander could not have been wiser in the way in which he exercised both mercy and yet firmness towards our captured enemies. But then again, I expect you've heard far too many stories about war to be interested in such a venture. Still you may be interested to know this is why we have the Sphinx on our caps. Because of our Egyptian campaign. Though there are not many of us left who were there.'

She looked up, as if wanting to know more, he thought. At last. He'd found something she might be interested in.

'I'm sure I've never heard anything about an Egyptian campaign.'

He took out and dusted down the story that used to entrance all new recruits without fail, one that Dermot Murphy used to tell, but which Fallowfield had now appropriated as his own.

'… And as a result of this some of our officers were presented to the Pope.'

Fallowfield, now quite relaxed, looked at the girl and smiled. It was like being back on the recruitment campaign trail, gulling young men, some of them only boys, persuading them to take the King's shilling. Acting a part, seducing your audience.

'Do go on, please, Serjeant Fallowfield,' Miss Rowlandson said, now looking directly at him. 'I'd like to hear more about your adventures in Egypt.'

~

Joanna had stifled her dismay at being hurried away from Serjeant Cowper. She hoped that their paths would cross again, though Louise had already advised her that it would not be proper for Serjeant Cowper to visit Boy while she was teaching him. Maybe he could bring in some medicinal herbs to show her class? Louise surely could not think that improper?

But then, no sooner had her aunt dismissed Serjeant Cowper because he wasn't an officer, than her father was welcoming Serjeant Fallowfield, one of his wretched Bible class group, though she had to admit that the fellow had made himself very agreeable to them all. He wasn't what you'd call handsome, but he did remind her of an old friend of her father's who used to tell such interesting tales about his adventures when she was a young girl. He had died at Waterloo; a hero's death, her father had said. Sometimes she persuaded herself that he was merely stationed somewhere else, like India, and they would meet him again one day. She missed him. Almost as much as her father did.

~

It was at times like these that Captain John Rowlandson regretted the loss of his wife most acutely. Possessed of considerable graciousness, she would have been able to weave her way between the officers' and the men's families without any discomfort. Once outside his own cohort in the artillery, he was neither fish nor fowl, he thought. He fitted in neither with the other ranks, nor with the officers. She would have known better than his sister or himself what to do about Joanna too, now she was becoming a woman. She certainly needed a chaperone in conversations with men. He hadn't liked the way she'd kept smiling at that batsman. His wife would have considered such behaviour vulgar, he was sure of that. And the man was scarcely gracious. Didn't even commiserate with him on their defeat. Not like Serjeant Fallowfield. Now there was a fellow who understood a man's feelings, with passable manners and affable in his conversation, yet completely serious in his faith after his own desperate experiences on the battlefield. Yes, he judged his daughter to be in far safer hands, engaging in an earnest discourse with Serjeant Fallowfield, than exchanging smiles with that batsman. And he was quite certain that his wife would have considered his old Peninsular acquaintance, Captain Haywood, an even more acceptable companion. Now where was the good captain? He looked round. Ah, there he was. He took Joanna's arm, and, making his apologies to Fallowfield, gently manoeuvred his sister and daughter in Haywood's direction. Now what would his wife do in this situation? 'Invite him to partake in a hearty meal, on a Sunday evening after your Bible classes, John. That's what you must do. And keep inviting him. Until he takes proper notice of our Joanna.'

14

The Soldier Needs A Wife

June 1816, Désvres, Pas-de-Calais. France

It was during another quiet evening with Freer, Louise, and Boy, a couple of weeks after the match, that Thomas finally shook himself out his months of despondency about Grace. With Boy resting his head against Thomas's arm and Billy sitting on his lap, he felt once again an overwhelming desire to have something to show for surviving the war. But what was different about this evening was a new-found determination. He was nearly twenty-eight years old. His pining for Grace had to stop and his courtship of Miss Rowlandson had to begin. He had to find a way to build a new life, to leave the last eleven years behind him, to cast off the old life that had caused him so much pain.

'It's time I looked for a wife, don't you think?' he announced.

Louise, busy mending officers' uniforms, her neat stitches skirmishing invisibly in the fabric, smiled. 'I couldn't agree more, Thomas. As long as she's the right wife.'

Louise and Freer were the only people Thomas had ever told about his attachment to Grace, although many of the men in his troop might well have guessed he'd had a sweetheart at home.

After a moment or two of silence, Freer looked across at Thomas. 'Tell me where you might find a wife in this damn place? The men can't get within a hundred yards of the French girls before their parents shoo them inside. And what with Vandeleur stopping the innkeepers serving us soldiers after nine, there's no chance of anyone getting to know their parents either.'

Freer tapped his pipe firmly against the hearth.

'As for the English lasses, they're like my Louise, mostly spoken for. Hardly any Waterloo widows left. Even Bonnie.'

Louise put her sewing down and looked Thomas straight in the eye. 'I know you both think Bonnie's only married Ashby because of his pension, but, whether that's true or not that's the reality of an army widow's life, isn't it? The number of times I've heard widows saying it was a choice between whoring or marrying as quick as they could back into the company.'

Louise picked up her sewing again and Freer tapped his pipe one more time on the fireplace. 'You might find yourself a widow back in England, but not here, though. There's not been many men dying these last few months.'

Thomas agreed. The horses had been dying off fast enough. But the men had kept remarkably well or, at least, stayed alive, in spite of the miasmas.

Freer continued to think aloud, as if this would conjure up more eligible women to be found in the Pas-de-Calais. 'What about sisters or daughters of the men, or maids of the officers' wives?'

Thomas seized his chance. 'Or a schoolmistress … or someone like that?' Thomas tried to widen the field.

Freer took the bait. 'Like that young lass who works with you, Louise?'

Louise adopted the same disapproving expression Thomas had seen when he'd said goodbye to her and Miss Rowlandson in front of the school a few weeks ago.

'That young lass is an officer's daughter. She won't be allowed near the likes of plain ordinary serjeants.'

Freer, though, became more, rather than less, enthusiastic. 'But Captain Rowlandson's an artillery officer, Louise. You know what they're like. They're just technical men. He could have started out as a butcher or baker, for all we know, and worked his way up. It's not likely he's a real gentleman.'

Louise became quite red in the face. 'He might not have been a gentleman once upon a time, but he's most certainly a gentleman now, and that'll be even more of a reason he won't want his daughter courted by a serjeant. No offence, Thomas.'

Thomas said nothing, stood up, shook down his trousers and gave Boy a hug. 'Must go. Before it gets too dark.' He had his answer. His hopes were just that. Not even worth crying over.

But as Thomas left Freer's quarters to make his way to his own lodgings in Haywood's billet, he still reflected on his unmarried state, the lack of a wife and baby, sitting side by side, cosy even, in spite of this incessant rain and dark skies. And tonight, with Littlethorpe away on other duties, he felt more alone than ever.

It was like that on most nights, even with Littlethorpe in tow. Once he'd left his old friends, he'd feel an immediate rush of loneliness. He'd normally greet Haywood in the farmhouse on his return. He found this helped steady him before retiring to sleep. But if Haywood had decided to dine out without his cover serjeant, Thomas's spirits would sink further, for Haywood was usually in and pleased to see him. Although Haywood preferred a quiet life and country pursuits rather than late nights flattering his superiors, he had often hinted that one day he hoped to rise further and then be able to support a wife and family of his own.

Sometimes Haywood talked of how, on his next leave, he might meet a suitable young woman, one prepared to accept a junior captain with little private money, though he too now seemed resigned to his lack of prospects. He thought it unlikely that a woman of breeding would wish to live where the land was half-submerged, threatening to turn the Pas-de-Calais itself into another Lowlands of mosquitoes and fever. It was something that Haywood often spoke of, unaware that this same topic was also worrying his cover serjeant.

But that evening, before he reached the farmhouse, Thomas stopped Fearless by the healing spring, fingered his Waterloo metal still tucked away safe in his sabretache and swore on his medal that he would find a suitable wife, that he would not let himself be discouraged and that he would find a way to woo Miss Rowlandson, in spite of everything. Maybe he could persuade Freer, even if not Louise, to act as some kind of intermediary, or even chaperone while he tried to get to know her better. After all, she had smiled at him several times now, though … and this worried him … he had seen Fallowfield at the cricket match being far too attentive to her father and aunt. What was that man planning? To gain influence, at the very least, over Miss Rowlandson. Thomas thought it would be just like Fallowfield to find a way to worm himself into the bosom of the officer classes. Thomas tightened his grip around his medal and told himself that there must be a way to thwart Fallowfield. And he would have to find it.

But, as he arrived back at the farmhouse Haywood greeted him, with some news that obviously pleased him.

'I have just received an invitation from Captain Rowlandson to dine with him and his sister and daughter next Sunday evening. Of course, I've already accepted. Tragic thing that Rowlandson has had to bring up his daughter unaided, except for the aunt, of course. Lost his wife when the child was scarcely two or three. Strange, though, that he never married again. He's an amiable enough fellow, who's also extremely clever with all that mathematics business you need in the artillery. Wouldn't have suited me, I can tell you.' Haywood beamed at Thomas. 'So both of us Sunday then, there and back.'

Escorting Captain Haywood back and forth along the forest roads to visit the Rowlandsons would be his penance for even thinking about Miss Rowlandson.

~

And so, as the coldest summer Thomas had known drifted into autumn, he and Haywood would visit Captain Rowlandson's house most Sundays, and on one of those evenings, on their way there, they unexpectedly came across Fallowfield leaving one of Rowlandson's Bible classes. Fallowfield, the last to go, was saying his farewells, laughing and joking with the Captain, but then he must have caught sight of Miss Rowlandson standing in the doorway, and Thomas saw him bow in her direction. At first she appeared to hesitate, but then Thomas saw her smile shyly. No doubt about it, she was smiling at Fallowfield. Thomas felt his temper rise and felt sure that Fallowfield was playing with her feelings most likely for his own ends – his pursuit of the troop serjeant-major's position.

Fallowfield, as was usual nowadays, was most affable and stopped briefly to pay his compliments to Captain Haywood, but merely nodding briefly to Thomas. It was at times like that Thomas had to repeat to himself that it was just a question of holding your ground, not letting those snake eyes force you into submission.

~

Thomas nodded back to Fallowfield, caught up with Haywood and retired to the stables for the rest of the evening. At least he had Fearless to keep him company whilst Haywood wooed Miss Rowlandson.

But on the way back Haywood seemed out of sorts. 'I don't know what Rowlandson thinks he's doing, convening those damned meetings at his own house. If the man wants to take up religion, he should at least have the decency to keep it away from his own front door. Unless he's a parson, of course.'

And Haywood was positively indiscreet in his complaints about Rowlandson's sister. 'She really is very forward. Constantly smiling at me and hinting that Miss Rowlandson is now of marriageable age.'

Thomas couldn't be sure whether Haywood's indignation was more to do with the aunt's breach of etiquette, or whether, after all these months, he still wasn't sure if Miss Rowlandson would be a suitable match. Thomas tried in vain to stop himself wondering about where Haywood's future, or his own, might lie.

It was as though he could never let down his guard. He was always watchful. When he was riding home at night, he'd listen out for the breaking of twigs, the rustle of an ambush. The woods were as dangerous as they were beautiful, and it would be easy for even two men to be set upon. And no one would be any the wiser as to the assailant.

~

Jack Fallowfield wondered how he might better use Rowlandson's friendship with Haywood to greater advantage. The girl, of course, was an added complication. Rowlandson clearly had hopes of Haywood as a possible husband, so Jack would have to watch his step there. After all, Haywood had been turning up most Sundays with Cowper in tow, covering his back.

Still, this order that everyone had to be on guard against footpads and stray enemy troops might prove to be useful … one of these days. Perhaps, one night, crossing the forest, Cowper might find himself separated from Haywood by one of these fellows. Who knows what might happen then?

15

Called To Account

October 1816, Désvres, Pas-de Calais, France

Thomas couldn't imagine a worse torture than accompanying Haywood to the Rowlandsons to court Miss Joanna, as Haywood called her now, though she usually greeted both of them with a smile. Thomas, of course, kept a respectful distance and took some solace from her friendly acknowledgment of him, but it wasn't enough to lift his mood as the nights shortened and darkness accompanied them both there and back through the forest.

By October, Thomas had taken to spending any spare evenings with Fearless, grooming her until her coat shone. Sometimes Thomas felt that she was the only friend he had left, for, though he was overjoyed to have Freer back by his side, Thomas grieved that their years of intimacy were slowly, but decidedly, slipping away.

One Monday evening, Thomas heard the stable door swing open. It was Littlethorpe, who now rocked back on his heels, as if to study Thomas's efforts.

'Not sure that's going to work. They've only got to look at her teeth to see how old she is.'

The six-monthly inspections were coming up. Tensions were running high. Soldiers who had still not mastered the lance would be sent away for further training, and any horses deemed to be unfit would be sent to the knacker's yard.

Thomas resumed his grooming. 'They still can't get hold of enough remounts, so as long as she looks like she can do the job, that'll be half the battle.'

Littlethorpe made as if to go, then paused. 'I hear they're already on their way. By tomorrow, they reckon.'

Thomas dropped his brush. 'Who told you that?'

Littlethorpe tapped his nose. And with that he left.

~

Haywood couldn't contain himself. The inspection report was damned unfair, praising those who had mastered their new weapons, whilst quietly damning their commander for the Regiment's shortage of good-quality horses and his officers' poor morale. It wasn't as though any of the occupying regiments, as far as anyone knew, had received any better reports, but anything less than full battle readiness had translated itself in the report into backsliding.

Whilst Haywood was very indignant, Thomas was much less so, as they had spared Fearless from their cull of horses. But Haywood was not to be cheered up and talked a great deal about transferring to another regiment. But that would cost him money, and money was one thing he certainly didn't have.

Acting Lieutenant-Colonel Bridges, though, seemed rather less downhearted. He decreed that morale would be boosted by a ball. This caused Haywood yet more grief. But Mrs Bridges had spoken, and with a great flurry of activity the date of the ball was set for the beginning of October.

Then one evening, a week before the ball, Freer took Thomas aside to tell him he had heard more news about Grey's troop serjeant-major post. 'He has to go back to the

Pension Board in a year. So we have another year to prepare the ground.'

'As does Fallowfield,' Thomas pointed out. 'And just look at what happened to Captain Webster, when you were promoted instead of Fallowfield. He got three months in a debtor's prison for his pains.'

Freer agreed. 'I can't believe how long he bided his time over that.'

Thomas nodded. They both knew only too well how long Fallowfield could hold a grudge, choosing exactly when to strike at a time that suited him.

'So now you must take him on properly, stop him going after Haywood.' Freer leant back against his chair. 'How many secrets does Haywood have?'

Thomas shrugged. 'Hardly any, I reckon.'

Freer sighed with some relief. 'So the man's not likely to be in debt to Fallowfield already, is he?'

'I shouldn't think so, though everybody knows he's short of money.' Thomas blushed at being thought indiscreet, as if Freer wouldn't have noticed Haywood's fraying shirt cuffs.

Freer replied as quick as a sabre's cut. 'So he doesn't gamble or do anything wild and reckless, as far as you can tell?'

Thomas couldn't recall anything that even Fallowfield could use as a gun to Haywood's head. 'Apart from shooting rabbits?'

Freer stared at the floor as if studying a battle plan. 'We both know that Fallowfield will move Heaven and Earth to get some hold over him before the year is out.'

'Haywood leads a remarkably blameless life.'

'Then Fallowfield will have to try hard, but try he will, so you'll have to protect Haywood in your capacity as his cover serjeant, in every aspect of his life.'

Thomas studied Freer's serious expression and knew he wasn't joking. Freer would never underestimate Fallowfield's skill in getting under people's skin.

'If nothing else, you owe that to the Regiment.'

Thomas nodded. 'You're right. Fallowfield has to be stopped. One way or another.'

Freer grinned and slapped Thomas on the shoulder. 'Good man.'

He stood up and stirred the spluttering fire back into life. 'I'd watch your own back and all.'

Thomas sighed. How on earth was he going to keep Haywood out of Fallowfield's clutches for another year?

16

The Ball

October 1816, Désvres, Pas-de-Calais, France

Henry Haywood hated these occasions. He'd never been extravagant, but nowadays he was finding it harder than ever to keep up appearances. For that reason alone, he spent most of his time quietly in his troop's farmhouse, with only the occasional foray out to hunt small game. In that way, he kept his expenses down and expectations of hospitality from his fellow officers low, except for kind-hearted John Rowlandson, who graciously accepted his gifts of game without expectation. So it was with some trepidation that Haywood had asked Freer's wife to smarten up his dress uniform and refurbish what she could of his shirts and linen. They came back almost as good as new, a transformation he could scarcely credit, but for which he was very grateful.

So now he was sitting in his almost pristine uniform, like a dummy set up for target practice, on the edge of a draughty salon with scarcely any remnants of gracious furnishing left to offset its faded walls. Still, the musicians were in fine form and he detected an air of gaiety amongst his fellow officers. He cast his mind back to that wayside breakfast before Quatre Bras, when all those old friendships had seemed more innocent. Haywood hastily rubbed the corner of his eye, and tried to concentrate on the business in hand … looking for a wife with her own means who would not expect him to provide a fortune equal to her own.

It was galling, but much as he'd expected when he'd been sent on his way with a cavalry commission, his only dowry. His father had also written lately to say that he was low on funds; the price of corn had now been regulated at a decent price by the government, but with yields low and costs high, and with the promise of another catastrophic harvest, his father had felt obliged to warn him that it was unlikely further subsidies would be forthcoming for several years at least.

He cast his eyes around the room. There's young Joanna Rowlandson, dancing with a stout fellow, in the leading pair. Poor man seems rather reluctant. No doubt her aunt has already instructed the girl to ensnare anyone with a substantial fortune. Still, if only she had money, he might be tempted himself. Haywood found all this a trying business. Perhaps there would be more enjoyment to be had, if he did not worry about it so much? He'd no sooner decided that he would leave all considerations of matrimony aside when he was accosted by Rowlandson, who insisted he join them on the other side of the salon.

~

Joanna found the whole business distasteful. Although she had sat patiently with her dance card, chaperoned by Aunt Rowley and the other officers' wives, she soon realised that she was being ignored. Occasionally an overweight lieutenant or sympathetic ensign felt it his duty to offer to partner her. But though Joanna knew she was good at maintaining a calm and contented countenance under fire, she was losing heart. Still, that is what you are known for, she told herself. Perhaps she could try just a little harder to look more animated? But Joanna had no talent for flirting, and had failed completely whenever she had tried. Besides, with no money or status to her name, she possessed nothing that would commend itself to a curious stranger. There was simply no point in fretting about her almost empty dance card; unlike her father, who'd exclaimed that he couldn't understand why so few fellows had asked her to dance.

It was at this point that Joanna realised that her father had little idea how finely graduated were the dividing lines between acceptance and rejection by polite society. She also disliked the brashness that the young men displayed when they came sniffing around the women, waiting to be asked to dance. Joanna could tell they doubted the quality of her dress, the tilt of her bosom, the truth of the smile on her lips, her desire to please. Joanna snorted quietly to herself. This was also why she was so rarely asked to dance.

But when her father came back he was in quite a different mood. He'd unexpectedly bumped into Captain Haywood. Perhaps they could provide each other, at the least, with a dancing companion.

~

Henry Haywood bowed and presented his compliments, as expected, to Rowlandson's daughter, but quickly found his eyes wandering to the young companion of one of the officers' wives. He recognised her to be the sister of Berwick, one of the fine fellows who'd taken breakfast with him that morning before Quatre Bras, and the only one, apart from himself, who had survived.

Turning away from Miss Rowlandson, he bowed to Berwick's sister. She smiled. 'I am glad to greet my dear brother's friend once again, and I see that you are no longer a mere lieutenant. You cannot imagine, Captain Haywood, how thankful I am that my brother, and you yourself, were spared, though, as you know, he did sustain injuries which restrict his active service.' She explained that Berwick was now a staff officer in another regiment nearby and she was visiting him.

Haywood bowed even deeper. 'Lady Catherine, I am delighted once more to make your acquaintance.'

Lady Catherine Berwick glanced down at her dance card and then quickly back to Haywood, who understood the signal sufficiently well to offer to mark her card and to sit down to exchange pleasantries.

~

Captain John Rowlandson studied his daughter. Handsome enough, he thought, but perhaps lacking that air of gentility that everyone seemed to think important. He looked over at Haywood, who was now engrossed in an intense conversation with a finely dressed woman. 'An old friend's sister,' he heard one of the officers' wives whisper. Even Haywood had hardly registered Joanna's presence. Rowlandson gazed round the ballroom: the women's ringlets bobbing, feet tapping, gauzy gowns swirling. Glancing again at his daughter, he began to fear that his fellow officers might think it not worth their while to get to know her.

~

Thomas stamped his feet. This waiting around for Haywood to pursue his courtship with Miss Rowlandson was getting him down. And, to cap it all, Fallowfield had contrived to act as an escort to another officer, who also lived beyond the forest. Last seen, Fallowfield had been standing near the main doors, chatting to the guards and scrutinising everyone who crossed the threshold. Thomas retreated away from the music and light cast by the shadows of the East Wing, listening to the creak of the great trees in the parkland, their branches silhouetted against the misty halo of the full moon.

But then he caught sight of Miss Rowlandson darting out of the front door, straight past Fallowfield. She had slung a flimsy shawl over her shoulders. Her sobs got louder as she moved towards the darkness. Soon she would be in the shadows too. She would not want him to see her so distressed. But it was too late. She skidded to a halt. He stumbled out an apology.

'Begging your pardon, Miss Rowlandson. I didn't mean to give you a fright. I'm ... waiting for Captain Haywood.' Thomas paused.

She was trying to rub away the tears.

'You must be cold. Would you like to borrow my cape?'

Miss Rowlandson nodded and allowed him to place it over her shoulders. It was not enough to stop her trembling, clearly now not just with the cold.

'You're very kind, Serjeant Cowper. Kinder than many a so-called gentleman.'

Thomas shivered. 'Sometimes things ... are easier if you don't have a position to keep up.'

'I'd always thought your Captain Haywood was better than that.'

Thomas swallowed hard. So Haywood was the reason for her tears. Had he, or hadn't he, declared himself? He wasn't sure he wanted to know.

'The Captain is a good-natured gentleman, who I am sure would not wish to upset anyone, but, sometimes, he just doesn't notice he might be causing offence. I can speak from experience about that.'

Miss Rowlandson brushed away more tears. 'You can?'

Thomas offered her his handkerchief. 'Oh yes. But, without any malice. Though, of course, that's not to say it's any less hurtful.'

Miss Rowlandson blew her nose hard in what, Thomas guessed, would probably be considered an unladylike fashion. 'It's not that I was expecting anything … Not like Aunt Rowley or my father. It's just that …' She stopped and blew her nose again. 'It's just that, if even an amiable gentleman like Captain Haywood cannot bring himself to dance with me, then will anyone ever …' She trailed off.

And Thomas found himself unexpectedly emboldened.

'Well, I certainly would, Miss Rowlandson. I would dance with you all night long if I could though …'he stuttered, I only know country dances.' He felt his face blush red.

Miss Rowlandson burst into more tears, then hastily dabbed her cheeks . 'Oh, Serjeant Cowper. No wonder Boy loves you.' And with that, she turned round, towards the light spinning out of the doorway. 'I must return, or my aunt will never forgive me. And that would never do, would it?'

'I expect not.' Thomas bowed.

Joanna handed him his cape. 'Thank you, Serjeant Cowper.'

'Thomas', he said.

Joanna straightened her shawl. 'Joanna,' she replied.

~

Jack Fallowfield thought it a strange business, but not entirely unexpected, as he watched the Rowlandson girl disappear into the darkness. When she brushed past him into the château ten minutes or so later, he noted the red eyes and traces of tears, but found no other clues as to what had upset her. But, at the end of the ball, he noticed Haywood nearly collide with Rowlandson, as the father, the aunt and the daughter came down the steps. Rowlandson was remarkably cool towards Haywood, keeping his greeting to well within the normal bounds of politeness. Fallowfield could feel the chill from where he was standing. Damn it. He'd been banking on Haywood and Rowlandson staying the best of friends. Building an alliance with Rowlandson to influence Haywood now looked unlikely. He would have to find another way.

Fallowfield scrutinised their faces for further clues. The aunt and daughter looked equally strained, though the daughter had, by now, wiped away any sign of tears. Haywood, though, was smiling, seemingly unaware of the Rowlandsons' mood. But that was Haywood for you. He never did notice what was going on right under his nose. Fallowfield stroked his chin. Haywood must have upset the daughter somehow. Still, there was no need to stop attending Rowlandson's classes. Bound to come in useful, one day. He walked forward to pay his compliments to the Captain, smiling at the aunt and daughter. Only Rowlandson acknowledged his greeting.

Not long afterwards, Haywood re-appeared, escorting a fellow officer and his wife and a much younger woman down the steps towards a rather fine carriage, Haywood talking most animatedly to the younger woman. Fallowfield knew that the officer and his wife were far from rich so … aha … the carriage must belong to the young woman. Fallowfield grinned. And how could a man without a penny to his name hope to impress a woman who could command such a grand carriage, just to leave a humble officers' ball? Fallowfield ran down the steps towards the stables to collect the horses. This was precisely the moment he'd been waiting for.

~

John Rowlandson couldn't believe how badly the evening had turned out. His best hope of finding a suitable match for his daughter had spent most of his time talking to another woman. As he undressed, he pondered as to what he might do next. It wasn't as though his sister would be any help in the matter. She clearly harboured very fixed ideas about suitable suitors. So, what would his wife have said? Well, John, he could hear her saying. It's not a question of looking for the ideal husband, but more a question of finding an acceptable candidate. He climbed into bed and recalled Fallowfield's steady expression as they'd left that evening. Now there was a man after his own heart, someone who knew the true value of being one of God's children. And he'd heard that Fallowfield might be in contention for the troop sergeant-major's vacancy coming up in Haywood's troop. And given that a troop serjeant-major could be promoted, without any commission required, to the post of cornet, Fallowfield's future prospects were decent enough. After all, it might be just as big a problem if Joanna married too far up the social scale. Officers like himself were not always acceptable guests around a gentleman's dinner table. Of course, now wasn't the right moment to approach Joanna. But, give it time, and matters might work out quite nicely. And with that thought he fell asleep, content.

~

Thomas hadn't seen Haywood so happy for some time, chatting about this and that as they left the ball, and then almost dropping his guard completely as they rode side by side through the woods.

'Do you remember,' Haywood began, 'those fine fellows I had breakfast with before Quatre Bras?'

'When I stopped your servant from pilfering?'

'Ah, yes, I should have got rid of him long before. Well, the sad fact of the matter is that only one of them, Lieutenant, now Captain Berwick, has survived. A great tragedy. All excellent soldiers.'

'I remember you telling me, sir.'

'Well, I've just had the good fortune to meet once again Captain Berwick's sister, Lady Catherine, a most charming woman, and she's invited me for dinner next Sunday to renew my acquaintance with her brother. He was indisposed this evening and couldn't attend the ball.'

'Instead of going to Captain Rowlandson's?'

'Yes of course, that's awkward, but I'll just have to offer my apologies. I'm sure they'll understand, for this once. Long lost friend and all that …'

'So where do they live?'

'Just a stone's throw from Captain Rowlandson's. I'll be needing you, just the same.'

Thomas now understood why Joanna had been so upset. He just wished he could make her feel better; that she wasn't an officer's daughter; and that Louise hadn't warned him against visiting her alone.

17

Devotion

November 1816, Désvres, Pas-de-Calais, France

Joanna Rowlandson was disappointed. She had hoped to have fallen in love by now with a suitable beau, though she had never been quite sure about Captain Haywood. Though Serjeant Cowper ... Thomas ... was probably right, that Captain Haywood hadn't intended to snub her. She smiled as she remembered what else Thomas had said; that he would have danced with her all night. Then she stopped smiling. She realised she was unlikely to be courted by anybody her father would consider unsuitable.

She was even disappointed at school. She had hoped to teach the girls elementary arithmetic or reading and writing, not plain sewing and knitting. The only saving grace to these mornings was the presence of Louise Freer, but as she marvelled at the devotion Louise's husband and Billy bestowed upon her, Joanna felt even more in need of being loved. And of someone to love.

And yet it was only today that she finally acknowledged to herself that she already had someone to love. Not a sweetheart. But someone she loved, as much as if she were his mother.

~

Boy looked forward to his afternoons with Joanna. But what he really looked forward to were the evenings, playing with Billy, or crouched by the wood fire, leaning his back against Thomas's knees, watching and listening. He knew it couldn't last. Thomas had already told him that Bonnie and Ashby wanted to take him back next year to England to learn a trade. If only Fallowfield had died instead of Dermot.

If only the dreams weren't getting worse … horses and men dragging him into a whirling tunnel of darkness. And the more he tried to make out the soldier who killed his mother, the more the fellow disappeared into a blur of blue uniforms and British flags.

~

When Joanna arrived she seemed flustered. 'Let me just tell you something before we begin.' She hesitated. 'You are such a clever boy. Your mother would have been so proud of you.' And with that she sat down and opened up his homework book.

Moments later, Thomas followed her into the room. He smiled at Joanna and then came over to gently ruffle Boy's hair, before quietly sitting down behind her.

Joanna planted a kiss on Boy's head. 'It's not as easy as everyone seems to think, to say what you really want to say to people, is it?'

She smiled. At him. And Thomas.

Boy was happy; he felt loved. Surrounded by love. Joanna was the second kindest person he knew. After Thomas.

18

Prospects

Winter had already set in; leaves shattered underfoot; heavy frosts weighed down branches, low enough to strike their faces, as the horses carefully picked their way over the frozen, rutted tracks.

It was Christmas Eve and Haywood and Thomas were on their way to the Berwicks, Haywood dressed in his brand-new uniform, carrying not only a brace of pheasants, but also a couple of well-wrapped parcels on the back of his horse. The invitation for Haywood to spend Christmas Eve and Day with the Berwicks had caused Haywood to become despondent as he surveyed his wardrobe. He'd grumbled, 'There is a point when a gentleman cannot give himself that title if his linen and uniform look as though they were the very same he wore at Waterloo.'

Haywood had exaggerated, but there was no denying his uniforms had lost their shine, despite Louise's efforts. 'And that he brings nothing to their table.'

Thomas had pointed out that Haywood's gifts of game had always been acceptable before. So why not now?

'But not good enough for a lady.' Haywood had declared. 'Not for a lady.' And, quite unlike his usual self, he said nothing at all for the rest of the journey.

The Berwicks' house was set back in its own grounds, with large stables and separate kitchens. Thomas had recently spent rather too many evenings there, grooming both Fearless and Haywood's horse, a handsome but nervous mare, who'd been almost impossible to ride when Haywood had first bought her. 'That's the second time you've saved my life,' Haywood had said when she'd bolted and would have tipped him into the Seine if it hadn't been for Thomas heading her off.

With Haywood invited to stay, it looked as though he would have to spend the night in the stable loft. That was no hardship, but he'd rather have been tucked up in Freer's cottage, with Billy and Boy playing at his feet. So he thought he was imagining things when he heard Freer's voice at the stable door.

'I thought I'd find you here,' said Freer. 'Berwick has cast his net to draw in Webster as well as Haywood.'

Without thinking, Thomas automatically took Webster's horse and started to take off the saddle. Freer didn't object. He has his own horse to see to and Thomas was still much quicker than Freer when it came to unsaddling horses.

'I suspect Haywood thought he would have Lady Berwick to himself.'

'I imagine he did, but then Berwick must have decided it was worth introducing her to another gentleman with not a penny to his name.'

Thomas began undoing the bridle. 'Tell me if I'm wrong, but I never reckoned that Webster was, let us say, interested in matrimony.'

Freer and Webster were close, not as close as he was with Thomas, but close enough.

'Hard to tell. But for my money, he'd rather handle a statue with a gold halo and a bleeding heart than fondle real flesh and blood. Besides, Catholic priests don't marry, do they?'

'But he's not a priest. Or even Catholic.'

'Give him time; give him time.'

'Then Haywood's got nothing to worry about?'

'Who knows? He might surprise us yet. I imagine Berwick must be hoping to find someone with a decent income, but there's not so many of them about nowadays.'

'Then how can anyone afford to marry?'

'Oh, Lady Catherine's got her own money, left to her by some aunt. Not a great fortune, but more than enough to live well on, so they say.'

Thomas smiled. Freer was back on form, gathering up all the gossip from God knows where.

'Just as well then, as Haywood must have used up all his credit by now, what with his new clothes, and presents suitable for a lady as he keeps saying.'

~

Berwick had invited a few more of his neighbours, as he put it, and soon the stables were overflowing with horses, grooms and escorts until their host finally sent word that food and ale would be provided for them in one of the back kitchens. It was a merry gathering till Thomas was astonished to see one of Rowlandson's grooms enter late to the feast. Lady Catherine had lent the Rowlandsons her carriage, but 'one of the wheels has been nothing but trouble, so I can tell you, we've practically slithered here,' said the fellow, filling a tankard.

~

Henry Haywood had been embarrassed to see Rowlandson and the Misses Rowlandson enter, with many an apology for their late appearance. But Rowlandson was in a surprisingly expansive mood and bowed very amiably in his direction. Haywood was much reassured, as he'd come to realise that he'd handled his withdrawal from their regular evenings most ungraciously. He hastily drank his third glass of wine. By the time Rowlandson made his way across to speak to him, he felt a good deal more relaxed.

Rowlandson bowed again. 'Delighted to see you, Haywood. Perhaps in the better weather we may resume our dining arrangement, even if it must be less frequently. So treacherous through the forest, I imagine.'

Haywood sighed with relief at the amiable Rowlandson's forgiving tone and swallowed another mouthful of wine.

'Now I do have a question or two to ask you about Serjeant Fallowfield regarding his prospects for promotion, and consequently for, perhaps, marriage.'

Haywood was surprised. He drank a little more wine.

Quite unexpectedly, a surge of warm fellow-feeling rose in him towards Fallowfield, who had been so very helpful of late. Indeed, he had saved the day when all had seemed lost. Such an enterprising fellow. And the good serjeant understood what it was like for an officer to be looked down upon and denied possible happiness because of a lack of fortune and status. Haywood indicated that Rowlandson should sit down where they could talk more comfortably.

'Serjeant Fallowfield is the most diligent of soldiers and I have no doubt, for example' … he suddenly found himself plucking possibilities out of the air …'that one day, he might well make an excellent troop serjeant-major. Indeed, there will be a vacancy at the end of this year in my own company. And I would consider him suitable. Most suitable.' Haywood felt by now so relaxed, and so happy to sing the praises of Fallowfield that he and Captain Rowlandson, over two or three more glasses of albeit modest Pas-de-Calais wine, established that each of them had found the attitude of some of their superiors discouraging and condescending to those less fortunate than themselves in wealth and connections.

'You must come hunting with me and … some other fellows … after Christmas. I'm expecting a couple of setters over from England. Quite soon. Magnificent breed … excellent gundogs. Lost my last two at Waterloo. Not much of the season left, though, and I'll have to train 'em first. Still, you'll be more than welcome.'

Rowlandson beamed. 'Delighted, my dear Haywood. Another glass?'

19

A Proposal

January 1817, Désvres, Pas-de-Calais, France

Jack Fallowfield tucked his knees as best he could under the table. Last week Rowlandson had suggested that he might join him in a simple supper of bread and cheese after Bible class. With Haywood's attention elsewhere, Fallowfield had wondered what advantage there might be in spending yet more time with Rowlandson, the aunt who talked too much and the girl who talked too little. Still, Rowlandson seemed to be on good terms with other cavalry officers besides Haywood. Fallowfield didn't fool himself that he would ever be accepted as an equal by an officer, though Rowlandson seemed to have developed a soft spot for him. But he was still surprised when Rowlandson took the opportunity to question him about his prospects. 'Now, Serjeant, I hear Captain Haywood may have a vacancy for a troop sergeant-major?'

Fallowfield tried to look as though this was not a matter of great moment to him. 'You mean Troop Serjeant-Major Grey's position, sir?'

Rowlandson hesitated. 'Is there another?'

Fallowfield continued to try and look dispassionate. 'I don't think so, sir.'

Rowlandson cleared his throat. 'Now, let me get this right. My understanding is that you are one of the most senior sergeants in the Regiment?'

He nodded and smiled as modestly he could muster. 'By many years.'

Rowlandson hesitated again. 'Then, what do you reckon your chances are of securing this position, Serjeant?'

'That's not for me to judge, sir.'

Rowlandson became a little bit more forthcoming. 'A position such as that would enable a man to live comfortably enough, particularly with the privileges for a wife and children that would come with it.'

Fallowfield looked down at the table. 'As you know, sir, I have no wife or children.'

Rowlandson looked awkward. 'Like so many men caught up in the War. But many are now taking advantage of the peace to find a wife.'

Of course, Rowlandson was on the look-out for a husband for his daughter.

'That is true, sir, but without prospects, an ordinary soldier can rarely make plans of that nature.'

Rowlandson spoke more earnestly. 'But consider, Serjeant, that a troop sergeant-major might even be promoted to cornet. I am surprised that Grey never was, though everyone says his lack of ambition was apparent from an early stage. But an energetic and courageous man could make much of himself.'

Rowlandson paused. 'And a man with such prospects would be welcome in many households.'

Fallowfield smiled again. 'That is, indeed, most gratifying to hear, sir.'

He couldn't believe his good fortune. Rowlandson would encourage him to court his daughter, if he became a troop sergeant-major. And no doubt Rowlandson would assist him in that endeavour. Of course, he would be a fool to turn down this opportunity. But as for marrying the Rowlandson girl? Well, he'd have to see how biddable she really was.

20

The Memorial

February 1817, Désvres, Pas-de-Calais, France

Waterloo, The Low Counties, January 1ˢᵗ, 1817

Dear Cowper,

Thank you for your letter and your news. Our Christmas here was quiet. As you can imagine, with this bad weather, we have had few tourists risking the roads to visit. But we have been much occupied. I was asked by Captain Webster to oversee the final touches to the Regimental Memorial in the church to ensure that, as a speaker of English, I could inspect the final carving of the names. Hard as it was to read the names of our friends on my list, I was much gratified to see that, unlike in many regiments, all our men have been remembered in stone at the site of their great sacrifice. I have noticed that most of the memorials being erected close to the battlefield commemorate only officers or noble gentlemen, whose families have raised the funds to ensure that they are not forgotten, and so it is to the credit of Captain Webster that he and Lieutenant-Colonel Pennington have contrived to raise enough money to ensure that all ranks are lined up side by side on the memorial much as they were lined up side by side on that fateful day.

Bonnie and I took great pride in attending the Christmas Eve service, where we could also pay tribute, not only to God's work, but also to our fellow soldiers. Bonnie, of course, enjoys finding herself once again among a Catholic congregation, so I do my best not to resent all the fripperies that go with that faith and the incomprehensible prayers of the priest. Bonnie takes great comfort in the mysteries of this religion, whilst I prefer my God to be represented by more plain-speaking and rough-hewn men of the cloth.

We are now making plans to return home in the early spring. I have saved enough to purchase two looms and Bonnie has declared she has finished with telling Dermot's story, whatever she means by that.

We have been delighted to hear how much progress Boy has made in his letters but we feel the time has come, for his own safety, to suggest that Boy should return to us as soon as you can make proper arrangements...

~

Jack Fallowfield stifled a shout of triumph and then read the last paragraph one more time, just to make sure he hadn't imagined it.

Once he was satisfied he had memorised all that he needed to, he carefully resealed the envelope and placed it back in the alphabetical letter slots to await collection. *"Vengeance is mine; I will repay, saith the Lord."*

21

A Conspiracy Of Silence

February 1817, Désvres, Pas-de-Calais, France

Once he had found Boy, everything else would be just between him and Cowper. So now it was merely a matter of elimination. Jack Fallowfield had already been working his way through each troop of soldiers, enquiring whether anyone might know what had happened to poor Boy, noting evasions and any shuffling of feet when asked. No one reckoned he was dead. No one reckoned he'd returned to England. Fallowfield had already decided that the complete absence of information pointed to a conspiracy of silence, and the quarry being somewhere close. But now he understood. Someone was teaching him his letters.

~

Fallowfield knew he would have to be careful. Freer's wife was not a woman to be easily persuaded. At the very least, he would have to be in possession of official orders before she would let him anywhere near the school.

Persuading Haywood, though, would be quite a different matter. After all, Haywood continued to be think him 'a fine chap' and be 'exceedingly grateful' for 'services rendered' … as well as not being the suspicious type. It would be just a question of spinning him the right kind of yarn.

'Excuse me for disturbing you, sir,' he began, ' but I have been hearing rumours that one of these feral children is running free in the forest nearby. Completely out of control. Like a wild animal.'

Haywood looked up, astonished. But Webster had told him that there were 'such phenomena in these vast forests of France.'

'Seen near the school, they think, clearly up to no good, sir. Perhaps, if you would give me the necessary authority to question the school children and teachers … and conduct a search of the school and its environs?'

Haywood hesitated, then took up his pen and reached for some paper. 'As you think fit, serjeant. We can't have a creature like that running wild near the school. Now tell me, will you require men to assist your investigation?'

'I don't believe so, sir. It'll be nothing I can't deal with myself. '

~

As he expected, he got a cold welcome from Freer's wife. The woman was a surly madam, if ever he met one.

'Good day to you, Mrs Freer. I've come to check your registers and search your premises for a missing child.'

Freer's wife just stood there with her arms folded. 'That is surely a matter for the School Serjeant to attend to.'

He showed her Haywood's letter of authorisation. 'I wouldn't know, Mrs Freer. I am merely following orders.'

Freer's wife continued to stare at him.

'I also need to speak to Miss Rowlandson. Would you be so kind as to oblige?'

Freer's wife protested, 'I'm sure I'll be able to answer any question you might wish to ask Miss Rowlandson well enough.'

'My orders, Mrs Freer, are to speak to everyone.'

Freer's wife turned her back on him. 'If I must, Serjeant Fallowfield.'

Whilst she was gone Fallowfield counted the number of children in attendance and, contriving to look serious yet friendly, told them he was looking for a little boy who couldn't speak. They clearly didn't know what, or who, he was talking about.

By the time Freer's wife had come back with Rowlandson's daughter, he was ready to spin them his tale about the wild boy and to question them all in case they'd seen anybody answering to that description, ready to sniff out evasive answers and suspicious looks.

~

Another frustrating afternoon. Nobody knew anything about anyone, they said, though he wasn't so sure about Miss Rowlandson. She had addressed him politely enough and both she and Freer's wife had made notes about the information he asked for. But there was something about her manner when he asked for the names of the children she taught…

Fallowfield thought he might possibly press her a little harder, if he returned later that day, when she wouldn't be with Freer's wife. But he would have to tread carefully. Perhaps he could offer to walk her back to her father's lodgings, which were only a short distance away, on the edge of the forest.

~

Joanna was surprised to see Serjeant Fallowfield waiting for her outside the château's gates, but he was now most gracious and solicitous.

'I must apologise for intruding on your lessons earlier today with my enquiries about the young boy. I am concerned that I might have alarmed you, so if you might do me the honour of letting me escort you home?'

Joanna thought the speech a pretty one. 'That is very kind of you, Serjeant Fallowfield. I was not overly alarmed by your account but I am happy for you to walk back with me to my father's house.'

'I was not only concerned that this child, who is closer to an animal than a human being, might cause mischief for those out walking alone, but also that the child himself might come to harm at the hands of a reckless huntsman.'

Joanna noticed how grave Serjeant Fallowfield seemed when describing this child. But this creature he was so concerned about was surely not Boy. He must be talking about another lost child.

'My only wish is to do my Christian duty and prevent any harm coming to either the child or to anyone else that encounters him.'

The Serjeant stopped briefly to look at her directly. 'So Miss Rowlandson, now you've had more time to think, have you ever happened across this boy?'

She began to waver. Had the Serjeant heard that Boy had come into these parts and was worried he would have been forced to fend for himself? Should she reassure him, and tell him Boy was safe? But she had promised Thomas and Louise that she would say nothing; and Louise had even whispered to her after the Serjeant had left this morning, 'Remember, tell no one about Boy.'

'The creature that does not speak. On your walks home perhaps? '

She heard the urgency in his voice, saw the quizzical look, the sharply defined features, the concerned expression and then the eyes … those grey eyes that never really smiled.

She twisted her hands together and replied carefully, 'I'm afraid I have never come across such a child, Serjeant Fallowfield, but I assure you, that should I do so I would tell the nearest soldier.'

Joanna comforted herself with the thought that this was not really a lie, as Boy did not answer the Serjeant's description. Still, she felt a little guilty, especially as her father, as the convenor of the Bible study group, always spoke of Serjeant Fallowfield most warmly. But her father wasn't always right about those kinds of things, she reminded herself.

~

The walk home had been pleasant enough. Serjeant Fallowfield had entertained her with his stories of skirmishes and battles, and colourful tales about the strange habits of the people of the Peninsula. He'd even asked her whether she was as clever at arithmetic as her father. It wasn't a question she had ever been asked before, and she hesitated before declaring that she did rather like mathematics.

'Well', he'd said, 'I could always put a word in with the School Sergeant, to see whether he might allow you to teach the children mathematics. How would that suit you, Miss Rowlandson?'

'Thank you, Serjeant Fallowfield. I am sure that would be interesting, but I'm not sure what Mrs Freer would think.'

But, when he'd suggested that he might accompany her again, she hadn't been sure about that, so she'd said nothing other than to wish him goodbye, before she'd turned towards home. But later that evening, sitting sewing with Aunt Rowley in the parlour, she almost began to wish she hadn't. Her life was so dull, apart from the afternoons she spent teaching Boy. Now that was really interesting. She was proud not only of him but of herself and could have happily carried on teaching him forever, or, at least, until he became a young man. She blushed. How had she come to love this child so intensely? But then again, she'd never expected to find herself apparently being courted by a man nearly as old as her father.

~

Jack Fallowfield felt it would only be a matter of time before she would confide in him. He'd always understood how to win a person's trust, how to exploit people's goodwill. He just had to be patient for a little longer and all would fall into his lap. That he was sure about. He had already sensed that the Rowlandson girl was hiding something. He'd detected a note of hesitation, a slight suppression of her natural spirit in her studied replies. He began to wonder if she too was being bound by this conspiracy of silence.

He could read people, could Jack ... except for that one time with bloody Cowper.

22

In Search Of Salvation

February 1817, Désvres, Pas-de-Calais, France

'Serjeant Fallowfield.' He turned. One of the school children was hailing him. He stopped his horse and dismounted.

'Yes?'

'You said you were looking for a boy that didn't talk.'

'Do you know where he might be?'

'I might do.' The lad shuffled his feet.

Fallowfield felt for some money and opened his fist wide to offer it to the lad, who swept the change into his own hand before beginning his tale.

'I've seen Miss Rowlandson come down this street, every afternoon. And this girl, whose mum looks after Billy Freer, says she goes to this house to teach a boy who doesn't talk.'

'And which house is that?'

'Mrs Freer's.'

'And which one might that be?'

'I dunno.'

Fallowfield gestured that he wanted his money back.

The lad clenched his fingers tighter round the coins. 'But I could take you there, near enough.'

Fallowfield got back on his horse and yanked the boy up in front of him. 'So, show me.'

But as he rode down the village street, Fallowfield realised that, whilst he needed to find out exactly where Boy was, there was no way he spirit him away without being observed by his young informant. He might have to wait a little longer for that.

~

Boy heard the horse and looked out of the window, expecting to see either Thomas or Freer. He turned and ran down the stairs into the long garden, winter cabbages still covered in snow, past the privy and over the bottom hedge into the fields surrounding the château. He headed for the school where he knew he would find Mrs Freer and Joanna. But too late. He heard Fallowfield roar and glanced back over his shoulder. Still riding forward, the big man was trying to set down the little lad who'd been riding with him. But the lad had got caught up in the stirrup and was trailing, squealing on the ground.

Boy realised that Fallowfield would have to stop and release him. It might give him just enough time to reach the schoolroom.

~

Joanna had stepped out that morning to pink clouds scattered against a brilliant blue over the eastern sky. And a light feathering of snow. 'Like fairy dust,' she said to herself, remembering her mother's words. She sometimes felt that she alone remembered that her mother had been more than a capable wife. Aunt Rowley had never been particularly close to her mother, so rarely chose to speak of her, and her father, who sang her mother's praises constantly, rarely celebrated his wife's spirited imagination. What he seemed to value were not only her domestic skills, but also her sense of how things should be done. Joanna wasn't sure that this was something she had inherited. Indeed, she had resisted Aunt Rowley's idea of how things should be done, ever since she had been able to think for herself. Ever since she could remember, ever since she'd first called her Aunt Rowley rather than her given name of Martha.

But then she and Aunt Rowley were cut from very different cloth. Aunt Rowley was more like her father, a practical down-to-earth woman, whose next task, she claimed, was to launch Joanna into the world by finding her a suitable husband.

As Joanna stepped out toward the school, it occurred to her that she too had lost a mother at Boy's age. And she too had been silenced. Nobody had ever allowed Joanna to talk about her mother. Aunt Rowley always cut her off if she ever began to ask about her, whilst her father chose only to remember what he wanted to.

Still, Boy's mother had died in dreadful circumstances, so maybe it was best not to jog his memory. Not that he would be able to tell her. Joanna had been trying to get him to express himself in writing, but he was resistant to putting words down in an order that might make sense. She was fairly sure he could read, for he seemed to understand what he had just read. But he was reluctant to write down sentences that had a beginning, middle and end. Joanna had decided that writing sentences from a beginning to an end would to him be just like speaking, and having to explain himself. She had, by now, come to accept his silence, just as Thomas had. It was what he did. He kept his own counsel.

But despite the crisp beauty of the morning, by the time she'd reached the school, Joanna felt weary. The thought of unpacking the sewing cupboard again felt as burdensome as ever. Yet as soon as she entered the classroom her spirits began to settle. She called out for her sewing monitors, Isabel and Bridie, to come out to the sewing cupboard in the corridor. Joanna had chosen them because they hated sewing too, but they loved helping her put things out and then away again. So, in the end, they enjoyed their sewing classes as much as anybody. Joanna smiled. That was what really pleased her.

But as she and the girls stood in front of the cupboard, Joanna heard a loud bang as the door flew open. She turned as Boy fell over the threshold. She saw the panic in his eyes. Grabbing his arm, she fumbled with her ring of keys to open the far cupboard door. 'In here,' she said, sweeping Boy inside. 'And don't move. Don't make a sound.' She quickly put her finger to her lips and addressed Isabel and Bridie. 'You are to say nothing. You understand, it is very important you say nothing'. They nodded. 'Now we must carry on putting out the sewing as if nothing has happened.' She turned and closed the school door.

Serjeant Fallowfield entered without knocking, and breathing hard. Unsmiling, his mouth seemed pinched and mean. As soon as he saw her he was back to his usual charming self, but with that glimpse of his unguarded expression she had seen enough. So, it's Sergeant Fallowfield, that Boy has to be hidden from.

'Ah, Miss Rowlandson, I am so glad to see you here.'

'Good morning, Sergeant Fallowfield. And how can I help you?'

'The wild boy. Remember, I've talked to you and Mrs Freer about the wild boy? He has been seen in the grounds and I suspect that he's come into the school building by this door. Obviously you haven't seen him or you would have told me, wouldn't you? So I need to ask the children if anyone has seen him.'

Joanna felt Isabel and Bridie huddle behind her. Hiding from the menace that Joanna saw lay behind his every word.

Now she understood. Serjeant Fallowfield, even if not particularly handsome, had always seemed so well mannered, charming and agreeable with his pleasantries and amusing stories. But in that brief moment she'd seen his mouth twist in anger, and his eyes flash with contempt.

'As I've said before, Serjeant Fallowfield, I am unable to help you in this matter. Neither I nor the girls have seen the boy you described.'

Fallowfield persisted. 'I am greatly concerned for the safety of your other pupils. The wild boy may be hiding here.' Joanna felt the two girls tremble behind her, and before Joanna could prevent him, he bent down and looked them both in the eye. 'Now girls, have you seen the boy who doesn't speak?'

Isabel started to cry, whilst Bridie huddled closer into Joanna's skirts. Joanna picked up her large sewing scissors and held them across her breast. If he was going to try and intimidate her girls as well as her …

'Serjeant Fallowfield, you are needlessly frightening these children. I must ask you to leave the school.'

Fallowfield stood up and walked to the door, but he did not leave. Instead he leant against the doorframe with folded arms and smiled at her. And his smile chilled her.

Trying to control her breathing, she recalled she'd seen Thomas ride with Haywood into the château grounds that morning. He would still be in the main stables waiting for Haywood's return. She bent down and whispered, 'Run Issy, run to the far stables and ask for Serjeant Cowper and … tell him to come here, urgently, straight away. And you, Bridie, fetch Mrs Freer here, right now, from her classroom.' As the girls scuttled away, she breathed as slowly as she could and tried to gather her thoughts. And it was only then that she remembered she had put Boy in the cupboard where the soldiers came in the evenings and stored their capes and any spare carbines.

Suddenly a clatter came from the far cupboard. Fallowfield, priming his pistol, walked over to the door. Joanna flung herself in front of the door, still holding her scissors. She had to stop him. Boy had to be kept safe. Whatever it took, she would have to find the strength to hold this man at bay.

'I asked you to leave, Serjeant Fallowfield. Please do.'

'And abandon you to the mercy of a wild creature?'

'I have seen no evidence of any such person.'

'What do you keep in this cupboard?'

'That, Serjeant, is none of your business.'

'I'm asking you to move out of the way, Miss Rowlandson.'

'I trust you're not going to shoot me, Serjeant.'

'I am merely offering to search your cupboard.'

'But it's my cupboard and I don't wish it to be searched.'

'This is a regimental school, Miss Rowlandson, and as a non-commissioned officer of the Regiment and on behalf of the Regiment, I would be very much obliged if you would move away from that door. I do have the requisite authority from Captain Haywood, remember.'

~

Thomas couldn't believe his eyes. Joanna Rowlandson was standing face to face with Fallowfield in front of a cupboard. She was holding a large pair of scissors. Fallowfield had drawn his pistol. Thomas would have to be careful. He signalled to Littlethorpe, who had come with him from the stables, to stay outside.

'I don't care what your orders are, Serjeant Fallowfield. So if you wouldn't mind I will be grateful if you could leave so that Mrs Freer and I can get on with our business of educating the Regiment's children.'

Fallowfield was not going to go away. 'If I tell you that this wild creature has committed a serious crime, are you prepared to bear the consequences of defying my orders?'

Thomas knew what he had to do. He was ready. 'Put your pistol down, Fallowfield.'

'Cowper. I might have known.' Fallowfield swung round. 'Since when did a senior serjeant take orders from a junior one, eh?'

' Since the junior serjeant finds him threatening a young woman with a primed pistol in his hand.'

But Fallowfield held his ground. 'As this child was last seen running into this building, and as my orders are to apprehend him, then I must, of course, search the school buildings.'

'You of all people, a professional soldier, threatening a young woman. If there are any arguments to pick, then pick them with a fellow soldier.'

Thomas moved forward between Joanna and Fallowfield's pistol.

Fallowfield suddenly seemed to remember whom he'd been threatening. He bowed. 'My apologies, Miss Rowlandson, for being perhaps over- zealous. I was merely concerned that you might be putting yourself in danger from a very wild young boy, whose actions are unpredictable, and whose sickness of mind prevents him from speaking. Some would say that it is the devil within him, the same devil that has led him to commit terrible crimes.'

Joanna stood firm, still holding the scissors in both hands. 'Be that as it may, I would like to remind you that I am an officer's daughter but that I am prepared to keep my silence regarding this entire incident, if you will now leave the premises immediately, and not return, or take it in your head to harass myself or Mrs Freer, in any manner at all, in the future.'

'Miss Rowlandson. We are agreed. I wouldn't dream of telling your father about … this incident. He would doubtless find it too distressing to discover you have been persuaded or indeed tricked into protecting individuals, who under any other circumstances would have already been dealt with in the most serious manner.'

Fallowfield bowed and left.

Thomas could scarcely speak. 'You are a very brave woman, Miss … Joanna. He is not a man to cross.'

Joanna turned and put the scissors back in the sewing cupboard. 'So I see.'

She sighed.' But I will keep my word and not say anything about this to anyone, so long as he keeps well away from Boy. '

Littlethorpe appeared in the doorway. 'Everything all right?'

'Everything's fine,' said Thomas. 'Just keep an eye out, will you? Don't let anyone pass.'

'Right you are,' said Littlethorpe and went back outside.

Joanna turned the lock of the soldiers' cupboard and lifted Boy out from under the capes where he'd been nursing one of the carbines. 'Good thing they're not loaded,' said Thomas, gently taking it from him whilst Joanna cradled him in her lap, stroking his hair, murmuring words too quiet for Thomas to hear. He put the carbine back in the cupboard.

~

Helpless in the face of Boy's distress, Thomas realised with growing admiration that Joanna had the situation under much more control than he had thought. He leant back into the shadows and began to study the two people in front of him. Joanna seemed unperturbed, her concentration staying wholly on Boy. Thomas wished he could hear what she was saying, but she had her head bent too close to Boy's for him to catch more than the odd word.

The longer Boy sobbed and the more Joanna comforted him, the more Thomas was reminded of another wintry day in the Peninsula. Captain Webster had told him that the only statue still intact in one of the half-destroyed churches was that of the Virgin Mary cradling the dead Christ. Webster had said it was as though the love of a mother for her dead son had somehow stilled their swords. Thomas often thought the religious Webster made too much of such things, but now seeing Joanna cradle Boy, he also remembered the statue of Virgin Mary and the dead Christ in the great cathedral in Paris, recalling not love but his mother's curses, how his mother's love for his brother Michael had turned to hatred. It was only in the great cathedral in Paris that he'd finally allowed himself to remember what he he'd put out of his mind for so long.

He wiped his hands briskly across his eyes but, at the very moment of doing so, Joanna looked up and saw him. He felt his cheeks redden, but she merely acknowledged his presence with a smile, as if to indicate she was grateful he had stayed. He made as if to move forward, but she gestured to him to step back, to wait and let her finish. Thomas scarcely had time to admire yet again her brilliant blue eyes, before she tucked her head down once more to comfort Boy.

He went outside and spoke to Littlethorpe, who seemed to be finding the whole business upsetting. He could see that Littlethorpe would have preferred to be dealing with Boy kicking and shouting, rather than in tears. That was his way, to shout, curse and threaten. Thomas remembered ordering Littlethorpe's friends to hold him down when his Maria was sent back with the other women. If they hadn't, Littlethorpe would likely have been shot there and then by the infantry sergeant in charge of the forced evacuation. 'Get your carbine, Littlethorpe,' he whispered, 'and go and find Freer. Tell him Boy must be got back to Ashby and Bonnie right away.'

Thomas went back inside and stood by the door. At long last, Boy raised his head from Joanna's lap and looked shamefaced as he and Joanna both rose to their feet.

Boy looked as though he wished the floor would swallow him up.

Thomas looked at Joanna. 'Thank you.'

'Thank you, Thomas.'

Thomas bowed. 'Joanna, would you mind if I speak to Boy alone. Just for a moment.'

Joanna patted down her skirt and smiled at Boy.

'I'll be waiting for you when you've finished with Serjeant Cowper.'

Boy watched her leave and then stared at his feet.

Thomas took a deep breath. He reminded himself of what Louise had always told him. Speak as honestly as you can.

'Boy, please listen carefully and try to understand. You know that Fallowfield is looking for you and that he very nearly found you. You and I both know what happened between him and me during the battle, and why it happened. You were there. You know what I did was necessary.'

Boy nodded his agreement.

Thomas hesitated. ' What you saw him do, before I arrived, puts you in danger. What I did puts me in danger. Now Fallowfield knows you're here, I can't keep you safe from him. No one can.'

Boy looked upset. Thomas put his hand on his arm. 'I know he did wrong but we can't rely on the officers either to keep us from danger. That's the way it is in the army. ' Boy still looked wretched. Thomas reached over and hugged him.

'I'm sorry but you must go back to Ashby and Bonnie, as soon as we can arrange it.'

Thomas hesitated. He should tell Boy how much he loved him. But how could he? Boy would be embarrassed. But no, Thomas thought. It's me. I've never declared my love to anyone. Not to my mother; not even to Grace. No wonder my mother hated me. No wonder Grace abandoned me.

They were so alike, he and Boy. Hiding behind silence. How could it be so difficult to say, when Boy was like a son to him? Not that his own father ever spoke of love.

'You know how much we all love you,' Thomas said and hugged Boy close, brushing his eyes vigorously with the back of his hand, 'and, you do know, don't you, I love you more than I can say.'

23

Consequences

February 1817, Désvres, Pas-de-Calais, France

Charles Webster sighed. He'd been as dismayed as the next man to find that Fallowfield had survived his Waterloo wounds and, much as he wanted to believe that Fallowfield, having found God, was a changed man, he didn't think it very likely. It was one thing, however, to nurture such thoughts in private, but to acknowledge these in public would be impossible; which was why he and Freer were dancing around the subject.

'You remember Boy, I'm sure, sir,' Freer was saying. 'Well, he has recently re-attached himself to the Regiment. He was at the battlefield with Corporal Ashby and Murphy's widow but Serjeant Fallowfield has developed some kind of grudge against him.'

'Oh?'

Webster had heard about the rumours concerning Fallowfield's injuries. Apparently one of their own. He'd asked Freer what he thought of them, but Freer had been unwilling to speculate. Surely Boy could not have been involved?

'If we could just get him back to Waterloo, sir.'

'You want me to authorise a leave of absence for someone to take him?'

'Ideally, sir. Perhaps Cowper, as he's a particular favourite of Boy's? Maybe with Private Littlethorpe, who has the strength to be an ideal escort?'

Webster felt uneasy. Whatever his feelings about Fallowfield, he would have to be careful how this spiriting away of Boy was handled. Best to choose men who had lain on the battlefield all night, or been taken to a field hospital, well before Fallowfield had been found.

'No, I want you to go… and take Corporal Byrne as an escort.'

'Understood, sir. We shall leave first thing tomorrow.'

Charles Webster shook his head. 'Best go now, straightaway.' He picked up his pen and signed and sealed the docket. 'Thank you, Troop Serjeant-Major.'

~

Joanna's knees were trembling and she felt sick, but as long as she stayed calm … She had to stay strong, even though she had seen behind the mask, and it frightened her. And she had been strong, even when Thomas came and she thought he and Fallowfield would come to blows. She had surprised herself.

It was only when Troop Sergeant-Major Freer came and told them he was to take Boy away there and then that she allowed herself to weep. Thomas and Boy too, as Boy clung on to him. But there was no time to waste, as they had to set off before it got dark. Thomas ruffled Boy's hair for one last time and then, searching in his sabretache, handed him his pocket-knife. Boy rubbed away more tears, and placed it deep inside the small bag in which Louise had packed all his belongings. The Troop Serjeant-Major swung Boy up to sit in front of him and they were off … back once again on the road to Waterloo.

Louise left to resume her lessons, but Joanna hadn't the heart for sewing. Thomas too, seemed at a loss. He looked at her.

' He'll be safe now. You know it had to be done.'

'Yes, I believe you. I can see … what that man might be capable of.'

As long as she stayed strong. And didn't cry in front of Thomas. But then he looked ready to weep too. She should try to say something, something that might comfort them both.

'I used to see him every afternoon,' was all she managed.

Thomas nodded. 'I used to see him most evenings.'

'I shall be lost without him.'

'We both will,' Thomas said quietly.

'Louise has told me to go home, but I'm not sure about going back on my own. You know, with things as they are….'

'I can walk with you, if you want, Joanna.'

'But what about Captain Haywood?'

'He's staying here all day and then going on to dine, at …'

'At Captain Berwick's?'

Thomas looked embarrassed. 'Yes, I'm to wait for him there. Later on.'

Joanna smiled, 'It's all right, Thomas. I don't mind. Not any more.' Joanna was surprised to hear herself say that, with so much conviction. 'No, it's perfectly all right. I don't care that I'm not a proper gentlewoman like Lady Catherine.'

'Nonsense. You're every bit a gentlewoman.'

She swallowed hard. She mustn't burst into tears. 'Shall we go, Thomas. I'm feeling … rather tired.'

Thomas moved closer and offered her his arm.

Joanna placed her arm on his and they walked in silence, so many things unsaid, down the track to the edge of the forest, the dark tracery of the trees glistening with haw frost, the sunset gashed deep pink and red across the sky.

~

Jack Fallowfield watched them leave, just as he'd watched Freer and Byrne ride away with the brat to God knows where. He rolled the lead ball from one hand to another. He couldn't settle. He couldn't banish the memory of Waterloo when the brat turned to defy him just before bloody Cowper came on the scene. It was as if the brat was trying to remember something, something maybe he'd seen in Spain. Fallowfield didn't like it, not one little bit. The brat already knew too much. And now he was beyond reach.

Well, that's buggered that. And as for that stupid girl, well, if bloody Cowper thinks he's going to persuade her to persuade her father to persuade bloody Haywood that he deserves the troop sergeant-major post … Fallowfield gripped his reins. He hadn't felt so humiliated in a long time. No doubt, both of them were laughing behind his back right now.

Bloody women and children pretending they're so innocent and then tricking you to within an inch of your life.

Fallowfield clenched his fists, remembering Ireland, where the young country girls went ragged and barefoot, smelling of peat smoke and the byre, but were so very beautiful, with their red hair and pale skin. And in the dark corners of Limerick, you could have your pleasure with them for pennies.

But then came along Cathleen. So beguiling. She bewitched him. He went back with her to a chimneyless cottage, with its bare earth floor, mud walls and straw bed, all ready she said, for him to lie with her. But no sooner had he stripped them both naked than her people came and set fire to the thatch, the straw boys chanting, the women and children shrieking, waiting for him to stumble naked into the yard, choking from the smoke of the burning turf and thatch, waiting to stone him to death; Cathleen now covered by her great shawl taunting him, his country and his God. But God and Dermot Murphy's patrol of soldiers saved him just in time, running their horses after them and firing their carbines.

'Bloody banshees,' Murphy called them. 'Bloody banshees.'

He pulled his thoughts back to the present. There was little he could do for the moment, as long as she could threaten him with her father's rank, though Captain Dickenson's rank hadn't protected him that day at Salamanca. And it hadn't stopped Captain Webster being clapped in jail. And it certainly hadn't protected the French officer, gibbering on his knees, begging for mercy. Or the rest of them. But, somehow, Cowper always managed to slip through his grasp. Didn't even desert after Fallowfield had put him in the firing squad that had executed his friend Quilley. And, as for Cowper and Freer managing to avoid the ambush that killed Sparrow, and then the business at Waterloo. How many lives can one man have?

So. The brat might have escaped, but there were more than enough ways left to deal with Cowper. As long as he could persuade Haywood that he would make a better troop serjeant-major than Cowper. By whatever means. God had already given him guidance. As long as he kept his mind clear and was ready to hear Him speak again.

~

That night as Thomas accompanied Haywood home to their billet, he found himself reliving everything that had happened that day. But now, it wasn't only Boy who occupied his thoughts. It was Joanna Rowlandson.

Captain Haywood too had been fretting all the way back, about whether a penniless junior captain like himself might win the hand of the daughter of a lord. He hadn't said as much in so many words, but Thomas knew exactly what he meant.

'I think sir, that any young lady who understands army life would pay little heed to the shine on an officer's jacket. She would realise that here's a man who has loyally served his King and country and would serve her just as loyally.'

Haywood sighed. 'If it were only that simple.'

Thomas felt a surge of fellow-feeling in his new determination to woo Joanna. 'I think we Waterloo men should be prepared to fight just as hard for our happiness as we did on the battlefield, sir.'

Haywood smiled. 'Quite so, Cowper. Couldn't have put it better myself.'

On reaching the farmhouse, there was another letter waiting for Haywood. He opened it quickly, but read it several times before dismissing Thomas for the night.

'Thank you, that's all, Cowper. I have some correspondence to see to before bed.' He picked up his writing case and took himself off to his rooms.

Leaving Haywood's quarters, Thomas, in his turn, began to fret. What was it Louise Freer had said months ago? He tried to recall the details of their conversation about the difficulties of courting an officer's daughter, falling asleep at last to the sounds of a heavy rainstorm, and the dull thudding heartbeat of likely disappointment.

24

An Industrious Place

April 1817, Désvres, Pas-de-Calais, France

German's Cottages, Heaviley, Stockport April 1817

Dear Cowper,

I trust Freer passed on our thanks for the money you sent towards Boy's passage. Having promised Freer faithfully that I would write regularly, I am sorry that I have not written earlier. But, on hearing your news, we decided to come back immediately.

I had already been advised that there was some work for handloom weavers in the silk and cotton districts of Manchester, so we made our way, as quickly as we could, from Dover to Stockport. We have now secured a sturdy cottage of two-storeys in a row of four, with good windows and a garden plot overlooked by open fields. Our cottage is situated high above the town, just before the road from London to Manchester plunges downwards into the valley.

Stockport is an industrious place, with many buildings and mills close together, where men, women and children congregate to work. But, up here, we can enjoy the freedom and fresh air that so many of our fellow townspeople lack.

Everything is built on a vast scale, as though to house hundreds, even the Sunday school, which serves mainly those of the non-conformist persuasion. Boy has already begun to attend and much enjoys it. The school occupies a prominent position on a hill, close to Sandy Brow, a large open space, which, I am told is often used for meetings. It is also near an old windmill, which scarcely turns its sails nowadays, as water power and steam have taken over the whole town, with many of its brooks dammed for water. I think it must be every man's ambition to open a factory of his own, so that he does not have to work himself, hour after hour, in such hot and humid conditions.

Nowadays, they spin mainly cotton, though there is still some silk, in the town, which should provide us handloom weavers with plenty of yarn for our needs. Yet, everywhere there are signs that trade has not yet recovered after the war that we fought so hard to end. Indeed, we had no sooner arrived on March 6th, and found temporary lodgings in the lower part of the town, than we were caught up in a great commotion at the only crossing over the river Mersey.

Men, who had been marching from Manchester to London to protest about the lack of work, were at this point prevented from journeying any further. These men, carrying only blankets on their backs, had been entrusted with petitions intended for Parliament and had taken particular care to divide themselves into small groups. This arrangement was made so as to avoid breaking the law, but they were still prevented from going any further by the Cheshire yeomanry.

There was little the men could do, trapped as they were in that narrow place, between the troops and the river. A number of them suffered sabre wounds, and an innocent bystander was also killed. Much was made of arresting these men, but, with the prisons full, there was nothing the magistrates could do, except threaten them with the vagrancy laws and send them home. But we have now heard that other men, sympathetic to their cause, have since been arrested and sent to London, in irons, charged with treason ... of all things. It upsets me greatly to think that honest men, who had broken no laws, should be treated so harshly. After our hard-won victory at Waterloo, I had hoped the government might now pursue not only peace, but also prosperity, on behalf of its people.

I fear there may be more disappointments to come, should we try to rectify injustices, only to be hauled away in irons, like common criminals.

It is fortunate, though, that there are a good many Christian souls in the town, and I was pleased to find three Methodist chapels. I have now settled on the one I wish to attach myself to. Bonnie, too, was delighted to find a small Catholic chapel, which she has begun to attend regularly. There is, of course, a parish church, not long rebuilt, with many showy flourishes, as well as another church, St Peter's, which is a good size, but more modest in appearance.

Boy has proved himself to be a reliable helper, and eager to learn my trade. So, you can see we are well settled here, though I pray every night that work will become more plentiful. I am told that employment is scarce like this in many of the manufacturing districts, and that, for the time being, men have agreed to reduce their wages until trade picks up again, just so that they might live.

May you go in God's love and peace.

Samuel Ashby

~

Jack Fallowfield carefully copied and then resealed the letter. He had never before thought of the Methodist Ashby as a man to support seditious mischief-makers. If only Freer or Cowper would show their hand as clearly as that. It was a pity the letter did not contain anything definite that he could make use of against them. He took out his Bible. *'God is my strength and power.'*

25

A Healing Spring

April 1817, Désvres, Pas-de-Calais, France

Henry Haywood was happy. Happy that Lady Catherine was encouraging his suit. Not even bored with the endless drills Wellington and Combermere required of them. Admittedly the six-monthly inspections were a drain on one's resources, and with Troop Serjeant-Major Grey more and more reluctant to fulfil his duties until the Pension Board declared him 'worn out', Haywood found himself relying on his serjeants more than ever. Cowper kept up the men's morale, whilst Fallowfield was proving to be unexpectedly helpful.

~

But as spring advanced Thomas was dreading their horses being inspected yet again. Most of them, he was sure, were likely to be declared unfit for service, including Fearless. But, after the inspectors left, Haywood came in, smiling as he waved the papers in front of him. 'Thought you'd want to know, Fearless has been spared.'

Thomas sighed with relief, but then pulled himself up. 'Aye, for this time.'

Haywood was not to be downcast. 'Now, don't you worry, Cowper. If she doesn't get through the next time, as long as she's still in reasonable condition I'll purchase her as a hack. After all, she's saved both our lives, eh?'

Thomas was surprised and even more relieved to hear Haywood promise this, but almost immediately began to wonder where Haywood's money was coming from.

~

Joanna didn't know what to do with herself, without Boy. She tried to transfer all of her affections now to Isabel and Bridie. But it was not the same. It would never be the same, she thought, except possibly with a child of her own. But, she had already snapped at Aunt Rowley that she would resist any attempt to marry her off to someone who didn't even want to talk to her. Reluctantly, but true to her word, she had said nothing to her father of her confrontation with Fallowfield. After all, she never expected to have anything to do with Fallowfield again.

So when she saw Fallowfield approaching their house as bold as you like, to attend the Bible class, and her father greet him with his usual courtesy, she felt her stomach churn, and when he looked straight through her and bowed, she thought she might vomit. She ran back into the house and locked herself in her bedroom, where she now stayed every Sunday evening for the duration of her father's meetings. Fallowfield had obviously calculated that if she were to tell her father about the situation, she and Thomas would be the ones in trouble, not him. If only Aunt Rowley hadn't rushed Thomas away at the cricket match before her father had a chance to get to know him better. If only it was Thomas who was welcome into their house. Not Fallowfield.

~

Thomas still felt lost, he confessed to Joanna, one evening on their regular walk back from school. Not that he could walk her all the way home. Just as far as the edge of the wood before the crossroads. 'I meant without Boy.'

Joanna had explained that her father might object to his accompanying her at all, although she herself seemed to care little about the difference in their social standing. If only she wasn't so young and an officer's daughter. But Joanna stopped and turned to face him.

'I feel the same,' she admitted. 'I miss him so much.'

'At least he's safe now, thanks to you, Joanna.'

'And you, Thomas. 'Mrs Freer and I have been, and still are, very grateful for your help.'

'It has been my pleasure. And I might add that I know of no other lady who would have been able to hold firm under such circumstances.' He smiled. 'Except for Bonnie Murphy, who'd never call herself a lady.'

'Boy's Bonnie?'

'The very one. If it hadn't been for her after Waterloo …' Thomas trailed off.

Joanna touched his arm. 'My father won't talk about it at all.'

Thomas frowned. 'Like most of us.'

'I'd thought he'd want to, you know, tell me how heroic everyone was and how his guns saved you all.'

' And they did too.' Thomas struggled with the memory. 'In front of our squares, when the French kept charging, time after time … firing away till the very last moment, running for their lives into the squares … Before the horses were finally upon them. Your father's guns did save us. Many times over.'

'Thank you for telling me this. I won't ask again.'

'Maybe, one day.'

'Only if you want to.'

They walked on in silence.

~

Joanna started to fret. How could they be sure there would even be a *one day*? Soldiers were moved around like chess pieces, all the time. With no notice. Just the thought of it was enough to make her speak out.

'I couldn't bear it if you had to move away as well.'

Joanna blushed. There, she had said it. She couldn't have said it more clearly, but now it was his turn to be bold.

Thomas started to blush too.

'I couldn't bear that either.'

'So, we must make the most of this time, mustn't we?'

'I never did bring in those healing herbs to show your class. Perhaps I could do that? Soon?'

Joanna edged a little closer, wondering how they might ever find some time alone.

She could see that she might have to be even bolder. Maybe approach the matter from a different angle. Her father was always talking about angles, trajectories and testing the target range before finally adjusting his guns. She would have to do the same. She would have to test the terrain first, perhaps try one or two gentle salvos before he would feel able to respond?

'And maybe we could visit the bluebell woods again? I loved those bluebells. They were just so … blue.'

Thomas laughed. 'Without the children?'

'Just you and me.'

Thomas cleared his throat. 'Yes. I'd like that.'

Thomas, at last, took her hand in his.

'Did anybody ever tell you that your eyes are exactly the same colour?'

'As bluebells?'

'The same.'

Joanna now wondered how she could let Thomas know she would be willing to be kissed. Be bolder still, she told herself.

'You do realise, don't you, that my father is being quite unreasonable about my prospects? After all, a proper officer is going to look for a proper lady with money and breeding. Both of which I lack.'

'But you've said yourself that your father wouldn't approve of you associating with a serjeant.'

'I think my father will have to be more realistic in the future.'

'But for now?'

She stretched herself as tall as she could and put her arms around his neck.

~

Fallowfield was beginning to think of himself as a creature of the forest who could slink silently behind the trees and find his way even in the dark. Like a cat. It was one evening in May that he first saw them, hidden from the pathway but not from him. He was on his way back from his shelter deep in the woods carrying an old writing case and a bagful of letters when he saw them. They both had their backs to him, Cowper with his arm around the girl's waist, and she with her arm around his, deep in conversation, unaware of his presence.

Fallowfield stood completely still and when they finally disappeared deeper into the wood he hurried on, imagining the letter he would now be writing to Captain Rowlandson.

~

As the evenings grew lighter, it was becoming more difficult to hide their growing attachment to each other from the rest of the world. Thomas hesitated to say attachment. It was not a word he had dared speak or even think of since Grace.

Thomas was bracing himself to visit the healing waters near the farmhouse. He would force himself to face the dead friars, the ghosts, the threats and the memories of his mother's screams. It wouldn't be called a healing spring for no reason, he told himself. So, if he wanted to gather medicinal herbs to show Joanna's class, this would be the first place to look. Clambering over the narrow stream ditches he would think himself back to happier times, in Stathern, picking herbs for his grandmother.

He wasn't sure he could see any plant he recognised. Maybe it was too early, though the signs of spring were everywhere. He could almost feel the sap rising, and see a multitude of leaves uncurling red on green and even the tight rolled beech buds beginning to open, leaving only the sharp spindled blackthorn and the cloven hooves of ash buds bare on the bone. And as soon the bluebells were out in the woods, he would take Joanna there and declare himself.

And after that, and only then, would he worry about her father.

26

The Letter

May 1817, Désvres, Pas-de-Calais, France

It was a Saturday. The steady pulse of the clock was slowly ticking away the hours before lunch. Sitting together in their plain living room, Aunt Rowley was busy sewing a shirt for Joanna's father, occasionally chiding her for being so slow with her own work. But Joanna was bored with sewing. She was even exasperated by the sampler she had been enjoying, stitching colour and ornament into its exuberant borders. She was beginning to resent her embroidery flourishing rather more than her life. She had wanted to go for a walk, pick some flowers, but what was the use of that if Aunt Rowley wouldn't have them in the house? Besides, Aunt Rowley had declared she was not intending to go out at all, on account of the afternoon rain her father's groom was predicting. Joanna would have to wait till Monday and pick some on the way to school.

But more than anything else she wanted to see Thomas. Yet he, like her, had no excuse to go to the château. Captain Haywood was spending the weekend at the Berwicks', where Thomas would also be in attendance. It promised to be a very dull Saturday and Sunday too … her father would be taken up with his afternoon Bible class, and during the morning service the regimental chaplain's sing-song voice would lull her back to sleep.

~

What she wasn't expecting was her father to storm in without even knocking on the door. He waved a sheet of paper at her. She stood up to greet him but he immediately ordered her to sit down.

'I've just received this letter, which informs me that you are consorting with a common soldier. Is this correct?'

Joanna feared the worst. 'I am not quite sure what is meant by the word consorting,' she said.

Her father looked angrier than ever. He hated it when she picked over words.

'You know exactly what I mean.'

'I'm afraid I don't, Father.'

He waved the paper again in front of her. 'This letter tells me that you are being courted by a non-commissioned soldier. Do you deny that?'

Joanna gulped in some air, ready to launch into her defence. 'Father, if you mean to ask have I been accompanied from school by a sergeant who has ensured I reach home in safety, then yes, that is correct.'

'You assured me it was perfectly safe for you to walk to the school on your own.'

'It used to be, but lately…'

'Lately, what?'

Joanna was cornered. 'There was an unpleasant incident at school … when I was threatened by another person on account of …'

Joanna wavered. It was hard to know exactly how to describe what had occurred between Fallowfield and herself without her father at once declaring she was never to return to the school.

'On account of something quite outside my control, and nothing really to do with the school, but it disturbed me, and, well, Serjeant Cowper, who witnessed the entire business, offered to escort me home, whenever I felt I needed … protection.'

Her father, initially stony-faced, now looked worried as well as angry.

'Why have you not told me about any of this before? What was this unpleasant incident, Joanna?'

'It concerned a young lad, scarcely more than eight, who had fallen foul of a certain person, and I judged it to be unfair, and there was some upset as a result.'

'Are you telling me that it is not safe for you to attend the school?'

'No, it's perfectly safe in school, but it is very reassuring to be escorted home.'

'This is exactly what I have been worried about: exposing yourself to unnecessary risks from locals and soldiers.'

'Father, I've already explained that Mrs Freer and I only teach very small children. The few older soldiers who attend in the evening are taught by the schoolmaster, not by us. We never set eyes on them.'

'But what actually happened, Joanna? Tell me. Did someone attack you?' He now looked and sounded quite perturbed.

'No, nobody attacked me. But please, Father, I don't want to talk about it any further. There's really no point, I can assure you. The young lad is no longer here.'

'And the person who caused the upset? Is he likely to trouble you again?'

'As I said, not now the boy has gone.'

'So who exactly is this fellow that has taken it upon himself, without seeking my permission, to escort you home?'

'He's one of Captain Haywood's most trusted men, his cover serjeant, Serjeant Cowper.'

'And you can assure me he is not someone who would abuse his position of trust?'

Joanna tried to keep calm. 'I can. But you can ask Captain Haywood.'

Joanna's father looked through the window of their farmhouse. ' I intend to. Because this letter tells me a rather different tale.'

What did the letter actually say? Joanna stepped as carefully as she could between truthfulness, omission and outright lying. How could they have been seen? And by whom? They had been so careful too, especially in the woods. She couldn't bear to lie, but what did this letter writer really know?

He threw it down for her to look at. 'You've been seen together, smiling, arm in arm. Do you deny it? '

Joanna read the letter. It was brief and polite but suggestive that more had occurred than the writer could be sure of. Still, she almost sighed with relief. Was this the most the letter writer could accuse them of?

'I've already explained, Father, that I was very much upset at the time, and needed considerable reassurance, which Serjeant Cowper was good enough to offer, when he was escorting me home.'

'If that is really the case,' he paused, 'and if you are so determined to return to the school, I will ask someone I know and trust to accompany you. Serjeant Fallowfield is a sterling fellow, and Captain Haywood informs me he is well respected. Enough to have a very good chance of being promoted soon to the position of troop sergeant-major.'

Joanna, almost dizzy with disbelief, spun round on her heels. 'In that case, I shall never leave this house again. I refuse to be escorted anywhere by … such a man. I'd never trust him. And you shouldn't trust him either.'

Joanna ran upstairs and locked the door of her room. She knew her father would send Aunt Rowley to talk to her.

Joanna didn't know what to do. Her father was bound to have thought her harsh words about Fallowfield were without foundation, and sure enough no sooner had she locked her door than she heard Aunt Rowley climb the stairs. Aunt Rowley was clearly not pleased to hear about the letter.

'Open the door, Joanna. Your father only wants to do his best for you. Surely you must understand that a girl of your age runs the risk of completely ruining her reputation. The writer of that letter was only thinking of your good name.'

Joanna felt instinctively that the letter writer was not thinking about her good name at all. In fact, the more she thought about it, the more she detected malice, not concern. Indeed, the more she thought about it, the more she recognised the same kind of polite poison that Fallowfield had so recently adopted with her. Whoever had written it had been spying on her and Thomas. Who else would do such a thing? Yes, it was undoubtedly his work.

'I do not believe that is true, Aunt Rowley.'

'But you do admit that you have been walking out, alone, with a cavalry sergeant?'

Does agreeing to marry someone not mean something rather different from just walking out?

' Not walking out,' Joanna felt able to retort truthfully. 'Just walking back home.'

'Well, if this is what just walking back home comes to, I can see why your father thinks it's time you stopped helping at the school.'

So had her father accepted she wasn't going to allow Fallowfield to escort her to school? But what would her little Isabel and Bridie do without her?

Joanna opened the door. 'In that case, Aunt Rowley, I should be very grateful if you would take a letter to Mrs Freer, to explain that I won't be able to help her any more.'

Aunt Rowley pursed her lips.

'I won't be carrying secrets for you.'

'Of course not, but I must, as a matter of courtesy, let Mrs Freer know my situation.'

Aunt Rowley surely could not object to this.

~

Louise Freer was surprised to see Aunt Rowley, as she too now thought of her, bearing an unsealed letter from Joanna.

Joanna had written briefly in her unmistakable round hand.

Dear Mrs Freer,

Unfortunately I am unable to continue helping you at the school. My father was concerned to hear that there had been a distressing incident a few weeks ago and that, as a result, I had asked Serjeant Cowper to escort me home. My father was naturally concerned to hear not only that there had been any trouble but also that a soldier whom he did not know was escorting me home. I hope you will understand my position and please give my apologies to all those I have inconvenienced.

Yours

Joanna Rowlandson

Aunt Rowley, who had clearly read the letter, tutted several times. 'She really can be quite a stubborn girl. My brother is perfectly aware of how much she enjoys helping at the school, and has suggested that Serjeant Fallowfield could escort her home instead. But she would not even agree to this.'

Louise felt her anger rising, but tried to choose her words carefully. Joanna had often commented on how close Captain Rowlandson and Fallowfield seemed to have become.

'I'm afraid I must take issue with that, Miss Rowlandson.'

Louise noticed Aunt Rowley flinch. She was clearly not used to being contradicted.

'I beg your pardon?'

Louise wondered what she could possibly say that Aunt Rowley wouldn't take offence at, and so cause Joanna more trouble.

'You should know, Miss Rowlandson, that the distressing incident your niece is referring to concerns Serjeant Fallowfield, and I can affirm that Serjeant Fallowfield was the cause of the upset. I will not say any more, except that it is perfectly understandable she does not wish to be escorted home by the very person who upset her. And not only her. I might add that he has also offended me.'

Aunt Rowley promptly sat down on the nearest chair and waved her fan vigorously over her face, which was now bright red.

'You cannot tell me any more about this … incident?'

'Let's just say it's over and done with, and best left that way.'

'But is this something that concerns my niece's honour, and that I should inform her father about?'

'Let me reassure you that your niece's honour has not been compromised in any way by the … incident. But it has left her, understandably, unwilling to spend time in the company of Serjeant Fallowfield. '

Aunt Rowley flapped her fan for quite some time, then put both hands in her lap. 'I see. I must say I have, on occasion, feared that the enthusiasm my brother has for his Bible classes might sometimes cloud his judgement.'

Louise felt her anger subside with both the suddenly pensive Aunt Rowley, and the pious Captain. Rowlandson would have been as hard-hit as the next man after Waterloo and, like the rest of them, was still trying to find his way.

'Of course, I realise that you and her father only wish to protect your niece from harm.'

'I confess I wish my brother hadn't become quite so devout.'

Louise nodded. Clearly Aunt Rowley seemed to feel rather the same as Joanna … 'those wretched Bible classes,' Joanna sometimes called them.

Louise tried to choose her words with particular care. 'All of those who were present at Waterloo … well, it has reshaped all their lives, and affected their minds, and some people are trying to find a God who understands the price that was paid.'

'But was it not a great victory?'

'But at a terrible cost, Miss Rowlandson.'

'Though surely one well worth paying to preserve the nation.'

'But, as I said, at a terrible cost.'

'And you think that my brother has been similarly affected?'

'As I said, I think all of us were.'

'All of us? So you were there also? On the battlefield?'

'I was indeed.'

'Really.' Aunt Rowley leant forward. 'If you don't mind my asking, Mrs Freer, how has it affected you?'

149

Louise felt the blood drain from her face. Aunt Rowley, in her clumsy way, had dared to ask the question nobody else had. Louise felt the nausea rising in her throat, gagging at the memories of what she and Bonnie Murphy had had to do that night, robbing from the dead to save the living. Turning over every corpse that looked in the least bit like Will or Dermot, running the gauntlet of the Prussians shooting the badly injured, the French peasants close behind, intent on taking their revenge for the loss of their livelihoods.

'It's hard to put into words,' was the best she could manage.

Aunt Rowley looked disappointed. 'I dare say it is. Still, this Waterloo business can be no excuse for improper behaviour. The plain truth of the matter is that my niece cannot consort with a common soldier. She is an officer's daughter. There is nothing more to be said.'

Aunt Rowley snapped her fan shut.

'Thank you, Mrs Freer. I shall, however, pass on the information that Serjeant Fallowfield has upset my niece in some way that neither of you, for reasons best known to yourselves, wish to divulge.'

'Let me assure you, Miss Rowlandson, that our reasons for doing so are more honourable than the man in question.'

Aunt Rowley rose to her feet. 'So you keep saying.'

'He's capable of considerable deception.'

Aunt Rowley turned to leave. 'Let me assure you, Mrs Freer, that I am not easily fooled by men whose only interest lies in charming their audience and who seek to conceal their true character.'

~

Joanna had never thought it possible, but when Aunt Rowley came back from her visit to Louise she asked her a good many questions about Fallowfield and Thomas and, for once, she dispensed with her fan and looked Joanna straight in the eye.

'So your father has reduced his expectations, and is prepared to accept a troop sergeant-major but not a sergeant?'

Joanna wondered why her aunt was bothering to ask about this at all, but nodded.

'Aunt Rowley, you saw what happened at the ball. All those bachelors, and none were interested in even dancing with me. You can't deny it. We are not considered to be gentlefolk.'

Aunt Rowley sighed. 'I must say I was ... disappointed. You looked so pretty, too. But is it true Serjeant Fallowfield will be promoted and Serjeant Cowper will not?'

'I don't know. It's what my father said.'

Aunt Rowley stood up to leave. 'In that case I need to clarify matters with your father.'

~

Louise chided Thomas. 'I told you this would happen, didn't I? She's barely seventeen and she's an officer's daughter. You could be court-martialled. And God help you, if you've ... lain with her.'

'You don't have to worry about that, I swear.'

'It's no wonder her father won't let her come back to the school. Or let her send letters without Aunt Rowley reading them first. It's just not possible, don't you see that, Thomas?'

'We were going to work out a plan.'

Louise gave him a hard look. 'For what? A plan isn't going to solve anything. I'm telling you, Thomas, you can't cross the gap separating you from her with any plan. It's not that easy. And I should know.'

'How do you know?'

'It's nothing to do with you.'

'It has everything to do with me if you're trying to persuade me there's no hope.'

Louise had never thought she would tell. 'It's only that Captain Webster, or Lieutenant Webster as he was then, used to give me his pictures when he ran out of cash. Like that one that used to hang in the back room at The Cock and Bottle. And we used to talk. A lot. I liked him. And he seemed to like me.'

'Are you saying you thought Captain Webster was paying court to you?'

'It was before I met Will.'

'But don't you realise? Has Will never said anything?'

'Said what?'

'Webster's not interested in women … in that way. It's not that he doesn't like them. But he doesn't seem to want to marry them.'

'You mean, it wasn't because I was an innkeeper's daughter?'

'Of course not. He told me Will was a very lucky man to be married to you.'

'After Waterloo?'

'Months before then. Though it doesn't hurt that you and Bonnie saved his life as well as Will's. But he really respects you.'

'He does?'

'Course he does. Why else would he go to all the trouble to make sure you got that schoolmistress position? He thinks a lot about you, you and Will.'

Louise felt the years of resentment slowly ebb away. She had always known she had made the right choice with Will, but the conviction that Webster had rejected her on account of her being an innkeeper's daughter had niggled away at her for years.

Thomas, her husband's friend, and hers too over so many years, looked completely lost. He'd been on his own far too long. The man does indeed need a wife. After all they'd been through, it was only right she should help Thomas find some happiness. She knew it wasn't one-sided. She'd seen Joanna's face light up whenever Thomas appeared. She knew what it was like to be parted from your lover. She shouldn't begrudge happiness to anyone, even herself.

She began to feel more alive and the shadow of that terrible night, when death encompassed everything, lifted a little further.

Louise smiled. 'So, do you want me to go and see her, and tell her …What shall I tell her, Thomas?'

Thomas was clearly surprised by her change of heart. 'Just ask her what I need to do to gain her father's approval for our marriage.'

'Marriage. It's far too soon to … And she's so young. As for her father and aunt … Thomas, have you taken leave of your senses?'

'Maybe I have.' Thomas grinned at Louise. 'But then Joanna has just said yes.'

27

Disappointment

May 1817, Désvres, Pas-de-Calais, France

Jack Fallowfield had expected more of Rowlandson. As far as he could see, all that had happened was that the girl had stopped working at the school. He'd expected him, at the very least, to demand that Haywood discipline Cowper, which would have put paid to Cowper's designs on the troop serjeant-major post. Jack Fallowfield despised any signs of weakness … in himself … or others.

But Jack felt the world slithering away from him, out of his grasp. He, who had always had fingers in every pie so he might bend everyone to his will, was losing his touch. It had started with Webster, who'd taken his punishment as a defaulting debtor rather than promote him to be his troop serjeant-major. But there was no going back.

God helps those that help themselves. Don't be fooled into thinking you can just let things take their course. You have been chosen to do God's work.

~

John Rowlandson was, truth be told, more than a little disappointed in his daughter. Locking herself in her room, after belittling a good fellow like Fallowfield, wasn't what he had expected. And then there was what could only be an infatuation, with another one of Haywood's sergeants. If only her mother were still alive. His sister hadn't been as helpful as she should have been. Quite unable to tempt Joanna out of her room. All she would say was, 'You'll have to give her a little more time.' He certainly didn't want Joanna to end up like his sister. An old maid and dependent on her brother. Not that Joanna had a brother. That was an even worse prospect to contemplate. How would she live once he'd gone? All he'd managed to get out of his sister was that Joanna kept asking if he had spoken to Captain Haywood about this Cowper fellow. He'd already spoken to Haywood about Fallowfield, whom Haywood had warmly recommended. No, he saw little point in bothering Haywood again.

~

Louise had never been to Captain Rowlandson's house before. A substantial farmhouse, it stood on the edge of the village beyond the crossroads, some distance from their modest cottage. It had been comfortably but not extravagantly furnished by its previous occupants. There was little evidence of feminine influence.

'My brother is used to living out of trunks in temporary accommodation,' Aunt Rowley had said once on their journey to the château.

Aunt Rowley poured tea, whilst Joanna held out her arms to Billy. 'Oh Billy, how you have grown.'

Louise cleared her throat. 'Isabel and Bridie were very excited when I told them I was going to see you. Look, they've made you a needle case cover.' Louise handed it over and Joanna looked as though she might burst into tears.

'I thought you'd like to know that all the children send their best wishes.'

Now what? How was she going to get the chance to pass on Thomas's messages to Joanna?

But Aunt Rowley now turned to Joanna. 'Joanna, would you be so kind as to take young William out to play into the garden for a little while.'

To her surprise, Aunt Rowley took the initiative once they were alone.

'I hear there will be a troop sergeant-major vacancy arising in your husband's Regiment.'

'I've certainly heard that Troop Serjeant-Major Grey is looking to retire. He is not a young man and says he's worn out. But the question is, will the Pension Board agree?'

'And the Pension Board sits when?'

'Sometime in the autumn. I hear he's going back to England to attend it.'

'I see. And in which troop is this possible future vacancy?'

'In Captain Haywood's.'

'And do all the sergeants in the Regiment have similar prospects of obtaining this promotion?'

'Were you thinking of any in particular, Miss Rowlandson?'

'My brother tells me that Captain Haywood has already spoken warmly of Serjeant Fallowfield and considers him an excellent candidate. My brother, who also thinks highly of Serjeant Fallowfield, has taken this as an indication of his prospects, and hence was willing to permit the Serjeant to walk his daughter home.'

'So Captain Rowlandson feels that a future troop sergeant-major is a suitable person to accompany his daughter?'

Aunt Rowley flapped her fan again. 'Indeed he does, but, as my niece is adamant, he has agreed that I, together with his groom, should accompany my niece to school, until such time as Joanna has recovered from the upset. My brother

156

feels, indeed we both feel, that returning to teach at the school will restore her spirits.'

'I'm sure it will, Miss Rowlandson.'

'So, I trust this resolution is satisfactory, Mrs Freer.' Aunt Rowley folded up her fan and tapped the table with it. ' But, as I've said on many occasions, my niece's reputation and affections are not to be trifled with, and so I trust that she will not encounter this Serjeant Cowper at any time while she is at the school?'

Louise stood up. 'Of course, I understand perfectly. Thank you, Miss Rowlandson. Shall I see if Joanna and Billy have finished playing in the garden?'

Maybe she would have chance to speak to Joanna on her own, after all.

28

Almost Summer

June 1817, Désvres, Pas-de-Calais, France

Louise took her news back to Will. Aunt Rowley had been emphatic on three points only. She now read out from her notes, only to make sure she had everything down as discussed, she pointed out to the impatient Will.

'Firstly, for the time being, Louise can return to school as long as aunt Rowley and one of their grooms escort her there and back.'

'Secondly,' she went on to say, 'Rowlandson has now widened his definition of potentially suitable suitors to include troop serjeant-majors.'

'Excellent.' Will jumped about.

'Not so fast, Will. Wait till I've finished.'

She paused to make sure Will was still listening.

'But thirdly,' Louise now fixed Will in the eye …'Aunt Rowley says Rowlandson thinks that Fallowfield is almost certain to become the next troop serjeant-major. Rowlandson says he'd heard it from Haywood himself that Fallowfield would make an excellent candidate. More or less his exact words.'

Will swore under his breath. 'Fallowfield's done it again. How did we not see it? Lady Catherine and all those new clothes? Of course he's exhausted his credit, but Fallowfield will have found someone to lend him money.'

Louise put her notes away in her pocket. 'So, Will Freer, what are we to do?'

'Talk to Cowper, I suppose.'

~

Thomas tried to stay calm. All was not lost yet, he told himself. Haywood had a more trusting nature than was probably wise for an officer. Fallowfield would have reassured him that he could pay back the loan at his own pace, without putting any immediate pressure on him.

'That's exactly how Fallowfield snared Webster,' Thomas muttered.

'It's not something you can easily point out to your senior officer, is it?' Freer lamented.

Thomas nodded. 'I know, I know. But I can't stand by and just watch, without trying to do something, can I?'

'I suppose I could try talking to Webster. Without mentioning any names, of course. '

'And I can speak to Haywood.'

'You have to choose your moment then. At least Webster knows we know.'

~

Charles Webster was puzzled. Freer didn't usually come to see him in the evening, but he obviously had something on his mind, though it wasn't clear exactly what he was worried about.

'I thought you should know, sir, that I have discovered that undue influence is being brought to bear on a officer by a member of his company. And, seeing as how you are aware of … some of the problems this can cause, I thought I should alert you, before…'

Webster was still baffled, but didn't want to press Freer much further. Since the business in Hythe, he knew that Freer was reluctant to ask for favours or special treatment, to avoid any accusations of exerting undue influence himself. His heart beat a little faster as he recalled that awkward encounter, years ago with Freer and Cowper, after they had discovered the company's spurious accounts.

'So how might I help in this matter?'

'I'm sure, now you are aware of the matter, you will be able to draw your own conclusions and decide on the best course of action, accordingly, sir.'

'Thank you, Troop Serjeant-Major. I shall do that.'

After Freer left, Webster could think of only one man who would have merited these concerns. But everybody keeps telling him, Fallowfield is a changed man. A sinner transformed. Forgiven. Now a man of God.

Webster sighed. He was not so sure.

As for the intended victim, Webster could again think of only one man Fallowfield would consider it worth his while to ensnare. But what to do about it without insulting a fellow officer, would be quite another matter.

29

The Wolf

June 1817, Désvres, Pas-de-Calais, France

With the hunting season over, Henry Haywood was at a loose end. Not that this stopped him taking his pair of setters almost everywhere with him in the day, with the occasional bonus of the odd rabbit. However, whilst the majority of evenings were reserved for dining with Berwick and Lady Catherine, he had some official duties that would also take up the occasional evening. The spot inspections he was supposed to make in the various hamlets, where the rest of his troop was billeted, took up some of his time. Checking that the village cabarets were not harbouring soldiers after nine o'clock, also took him out several evenings a month. When visiting the cabarets, he usually took Littlethorpe, who, by sheer size, could immediately scare off potential pugilists. Otherwise, he preferred Cowper's companionship, and marksmanship, to provide him with protection.

He had just set off from the Berwicks one evening with Cowper, when his horse began to fidget, almost as unhappy as she'd been when he'd first bought her. Cowper wasn't far behind, and although Fearless also began to whinny, Cowper seemed to be more in control of his mount.

Cowper tried to get Fearless alongside his mare.

'She's been spooked', Cowper said, as he leant over to try and grab her bridle.

'I don't care if she thinks it's Boney himself but she's going to throw me the way she's going on.'

The mare suddenly reared and bucked, eventually tossing him off her back and galloping away.

Only winded for a moment or two, Haywood got up and brushed himself down. He tried to look dignified. Still, when you've had to hang onto your cover serjeant's stirrup and be hauled up the hill to avoid a French lancer, he was beyond feeling foolish in front of Cowper.

'She's going to lame herself. And that's the last damned thing I need.'

'She's not been like that for a long time, has she? Something's upset her. Fearless is not so happy either. Maybe it's a wolf? We should get on our way as soon as we can.'

Haywood didn't like the sound of wolves. Cowper heaved him up onto Fearless's back, offering him the saddle. But Haywood insisted on Cowper taking the reins. He didn't want to upset Cowper's horse as well.

'And if it is a wolf?'

'It'll have to be injured or desperate to come for us.'

'But, if there's a pack of them?'

'I've got my carbine.'

So this was why you need a second man with you. Not to fight off the French but to defend yourself against the damned forest wolves.

Haywood swore. 'Damnation. Mine's on my horse. It'll be a damned expensive business, if I lose everything on account of her nerves.'

Cowper spoke quietly, but thoughtfully, just as on the way from Waterloo they had bivouacked and Haywood and Thomas had talked, staring into the fire.

'That, sir, would be a dreadful business, when you have been so careful all these years to manage your affairs and keep them in good order.'

'Exactly.'

'Debts can leave a man at the mercy of all kinds of scoundrels.'

Haywood felt sick. Thank God Cowper couldn't see his face.

~

Thomas knew he had to speak up now or he might never get another chance. These moments when a subordinate can broach such a subject with a superior rarely happened, so he decided to carry on, hoping that Haywood too would remember the confidences shared over the campfire. 'None of us will be quite the same fellows we used to be.'

Thomas took another deep breath. 'This is exactly what happened to Captain Webster, sir. And it couldn't have happened to a more upright and honest gentleman.'

Thomas hoped that praising Captain Webster would reassure Haywood that he thought no less of him for succumbing to Fallowfield's enticements.

'For there are some scoundrels who are adept at setting traps for the honest and unwary, traps that they would not normally fall into except under the most extreme circumstances.'

Haywood sighed. 'It is the very nature of traps to make it difficult for a creature to escape them.'

'Indeed,' Thomas agreed.

Thomas remembered only too well how years ago, in Hythe, Webster had been caught up in a bookkeeping fraud over regimental provisions. It had left Webster at the mercy of the very man who'd encouraged him to incur the debts and then acquiesce in the fraud in the first place. Not that he would ever betray Captain Webster's part in that.

'I understand this particular individual makes it his business to seek out moneylenders in whatever town he finds himself and arranges to be an intermediary between those in need of money and the moneylender. All seems favourable for quite some time until the extraordinary interest rates make the debt unpayable and thereafter the gentleman in question is forced to comply with the scoundrel's requests for advancement or other such services.'

Thomas could hear Haywood's voice tremble, 'And what pray might these gentlemen do to avoid such a fate?'

Thomas hadn't much of an answer to that. 'Only to avoid incurring the debt in the first place.'

Haywood hesitated. 'But if it is already too late?'

'Perhaps to seek the advice of others, who have suffered similarly?'

There, it was done. Thomas had breached all manner of protocols but Haywood had not taken it amiss. At least so far.

Suddenly Fearless stopped. Skulking on the edge of the forest there was a lone wolf gorging on a young lamb.

~

Haywood heard Cowper cock his carbine. 'Last resort. Not accurate enough to be sure to kill it,' he heard him mutter. 'And they say they can out-run horses. So are we agreed that we do not turn our backs? That we face it down?'

'Agreed,' Haywood mumbled.

Cowper managed to persuade Fearless on, and, like the steady war-horse she was, she obeyed, edging slowly towards the wolf, Cowper yelling loudly at it.

The creature stared at them, long and hard, until it eventually turned tail, with the lamb still in its jaws. Haywood took a deep breath, but took it as a sign that all might not be well in his world.

~

The wolf stalked his dreams, unsettled him, made him worry about his future. The advances of money had been so easy, so lacking in fuss, with the envelopes delivered to his door, in exchange for a careless flourish of his signature. But Haywood was unnerved. The wolf was closing in, and nearly at his door.

30

The Review

June 1817, Désvres, Pas-de-Calais, France

'We are to be the French?'

'Not exactly. We are to be the Polish lancers,' Captain Haywood repeated. 'The staff officers, spare artillery fellows, sappers and engineers will be the French. As usual.'

The plans for the review at Denain had just arrived and Haywood was sharing them with Grey and his sergeants, but clearly was only just beginning to digest them himself.

'We are to conclude the review with a cavalry charge, including lancers ... that's us ... against infantry squares.'

'Like Ney's charge? Unsupported by artillery or infantry?' Grey queried.

Haywood looked up from his papers. 'So it would seem, Troop Serjeant-Major Grey.'

None of the sergeants or Grey looked pleased.

To be informed that they would therefore be attacking their own cavalry squares, as in the infamous cavalry charges undertaken by Marshall Ney's troops, drew a murmur of discontent.

Why would we want to do that, Thomas thought, when Waterloo was only just won? What lessons could be drawn from that particular near miss? Other than they were lucky that Ney thought he was turning a retreat into a rout and came unprepared to meet opposition.

'So what is it we are supposed to be learning?' Grey persisted.

Thomas was surprised to hear him voicing his opinion so strongly but Grey was becoming noticeably more irritable as his likely retirement from the Regiment drew closer.

'And, how big a part do the Prussians get? The Duke, himself, has wavered on this point several times or so I understand,' Grey continued.

Haywood tried to be diplomatic. 'My understanding is that Prussian troops are unlikely to be there at the review.'

Thomas knew that this was not the question Grey had been asking. Although they had no love for the Prussians, many of those holding the line during those last few hours thought it shabby the way the Prussians' crucial part in their victory had been played down. They would not have liked to have been treated so.

Haywood battled on. 'We shall also try the new formation that the Duke of Wellington has suggested.'

'Which formation is that?' asked Grey.

Haywood returned to his set of papers.

'He has suggested that although we must adhere to our own regulations, which allow a looser formation than in other armies, we must adhere to it strictly, and not allow ourselves to become more extended.'

Haywood continued to outline to within yards, the maximum distances Wellington required between his files and lines in such fine detail, that even Thomas with his usually close attention to such factors began to lose concentration. The brief Wellington had given their commanders meant they had to rethink the distance they maintained between the files. Their instinctive feeling for where the next fellow should be, had to be re-learnt, re-imagined even.

This re-enactment of Ney's charge had clearly been designed to test the 36th dragoons' final transformation into a lancer regiment. The British infantry would be deployed in squares, much as they had been at that point during the battle. Their task was to charge the infantry with as much power as the massed French cavalry and Polish lancers, but without damaging anyone, though every soldier knew that men can get killed during reviews. Just as everyone knew that training exercises provide the ideal opportunity to settle old scores.

~

With Grey almost certain to go in the autumn, the question of the vacancy was assuming a new urgency. Without the promotion Thomas would be a dead man.

Thomas, though, wasn't the only one who sensed danger.

That evening Freer tapped his pipe hard against the fireplace. 'This damned charge in close order files is too good an opportunity for Fallowfield to make mischief, but what's to be bloody done, with sour face Troop Serjeant-Major Grey in charge of dispositions?' muttered Freer. He paused. 'You know, of course, what the best option would be?'

It wasn't something that could be directly expressed in words, even between two good friends. But it was, Thomas concluded, the only logical position for a military man like Fallowfield … or, for that matter, himself to take. To kill or be killed. He could justify to himself the one time he had tried, but this time, if there were to be another time, it would have to be planned and in cold blood. Not the same at all. Besides it carried its own risks of a public disgrace and a military execution.

Better to take defensive action than offensive, Thomas concluded.

'Maybe have a couple of good lads covering my back?'

'I'll see what I can do but whether Grey'll take any bloody notice … 'Freer shook his head.

Thomas too expected little but the night before the march over to Denain, Freer walked into the stables. 'I've persuaded Grey to place Littlethorpe and Byrne behind you in the charge.'

'How did you?' Thomas began. Freer silenced him with his finger to his lips.

'I've told them they're to stick to you like limpets on a rock.'

Thomas raised his eyebrows. During a charge it was nigh impossible to stick to anyone. But Byrne and Littlethorpe were tenacious fellows and they would do their best. Thomas and Freer had already seen the provisional plan for their deployment, and Fallowfield was uncomfortably close to Thomas, in spite of Freer's efforts to get Grey to shift him further down the line.

Freer grimaced. 'It's the best I could do.'

31

On Show

October 1817, Denain, Nord, France

The day came to demonstrate that they were ready. They had taken their time to march to the Denain plains. These open lands couldn't entirely mimic Mont St Jean with its ridges, sunken lanes and flanking farms and villages but Wellington was determined to demonstrate to the allies, as well as the French, what they could do in the centre ground, should they be called upon once again.

The newly formed lancers lined up nervously. It would be a public judgement upon them, if they didn't perform well. Wellington and assorted dignitaries were standing there, telescopes at the ready. They were to be judged.

Thomas, thankful he still had the steady Fearless under him, held his lance, feeling rather like one of the mediaeval knights Captain Webster said were at Agincourt; 'though,' as Freer kept insisting, 'it was the English longbow men who won the day, not bloody knights with long poles.'

Thomas and the other sergeants were to be out in front. They, unlike the French officers took the lead from the start. He fingered the grain of the ash pole and remembered the ash trees, scattered amongst the fields and hedgerows in Burton, back home. Ridiculous, though, to still call it home, after all these years away. Ridiculous too, to be sentimental when it was only an exercise, and not war itself. But, to re-enact even the smallest part of that long day and night at Waterloo, would be to re-open wounds.

He wondered how Freer, Webster and Byrne felt. Did they feel the same rush of blood tingling through every limb, heart beating faster than you ever thought possible; the crushing pains in the chest, the difficulty breathing? The sense of dread? Thomas told himself to nurse the rush of blood over the pain, to focus his eyes ahead, and keep his ears alert for the signals. He made sure his sabre was in position and readjusted his lance, safely stripped of its tip, so it rested easy in his hands and waited.

He was just about to take his place at the front, ready for the men at the back to follow up their lancer charge, with their sabres unsheathed, ready for the close combat required in reality. It was then that Thomas heard the long-dead French officer whispering over his shoulder. 'You mustn't fall. You mustn't lose your mount. That is when someone will cleave your skull in, however much you plead with him, however much your eyes stare directly into his, you will be killed.'

~

'Prepare to receive cavalry.' The infantry wheeled into squares. John Rowlandson ordered his men to uncouple the nine pounders, now well out in front at twenty-yard intervals. Of course, this time they had no canister or shot to load, just black powder. And, this time, although the lances and sabres would be real enough, the lances would be stripped of their steel and the sabres sheathed by the time the first line of cavalry reached the infantrymen's bayonets.

He watched and ordered his men to keep loading their black powder and fire as each squadron moved forward …

two hundred and fifty cavalry, a hundred yards across, two files deep, a hundred yards apart, advancing slowly, at just a walk, the waterlogged ground much like that at Waterloo. But unlike the French, they had managed to preserve their formation. The French in their thousands had been so tightly bunched that horse fell upon horse, man upon man, the dead upon the wounded.

~

At a hundred and fifty yards, the buglers will sound the gallop and the cavalry will run at the guns till they break through, wave after wave of horses and men surging towards us, the earth vibrating.

Time to run back, to seek shelter in the squares, carrying our spikes, rams, and port fires away with them, whilst the French had not even brought so much as a nail to spike our guns or a piece of rope to tow them away.

And so it would go on, holding our nerve, firing the guns, and taking shelter before returning to the guns, until the French horses were incapable of another assault.

~

This time the horses were not to be run into the ground. A halt would be called surely when Wellington had seen enough, thought Rowlandson.

~

But still they rode on, and still we ran backwards and forwards between the guns. He saw the Polish lancers right behind the armoured chasseurs, heard his canister shot shattering lives. He prayed to God for His forgiveness, to show him mercy for all he was about to do.

On the ridge, our field guns no more than twenty yards apart. Twenty-five squares of infantry laid out behind us like chessboards.

The Grand Battery. Cannonballs and shells. Straight at them.

First charge. Massed ranks of horsemen firstly at a walk, then at a canter. Up the hill.

Load and fire, scatter their horsemen, run to the nearest square. Horses and their riders pushed between us, side-by-side. Infantrymen cut them down. Our dragoons press them back down the hill.

The Grand Battery. Cannonballs and shells into the squares. The dead and wounded fall as they fight.

Second charge. And still they come, firstly at a walk, then at a canter.

Run out, re-load the guns. Fire. Scramble into the nearest square. Horses and riders swirl side-by-side. Infantrymen pick them off. Our cavalry force them back down the hill.

The Grand Battery. More cannonballs and shells into the squares. The dead and wounded pile up higher.

Third charge. Rank after rank at a walk then a canter of heavy cavalry up the hill, all red-crested brass helmets and cuirasses.

Load, fire, kill with canister. Pain; pain in the shoulder, pain in the arm, pain in the knee. Can't run; must run. Lancers kill everyone found outside the square. Crawl back. Men and horses squealing. Darkness.

I'm praying. 'God is my strength and power; and he maketh my way perfect.'

~

Through the haze of black smoke, Rowlandson sees a lancer come straight towards him, then swing his weapon sideways, sweeping one of his fellow lancers straight off his horse, into the path of those following. He blinks and rubs his eyes. That was the trouble with exercises. Remembering things. Seeing things that aren't there.

~

Thomas was tumbling, falling. Hooves, fetlocks, mud. Body broken. Breath taken. Darkness.

32

Secrets

October 1817, Denain, Nord, France

Henry Haywood rushed in late, quickly checking the crowded salon for the Berwicks but, surprisingly, they weren't there yet. He could see all three of the Rowlandsons, and, more surprisingly, Captain Webster. Webster was not a man who enjoyed large social gatherings. Not that Haywood was in the mood for celebrations, either.

Captain Webster walked over, smiling. 'Wellington, himself, has just sent his compliments. He now feels that, under the command of Lieutenant-Colonel Pennington once again, we have acquitted ourselves well. Apart from that bit of a tumble.'

Haywood nodded politely. Webster clearly hadn't heard. 'Excellent news, sir. But,' he paused, reluctant to change the mood. 'Unfortunately, we have suffered casualties in that bit of a tumble. Following orders, of course. But with not enough distance between the files, in my opinion.'

Webster looked shocked. He'd been far away on the other side of the field.

'You said we had casualties?'

'One dead, a serjeant, three seriously injured, a number of minor cuts and bruises.'

But before Webster had chance to say anything else, Captain Rowlandson, standing right behind them, stepped forward

'You've lost some of your men?'

'A serjeant, for sure, and three others we don't know about yet. No gunshot wounds of course, but at least one of them is barely conscious.

Miss Rowlandson, looking shocked, moved in between them.

'Which serjeant, Captain, which serjeant has died?'

Haywood was puzzled by her agitation but then remembered she knew both Cowper and Fallowfield.

'I'm afraid Cowper…' her face began to drain of colour, 'has been badly injured.'

'But he's still alive?'

'Just about,' Haywood shook his head, 'but he's barely conscious.'

Then Rowlandson spoke up.

'It's no wonder, the way it happened.'

'You saw it happen?'

'I saw the collision.' Rowlandson paused, as though struggling to say more.

'The leading group were our strongest and best lancers, so if you can remember anything …'

Rowlandson cleared his throat, as if also trying to clear his mind. 'I think I saw it. I can't be really sure. You know what it's like.'

Haywood smiled at his old friend, remembering again why he was such a fine fellow.

'Exactly.'

'Well, I could have sworn that I saw one of your lancers push another one off his horse. As quick as a flash with his lance. Sideways. The other fellow didn't stand a chance. But maybe I just dreamt it.'

Haywood felt his heart jump as he saw Webster's face blanch.

Haywood leant forward. 'Somebody riding close and in the same formation?'

'It must have been, I suppose, but I couldn't say.'

'You didn't see who it was, then?'

'Not in that press of horses and men. You all look the same in your uniforms.'

Rowlandson paused. 'To be honest, I thought I'd dreamt the whole thing, you know, in the heat of the action.'

Webster intertwined his fingers. 'No. I don't think you did. It's rather too easy with one of those lances, even without the tips, to wreak havoc in a charge. By accident or design.' Webster was clearly troubled. 'Thank you, Captain Rowlandson. That was most helpful.'

'Where are they, where have you taken the wounded?' Miss Rowlandson asked Haywood.

But before he could reply, the aunt seized Miss Rowlandson's arm and guided her firmly out of the salon. Seeing this, Rowlandson bowed and followed them.

Haywood, nodding to the departing Rowlandson, whispered to Webster. 'Do you think he did see something?'

'It sounds like it. So, apart from Cowper, who were our casualties?'

'They were all in my troop. Poor Serjeant Riley killed instantly, they reckon, Byrne and Littlethorpe badly, but not critically hurt and Cowper, as I said, barely conscious. Littlethorpe and Byrne were behind the leading group. Got most of their injuries helping Cowper. Broken ribs, an arm or two, that kind of thing. But the two of them reckon that, if it hadn't been for Cowper's horse, Cowper would be dead. She must have managed to pull back enough to protect him, forcing the other horses away from him. As it is, the doctors can't be sure of Cowper's full recovery.'

Haywood straightened his back and tried not to think about losing Cowper.

Webster still looked shaken. 'So, was it Serjeant Riley or Cowper, do you think, who might have been pushed off his horse?'

Haywood shook his head. 'No idea, sir. Both good men. And well liked.'

Webster sighed. 'It's not such an easy business pretending to wage war, is it?' He unfurled his fingers. 'So, we must pray for our brave Irishman's soul, and for the recovery of our other men.'

~

Everything he'd heard that evening confirmed Charles Webster's worst fears and suspicions.

But Haywood was now looking distracted. 'You haven't seen the Berwicks this evening, have you?'

Webster threw up his hands. 'My deepest apologies, Haywood. I was to pass on their message to you. I'm afraid Lady Catherine is unwell and Captain Berwick is unwilling to leave her.'

Haywood looked worried. 'Something serious ?'

Webster shook his head. 'I don't think so. She hopes to be fully recovered in a day or two.'

Haywood tried to smile. 'That's good.'

Now, Webster urged himself on. Better get it over with.

'I'm told that these days, you are a regular visitor to the Berwicks.'

Haywood smiled. 'Indeed, I am. '

Webster took a deep breath to steady himself. 'These kind of social engagements can sometimes lead young officers into difficulties. Keeping up with those with a little more income than oneself can be an awkward business.'

Webster saw the relief on Haywood's face, when he talked about this as a general problem. But he still looked somewhat embarrassed.

Dare he say any more?

'There are so many traps impecunious young officers can fall into, especially if they happen to be approached by a certain kind of man, who can worm his way into their lives, through their pockets. Encouragement to spend; cash advances at the flick of a signature, loans never paid off on account of interest rates always rising.'

Webster paused before making his most important points. 'And worst of all, there are hidden loans left on the books, accruing vast amounts of interest, impossible to pay back. Unless the man concerned is offered an advancement, which would compromise the officer's honour. Unless he is willing to call the other man's bluff.'

Webster noticed Haywood redden. 'And how would you advise these young officers, should they happen to be in this man's debt?' asked Haywood.

'To swallow their pride, to write to their parents, explain that they are in urgent need of funds. They will, of course, have to pay them back over time, but parents are unlikely to land their own sons in a debtors' prison.'

'So how would you advise guarding against these hidden loans?'

'I would strongly suggest that any officer, intending to repay his loans, should commission a legal document, duly signed in front of a notary, which states that all loans and interest are agreed by all parties to have been repaid.'

Webster smiled, as encouragingly as he could, and refilled Haywood's glass of wine. Webster liked Haywood, in spite of his gossipy, indiscreet ways. He had always shown himself to be an obliging kind of fellow, without malice, which in a small officers' mess was always welcome. He hoped that neither Haywood nor the Regiment would be paying too great a penance for his indiscretions.

For once, Haywood seemed lost for words and sat quietly, drinking his wine, before he finally spoke.

'Just a query, but I was wondering if you had any thoughts about Fallowfield, whether you think there might be any problems, should he become my troop sergeant-major?'

Webster leant forward. 'I think you know what my answer would be.' Haywood nodded. 'I'm just trying to think ahead, be prepared. Especially if Cowper has not recovered, by the time decisions have to be made.'

~

Joanna rushed straight up to her room. John Rowlandson knew at once that this must have been on account of the incident he had witnessed. Witnessed, though, was not quite the word for it because it had been such a fleeting glance, that he could hardly persuade himself that it had happened at all. It clearly had, however, and the more Rowlandson thought about it, the more he knew that malice had been at work. Then when he'd said as much to his sister, she'd declared that the whole business might well be on account of Joanna. 'How on earth,' he'd exclaimed, 'Could this possibly be anything to do with Joanna?'

But his sister had held her ground. 'Do you not think it a little strange that this Cowper fellow has been injured in this way? This is clearly very same man Joanna has an attachment to, and the one you received a letter about? Somebody doesn't like this Serjeant Cowper. Indeed somebody so dislikes him that they have tried to kill him. Somebody is jealous.' She had snapped her fan shut and left him to his own thoughts once again.

All on account of his Joanna? Rowlandson was horrified to even think of this and went over what he'd seen again and again to see if he could remember anything more about Cowper's attacker. But, as he had said, it was far too difficult to distinguish the men in their uniforms from each other. But then he suddenly recalled their sergeants' insignia. The attacker and the attacked were both sergeants. Of course, he could see their uniform markings quite clearly now. So it was one serjeant against another, but there are a number of sergeants in any one troop of cavalry. It could have been any of them. John Rowlandson began to feel protective towards Serjeant Cowper. It was a murderous act. And by a fellow soldier. Perhaps he should talk to Captain Haywood, after all, to tell him he had remembered that detail. He supposed though he should also ask him more about this Cowper fellow and particularly as to whether his conduct could have merited such an attack.

~

He had no particular cause to seek out Haywood, but the very next morning before they all returned to Désvres Haywood called on him at their lodgings. Haywood seemed eager to talk.

'Captain Webster asked me to come to see you in case you are able to remember anything else about the accident during the exercises.'

Rowlandson sighed. 'As I said, it was too difficult to distinguish your soldiers apart, though I have just remembered that the assailant was another serjeant.'

'I see. And you are sure that you do not remember anything else?'

'Sadly, no. But I was wondering though if this Cowper had done anything to provoke such an attack from one of his fellow serjeants.'

'Not at all, as far as I am aware. Indeed, Cowper is my cover sergeant. He has saved my life at least twice.' Haywood looked upset. 'So you understand why I would like to believe that I have left no stone unturned, as to who did this. But, as you say, that will be a difficult matter to prove'.

Rowlandson held out his hand. 'I'm sorry I cannot help further other than to confirm it was no accident. But you said that this fellow Cowper is your cover serjeant?'

'Yes. He's always been the most obliging, honourable man.'

'Then you think highly of him?'

'I do indeed. Very highly. I had hoped he might become my next troop serjeant- major.'

Rowlandson cleared his throat. 'Not that I would encourage her interest in a mere sergeant, but my daughter also seems rather impressed by him.'

'Then I'm sorry to hear that, Rowlandson.'

'So he is not a man you would vouch for?'

'Oh, I would vouch for him, all right, but I am not sure of the prospects for his recovery. He may never be the man he was.'

'Captain Webster is keeping back Cowper's good friend, Troop Serjeant-Major Freer to watch over all three men in the convent, and to keep us informed. We thought it best it should be somebody Cowper knows … just in case we lose him altogether.'

'It's as bad as that?'

'Apparently.'

Rowlandson noticed Haywood briefly brush his hand across his eyes.

'So my apologies for being the bearer of bad news, but I must be on my way.'

As Rowlandson escorted Haywood to the door, he caught a glimpse of Joanna running back up the stairs. She had probably been listening at the door.

~

Joanna had heard enough of what Captain Haywood said to realise Thomas might die. Of course she would not be allowed to visit, but she must write him a letter immediately so Troop Serjeant-Major Freer could take it to him.

33

Wounded

October 1817, Denain, Nord, France /
October 1817, Désvres, Pas-de-Calais

Littlethorpe turned over. 'Aah. That bloody hurts.' Bloody horses trying to mow us down. Me and Byrne heaving Cowper, bleeding like a stuck pig, on to Fearless, a dead bloody weight, if ever there was one, grabbing on to Cowper whilst Byrne wriggles him on to her back, still bellyaching like hell but hanging on to him like an old granny, with me trying to stop the rest of the bloody horses charging us before I can get back on Byrne's horse. Don't know where mine went. She always was a bad-tempered bugger. Ran off first chance she had. With the rest of them. Not like Fearless. Just stood there solid as a rock.

Still, Byrne must be getting better. First thing he said this morning, 'I'm never back in a bloody convent again?' But they say Cowper's still gabbling and doesn't know his arse from his elbow. They reckon he's cracked his skull, way he's going on.

~

Will Freer sat by Cowper's bed wondering whether to read Joanna's letter to him. Cowper didn't even appear to know him, never mind understand a letter written by his sweetheart.

My dearest Thomas,

Your great friend, Will Freer, has agreed to read this to you. I am sure he will think it strange to repeat my words but I know how much he loves you too and would not feel shy to admit this.

I wish I could be with you and sit by your bed and hold your hand. But it is not to be. There's not been a day gone by since we were forced apart that I have not thought of you. It is hard to explain to anyone how much I have missed you. But I know that you are strong and a good man and I pray to God that he will remember this and restore your body as well as your soul. My father too has said he will pray for your recovery. He seems quite shaken by what has happened to you and has spoken to Captain Haywood who has again said many wonderful things about you – all true of course. I know that my father listened hard and asked him questions and understood what Captain Haywood had to say. Captain Haywood said that he had hopes that you would become his next troop serjeant-major. My father, of course, was impressed and I know that this has been our hope as well that you will secure this well-deserved promotion and we shall be able to be married with everyone's blessing.

So I urge you, dearest Thomas, not to give up the fight, and to remember how much I, and all your friends, love you. I have sent a token of my love, for you to hold tight, in place of myself. It belonged to my mother and was a very special thing for her just as you are a very special person to me.

Remember, dearest Thomas, that we have promised to share our lives together and that your strength will be my strength and my strength will be yours. I send all my strength now in this letter and tell you yet again how much I love you and pray for your recovery.

Your loving Joanna

As he had been instructed Will Freer tucked the little silver bird into Cowper's hand and was astonished to see Cowper's hand grasp it and hold it tight in his palm.

'Bloody hell, Thomas, come on, wake up.'

Cowper stirred, moaned a little but still held tight onto his little silver bird.

What was to be done? Will Freer decided the only way he could haul Thomas back into the present would be talk about the past, to remind Thomas of everything they'd done together over the last ten years.

It was not as easy as it sounded. Indeed Louise regularly scolded him for living too much in the future, whereas Thomas had always lived far too much in the past. But, when he eventually settled down to it, he was almost overwhelmed by the memories. No wonder Thomas sometimes got lost in the past.

'Right Cowper,' Freer began, 'do you remember that first time we met in Leicester, watching the recruiting party come into town? Captain Dickenson was in charge? Remember him? Killed at Salamanca. He used to call me his boot maker, which I was, of course. But my master had just thrown me out. Remember?'

Thomas grunted crossly, as if to say of course he bloody remembered. Freer felt encouraged. The more he talked, the more Thomas seemed to respond. The more the nuns kept telling him he was disturbing the patient, the more he kept telling them it was good for this patient to be disturbed. And so it seemed to be, as Thomas began to respond with single words to Freer's stories.

By the time Freer had reached 1812 and the Peninsular Campaign, Thomas was regularly joining in with the odd word and phrase. By Portsmouth he'd remembered Littlethorpe swimming the horses out to the boats. And then navigating his way across the Tormes. By Salamanca he'd remembered the fires burning into the night.

He even remembered ending up in the general hospital in Lisbon, after being off his head with a fever. And now he was off his head again with a fractured skull. But he'd got better before, so no reason he wouldn't get better again. Freer cheered himself up and carried on talking.

Out of consideration for Thomas's delicate state Freer had omitted the lifting of the siege of Badajoz. Suddenly Thomas mumbled, 'Badajoz. You've missed out Badajoz. And Boy. You've missed out Boy.'

And so Freer, at Thomas's insistence, went back and told of the carnage the troops had visited upon the fortress town. Thomas now became quite agitated. 'Boy,' he kept saying. 'Is Boy safe?' He kept asking and Will kept reassuring. 'With Bonnie Murphy and Ashby. Remember?'

But it was the reading of Joanna's letter that Freer read again and again that seemed to penetrate his consciousness the most. Freer could have recited it off by heart by the end of that second day … when Thomas finally began to wake up.

~

Swirling, dancing, dizzy, moving. Nothing staying still. Dreams, always dreams. Joanna at the cricket match. People talking. Questions. No one staying still. Joanna. In the woods. Kissing her. Bluebells. But the trees keep moving, spinning round and round. I'm tired. I want to sleep. I want to sleep.

'Cowper, wake up, you need to keep awake.'

'I am awake.'

'No, you aren't.'

'Who says not?'

'Me, Will Freer says not. You've been drifting off the whole time I've been here.'

'I'll prove it.'

'Go on, then.'

'Help me up.'

'Not likely. You've fallen over at least three times today.'

'How do you know?'

'I've been here all day.'

'Have you?'

'You've cracked your head. You're not yourself. You need keeping an eye on.'

'I got bowled out ... the ball hit my head. Came out of nowhere. Mustn't have been looking.'

'You got hit on the head before you fell off Fearless?'

'It might have been a cricket bat?'

'Like a ten-foot-long one made out of ash?'

Thomas laughed, 'That's a stupid question.'

'Well, it was a bloody stupid answer.'

'Will Freer?'

'That's me'

'I'm Thomas?'

'That's right. Thomas Cowper.'

'I remember now. I'm going to marry Joanna.'

'Thomas, don't bloody say that.'

'But I asked her and she said yes.'

'I know she did. But it's a secret. You can't tell anybody. Not yet. Understand?'

'Can I see her?'

'When you're a bit better and we can get you back to Désvres.'

'So where am I now?'

'Denain. In a convent.'

'What happened?'

'You mean apart from you getting hit by a giant cricket bat?'

'You always did have a dreadful sense of humour, Will Freer.'

'Well, if you can remember that, if you try even harder, maybe you'll remember a few other things?'

It would be easier if the room would just stop spinning around quite so much.

~

The letter was from his father. Haywood opened it carefully. He didn't want to risk damaging it. But there was no need to guard its contents. His father was clearly angry with him, reminding him, with several underlinings, that he had already written to say he was struggling to gather in rents from his estates in Ireland, whilst, after this damned peace, his English holdings were equally unfruitful. His father was right, of course, he had already written to explain all this, which was why Haywood had got himself into this mess in the first place.

But Grey would be off to the Pension Board any week now. And decisions would have to be made, though it was beginning to look as if it would have to be Fallowfield, after all. Not that Webster would approve. Cowper would have been the first choice of both officers. He knew that. But with

Cowper not being entirely straight in the head yet and with all this other business …

Of course, Fallowfield had been charm itself, most helpful and ingratiating, ever since he'd returned from Brussels. Until Haywood, trying to pull back a bit, had refused any more offers of money. He was also beginning to think that even promoting him to the troop serjeant-major post might not prove to be enough to write off his debts. He would be trapped like a rabbit in a gin. He stood up, walked to the window and thought of Cowper, still in the convent back in Denain, fighting hard to get well again, as Freer reported.

For God's sake. He picked up his father's letter and tore it to shreds.

~

Back in Désvres, John Rowlandson thought it was time he consulted his wife. He paced up and down the study, throwing out question after question. He'd begun by summarising, in proper military fashion, all that had happened, as he understood it, between his daughter and Serjeant Cowper, concluding with his question as to whether it would be kinder to discourage his daughter's interest altogether rather than display any sympathy or investigate the man's prospects any further. He waited patiently. Eventually he imagined what she would have said to him. 'Now John, remember when we first met you were only a serjeant, with prospects mind you, with a lot of prospects, you being as clever as you were to pass all those exams. But did my father say no, you could not come and pay me visits? Even though I was the daughter of a very prosperous grocer. No, he did not. He could see that I already knew that I would be satisfied with no other. And being the father that he was, he wished for my happiness regardless of whether you would have secured another promotion by the time of our engagement. Now he was a man that cared nothing for status, little even for money and a very great deal for his daughter's and wife's happiness. So I ask you again, John. Is this man Cowper, should he survive, a man who will make our daughter happy and of course, be able to provide for her?'

So long as he becomes a troop serjeant-major, John Rowlandson found himself answering. It's the only way she will be offered somewhere decent to live. You wouldn't want her living her married life behind a curtain in some barracks block, would you?

'I agree,' his wife argued back. 'So, if he does become a troop serjeant-major and if Joanna continues to have this strong attachment to him and he is of good character then you will have no grounds at all for preventing this match.'

John Rowlandson sat down at his desk, exhausted. Geometry was so much easier than life. He'd always left life to his wife. But now at least he'd had some guidance. But there would be no point telling Joanna for the moment, in case the poor man dies. No point in raising her hopes.

~

When after ten days or so Littlethorpe and Byrne were well enough to return to Désvres, Freer decided to write to Haywood. In this current atmosphere of distrust, Freer felt it wiser to give his letter for safe-keeping to the two men who, undoubtedly, had saved Thomas's life.

Denain, November 8th 1817

Dear Captain Haywood,

You asked me to report on Serjeant Cowper's progress as soon as I could. According to the regimental surgeon Sergeant Cowper suffered a fracture to his skull, most likely caused by a single heavy blow to the back of his head, sustained during the charge but not through the subsequent fall to the ground. Fortunately this blow did not result in an open wound to his skull, which means that the surgeon is confident of a good recovery. In due course.

When you saw him last, he was only just able to recognise us and say a few words. Over the last ten days or so, he has made a good deal of progress and I am hopeful that he will return to health by the end of the month. I will keep you informed as to when we plan to return. Obviously it may be beneficial for him to resume lighter duties on his immediate return but the surgeon and I are confident that he will be fit and well enough to resume his full duties during the month of December.

Yours

William Freer, Troop Sergeant-Major

Having promised Haywood, in effect, that Thomas would recover in time to be considered for the troop serjeant-major post, Will Freer now walked slowly back to Thomas's room. 'If I have anything to do with it,' he kept saying to himself.

Thomas was sitting on the edge of his bed, half dressed. He looked upset. 'I'm not sure I can remember anything any more.'

'Nonsense,' Freer said. 'By the time I finish with you, you'll be back to the man you were. In mind and body. I've promised not only Captain Haywood but also Joanna.' Freer passed Thomas his boots. For his walking exercises. Round the grounds. The walking exhausted Freer, but seemed to be doing Thomas some good. He seemed to remember things best when he was outside. He had recovered his past memories all right but not those of only half an hour ago.

34

Testing Times

November 1817, Pas-de-Calais, France

Henry Haywood was running out of time. Cowper was returning from Denain in a couple of days, much improved by all reports, but he would have to see. Troop Serjeant–Major Grey was, at long last, leaving for Britain next week, and unlikely to return, and now Rowlandson wanted to see him as well. To do with Cowper's prospects, he'd said in his brief letter. If only Haywood knew what to do himself, that would help. So he'd put Rowlandson off until next week.

As for next week, well, almost everything should follow from today. After he and Webster had met in Désvres to make the final arrangements.

~

The ride back with Freer would be the first test. The broken bones in his wrist had knitted together but his grip was still weak. Freer said he should ride Freer's far less obedient horse, rather than Fearless, whose temperament didn't need managing. And to use his hands rather than his legs to control her. So far, so good.

The next test Freer had set him was to remember as many army regulations, drills, and requirements as possible. In fact, anything he chose to ask him. This was considerably more taxing, but as they bumped along, Thomas found things coming back to him in a way he would never have imagined only a few weeks ago.

'So now,' Freer teased, 'what do you remember about being hit by that giant cricket bat?'

Thomas smiled. 'Is that what I said?'

'Indeed, you did.'

'I didn't see a thing, but if I had to try and describe how it felt, being hit across the back of my head with a giant cricket might well answer it.'

'Hmm. So the final part of today's test?'

'All right.'

'What have you not got to mention to anyone about you and Joanna?'

Thomas thought for a moment, and then smiled.

'We're going to get married?'

'Yes, but it's secret, remember.'

'I know. And I've got to get promoted first.'

Freer declared himself satisfied that Thomas had now fully recovered all his faculties and it was 'about bloody time he got promoted and got wed.'

Thomas nursed his wrist and massaged the pain away. If only it was that easy.

35

The Revenge Of The Israelites

December 1817, Désvres, Pas-de-Calais, France

Jack Fallowfield was furious. By rights, Cowper should be dead and Haywood in his pocket but the bloody worm's gone and turned, refusing every offer to procure him another loan. And now Cowper's on the bloody mend and all. But all was not lost. Yet. He would continue to make himself agreeable until the time came, if forced, to remind Haywood he was still considerably in his debt.

So he could hardly believe it when he and the money-lender were summoned to attend a notary's office in Désvres. There they were handed a banker's draft supplemented by an agreed amount of cash, in return for signing documents stating that all Haywood's loans and any outstanding interest had now been paid in full. The money-lender might have been satisfied, but Jack saw his hold over Haywood slipping away from him. Though he would now have to act pleased that he'd been able to assist him, in these temporarily difficult times, to court Lady Catherine. So the last thing he wanted to do was to risk upsetting Haywood before Grey's pension board next week.

But where the hell did he get the money from? From all accounts, Haywood's father was practically bankrupt himself. And then he realised. Last week, the hunting dogs disappeared, and he wasn't wearing his signet ring or gold pin. Haywood must have sold them all, and more, to pay off his debts.

He must have been warned off. The only one who might have done that was bloody Cowper, now back from the convent.

~

So a week later when Cowper was appointed Haywood's troop serjeant-major, he could hardly contain his rage. God knows it should have been me. *'Vengeance is mine; I will repay, saith the Lord'* … everything and more that you have cost me, Cowper.

~

Thomas had never been happier. He and Joanna were to be married by licence by the Army chaplain on Monday, just a week after he gained his promotion.

He was still nervous, though. It was all well and good being sweethearts, but being man and wife was a different matter. Thomas was sure Joanna would be happy to lie with him. He knew her already to be a woman of some passion. He was more worried about whether her father and aunt would ever truly accept him. He liked Captain Rowlandson and he could see that the Captain had begun to warm to him, but Aunt Rowley seemed as stiff and formal as ever. 'He has so little charm,' she had said to Joanna. Thomas knew exactly what Aunt Rowley meant. His brother Michael had been the charming one in his family. Everyone had said so. Joanna, though, was indignant on his behalf and had told Aunt Rowley that, in her experience, 'charm was an unreliable indication of a man's true nature.' But then Aunt Rowley had almost agreed with her, saying Joanna might well be better off with Thomas after all. It was a grudging acceptance but still some kind of an acceptance.

But, it wouldn't be him, Thomas reflected, if he didn't find something to worry about even on the happiest day of his life, the day when everything he had hoped for over the last two years was about to happen, when he would have a future rather than just a past. When their sons and daughters would be born and their future and their children's future would stretch on and on, making all, good and bad, that had happened to him worthwhile. His life would make sense. Joanna had brought joy into his life. And now he was about to pledge his loyalty and allegiance "till death us do part". He hoped beyond hope that he would make her a better husband than his father had ever been and be a better parent than either his mother or his father.

But on this beautiful winter's day, with a brilliant blue sky, and sun streaming through the trees, the beech buds as tight as a chrysalis waiting for spring, waiting for life to begin once again, Thomas was content. Almost.

~

Joanna couldn't wait for her wedding day to be over. To lie with Thomas all night, in their own small cottage at the edge of the woods, the woods where she had first discovered how love feels.

'Don't expect too much,' Louise had warned her. Like so many, he still bore the scars of a long war and a brutal end to it. And scars from his early life too, Joanna guessed.

Joanna was wearing her ball gown, the one she had been wearing the night Haywood had neglected her, the night Thomas had blurted out he'd have danced with her all night, the night they had exchanged first names.

Joanna's father was to give her away.

'If only Boy could have been here too,' she whispered. 'If only.' Thomas squeezed her arm.

Louise sat in the front row with Billy, Isabel and Bridie, and the cheerful chatter of cavalry and artillery men filled the room with an anticipation and liveliness he'd not known for a long time.

Freer and Littlethorpe were to be their witnesses. Littlethorpe had said he wanted to try out his newly mastered signature, and as for Freer, how could he not ask him?

A small wedding breakfast, arranged by Aunt Rowley for those above troop serjeant-major rank and their ladies, was held at Captain Rowlandson's house, after which Thomas and Joanna were to be released to return to the party for other ranks organised by Byrne in the school room, which was to last all evening.

It was when Captain Haywood walked in, smiling, with Lady Catherine on his arm that Thomas realised that they had chosen to announce their engagement on Thomas's wedding day. 'I would like to interrupt these celebrations to honour the man who has saved my life at least twice, and his lovely wife, by telling you all that their fine example has encouraged Lady Catherine and myself to announce our own engagement. The printed announcement has already been placed in *The Times*, but we thought that Troop Serjeant-Major and Mrs Cowper would not object to our joining their happiness with our own.'

Thomas rushed up to shake Haywood's hand. 'I couldn't be more honoured, sir,' and then, bowing to Lady Catherine, 'many congratulations on your engagement.'

Lady Catherine smiled. 'Delighted to see you again Troop Serjeant-Major.'

~

Will whispered to Louise, 'She'll be relieved to have a decent fellow with modest habits like Haywood spending her money rather than some spendthrift young buck.'

Louise whispered back, 'And when you're blessed with intelligence and reach a certain age you want someone who's entirely amiable and thinks the world of you and not of your money. And she was impressed that he'd sorted out his debts too before he proposed.'

'How do you know all this ...'

Louise smiled. 'Oh. Captain Webster and I worked out a plan together.'

Will couldn't believe what he was hearing. 'You did what?'

'He said he wished he'd talked to me about his own debts all those years ago, and now that he was in a position to help Haywood, he would. An uncle had just died and left him some money as well, so if Haywood cut his losses, he would offer him an interest-free loan.'

'I suppose you knew when Haywood was going to propose as well?'

'Of course I did. He talked it over with Webster first. And Webster talked it over with me. In strictest confidence.'

'I always did reckon Webster had a soft spot for you.'

'You're right, Will, he does seem to. I like him too.'

'But not as much as me?'

'Definitely not as much as you.'

~

Light-headed with rage, Jack Fallowfield retreated into the woods with two flagons of wine. The un-soldierly Cowper was now in charge of men. By rights, his men.

Fallowfield threw himself onto the ground, hugged his knees, and summoned every muscle in his body to regain control. Rage had to be channelled. To smite down sinners. He rocked slowly back and forth. What to do?

He took his Bible out of his sabretache, and opened it, savouring every word. He declaimed its text into the darkness, drinking fully of His holy wine, but other thoughts came unbidden, unwanted, tormenting.

And the Lord said unto Joshua,
Be not afraid because of them: for to
morrow about this time will I deliver
them up all slain before Israel: thou
shalt hough their horses, and burn
their chariots with fire.

Bare earth floor, straw, naked.
Turf burning, choking …

So Joshua came, and all the people
of war with him, against them by the
waters of Merom suddenly; and they
fell upon them.

Faces blackened with burnt cork, woven straw plaited over their heads, running, yelling.
Turf burning, choking …

And the Lord delivered them into
the hand of Israel, who smote them,
and chased them unto great Zidon
and then unto Misrephoth-maim, and
unto the valley of Mizpeh eastward;
and they smote them, until they left
them none remaining.

Women and children laughing, Cathleen taunting. Stones flying. Banshees all of them.

Turf burning, choking …

And Joshua did unto them as the
Lord bade him: he houghed their
horses, and burnt their chariots with
fire.

Black peat swallowing everything.
choking …

Lucky to be alive. God was speaking to him, just as he had spoken to Joshua. Fallowfield knew what he had to do. But he would need courage. He drained both flagons dry. He took out a knife from his sabretache and walked back towards the château. He was ready to serve his God.

~

Aunt Rowley had asked Louise, being a married woman, to prepare Joanna for her wedding night, to explain, she said blushing, what would happen. Louise wasn't sure she would have to explain absolutely everything, but she agreed to walk Joanna back to her cottage and, as requested, to do her duty.

Thomas was to follow as soon as Will judged him to be sober enough, though Will, Louise sighed, was almost as far gone as Thomas, slapping his back, telling him it had been a long time coming but was going to be worth the wait, Littlethorpe and Byrne winking behind their backs and encouraging Thomas to drink yet more toasts to his beautiful wife.

It was Freer who had the idea of drinking the last toast of the evening to Fearless, 'who has saved your life on far too many occasions to mention.' Leaning on each other, Freer and Thomas made their way to the stable block, which was, after all, Freer declared, on the way to the cottage. The bitter December air was rapidly sobering them up. Thomas, now fully alert, thought he'd waited quite long enough to give Louise time to leave and wanted to get back to Joanna straight away, but Freer hung on to him. 'Shouldn't take long,' Freer said, swinging his lantern.

They heard Fearless before they even got to the stables. She was the only horse there. Thomas rushed through the door to her stall. Freer followed close behind. There was blood everywhere, spurting into the stable gullies. Fearless was thrashing about in pain, lying on her side unable to stand, soaking in her own blood. Thomas fell to his knees in disbelief. 'Who could have done this?' She had been hamstrung, as surely as if the enemy cavalry had severed her sinews themselves. He could see there was nothing to be done. And the pain she was in …

Freer put his hand on Thomas's shoulder.

'Freer, have you got your pistol?'

'No.'

'Then go and get mine from the house, and tell Joanna what's happened. I will stay with her, see if I can do anything at all.' He stripped off his uniform.

Of course there was nothing that could be done. Except talk to her, stroke her neck when she was still for a moment. ' Now, don't kick me to death, neither.'

It was Joanna, wrapped up in his cape over her shift, who came back with his gun.

'I can walk faster than Will. So I told him to get back to Louise.'

She moved closer. 'Oh, how terrible.'

Thomas loaded the pistol. ' You might not want to stay.'

'But that's why I came. To stay.'

Thomas put the pistol against Fearless's head.

'Thank you, my friend, for… everything.'

He wiped away his tears and pulled the trigger.

~

He didn't want to leave her. Joanna could see that. After he'd cleared away the bloodstained straw, he laid some fresh sheaves around her body, as though making her more comfortable. 'Did I tell you that Haywood said he'd buy her as a hack if she didn't pass the next inspection? Spare her from the knacker's yard for a bit longer. Talking of which, we'll have to send for him, first thing. Good job it's not summer. She'll be fine till morning. She'll be fine.' He patted Fearless's neck. 'You'll be fine, eh?'

Joanna sat down on some sheaves. 'Why don't we just stay and keep her company till then?' Joanna patted the straw. 'We could sleep here.'

'But it's our wedding night.'

Joanna tucked herself under the cape and a couple of horse blankets. 'Just come when you're ready.'

He stayed with Fearless until she began to lose all her warmth, praying for forgiveness that she should die this terrible death, because of him. Of course, she could have died many terrible deaths long before now, but then how many times had she saved his life … when she'd carried him and Haywood up the ridge away from the Polish lancer, when she'd stood over him at Denain. And all the times she'd been his absolute rock in all his sorrows. He laid his head against her neck and sobbed.

Who could have sunk so low? But Thomas recognised the hallmarks of a bitter man, one who knew how to wound him most grievously. And on his wedding day. After all, no one would suspect Fallowfield of killing a horse. No one except him and Freer.

Thomas took one last look at Fearless, slithered off the rest of his blood-splattered clothes, washed himself in the water bucket, and, shivering, bolted the stable door before returning to Joanna. She was asleep. He huddled next to her, wriggling his hand under her shift. She woke up and kissed him.

36

An Empty Sky

3 November 1818, Serques, Pas-de-Calais, France

Joanna Cowper cradled her swollen belly, listening to the sound of packing up all around her. Even Louise had abandoned her, returning to school to parcel up the slates and books. As for Thomas, he was away rounding up his men from the billets dispersed across the villages. Now that he was a troop serjeant-major. Joanna sighed. Sometimes she wondered how it came to be that she was married, pregnant and about to be shipped back home to England, in less than three years. Aunt Rowley and her father had already left for who knows where. All their letters were now being held at Calais. She didn't even know when she might see them again. She felt very alone. If only her mother were still alive. If only mothers didn't die before their children were safely launched into the world. She sniffed, wiped away a rogue tear and told herself not to be so silly. Of course she and the baby would be fine. She was not the kind of person who dwelt on possible tragedies. That was what Thomas said he admired. Naturally optimistic. Not like Thomas. But she was beginning to understand how Thomas must feel. Recently, she'd found herself prone to tears, in the certain knowledge that the baby she would give life to would one day die; that death and life were but two sides of the coin. She stood up.

This really wouldn't do. If only this baby would hurry up and be born. She was sure it would be better to face the voyage with a new baby than risk giving birth on the boat. Or, even worse, by the wayside.

The wind was getting up. Time to take a walk before it became a gale. She pulled her bonnet tight and stepped out into this great endlessness of fields and yet more fields, with only the occasional tree to indicate the road. She would walk down to the river and then back to the village. But it was no good. The more she walked and was buffeted about by the wind, the more she feared being blown away as if a mere speck in this vast emptiness. Even the farmhouses seemed battened down like fortresses. She told herself not to be silly, but still turned round and headed briskly back to the village, hoping that a more vigorous pace would encourage her labour. But then she saw the dark spire of the sturdy village church appear above the cluster of low cottages.

She bobbed in, nodding, as respectfully as she could manage, to a statue of the Virgin Mary, and knelt down to pray, 'Please, please, let this child be born before the tenth of November.' It was only as she tried to get up that she noticed the contractions.

37

Distress And Discontent

9 November 1818, Calais, France

German's Cottages, Heaviley, Stockport, October 11ᵗʰ, 1818

*' … Our labour has been essential to the production of your
wealth and that we cannot, without remonstrance, at least,
suffer ourselves, like bees to be smothered in the hive which
our exertions have so essentially contributed to fill.'*

Dear Cowper,

*I have added the above from the Jenny Spinners' address to
the Master Jenny Spinners of Stockport in great sorrow as
our hot summer of much distress and discontent ended in
rain on Sandy Brow on September 1ˢᵗ. Some of our Stockport
weavers welcomed the five hundred or more striking mule
spinners from Manchester to Sandy Brow. These men, for
they are mostly men as the strength required to lift a full-
sized mule into place is beyond that of most women and
certainly children, had marched in peace from Manchester
with music playing and banners flying. Our task was to
escort them as quickly and safely as we could, over the river
bridge from Lancashire in case of attack by the Cheshire
Yeomanry. You will remember I wrote to you about the*

vicious assault on the Blanketeers at this very crossing of the Mersey only two years ago.

Having safely guided them across the bridge, we then led them up into the marketplace to march in defiance past the Court Leet and Dungeon, until we reached St Peter's Church at the foot of Sandy Brow itself, the open ridge in the very heart of the town. There must have been several thousand or more spinners, hatters, coalminers and we handloom weavers, gathered to hear the speakers urge us to stand firm against our masters. For these same masters have failed to honour their promise to reinstate our full piecework rates, sacrificed at the time of the post-war depression. They also urged us to stand firm in the face of the tyranny of Lord Liverpool's government, itself, whose resolute refusal to entertain Peel's Short Time Bill confirms that Parliament is no friend to the working man.

For many of us, The Manchester Observer has now become our champion instead, advertising and reporting on our meetings. For those of us scattered across the many manufacturing towns in this area, the open-air meeting serves as our very own debating chamber, something the magistrates abhor. We working men and women, though, consider it to be a far better way of bringing matters to the attention of the authorities than rioting. Our aim, of course, is to keep our meetings legal and peaceable and to secure our cause by virtue of patient and peaceable petitioning.

Many of us have been serving soldiers and know how to organise and conduct ourselves in large groups. But our passions are no less roused. After all, what kind of civilisation is it that condemns women and children to work themselves to the bone for over-long hours in hot and humid factories?

Nevertheless, over this difficult summer, there have been some examples of ill-temper from those men who have been tipped out of their jobs and replaced by others willing to accept less than their dues. There was much singing of songs, accompanied by a blind fiddler, and threats as well as stones and mud being freely hurled at one of the offending manufacturer's premises. The magistrates responded by reading the Riot Act and by trying to persuade the cavalry to intervene before they themselves beat a retreat.

Opinion is divided as to how much we steady reformers should link with men of a more fiery temperament, to achieve our aims. Dissension too, I am sad to say, has worsened now that the many strikes in this area are gradually coming to an end, some achieving their aims, many not. But, as we stood on Sandy Brow with the rain streaming down our faces, I was reminded of the night before Waterloo when we suffered such hardship, but then, through God's providence, we triumphed in spite of our many reverses. I have to hope that all will come right for our cause in the end, though with far less bloodshed.

We are all as well as can be expected, though, as we live side-by-side with increasing numbers of weaving sheds, I fear our cottage trade of handloom weaving is dying all around us.

We are much supported by the Reverend Joseph Harrison, who used to teach at Bagguley's school, and who has embraced the reformers' cause. Our three speakers at Sandy brow, Bagguley himself, Drummond and Johnson, are presently incarcerated in Chester gaol. I am not fully aware of what the charges are, but I imagine their imprisonment is on account of denouncing the tyrannical government of Lord Liverpool. There are of course, many spies amongst *our number, some of whom are recognised and are chased away by the crowd though some will remain entirely unknown to us.*

Parson Harrison has most recently formed, with others, The Stockport Union for the Promotion of Human Happiness. It is similar in spirit to our Methodist societies with its classes, class leaders and penny subscriptions. This union has now launched a campaign to set up a national subscription fund to come to the aid of our three imprisoned speakers.

The Union has a number of other noble aims but is as yet in its infancy.

Boy and Bonnie are well and send their warmest greetings.

With peace in our hearts.

Samuel Ashby

~

Jack Fallowfield wasn't able to believe his luck. Lord Liverpool's government described as tyrannical. He began the laborious task of copying Ashby's letter before the others arrived. He looked forward to some unguarded comment that Cowper or Freer might make in response to Ashby's tale of woe. Besides, it wouldn't be long now before they would all be back and he would be able to deliver copies of Ashby's letters, perhaps even in person, direct to the Home Department.

38

Homeward Bound

9 November 1818, Calais, France

'Thank God, somewhere warm, at last.' Freer shifted his skinny frame a little nearer the fire and looked at Thomas, who'd just opened a letter.

Thomas muttered, 'It's from Ashby. Just caught up with us in time.'

Lodged at an inn, alongside the other non-commissioned officers and families, Thomas and Freer were sitting in the taproom in front of a large fire with two pints of small ale. They had just returned from duties at the encampments that encircled Calais harbour, the bell tents beginning to billow in the wind like the clouds, which promised heavy rain.

'So, what news?'

'I haven't had time to read it properly, though they all seem well enough. But as for news, unrest and more unrest.'

'That's all we bloody need to come home to. Are they sending troops in?'

'I don't know about troops. Ashby mentions the yeomanry.'

Freer sighed. 'We're never back to keeping the peace with any Tom, Dick and Harry who can afford a horse, are we?'

'Seems like it. Look, you read it.'

Thomas handed over the letter. 'Ashby's quite the reformer, nowadays.'

'Who wouldn't be?'

Freer ran his finger over the letter, exclaiming and grumbling.

' Good men put in prison just for voicing their views.'

Thomas drained his tankard. 'I'm beginning to think I'd rather stay put.'

Freer frowned. 'Then you won't be the only one.'

Thomas tucked Ashby's letter away to read with Joanna later and wondered where they might end up next. Scattered between the fields and woods, the quiet villages and small towns of northern France had reminded him of Burton Lazarus. Home. Not that he usually wanted to remember Burton.

He stood up and pulled his cape on. 'Time I went to bed.'

~

Examining his baby daughter's scrunched up-face, peeping out of the folds of blanket, Thomas remembered all his mother's babies, but Hannah in particular, and couldn't quite believe that she was truly his. 'Do you think we should shorten her name to Annie,' he asked Joanna. 'It doesn't always do for a child to have the same name as a parent. Look at my father and me.'

Joanna laughed. 'I would if I could, but from what you tell me, I don't expect I ever shall see your father and you together. Anyway, I certainly don't plan to be as ill-tempered with little Joanna here as he was with you.'

Thomas leant over and kissed her on the forehead. 'Is that a promise?'

Joanna tugged her shawl tighter over her shoulders and nodded. 'It is the most solemn promise I shall make to you, Thomas Cowper.'

'Then I shall also promise that I will be much better tempered than my father was with my mother.'

He reached over and kissed her on the mouth.

Joanna pretended to be indignant. 'I should truly hope so. From what you tell me they were not matched well.'

Thomas nodded. 'No, they weren't,' and walked towards the window to watch the waves pounding against the harbour wall. How could he ever tell Joanna quite how ill-matched his whole family had been, though Grace had written to him telling him his father had been much distressed over his mother's death. Had he completely misjudged his father?

'Then you must promise never to grow old and crotchety with me.' Joanna smiled. 'I couldn't bear that. I really couldn't bear that.'

Thomas turned around saying, 'Of course I promise. Besides we soldiers never survive into old age.'

Joanna stood up. 'Don't you dare say that to me. I have every intention of us spending our old age together in a little cottage in the middle of a beautiful village, with our own gardens and orchards and our grandchildren playing at our feet.'

He glanced back at his daughter and made another promise. To himself. To love and protect her till the end of his days.

It was only then he remembered Ashby's letter.

39

The Queen's Funeral

2 December 1818, Windsor, England

The good Queen was dead. And their regiment was to provide the escort for her funeral. 'A great honour,' Haywood had announced. And so the horses of the 36th clattered, like death itself, down every High Street between Kew and Windsor, flanking the torch-lit procession as the eight horses pulling the dark coach drew closer and closer to the Queen's final resting place.

Thomas shivered. He'd had enough of dying for one lifetime. He looked around him; the streets were lined with people, who'd come to watch but who'd probably never even thought about the old Queen when she'd been alive.

And still they rode on…

He remembered the summer in 1808 when they'd last acted as an escort. A lifetime ago, Thomas sighed. It was before the King's illness had set in. But even then Thomas had been worried about the King. Or more precisely he was worried about the King's eyes. Of course, they were the eyes of an old man, almost opaque, like his grandmother's had been; and whilst his body was somewhat stout, his hands a little swollen with the rheumatics, his general demeanour was that of the ruler. But then Thomas noticed the King's eyes; the way they danced and scanned the horizon, without apparent comprehension, the way they stared into the middle distance, as though defending themselves from invisible enemies. They could have been his mother's eyes. He remembered seeing almost the self-same look on her face when she'd accused him of murdering Michael ... filled with guilt, grief and madness.

And still they rode on...

He felt sure it was madness that had begun to afflict the King. Not that anyone would have said, least of all the Queen, though Thomas was sure from her bewildered face, that she feared as much. He wondered how she'd managed to live with a spouse who had lost his mind. Better than his father had done, he imagined. But then Haywood had said she'd often lived at the Dutch house at Kew whilst the King lived in Windsor, where the Queen was to be buried. The end of a life, the end of a marriage ... the end of an era.

And still they rode on...

Thomas doubted, though, that the King would be at her funeral. He probably didn't realise she was dead. Haywood had said they'd covered the Windsor courtyards with straw so he wouldn't even hear the horses. So he couldn't even be angry at his loss. Not like Thomas's father, who could and did blame Thomas as well as the rest of the village for his wife's early death; her funeral procession trailing behind a cart, round Burton Lazarus in broad daylight, with none of this burying at night business ... as if the Queen were a suicide, fit only to be buried with a stake through her heart at the village crossroads.

And still they rode on...

Thomas wondered if there was anyone at Court who'd loved the old Queen enough to blame one of her children for her death. Still, he wouldn't wish that on anyone, never mind his own daughter. Scarcely a month old, she was already so much part of his life. He thought of his mother again and wondered what she would have made of Annie, born and baptised in France, the very air drenched in the Catholic faith. Doubtless his mother would have thought it a bad omen, as Catholics, in her opinion, were kissing cousins of the Devil himself. Thomas almost laughed at the thought of Dermot Murphy being on such familiar terms with Beelzebub. Then he remembered where he was. For right now, he and his men were the only mourners the Queen had on her last journey.

And still they rode on…

It was just after seven when they finally entered the Home Park where the Princes joined them from Frogmore House. Thomas glimpsed the portly profile of the Prince of Wales, and wondered if he'd treated his mother any better than Thomas had treated his own.

He wiped his hand across his eyes and looked back along the lines of men but saw only ghosts.

40

To London

13 December 1818, London

No sooner had Thomas, Joanna and Annie settled in their room at Hounslow Barracks than Thomas's and Freer's troops were ordered to central London.

It was Haywood who brought the news.

'Merely as a precaution. On account of loose talk on the streets. Not that there is any space in the London barracks, especially for married men. So Mrs Freer and Mrs Cowper will have to stay behind for the time being. My own wife too, until such time as we have all secured ourselves proper accommodation. Captain Webster is, of course, untroubled by such personal considerations. Therefore he has kindly agreed to ride to Pimlico tomorrow to see what can be arranged for the men and horses, and we shall join him as soon as he sends word.'

Freer didn't seem surprised at the news. But then again, Thomas thought, if anyone was going to have his ear to the ground about unrest, it would be him.

'So are we to be scattered across the entire city or concentrated in one or two areas, sir?' asked Freer.

'Hard to know yet. They say discontent has a habit of showing itself in the most unexpected places. There was an attempt on the Tower a couple of years ago. Some misguided wretch thinking he was Wat Tyler, no doubt.' Haywood sniffed. 'And we all know how that ended.'

Thomas glanced at Freer, who briefly turned away from Haywood, drawing his forefinger across his throat.

Haywood was now thinking aloud. 'The way things are, we may have to find our own lodgings and stay for, at least, the next year, so best to get settled as soon as we can, eh? Mind you, it's a damned expensive place to live for us married men.'

~

'The centre of London?' Joanna hugged Annie to her. 'They say the air there is very stale.'

Thomas stroked Annie's head. He'd thought the London miasmas quite bad enough three years ago. 'Well, if we are to find our own lodgings, we must find the best neighbourhood we can.'

Thomas had never enjoyed being in London but, as the old King had favoured the Dutch house at Kew, or Windsor, on the few occasions they'd escorted him into London, they had quickly returned to the countryside at Hampton Court or Hounslow. It had been bad enough billeted in Pimlico during their lancer training. But this was different. They were to live in the place.

Webster sent word all too quickly. The two troops, each ninety men strong were to be dispersed over several barracks, but with horses stabled as close to the men as possible. Webster's and Freer's troops and horses were to be billeted in the old Savoy Palace area and in Somerset House's coach houses, and Haywood's and Thomas's men and their mounts at the King's Mews near Charing Cross. But Freer and Thomas, as well as the officers, would have to stay in lodgings, which the barracks masters would arrange for them.

~

After they'd left the heath, it was a dreary enough ride, but once they'd passed through the Kensington turnpike, the very buildings seemed to close in on them with not even a glimpse of the Thames to open up the sky. Freer, however, seemed to become more and more animated by London's noise and stink, exclaiming under his breath. After the briefest of stays in Pimlico barracks to collect further orders, they resumed their ride into the centre, up Whitehall and past Horse Guards.

Freer's men were now due to leave for Somerset House by St Mary le Strand, but before they turned away, Freer rode over to Thomas and gestured towards the huge equestrian statue of Charles I facing down Whitehall. Freer whispered to Thomas, 'Maybe he's looking at the Banqueting Hall to see if he can recall exactly where it was he lost his head.'

Thomas stifled a smile and looked around to see if anyone else had heard. Freer's irreverence had got him into trouble on several occasions.

But, by the time they reached the statue of Charles, astride his horse and still with his head on, there was another kind of trouble brewing. Two men had been suspended in a pillory at its foot and the crowd were whooping with undisguised pleasure at the chance to hurl mud and enormous stones at them. They would be lucky to escape being killed or seriously injured. Thomas wondered aloud what the two men had done. Haywood, who liked to keep up with changes in the law, tutted, 'Who knows whom they have offended? But somebody important, I warrant, as only perjurers or blasphemers are sentenced to the pillory nowadays.'

Thomas wasn't sure the crowd was interested in perjury or blasphemy. More likely they had seen a chance for some sport or to vent their frustrations on the helpless men. The mood was certainly ugly enough.

Haywood, too, was beginning to be more concerned. 'Perhaps we had better wait a while longer and keep an eye on matters. We don't want another king to lose his head, do we?' Thomas nodded his agreement and, as they saw the back of Webster's troop, including Freer, ride up the Strand, he rather hoped matters would not get any further out of hand.

Thomas and Haywood edged closer to the railings protecting the great statue and Thomas felt Mam'selle shift under him. Her legs began to tremble. Unlike Fearless, she was as yet untested in battle or riot but he wondered if she too had sensed that the crowd's vengeful exuberance might turn at any time. He stared again at the statue. The horse was magnificent with his strong neck and crooked foreleg, black as a Leicester dray. Haywood too stopped to admire it.

'That horse is quite superb, don't you think, Cowper?' Haywood was in a talkative mood. 'Captain Webster tells me this statue replaced one of the Queen Eleanor Crosses that Edward 1 had put up wherever his wife's coffin rested on the journey back to London.'

Thomas smiled. 'I remember now, sir, being told of a Queen Eleanor dying in a village called Harby, close to Stathern where my grandmother lived.'

Haywood beamed back. 'And is there a cross there?'

Thomas shook his head. 'I don't think so.'

Thomas found himself unexpectedly regretting its loss. The replacement of a monument to love with one representing what? Guilt, defiance, regret? But the fact they still needed to protect a statue of the executed monarch with iron railings raised yet more questions.

Thomas squinted at the great white plinth carved with angels and shields and mottos in Latin. Haywood or Webster would have to translate for him; but no, he now saw that the language was French. Thomas could just about see some words he could make sense of. Something about thinking ill? Of what, Thomas wasn't sure. Perhaps he would have to ask Haywood after all.

By now Haywood had turned his horse away. 'Let's leave them to their punishment, Cowper,' he said and headed towards the King's Mews. As Thomas automatically ordered their troop to follow, Haywood's words preyed on his mind. 'We don't want another king to lose his head, do we?' Was Britain that close to a revolution? Someone must think so. Why else were they there?

The crossroads were dominated by the great coaching inn, The Golden Cross, but moving on they soon found themselves in an open space bordered by a double-fronted set of stable blocks. The King's Mews, though, turned out not to be quite as regal as their name. Though the entrance was grand enough, the blocks themselves were cramped, the barrack rooms containing more beds than usual to accommodate the extra soldiers being drafted into the capital. Thomas felt sorry for the men, but once the roll call had been checked, Thomas and Haywood handed over to their serjeants. Thomas, however, now on high alert, suggested that as they left, they might usefully reconnoitre outside for any weak points that could pose a risk.

'My thoughts exactly, Cowper.' Haywood replied as he gathered up his reins to leave, summoning his groom to follow them.

They doubled back sharply where a ramshackle collection of old barracks buildings and assorted low structures gave on to St Martin's Lane. But it soon became clear that, within sight of the grand church with its soaring portico, and a decent array of small shops and pie houses, there stood, cheek by jowl just behind the Strand, some of the most wretched slums in London.

'Don't like the look of them, Cowper,' Haywood pronounced. 'Most likely where that rabble stoning those fellows came from.'

'Though I did notice as well, sir, some ladies in carriages who seemed to have come to watch the spectacle.'

'Well, shame on them.' Haywood snorted and rummaged about his person for the sketch map they had been issued.

Haywood studied the now crumpled sheet of paper. 'Up the Strand first. Then past Somerset House, where Captain Webster's troops are. He and I have lodgings in Surrey Street opposite St Clement Danes, on the same side as a rather large establishment called The Crown and Anchor. You and Freer are on the opposite side just past St Mary le Strand, number 27, Wych Street. Look for the Angel Inn at the bottom of the street.'

'Thank you, sir. I have arranged to call on Troop Serjeant-Major Freer first so that we may both make our way there together.'

'Quite. Two heads are definitely better than one at finding your way around this damned labyrinth.'

As Thomas and Haywood made their way up the Strand, Thomas admired the prosperous-looking houses and shops, narrow and mostly built of wood, three or four stories high, some with projecting bays of timber with bow windows, some set back in stone. The shop windows were practically the full height of the ground floor, their hanging signs advertising everything a man or woman could hope to buy. And everywhere there were building works. Knocking things down, or digging them up. Thomas, assailed by the occasional smell of biscuits, sausages and pies mingling with the city's usual stink, was almost overwhelmed by the incessant racket of horses and carriages bumping and clattering rapidly over badly-laid granite setts. He was relieved at last to glimpse St Mary-le-Strand, or so he presumed, which Haywood had thought was more or less opposite Somerset House.

But before he could say anything to Haywood, they'd both stopped to stare at a huge building advertising a menagerie and all kinds of wonders, with its own footpath running straight through the middle of it: the Exeter Exchange. He wondered what it was about London that left him both intrigued and appalled in the same breath. Well, the stifling air often left him gasping, but then there were all these grand buildings and exhibitions of curiosities that couldn't be found elsewhere.

Haywood turned and pointed to a grand stone frontage with a more modest set of buildings to the side. 'I think this is where you stable your horse, Cowper.'

'Until tomorrow then, sir.'

~

Jack Fallowfield felt the spring in his step as he passed Horse Guards, a building standing as proud as a well turned-out squadron of men, the central tower presiding over its pairs of flanking buildings. Understated, well disciplined, unlike its near neighbour, the Treasury, grand and self-important. The Home Department looked like the poor relation, but that was where Jack was headed. He tapped his sabretache. Should get his proper reward for these … Not to mention another retaining fee for rooting out insubordination and sedition … As long as Cowper and Freer's mail was still being directed via Pimlico barracks. If not, he'd have to think of another way. Never mind, he thought. London's overrun with damn radicals trying to persuade soldiers to join their cause, and for sure, it wouldn't take much to turn Freer, and maybe even Cowper. And when I get to hear about it then they'll be mine for the taking.

41

Wych Street

13 December 1818, Wych Street, The Strand, London

'So how were the King's Mews?' Freer asked as Thomas wiped down Mam'selle.

'Crowded and better appointed for the horses than for the men.'

'Just like here then.' Freer clapped him on the back. 'I have the map. Let's go find our lodgings and hope for better things.'

Wych Street, too narrow for carriages to pass each other safely, was neither as grand as the Strand, nor as abject as the rookeries behind St Martin's Church. Its houses, with attic windows set high under pointed gables, as sharp as teeth, were mostly plastered, their upper storey window overhangs tilting slightly forward and sidewards as if in secret conversation with their neighbours. And below them, shops: some with low, some with high ceilings, with plain fronted windows, and between them narrow alleyways and courts disappearing off into the darkness.

Freer stopped. 'Remind you of anywhere?'

Thomas wasn't really concentrating. 'Should it do?'

'Where we first met?'

'Of course. Leicester.' Thomas smiled, recollecting the half-timbered streets that had so reminded him of Melton.

'But a bit more down-at-heel?'

'Well, we were never going to be billeted in one of the grand houses, were we?'

Freer looked at his map and instructions again. 'Look for the second-hand-clothes shop on the north side … Number 27…just past an opening to Clare Market.'

Thomas peered through the now drifting gloom. 'Can't see any numbers.'

'Try looking for the second-hand-clothes shop then.'

Thomas, spotting a shop window displaying every kind of clothing imaginable, shouted back. 'Got it.'

Number 27 turned out to be one of the larger houses, four stories high with narrow gables, but considerably wider than its neighbours. It had been plastered in stucco, a timber lath occasionally thrusting through the overhang, which supported a large angular window on its first floor. There were two windows with many small panes on the next and attic windows above them. If it hadn't been in need of re-plastering, it would have been the grandest house on the street.

They walked in to the faint musty smell of worn clothes.

A bell rang, but nobody came and there was no one to be seen, apart from a skinny-looking fellow, with a peg leg and fair hair that almost hid his eyes, bending over a large table at the far back. He appeared to be colouring a print, his pigments arrayed in small cakes of colour as if in regimental squares, shades neatly stacked against their closest fellows.

'We're looking for a Mrs Mary Booth.'

'Ma's out.'

'We've been told by our barracks master that you have rooms to rent.'

'That may be so, but Ma will have to look you over first.'

As Thomas saw how closely the fellow was examining

them, he began to wonder what extra level of scrutiny his mother could offer.

'Waterloo men then?'

Freer nodded, looking at the fellow's peg leg. 'And you?'

'Infantry. Shot to pieces by their damned artillery. Still we held the line. That was all Wellington wanted, wasn't it, for us to hold the bloody line?'

He returned to his print, loaded his brush with a brilliant pink, which he applied to the cheeks of a woman clambering into a large coach. He turned his gaze back to them.

'Pink enough for an over-excitable lady? What do you reckon?'

Thomas craned his neck but couldn't make any sense of the picture. There seemed to be a multitude of women and men scrambling over each other in a frenzy of excitement to get into and on top of a stationary coach; women with great feathers springing out of their bonnets, men waving their hats, a soldier with his sword and shako watching the spectacle, with smaller groups examining various boxes and a shirt as reverently as if it were the winding cloth of Christ himself.

'They can't get enough of this one. Third or fourth print run, I'd say. I could colour this in now with my eyes shut.'

'But what's it all about?'

'Ah, you weren't here then, when Napoleon's coach was exhibited in Piccadilly? 1816.'

'Napoleon's coach. I thought the Prussians grabbed that. How the hell did it get over here?'

'I dunno but it did,' Booth snorted. 'Everywhere you look people seem obsessed by the fellow.'

'That must be a bit galling for a Waterloo man.'

'Some people think he's a greater general than Wellington. Others simply worship him and are in mourning for his defeat.'

Freer nodded. 'There was a time once when I thought Napoleon was the true champion of liberty. Then, like so many, he became a tyrant, the very thing he had fought against.' Freer bent closer to look at the print. 'Though I reckon this artist is more interested in making fun of the visitors than anything else. So what happens to these when you finish them?'

'Oh, they'll go on show at some print shop or other on Old Bond Street or St James's, where those with money buy them, and, those who haven't, stare at them through the window and mock.'

Thomas was still staring at the print. 'But this is amazing. Such careful work.'

'Sadly, I fail to see what is amazing about colouring another man's print following a template. Let's face it. I'm a hack.' Booth sniffed. 'Still, it's a living. And I'm supposed to be especially grateful for the work, now I can do little else.'

Freer joined in. 'But you and the artist are making an important point.'

'Really?' Booth blew his nose. 'If only that were so.'

Freer smiled. 'You speak like a man who knows his own mind.'

'I wasn't a serjeant destined for serjeant-major without being able to tell a fool from a rogue.'

Booth suddenly held out his hand. 'Enoch Booth. Not a name to be ignored … one who strives to do good, but is too easily persuadable to do bad. My father doubtless gave me this name on account of my mother dying when I was born.'

Freer offered his hand. 'And mine is Will Freer. Orphan, parish boy apprentice.' Freer looked defiant, then chastened. 'But, at least, I have some memory of my mother and father.'

Booth turned back to his colouring, shaking his head. 'And then, with my father being a martyr to the cause, as well…'

'What cause?' Freer queried.

'Oh, you know, being in the right, that kind of cause.' And with Freer's enquiry dismissed, Booth swished his paint brush clean and began to colour in the soldier's uniform.

Thomas was getting hungry. ' Is there somewhere we can eat while we wait for your mother to come back? I mean…' Thomas realised too late his slip of the tongue.

'Stepmother,' Booth drawled.

'Of course. Stepmother.'

'So where do you want to go? The Crown and Anchor, where reformers, mostly gentlemen, meet, or The White Lion, where they are decidedly not gentlemen.'

Freer looked up. 'I've heard of The Crown and Anchor. Isn't that where Major Cartwright's Hampden Club delegates met a couple of years ago?'

Booth nodded. 'January 1817. When they were persuaded to campaign for universal rather than just household suffrage.'

'At least for men,' Freer added. 'Remember, Cowper, Ashby wrote to us about one of his pals who'd been a delegate?'

Thomas did remember for once.

'Yes, that's right.'

Booth shrugged his shoulders. 'We had a few of them staying.'

Freer stood up. 'So, decision made, then, Cowper?'

42

The Crown And Anchor

13 December 1818, The Strand and
Arundel Street, London

Booth had advised entering through the main entrance on Arundel Street, rather than down the long corridor off the Strand. They emerged into a spacious hall, where huge columns supported a gallery. A great lantern overhung a staircase of stone and iron, its banisters leaping dizzyingly upwards. Booth had recommended they inspect the great assembly hall as well as the enormous dining room.

As they eventually made their way into the far more humble rooms where passers-by like themselves might be served with ale, Thomas began to detect phrases he hadn't heard even Freer use for some time: talk of the rights of citizens and holding the Regent to account. A definite buzz of discontent. It had started as soon as the two men had entered. Soldiers were clearly not welcome here. Freer looked at Thomas, signalling silently with his head and eyes. It was time to leave as quickly as they could. Thomas casually cancelled their order with the maidservant.

Freer smiled at her, muttered an excuse and led the way up the corridor towards the Strand.

Freer smoothed down his jacket. 'Well, now we know we can't pass ourselves off as gentlemen.'

Thomas shook his head. 'It can't just be that, can it? After all, if Ashby's friend and others like him were happy enough to be there?'

'Probably weren't wearing soldiers' uniforms.'

'So what are we to do? Not wear them?'

Freer shook his head. 'And be thought spies?'

'Like Ashby says, people either hate you because you're a soldier or because they think you're a spy. So we take our pick.' Thomas grimaced. 'Anyway, I'm still hungry.'

'So am I,' Freer agreed, and stamped even more vigorously up the narrow passageway, Thomas following.

'Feels like the whole place is going to explode around us. Like that powder keg you keep talking about.'

They were almost at the exit to the Strand. The walls were covered with posters and advertisements. One particular playbill caught Thomas's eye as he passed it.

The Theatre Royal, Drury Lane, it blazoned, *introducing Miss Burbage in the part of Ophelia in our production of Hamlet with our esteemed Mr Wallace playing the title part.*

He turned back. 'I just need to check something.' He ran his finger over the text to see if he might be mistaken. No, it must be Grace. It must be. As he stood there wondering what to do, Freer came up beside him. Both men stared at the poster. Thomas blushed.

Freer leant a bit closer. 'Is that her?'

Thomas felt his face getting warmer.

'I think it must be.'

Freer paused for a moment. 'So it was true, what she told you. That she was joining a respectable company.'

Thomas nodded. 'I'd hoped that was so, but I was worried that some rogue might have deceived her.'

Freer turned round to leave. 'Well, you can put your mind at rest now.'

'I suppose so.'

'The Theatre Royal. A highly reputable company. Doesn't that alleviate your fears?'

Thomas pulled himself together and did his best to sound reassured.

'Of course, that is excellent news.'

Freer began walking back along the corridor. But when Thomas still lingered in front of the poster, he turned round.

'Cowper, come on now. You've a wife and child. Remember?'

Thomas turned away and followed Freer down the passageway.

'Just curious.'

Thomas paused and gestured towards the ragged street sellers at the roadside. 'Look at them all, desperate to make a sale before they fall into their cots. Just look at them.'

Freer threw a penny and picked up some apples. He handed one to Thomas. 'Instead of the pies,' he grunted.

Thomas wiped the apple on the sleeve and bit hard. Its sweet, sharp taste took him back to his father's scrubby patch of apple trees where he and Grace used to gather up the windfalls. He looked around him and wondered how anyone could call this place home.

'One of these days, people will take their revenge for the lives they have to live here.'

Thomas, taken aback to hear the anger in his own voice, saw the surprise on Freer's face to hear him speak out so strongly. But Freer didn't like what he saw either.

'Aye. You're damned right about that. It's not a place where I'd want to end my days.'

Thomas threw his apple core to the ground. 'Who would?'

43

'I would give you some violets'

15 December 1819, The Theatre Royal,
Drury Lane, London

Having committed to memory the exact address, time and
date of Miss Burbage's next performance as Ophelia in
'Hamlet, Prince of Denmark', Thomas knew himself to be
more than curious, but had persuaded himself that there
was little point in saying anything when it would likely
come to nothing. Indeed, he had not decided yet whether to
go. And, even if he did, he might not speak to her. Anything
might happen. After all, he should be angry with Grace, and
he was angry with her, and himself. He now accepted that
he might have wronged her by failing to declare himself.
But then, she had rejected him in favour of taking up the
acting life. Without a word of warning.

~

He hurried down Wych Street, turning into the more
substantial Drury Lane, which took him directly to the back
of the theatre. Making his way round to the front, he thought
the building not as grand as some of those he'd seen in Paris,
but it was grand enough.

Crowds of both gentle and not-so-gentle folk were
already clustered outside. Thomas fingered his precious

shilling. He would pay for the best seat he could afford and for the full performance. He most certainly didn't intend waiting until the second half, just to save money.

The auditorium was gigantic, the slenderest of pillars supporting tier upon tier of balconies with narrow balustrades. He could scarcely see them all from where he was sitting. He wondered how Grace ever came to imagine herself performing in such a vast space. In the pit below people milled and chatted while waiting for the play to begin.

But as soon as it did, the audience quietened. Thomas was transfixed. To his surprise, he found listening to Shakespeare no more difficult than listening to a vicar read the Bible, though he did not always understand everything that was said. But it mattered little, for his attention was focused on Ophelia. As far as he was concerned, the entire play centred upon Hamlet's rejection of Ophelia. Or Grace. She was the rejected lover. She went mad. She surrounded herself with beautiful flowers and still they could not heal her.

As he saw her move around the stage, incoherent and distraught, Thomas marvelled at her skills. She had to speak loudly enough for all to hear, yet Thomas was aware only of the tenderness, the simplicity of her manner. It was as though she was talking to him directly. She spoke about rosemary for remembrance, begging Hamlet to remember. She talked about pansies and daisies, and violets withering. He remembered the flowers he had sent her from Portugal. He remembered those words she had sent him to read. From Shakespeare she'd written: ' I know a bank where the wild thyme blows.' He remembered leaving her behind in Burton's churchyard. He remembered clambering down stream banks to pick his grandmother's healing herbs.

He watched her die on stage, the tears running down his cheeks. He was entranced again by her auburn hair, her pale complexion. And as Ophelia lay dying Thomas saw the madness of his mother, her eyes like his mother's staring into the distance. Questions filled his mind. Is that how you learn to act? Do you just copy what you have witnessed? Or must you have suffered it yourself? Might Ophelia's sadness be her sadness at their parting? How could he have been so cruel, as cruel as Hamlet himself?

Thomas thought his heart would break, as the crowd surged forward and carried him out of the theatre, back again into the thick fog.

44

The Scolding

15 December 1818, Wych Street, London

Freer guessed immediately where he'd been. 'What the hell did you think you were doing? The past is past, Thomas. You can't go back. Ever.'

Freer rarely addressed him as Thomas, and Thomas understood that Freer was both furious and concerned. But then, Freer never could understand how often the memories kept surfacing, dragging Thomas beneath the past's murky waters again and again.

The thing about Freer was … was that he never looked back. He believed in progress, mankind moving forward; life would eventually get better if we would all just battle on for long enough. Freer was a believer in the basic goodness of Man. A true warrior on behalf of all the backsliders. amongst whom Thomas numbered himself.

It wasn't as though he hadn't tried to shake off the chains of the past, as Freer described Thomas's propensity for backwards-looking gloom. It wasn't as though he wanted to be miserable. Just as an army needed to identify its fall-back position should it need to retreat, so being worried, for good and for bad, was his fall-back position. It made him a useful fellow to have about if your men needed to watch their backs. Less useful if your commanders wanted your men to risk their very lives regardless of the odds.

Thomas took Freer's scolding much as he usually did. As a sign of friendship. But not always to be taken notice of.

45

The Women To Follow

17 December 1818, London

Joanna was tired. It had been a hard journey from Hounslow, stopping at every tollgate, with the lumbering baggage wagons taking nearly ten hours to cover the fourteen or so miles. They'd stopped, at last, at Pimlico barracks, Thomas's and Will Freer's home depot, to see to the children and send a message ahead. They were then directed to another, smaller wagon, which waddled along even more slowly before turning, as the driver informed them, into the Strand, now glittering with a multitude of lights in the darkness. Their driver at last deposited them and their baggage outside a crooked kind of house with a large shop window full of clothes.

They were greeted by an elegant woman about fifty years old, balancing a small child about Billy's age on her hip, followed by a much shorter dark-haired woman. Lucy, as the tall woman called her, then proceeded to carry their bags up some cramped stairs, that wound their way upwards from the middle of the shop.

The tall woman held out her hand. 'Mrs Mary Booth. And this young man, who really ought to be asleep by now, is Lucy's Sam. We received your message, but scarcely ten minutes ago, so I'm afraid your husbands are not at home.'

This news troubled Joanna. Where were they? Surely their evening duties would have been over with by now?

'But you're expecting them back soon?'

'Troop Serjeant-Major Freer has just gone to fetch Troop Sergeant-Major Cowper. I don't expect they'll be very long now.'

Joanna couldn't imagine where Thomas could be if Will had to go and fetch him.

Lucy's Sam wriggled himself down on to the floor and inspected young Billy, who'd done likewise. Both ran off to play peek-a-boo amongst the clothes. Louise made to chase after Billy.

'Leave him be, if you want. As long as he has clean hands, he won't hurt anything.' Mrs Booth now gestured towards a partly closed-off space beyond the dresses. 'My stepson, Enoch, lives … and works at the back of the shop. To the right is the yard door. To the privy. As for our water, on account of all the laundry we have to do, we draw ours mostly from the rainwater butts at the back.'

She turned towards the middle staircase and led the way up.

They soon passed a substantial panelled room on the first floor, its door wide open. 'My room,' said Mrs Booth. 'But it's also where we sew under the light of the big window. In between everything else there is to do, I'm teaching Sarah and Lucy my trade. I used to be a seamstress and then a mantua maker. Although I will only buy my clothes in the very best condition, I find they usually require some repairs before they can be washed and made ready to sell.'

Their rooms were on the next floor, still smelling a little sour from newly white-washed walls. Louise, Will and Billy were to be at the back, and she, Thomas and Annie at the front.

But Joanna was still preoccupied. Where were the men?. 'Have you no idea where our husbands might be, Mrs Booth?'

Mary Booth turned back from the stair and shook her head. 'I can't be sure, but I suspect that Troop Serjeant-Major Cowper had a fancy to go to the theatre. I believe I saw him checking a playbill this morning. That's what I advised Troop Serjeant-Major Freer.'

Louise threw up her hands. 'To the theatre. Oh, for God's sake, not Grace. He's not gone looking for Grace, has he?'

Joanna sat down with a bump, still clutching the sleeping Annie.

'Grace. Who's Grace?'

Louise paced about the room. 'Hasn't Thomas ever told you?'

'Told me what?'

'About his childhood sweetheart, who ran off to be an actress. '

'Oh, her. He did say something about a girl in the village, when they were practically children, but after some years of him being away, it came to nothing. He made light of it.'

'He did, did he?'

'What do you mean?'

'From all accounts, he didn't take it that lightly.'

'You mean he was still … smitten?'

'I don't know about that, but he seemed very upset by the whole business. Then again, as you know, he's a man who gets…distracted over such matters. Will told me he grieved for his mother and his brother Michael for years. Still does, for all we know. Will reckons he's got better at keeping things like that to himself nowadays.'

'So you think Will might have gone to look for Thomas at the theatre?'

'I suppose he might have.'

'Perhaps I should go after him?'

'And you know the way?'

'No, but I have a tongue in my head.'

'I think it's better you let Will catch up with him.'

'Supposing he doesn't?'

'Then he'll come home and tell us, won't he?'

'And Thomas?'

'Thomas will come home before the night is out, for sure. Don't you worry.'

'But even if Will does find him? Will either of them tell me where's he been?'

'I promise you, Joanna, that my husband will definitely tell me everything. And then I will most certainly tell you.'

Annie woke up and began to cry. Joanna clutched Annie to her and stood up, rocking her instinctively, swinging from one foot to another.

'I must see to Annie now. Thank you. Good night, Louise.'

Joanna tucked her head down to enter through the low door to her room, which seemed to be buttressed with sturdy timber beams at every turn, and sat on her bed, nursing Annie, staring into the darkness.

46

Ice

Thomas went straight after evening duties and loitered outside. The least he could do would be to pay her his compliments. But, as he bided his time, he noticed others also waiting, one of whom seemed familiar. Thomas peered harder, but still couldn't make out the man's features.

Suddenly, there she was, framed in the doorway, her bonnet tied firmly under her chin, her flowing cloak concealing any finery she might be wearing. He hesitated, still couldn't bring himself to step into the light. And then, as she moved forward, she was smiling, smiling and walking towards the outstretched arm of Squire Rearsby's younger son, Master Andrew. Older, and with an empty sleeve with a captain's insignia dangling from his coat, but unmistakably his father's son.

Of course. Her letters were full of chatter about him. How Master Andrew had been dreadfully injured at Corunna; how he'd recuperated for months at home; how he'd put on amateur theatricals, cast Grace and the other servants to act alongside his friends; how his actor-manager friend had persuaded her to join his company in London. And as the Captain greeted her, he bent low and kissed her on the lips. Thomas could hardly bear to look. Both were smiling. He shrank back into the shadows. He remembered when he and Grace used to play under the table in Jake Wiseman's kitchen, learning their letters; when he'd gathered up orange blossoms and sent them from Portugal; the sharp acidity of apples, the trees creaking as he climbed up and shook the fruit down for Grace to catch. But did she remember? Did she ever think of him?

Probably not. After all, she, like him, had left the cow byres of Burton far behind. He sighed. And she seemed happy. He wiped away a tear but felt more come, and brushed them away with his sleeve, its roughness scouring his cheekbones. He sniffed, blew his nose, spat out a gobbet of phlegm into the muddy street and tried to compose himself. He looked up. She was gone.

Thomas walked back to the playbills, looked at the other dates when Miss Burbage was playing Ophelia and entrusted them to memory, but doubted he would be coming back. Huddled into his cape, he walked back down Drury Lane. But as he got closer to Wych Street, he felt an overwhelming urge to go to the river, to stand at the top of the steps down Essex Street and watch the watermen go by.

~

Will Freer hadn't been particularly concerned at first when there was no sign of Thomas that evening. He and Cowper would often be held up talking with their serjeants or inspecting a horse they were worried about. But now Thomas was really late. Will began to fret. It was possible that he'd set upon by footpads but unlikely; they usually kept clear of soldiers who were clearly sober. There were easier ways to make their money. Some major problem with the men? Again, possible, but unlikely. There were usually clear signs when discipline was slipping and he and Cowper always talked over matters like that together. Haywood stopping him for a prolonged gossip? Not so likely now Haywood was married and his wife organised his life for him. No, another, more persistent thought was beginning to nag away at him. Grace. In spite of everything, he must have gone back to the bloody theatre again. Will despaired of him. And then, when Louise and Joanna's much-delayed note came, saying they were on their way, he knew he had to do something, though he wasn't sure what. But, at least, try to and get Thomas back in time, to greet his wife. He mumbled some excuse to Mrs Booth, after she'd confirmed that Thomas had been looking at a playbill, and rushed out of the door.

He was just in time to see Thomas moving away, much further down Wych Street, and too far away to shout. Thomas was almost running. Where? Towards the river? Freer cursed his bloody leg; the pain was slowing him to a hobble. He had to be content with keeping Thomas in sight, however distant. Yes, he was heading towards Essex Street. The river. Freer stopped for a moment, gasping, and remembered the time he'd caught him staring into the sea at Blatchington, when he thought might lose him to the waves. He started to run. Never mind the pain. Run.

~

The river was high, flowing so fast Thomas wondered how anyone could ply a boat across it. Already he could see ice beginning to form at the edges of the fast-flowing currents. Thomas watched, fascinated as he counted the small islands of ice bumping into each other like so many inconsiderate wherrymen. He saw his breath dance away from him, the warmth of his life force disappear into nothingness.

And, in that moment, even the smell of the Thames seemed benign, as though the river was rinsing away all earthly imperfections down into a great sea. He remembered the marshes at Romford, how he and Freer had thought this wide stretch of water a marvel beyond anything they had ever seen. He remembered the sea coming in at East Blatchington, and how the sea and sky had merged together like a single force of nature. And how it might feel to be part of that …

~

'Cowper. What the hell do you think you're doing? Just get away from those steps, will you? Joanna and Annie will be here any minute. They'll be looking forward to seeing you. Come on, it's too bloody cold to be out.'

Thomas turned to see Freer holding out his hand towards him. He instinctively held out his own.

47

The Row

Thomas crept up the stairs, but, in his fevered state, each wooden step seemed to creak louder than a gunshot. He opened the door as quietly as he could, praying that Joanna and Annie would, by now, be fast asleep in their bed. It was not to be. Joanna was sitting bolt upright, her eyes glimmering in the candle light.

Thomas told himself not to lie. He was a terrible liar, anyway, and Joanna deserved better.

'You were out.'

'I didn't know you were coming.' Which was true.

'We sent a message ahead.'

'I didn't get it.' Also true.

'So you were out already?'

'I must have been.'

'So you've been making the most of your freedom, while Louise and I were left behind in Hounslow.'

'I just went to the theatre.'

'I know.'

How did she know? Who told her?

Joanna now looked as though she might burst into tears.

'But it isn't a question of only just, is it?'

'How do you mean?'

'I mean, you weren't just going to the theatre. You were going to meet your childhood sweetheart.'

Thomas started to redden. He was glad of the darkness. 'But I didn't. I didn't meet her.'

Joanna pounced. 'But not for want of trying.'

'I did tell you about Grace,' he muttered. He'd felt compelled, as any man his age might, to explain his bachelor state to his new bride. 'How she and I, once … we didn't exactly have an understanding, but then, after the War, everything changed anyway, and she came to London to become an actress.'

'But you couldn't resist going to see her at the theatre. In the flesh.'

Thomas reddened more. It was as though she had been there and seen his desire, desire that only began to weaken after he'd seen Grace greet another man with a kiss.

It must have been Louise who told her, Thomas decided. Louise must have guessed after Freer had run off to find him.

'It was curiosity, more than anything else,' he stammered. 'We'd been friends since we were children.'

'So?'

'We wrote letters to each other. All through the war.'

'So were you or were you not … betrothed?'

Joanna clearly knew what betrothed, in its fullest sense, might mean.

Answer her honestly. 'I've never lain with her, if that's what you mean.'

'But now you wish you had?'

Thomas took a deep breath. 'Of course not.'

'I don't believe you. Why else would you go to see … an actress?'

Thomas was sweating now. He'd asked himself that, all the way to the river after he'd seen Grace with the Captain.

His family would never have countenanced his marriage to a village girl. She had to be his mistress. And yes, Thomas did regret she'd never been his.

'But, nowadays, being an actress doesn't have to mean …'

'I think you'll find it usually does.'

'After I was obliged to leave home, and I joined the army, she was the only friend I had left.'

'Did your family not care about you?'

'I've told you. My mother was ill, and my father and I didn't get on. He blamed me for … many things.'

'And were you to blame?'

No need to burden Joanna with the details of Michael's death, thought Thomas. But I'll have to explain more than I have so far.

'Not for everything. My mother was a very loving person, but much affected by grief for the loss of so many of her children … including my brother Michael. And she took his death badly, and I took her anger and grief even more badly, so we parted … on very bad terms. And then she died, less than a year later, so I never had chance to … apologise. We were never reconciled.'

'Oh Thomas, why didn't you ever tell me all of this before?'

'I didn't want you to think badly of me, or my family. Besides, as Freer keeps reminding me, it's over … all in the past. Near enough fifteen years ago.'

'But it's not over, is it? Not with Grace?'

'Of course it is, Joanna. I swear it is. But she has been, had been, part of my life for so long, I only wanted to ask how she was, how she liked being an actress … and tell her my news. That I was married now, with a young daughter. And that I think the world of both of them. And I do, Joanna, believe me.'

He opened his arms and moved towards her but Joanna burst into tears, turned away and retreated into their bed, where she made it quite clear he was not welcome.

Thomas laid down his cape on the floor, tucked his sabretache underneath to serve as a pillow and wrapped himself up as best he could. As if this was another night on campaign. He'd meant everything he'd said to Joanna, except … she was right about one thing. As hard as he tried to make it so, in his head it wasn't really all over between him and Grace.

48

Women Alone

18 December 1818, Wych Street, London

Mrs Booth had invited them to join her in the front room. 'Any time you like, in the day, and bring your own sewing, of course,' she said. 'I would hardly expect you to undertake any of mine. The children can all play under our noses whilst Sarah helps mind them.'

Joanna arrived first, placing Annie carefully in her crib a little distance away from the fire. Sarah was already pulling the chairs into a circle by the window and by the time she'd finished, Louise had found some threads that would match a dress of hers that needed taking in.

Sarah's own child was scarcely older than Annie and she placed her next to Annie. There was no sign, as yet, of Louise and Billy or Sam.

Joanna asked the child's name. 'Mary', said Sarah. 'After Mrs Booth.'

'That's kind of you,' Joanna smiled.

'Well, Mrs Booth has been more than kind to me.'

'She has?'

'Took us in after my last mistress threw me out on account of me expecting. She does that, you know.'

'Does she?'

'Oh yes. We're all what respectable people call fallen women round here, Mrs Booth included, as she keeps reminding us. Why does nobody ever talk about fallen men? That's what she says.'

Joanna remembered Thomas's face and how guilty he'd looked about Grace.

'I thought she was a widow.'

Sarah took out her sewing, now more than happy to relate Mary Booth's story. 'She is now but she didn't used to be. She wasn't always married. What I mean is, as soon as Mr Enoch was born, his mother went and died. So his father was desperate for a wet nurse but he'd heard such terrible tales, he didn't want to farm him out. So he took Mrs Booth in, with her own little one, so she could nurse Mr Enoch and all. Then he married her, a year or two later. But I'm not surprised. On account of her liking books and all.'

'But she is a widow now?'

'Definitely. Her poor husband died in Cold Bath Fields, years ago now. During the War. Prison fever, they said.'

' He died in prison?'

'On account of the books he used to sell. A lot of his friends were in prison so Mrs Booth couldn't ask any of them for help, so she had to find another way to support herself without ending up in prison like Mr Booth. That's when it all started.'

Sarah examined her sewing.

'What started?'

'When she realised there was a living to be made buying up cast-offs and making them fit to wear again. At the same time as helping us girls get on our feet, learn a trade, then pass ourselves off as respectable widow women if we want to.'

Joanna nodded. Of course. Clothes were too precious to be thrown away and were always passed on somehow or other.

'And when a girl moves on and she has room for another, she stands outside the poorhouse waiting to see who's been forced to come along,' explained Sarah. 'Then she eyes you up and if you're lucky you might get taken in.'

Joanna smiled at Sarah's child, who was now smiling at her. 'So how long have you been here?'

'Just before I had Mary. But she doesn't take in just anyone, you know. Mind, I reckon Lucy is going to stay forever, and take over the shop one day. Mrs Booth loves Lucy's Sam like her own. I think it's on account of her losing Mr Jacob only weeks after Lucy came.'

'Mr Jacob?'

'Mrs Booth's own boy. Two weeks older than Mr Enoch. Shot stone dead standing next to him at Waterloo. Lucy says Mrs Booth reckons Mr Enoch's not been the same since, what with that and losing his leg as well. I wouldn't know, of course. But he is a bit queer with his moods.'

Joanna threaded her needle and leant forward. 'But you like it here?'

'Oh yes. I mean, it's hard work, keeping on top of all the washing and mending and ironing for the shop, especially as Lucy sometimes goes out buying as well now. Me, I'm still learning.' Sarah bent her head over her sewing. 'We have to mend the clothes first or we could destroy them in the wash. That's why they smell none too fresh. When they arrive, I mean. Before we get our hands on them. You have to be strong as well. That's another thing Mrs Booth has to take into account when she's choosing her girls. You have to be strong, yes, and clever and all. Strong 'cos of filling and emptying the pans and clever 'cos you wouldn't credit the number of ways you can ruin nice clothes.'

Joanna nodded in agreement, but she wasn't thinking of Mrs Booth and her girls. She thought of Issy and Bridie and wondered: how would their lives turn out, and if her sewing classes would be able to help them? She thought of Boy and wondered: was he missing her? She thought of Thomas and wondered: did he still love her? Had he ever loved her?

49

The White Lion

18 December 1818, The White Lion, London

Thomas and Freer had been leafing through prints for ten minutes or so in Enoch Booth's workshop, pretending all was well between themselves and their wives, when Booth stood up and reached for his coat. 'Come on, let's be off to The White Lion.'

Thomas didn't need any encouragement. Even a tavern favoured by the decidedly 'not gentlemen reformers' was going to be better than staying in.

It wasn't far away … on the north side of the street, along the passageway to the New Inn. The passageway itself was scarcely wide enough for them to pass down, a windowless channel of puddles of piss, snaking between high brick-backed buildings. Freer cursed as he slipped on a turd. 'Shit.'

Booth laughed. 'Can't rely on your horses to see in the dark round here.' Booth turned into a slightly wider court, and headed towards a left-hand-corner door, under an upstairs veranda, facing on to the yard. The wood-panelled veranda, only held up, it seemed, by a single narrow pillar, overhung some crude wooden shuttering pulled across the lower floor windows, its broken guttering suspended above a barrel that had once been used to catch the rain. With its wooden shingle tile facing and roof, it reminded Thomas more of one of the fisherman's cottages found on the south coast than a city dwelling.

Booth pushed through the door into the tap-room. It was an austere space, bare of furniture but for a couple of trestle tables and benches, and a few small tables and stools wedged into its corners; yet it was brimming with a warm fug of smoke and noise. Booth gestured towards one of the small tables, well away from the fire, so as to avoid the regular bombardment of jumping sparks from its poor quality slack. They sat down and Booth began to speak, but the din drowned his words.

Freer made a sign to show he was having difficulty hearing what Booth was trying to tell him. Booth laughed and almost shouted. 'What do you expect when we're all in our own corners, putting the world to rights? Mind you, if you really want to change the world you'll have to book the back parlour. Anyway, you ought to be glad the landlady doesn't allow singing.'

The landlady, a solemn-looking woman in a high-waisted, low-cut dress made more modest by a large apron presided, whilst a young girl and even younger pot-boy served them dark bitter ale as rich as the earth itself. Thomas leant back against the wall and watched the world go by, whilst Booth interrogated Freer, whose limp he'd only just noticed as they walked to the tavern.

'Suffered a bit of damage yourself then?'

Freer nodded. 'Lucky it was a clean break. No shot to dirty the wound.'

Booth stared into his porter. 'Once you realise you've got lead in your leg, you're practically begging the surgeons to take it off. That, or prepare to meet your maker. Blood flowing everywhere, legs and arms piled high in a corner, you're past caring by the time they lay you out on the table, hoping for grog, getting the gag, telling yourself you're still alive … not like poor Jacob, blown to bloody pieces right beside you.' Booth drained his tankard. 'Still hurts though … like knives jabbing at a leg that's not there any more. Can you believe it? And all the nuns would say was You must pray to God. For his mercy. Tell you what I think. All their pictures of hearts stuck through with arrows, sacred or what, they reckoned pain and suffering would bring you closer to God. Well, they were bloody wrong.' Booth beckoned the serving girl over.

Freer gently tapped the table. 'So right, my friend.'

Booth straightened his back. 'Still, your leg's none too clever, is it? Slows you up?'

Freer nodded and sipped his beer. 'Need to build up my boot again. I could do it myself, if I had the tools and the leather.' He cast his eyes around at the many working men joshing with each other at the tables. 'You don't happen to know a decent shoemaker, do you?'

Booth grinned. 'I most certainly do. The very man.'

'Oi,' Booth shouted. 'Owens, I've someone here who wants to meet you.'

Booth summoned another ginger-haired fellow, maybe in his forties, over to their table. 'May I introduce Daniel Owens, master shoemaker … Troop Serjeant-Major Freer and Troop Serjeant-Major Cowper. Now, Owens, my friend, Freer, needs one of his boots building up. Got a nasty limp.'

Freer explained, 'I was an apprentice bootmaker once, but as I have no tools of my own now, I can't repair it myself. But if you'd allow me to use your tools and materials and pay you accordingly?'

Owens looked Freer up and down. 'I don't let neither man nor beast get near any of my tools, but you're welcome to come to my workshop and I'll provide you with a built-up boot, at,' he coughed, 'a very reasonable price suitable for a military man.' Thomas detected a slight edge in his manner, but Freer seemed happy enough and they soon decided on a time when he might go to Owens's workshop, and the bootmaker returned to his chair.

Thomas looked around the room. Men jabbering and debating, others scribbling down notes of the discussion, some reading papers out aloud; this tap-room was livelier than any he'd been in. Suddenly the door opened wide and in came a tall man with an angular nose and awkward hands, carrying a bundle of pamphlets.

Booth leaned forward. 'If you want to buy a copy of *Sherwin's Political Register*, now's your chance. Crowe there works with Richard Carlile, Fleet Street way. He and Sherwin publish the *Register*. It's full of reports, essays, even poems, everything you could possibly want to know about the present state of affairs. Crowe brings in copies every week. Lives with the sister, who runs a dame school over Covent Garden way.'

Thomas inspected Crowe further. He was balding, the tufts of hair barely managing to cling to the back of his head, with glasses and ink-stained fingers. Booth leaned closer to Freer. 'I take it from our earlier conversations, Troop Sergeant-Major, you would not be averse to reading about the true state of affairs in this country?'

Freer rummaged for money. 'How much is it?'

'Twopence. Griffin, over there, will take it. Crowe's never been good with money. A lot of people rely on Griffin to keep their books.'

He waved to a distant corner. 'There he is, see. Jeremiah Griffin, apothecary and book keeper.'

Thomas could just about make out a small man hunched over documents in which he was examining what were probably columns of figures. Freer made his way over to Crowe, who handed him a copy of the *Register* before waving him across to Griffin.

Griffin glanced up, put Freer's money into one of several canvas pouches, then quickly turned to another document to enter Freer's two pence into Crowe's accounts. He added the date with a surprisingly flamboyant flourish, looked up and smiled. Then he saw Freer was wearing a uniform and his mouth tightened. 'You do realise, don't you, that one day you'll have to make a choice? To stand with us or stand against us?'

Freer looked him in the eye. 'Or we'll all stand together.' He tucked his *Register* under his arm and turned back to Thomas and Booth.

'Time to go, eh, Cowper?'

50

Bear

18 December 1818, Haughton Street, London

Thomas and Freer turned left rather than right after leaving The White Lion.

'I thought we'd take a stroll. Keep out of the way of the likes of that Griffin,' Freer grumbled.

Thomas agreed, but rather regretted leaving his ale half drunk. Things had seemed to be going well enough, till that Griffin fellow took against Freer's uniform.

Still, neither of them was enthusiastic about going home straight away. Joanna was hardly speaking to Thomas, whilst Louise still thought it unfair of Freer to blame her for telling Joanna about Grace.

It was just as dark, and no more pleasant than the way they'd come. And it might not be safe. 'But at least this way,' Freer asserted, 'we can explore an alternative route, if we ever need to leave in a hurry.' Thomas thought it made no sense to risk the unknown just to avoid bloodthirsty reformers who might be skulking in the passage, but, for want of a better suggestion, trailed after him round the far courtyard looking for another exit.

At last they were able to find another opening, as narrow and stinking as the one they'd entered by, but which led out to a wider thoroughfare than Wych Street. But, as they turned back towards their lodgings, Freer spotted a stout figure, with his back to a handcart full of books and pamphlets, scrawling something on the wall.

'What the hell is he up to?'

Freer walked over to the man. 'Bit late at night for selling books?'

The fellow turned round to face Freer. He looked offended.

'I'm not selling.'

'But … your handcart?'

'Where I go, it goes, whether I'm selling or not.'

Thomas could see that, in spite of his ample belly, his face was pale and pinched, the mark of a man used to going hungry for days on end.

Freer moved closer to inspect the man's handiwork, chalked in a schoolmasterly clear and elegant script: *Spence's Plan and Full Bellies.*

Freer pointed to the writing. 'And this means what, exactly?'

The stout man recited his explanation without pausing for breath. Clearly learnt off by heart, rather like the creed, Thomas thought, as if to forestall any hecklers and disbelievers.

'Well, as we are all by nature born equal under the sun, it is therefore perfectly clear that nature intended us all to share her bounty equally and then use it to benefit everyone. So therefore all land constitutes the People's Farm, which all of us must hold in partnership with each other.'

'And is this what all these pamphlets explain?'

'The ins and outs of everything.'

'So, you're a follower of Tom Paine.'

The stout fellow looked uneasy. 'And what would two soldiers want to know that for?'

Freer threw up his hands. 'Forget our uniforms, friend. We too wish to see a more just society. So, are you a follower of Paine, or not?'

'You can't be too careful, the law being as it is. Let's say it's a matter of public record that I used to sell his works. Split into booklets. Made them more affordable. Avoided the tax and the risk of prosecution. Or so I thought. They still managed to clap me in gaol on his account … Tom Paine's, I mean. Still, it gave me the opportunity to study the many other injustices we labour under.'

'What kind of injustices?'

The stout man drew himself up to his full height and puffed out his chest, though he still looked uneasy, and Thomas now saw how ragged his once respectable fustian coat was around the sleeves. He clearly made little money in his calling. 'Let us say I am not a exactly an official member … on account of the membership fee… but I am, as it were, an associate of the Society of Spencean Philanthropists, which, to quote one of its founders, Thomas Evans, 'established itself for the purpose of discussing subjects calculated to enlighten the human understanding.'

'And where is this Society to be found?'

'Everywhere and nowhere. Makes it harder for the spies.'

Thomas felt maybe they should introduce themselves. 'And your name, sir?'

'Best to avoid names.'

'But what do your friends call you?'

'Bear. They call me Bear. Those I have left. But, as I say, sometimes it's better not to know a fellow's name.'

Freer took the hint. 'Then we are Will and Thomas. And we have been much pleased to make your acquaintance.'

Freer shook the man's chalky hand. Thomas hesitated. His first instinct had been to hand the old fellow a penny for a hot pie or two, but he now realised that this would offend him. He also held out his hand

'We shall look out for your friends too.'

'Outlived most of them. Even Tom Paine's been gone near enough ten years now, and Tom Spence close on five.'

'What an interesting fellow,' Freer enthused as they made their way back to Wych Street.

'But half-dead on his feet, I recko,.' Thomas muttered. He felt uneasy too. This old man could be dangerous to know.

51

The Garret

20 December 1818, Wych Street, London

Owens's workshop was up several flights of the steepest steps Will Freer had climbed in a long time. He finally reached the top floor, pulling himself up by the newel post, to find Owens sitting quietly sewing under the window.

Owens stood up, his leather apron trailing almost to the floor. 'You managed the stairs then?'

'Just about.'

'It keeps us pretty private.' Owens pointed to a small canary high above in an elaborate cage, and smiled. 'Me and Geordie, my only company. Now there's no trade for army boots, we've disbanded our combinations, when we could share the tasks between several men. I fear, too, with the end of apprenticeships, the gentle art of shoemaking will soon be no more.'

Freer remembered his own shoemaking days. 'The peace has come at a high price.'

Freer noted the orderly workshop, sign of an organised mind as his old master used to say. Owens's tools were laid out in a rack, his lasts lined up close to hand. In the far corner a neatly made bed. Freer felt reassured. Here was a man who took a pride in his profession.

Owens tidied his work away. 'Trade's been getting worse anyway and more so since the Northamptonshire manufacturers opened their warehouse in Smithfield. And they even say some young ladies are taking up fancy shoemaking in place of needlework, and that the workhouses are teaching wounded soldiers how to make boots. Still, you haven't come to hear about my woes. Let's have a look at you.'

Owens checked Freer's feet and boots with his sizing stick and then measured his leg. 'You say you have an existing lameness as well as your injury at Waterloo.' Owens scratched his chin and stood back to look again. 'I expect you have accommodated to your old lameness for many years and your body will be used to this. But with the new injury, let us hope we're in time to remedy it.'

Owens signalled him to sit down before walking over to his bench to select a substantial piece of leather. 'This shouldn't take too long.'

Freer, as he always did, felt vulnerable without his boot. He certainly wouldn't be able to go anywhere now without it being remedied.

Before long, there was the sound of footsteps and a knock against the top stair as the pot-boy from The White Lion swung himself into view.

'Same as usual, Mr Owens?'

Owens looked across to Freer, who nodded. 'And for my friend too. I will stand surety for the tankard.' Owens threw him some coins.

The boy offered him a ragged publication. 'Not very old.'

Owens threw some more coins and the boy dashed off.

Owens passed it to Freer. 'While you wait.'

'Then I must give you some money.'

'No, I shall sell it on for practically the same. Sherwin's Register, however old, always gets a good price.'

Freer began to browse and soon a familiar name caught his attention. *Stockport Union.* He quickly read on.

Declaration of the Object and Principles of The Union formed at Stockport in October 1818 for the Promotion of Human Happiness; with the Rules for conducting the same:

He ran his finger over a great number of regulations, which were carefully outlined over the next few pages, in pursuit of its declaration of belief, *'Do unto others as you would they should do unto you.'*

The document ended, *Approved by Major John Cartwright of London.*

NB All communications to be addressed to the General Committee, Union Rooms, London Place, Stockport.

Freer looked across at Owens. 'Endorsed by Major Cartwright himself, eh? My friend, Samuel Ashby in Stockport, has already informed us about the Stockport Union Society. He has high hopes for its success.'

Owens paused in his work. 'You are a friend of reform?'

Freer ran his fingers over his uniform. 'Forget this. Many of us, though not all, I admit, think that we who fought for our country should be trusted to vote for its government.'

Owens put down his tools. 'But you can't blame us for harbouring some suspicions of the uniform and those who wear it.'

'Perhaps it's more honest to advertise our profession openly rather than risk being considered spies.'

'We are plagued by spies. That is why our members choose to meet as we do, in different sections and in different taverns, scattered across the city. My good friend Evans arranged it like that, so that every man only knows his neighbour, but no further.'

'But what have you to fear?'

'Excepting a few hotheads, we are men of peace, but because we seek urgent changes to our lives we are considered dangerous … and thereby banned by law.'

'Like Paine?'

Owens nodded. 'But under Spence's plan …'

Freer interrupted. 'Spence's Plan? The Land is the People's Farm?'

Owens smiled. 'Then you've heard of us?'

'Not exactly. Cowper and me, we've just met a man who was chalking that on a wall. Called himself Bear.'

'Oh, Bear. Yes, he's from the old days. Ruined after being in prison. For selling the wrong kind of books. Like Enoch Booth's father. But he went and died.'

'In prison? Booth never said.'

'Na, he wouldn't. He says he hates being the son of a martyr to the cause.'

'Right.'

'He reckons we'll all end up the same way. Penniless or dead. He says, if it hadn't been for his stepmother they'd all have ended up in the poorhouse. But Mary Booth's a fighter if there ever was one.'

'And this Bear fellow isn't?'

'Yes and no. But he's an old man now.' Owens sighed. 'Those of us who remember him as a friend to Tom Spence do what we can. But he's proud. And he won't accept charity, as he puts it.'

'So, what is this Plan?'

'Well, both Thomas Paine and Thomas Spence agree that the land is the common property of mankind, but they differ in the ways this is addressed in practice.'

'And how is that?'

'Well, Paine thinks taxation is the best way to redistribute the wealth that has accrued to the land, in order to pay for the needs of those with no land. This money would then be distributed as pensions to the old and those incapable of work.'

'And Spence doesn't?'

'Exactly. Spence argues that his plan will ensure that people will receive the whole of their inheritance through the rents levied on the land, that is the People's Farm, hence the machinery of government will be simplified, with no need for taxes to be raised on basic necessities.'

'But what about the right to vote?'

'Spence maintains that universal suffrage will inevitably follow, as all governmental powers will derive from the parishes which hold their lands on behalf of the people. Therefore government must, of necessity, be democratic. But as Paine accepts that land can be privately owned, he can't specify what kind of government is likely to result from his arrangements.'

Owens paused, as he heard footsteps on the stairs, but slower this time. The pot-boy eventually stumbled in, carrying two tankards and warm pies tied in a kerchief.

Owens thanked him and gave him another coin. The boy scuttled away downstairs.

'And tell me, where does Paine make it clear that his plan will ensure the protection of the most important rights of all, those of infants and their mothers, so that the young may be raised in decency and good health?'

'I couldn't agree more, Owens. They are the most important of all.'

Freer thought of Louise and Billy, how they had been warned that Louise might well lose her life if she had another child … like her mother and grandmother before her. He and Louise had decided there would be no more children. Now they would have to work to bring about a better future, a better world, for themselves and Billy.

52

The Fever

Thomas came back late from The White Lion. Joanna was still scarcely speaking to him. He'd even offered to help with Annie. Being the eldest child, Thomas knew all about bawling infants. But Joanna spurned him. ' So you think I can't look after her?'

Since the row over Grace, Joanna's anger had turned in on itself to become self-doubt. But now she was low and dispirited, he still didn't know how to help. In another situation he might have asked Louise to talk to her, ask what he could do. But Louise seemed almost as cross with him as Joanna. He felt helpless, and none of his attempts to seek forgiveness had had any effect. He'd tried bringing her tokens of his love, coloured ribbons and lace, but she'd just shut them away in her sewing box without a word. Nothing seemed to make any difference, though Joanna had kept up her care of Annie and had made it quite clear that she didn't want Thomas taking this away from her.

But tonight was different. Joanna was lying on the bed, seemingly unaware of Annie sobbing in her crib. 'Joanna.' Thomas rushed over to her and shook her gently. She was barely sensible. She had a fever. He rushed across the landing and knocked on Louise's and Freer's door. 'Joanna's ill.'

Louise threw her shawl around her shoulders and followed him. She felt Joanna's brow. 'Get me some water and cloths,' she commanded. Thomas, hands shaking, poured water into the bowl from the ewer and handed it to her. She knelt down by the bed.

Louise gently scolded her. 'Why didn't you say you were ill, Joanna? You know I would have come.'

Meanwhile, Thomas picked up the still crying Annie and carried her through to the landing, where his campaign box stood. Balancing Annie precariously against his shoulder, he flung open the lid and rifled through the various papers and found the containers where he kept his medicinal herbs.

He'd scarcely any left. How could he have been so careless as not to have re-stocked when they were in France, close to the woods and streams? Where in this great sprawling city would he ever find comfrey, beech leaves, ramsons, and feverfew ? He felt the cold sweat of despair and walked back to Joanna's bed. His heart jumped as he saw her, naked as a corpse. But Louise was just sponging her down. Freer suddenly put his head round the door, and Louise quickly threw a sheet over Joanna to protect her modesty.

'I've had a word with Booth. If you need medicines try The White Lion and ask for Apothecary Griffin, you know, the grumpy fellow with a grudge against soldiers. Booth reckons he's always the last to go, so he should still be there.'

Thomas quickly handed Annie to over to Freer. 'I think she must be hungry. Sometimes we had to feed the little ones a sort of gruel when my mother was too ill.' Stopping only to find some money, he headed back to The White Lion, Louise calling after him, 'I'll ask Sarah to feed her.' Of course, how could he have forgotten about Sarah?

He just wished he wasn't wearing his uniform.

True to Booth's predictions, Apothecary Griffin was still there in his usual corner, filling his columns with figures.

'Please can you help?' Thomas gabbled. 'My wife has a high fever. We have a child, not four months old, but it doesn't appear to be on account of that. I usually keep some herbs by, but now I have none.'

Griffin didn't even look up. ' My wife went back to her mother's when my son was that age.'

Thomas feared the worst; that he even begrudged him having a wife and child at all, never mind his being a soldier.

'I have money.'

'No point wasting it, though, is there?'

Thomas could have shaken him. 'Please, can you help? Please,' Thomas begged.

Apothecary Griffin looked up slowly from his columns, and scrutinised every inch of Thomas's uniform before speaking again. 'Is anybody else ill in the household?'

Thomas shook his head. 'No, nobody.'

'And the child seems well?'

'I think so.' Thomas began to panic. Had he checked for fever, or had he just assumed her red-faced fury was on account of hunger?

'Then you have no notion of how she became ill?'

'None.' Thomas wished the man would finish asking all his questions. But at least he hadn't refused to help him. So far.

'Come with me to my shop and I will see what can be done.'

He gestured to Thomas to follow him back the narrow passage on to Wych Street. Heading towards Drury Lane, he turned down another dark alleyway that opened up into a dank courtyard. His shop, if it could be called that, was in a low-fronted, crooked building with a dark green door.

270

Inside, Thomas could just about make out the usual glass bottles and drawers of an apothecary's trade though this one he realised, scarcely made a living. But what choice did he have? There would be nowhere else at this time of night.

After what seemed a lifetime of waiting, Griffin lit a couple of lamps and took one of them with him so he could survey his stock more closely.

'A high fever you say?'

Thomas nodded impatiently. 'Yes, very high.'

'And you have somebody sponging her down right now?'

'Yes, yes, a good friend.'

'Is she able to drink?'

Another question he didn't know the answer to. 'I think so.'

'She must drink.'

'Of course. But what if she can't?' Thomas could hear the panic rising in his voice.

'If she can't, I agree that is a problem. If she can, I would recommend a tea made from yarrow and ginger, which should promote more sweating to drive the ill humours out. Eventually.'

'Do you have any feverfew or comfrey?' Thomas asked.

'Possibly.' Griffin ran his fingers down the list he kept on his counter. 'But I'm not sure I would recommend them.'

'And beech leaves? I've used them as a poultice before now to draw away inflammation.

'You didn't say she was suffering from inflammation.'

'I don't know what she's suffering from, but until I get back and can look closer, perhaps I should take everything that might do some good.'

'That will be expensive.'

271

'I don't mind. Please, anything that might help.'

Griffin fussed slowly over his bottles and scales, weighing out each item as slowly, Thomas felt, as a man could, before painstakingly inscribing something on each of the packets. No wonder the man had little trade. For God's sake hurry, thought Thomas but said nothing.

Thomas resisted the temptation to offer to help speed things up. He just hoped that he had enough money with him. Apothecary Griffin seemed the kind of man who would insist on being paid in full.

Griffin looked at him. 'How much do you have on your person?'

Thomas showed him.

'That'll do. Now I have written instructions for you, but you seem as if you would know how to differentiate between internal and external remedies.'

Thomas thanked him, grabbed all the packets and managed not to dash out of the shop before running full tilt down the alley.

He heard Griffin shout after him. 'You said you have a young baby. Is she feeding the child herself?'

Thomas turned round 'Yes.'

'Feel her breasts. If they are hard and inflamed, bathe them in warm water and empty them of milk. And she must keep drinking the tea.'

Thomas raced back to Wych Street and up the winding stairs to their rooms. Louise was still sponging Joanna down. Freer had taken Annie up to Sarah, who was now feeding her along with her own daughter.

Thomas repeated what Griffin had told him. Louise had already noticed Joanna's breasts were inflamed and they now began to follow the apothecary's instructions. But how to empty them of milk? Griffin must have meant they should be massaged. And since Joanna was too ill to feed Annie they would have to find another way.

'You'll need to ask Sarah again, if Joanna' ... Thomas caught the hesitation in Louise's voice, as though she was doubting Joanna would live ... can't take Annie on to the breast by tomorrow morning. But, for the moment, Sarah can feed Annie, and you must go and get warm water from the kitchen, while I'll carry on here.' Thomas crept down, trying not to wake Booth.

He grabbed two tankards. In one he placed feverfew leaves and a scattering of the flowers and in the other the yarrow and ginger. He stoked the fire, and waited for the kettle water to become hot enough to mash the herbs thoroughly. In another bowl he prepared the comfrey and beech leaves, soaking them to make a poultice to draw away any infection. And another one he filled with warm water to massage Joanna's breasts free of their milk.

When he came back for the second time, he found that Louise had managed to cool Joanna just a little more. He put the tea in a child's drinking cup, and he and Louise were able to lift her up and drip the tea down her throat. Then she began to swallow the liquid on her own account, gasping and opening her mouth for more. Thomas brushed her hair away from her face, leant over her and whispered, 'That's right, Joanna. Keep drinking. You must drink. Please. I love you. I love you more than anything.' And he placed in her hand her mother's little silver bird that had been a token of her love for him when he'd been so ill in Denain.

53

The Company Of Women

21 December 1818, The White Lion, London

Thomas woke up in a panic, the candle guttering in its holder, Louise dozing and Joanna tossing from side to side, Annie restless and grunting.

Annie so small and so helpless. He couldn't imagine what would happen to her if Joanna died. He couldn't imagine what would happen to him if Joanna died. He jumped up. Should have contacted her father. Why hadn't he sent to Woolwich straight away? Ah yes, because the Captain and Aunt Rowley were already on their way to Bristol, bound for Ireland. Should he send for them now? Maybe. Yes, he must. By the mail coach. A letter at once but first, first, see to Joanna. Louise had fallen asleep with the sponge still in her hand. Her hair falling out of her cap in tangles, she looked exhausted.

He walked over to Joanna, felt her forehead which was still burning, and began applying the poultices to her breasts, trying to release their milk. As he started to sponge her forehead, he brushed against Louise, who woke up with a start. Thomas signalled that she should continue to rest.

'Please God,' he found himself praying, 'Don't take her from me. Please.'

As he sponged her brow, Joanna murmured and opened her eyes though not seeming to recognise him.

'It's Thomas,' he whispered. She closed her eyes and turned her face away. He gently moved her head towards him, sponged her face and then the rest of her. So beautiful, so young … and so dear to him. He couldn't imagine losing her to the dark, rotting earth. He began to sob.

This was all his fault. He'd married her when she was scarcely a woman. Maybe she'd been too young to have Annie. Maybe her constitution was too like her mother's to bear the strain of childbirth.

If only he could speak to a God he could be sure about. He muttered remnants of prayers from all the church parades and services he'd ever attended, seeking forgiveness, hope, mercy, the love of God and Joanna's life, all muddled up into one long desperate plea. Save her.

By the time Louise woke up again, Thomas had written his letter to Joanna's father and was pacing the room, willing Joanna to survive.

Louise took just one look at him and said, 'You need to occupy yourself, Thomas. Go and look after your horse, find Will and tell him to advise Webster and Haywood that your wife is gravely ill and that you're needed at home. I don't think either of them would expect you take your men out on patrols today.'

'But how can I leave Joanna? Anything might happen.' He couldn't say die though it was what he meant and what Louise knew he meant. 'And what about Annie?'

Louise gave him a long hard look. He bowed his head, allowing her to take control. 'Take Annie to Sarah, then go to the stables and see to Mam'sell and do what you have to do, then come home.'

But Thomas still wasn't sure he should go out at all, except to the receiving house.

'I have to post this letter to the Rowlandsons first, before I do anything else.'

Louise nodded. 'Of course you must.' She pressed her hand to Joanna's forehead. 'Thomas, I think she's a little cooler. Come and feel. Don't you think the fever is lessening?' Thomas heard the note of hope in Louise's voice. He ran his fingers over Joanna's forehead. Maybe, maybe the fever was a little less. He wanted to believe. Let it be true.

He left for the receiving house and stables as reluctant as any man could be, but when he got there, Freer agreed immediately to cover his duties, though Thomas insisted on grooming Mam' sell himself. He would try and steady himself. But his worries about Joanna and the memories of losing Fearless that terrible night overwhelmed him. Grief welled up. He laid his face against Mam'sell's neck and let the tears run dry. Then he brushed every inch of London dirt out of his horse's coat, bade Freer farewell and forced himself to walk back home, though he wanted to run.

Louise was sitting holding a grizzling Annie. 'Good job you're back,' she said. 'Annie needs to go to Sarah.'

'But Joanna, how is Joanna?'

'Just about drinking your concoctions, when I force them down her, but she's still rambling and doesn't seem to know who any of us are.'

Thomas walked over to kiss her forehead. 'But she's a bit cooler, don't you think?'

'A bit,' Louise agreed, handing him Annie, 'but not quite enough for my liking.'

It was laundry week and Sarah would be in the cellar. Thomas, clutching Annie to him, stood on the bottom step and watched as Sarah and Lucy carted pans of water back and forth, filling them from the butts outside, then lugging them back into the steaming heat and on to the fire grid, before taking yet more pans outside to empty the dirty water into the soakaway.

Sarah's Mary was grumbling in her crib, whilst Sam and Billy, paddling in the puddles, were getting under everybody's feet. Thomas could see it was heavy, hot and remorseless work, needing both Lucy and Sarah, so, as he handed over Annie to Sarah, he offered to take her place alongside Lucy. Lucy frowned and looked very doubtful. 'As long as you do exactly as I tell you,' and she handed over Sarah's wooden paddle to beat the clothing.

Lucy told him that Mrs Booth had already supervised the sorting and soaking the day before, checking for holes and rips. So all he had to do now was follow Lucy's orders ... as she got hotter and more ill tempered by the minute. Nothing would be cooked that day and everywhere stank of piss, potash and whale oil. It was just as hard, if not harder, as mucking out half-a-dozen horses one after another, and there was nothing that could be done to make it any easier. But Thomas had never been more grateful for the company of women.

During the second night of Joanna's fever, as Thomas took over her care from Louise, he tried to apply some reason to her situation. First, his grandmother's herbal remedies had proved their power time and time again. After all hadn't Littleworth and Ashby administered them to him after his injuries and fever at Salamanca? They had helped Freer, and even Fallowfield, after Waterloo. He tried not to think of Sparrow. They hadn't been able to save him. No. Don't think of failure. Joanna is strong.

Yes. Second, Joanna was strong. She wasn't ready to die and he wasn't ready to lose her. He would fight so hard that she couldn't fail to get better.

Third, she was a good woman. A loving God wouldn't take her. A loving God mustn't take her, he found himself praying.

He stood by her bedside, the new poultices ready, the fresh water ready, and felt her forehead. Too hot. He shivered. How long could a woman go on with this high fever without it sapping all her strength? He set to once again, sponging her down over and over again, drying, cooling, applying the poultices, raising her head in his arms, making her drink his herbal teas, telling her he loved her. Annie was now with Sarah, Louise asleep in her own bed. It was a longer night than those before and after Waterloo and they had been unbearably long. But he kept telling himself that he had survived that battle and Joanna would survive this one too.

By morning Thomas was relieved that Joanna was no worse. When Louise took over, he went down to the cellar again to find Annie, to take her back to sleep beside her mother, her grunting and snuffling another reminder to Joanna that she had more than one reason to stay alive.

But once a happy, sleeping Annie had been handed back to him by Sarah, Lucy grinned. 'By her next feed you'll be on wringing-out duties.' Which he was.

~

And the feed after that, he was hanging out the wet washing to dry inside, away from the London filth. When hauling down and loading up the wooden drying racks that hung below the ceiling, Thomas was only trusted to hold the laths steady, whilst Lucy arranged the clothes. Thomas suddenly remembered helping young Hannah lay their family washing out to dry on the hedges in the sun. So many years ago now.

He marvelled at how strong the women were, how well they worked as a team, sweating and spluttering in the heat, bonded in a community. Unlike his mother, isolated in the village because of her weird ways, shunned in her grief and madness by all except Grace's mother. A kind and homely soul, she must have understood somehow that his mother was mad for a reason, not taken by the devil, as the rest of them said, turning their backs.

He remembered Hannah again, remembered he and she working together to help the little ones. He wondered how she was, if her life in the village perhaps had changed for the better? He hoped too that Hannah had escaped his mother's grief in spite of everything, in spite of Michael's death and what Michael had done. He too loved Hannah but as a sister.

By the morning of the second day, Thomas could hardly believe that another night had passed and Joanna was still with them.

He began to hope. The fever was definitely less. She was more awake. Even called out his name. She cried out for Annie but was still too weak to nurse her. But there was hope. But with hope came remorse. Thomas couldn't believe how he'd sought out Grace for the second time and then had been, at best, less than honest with Joanna. No wonder she'd been furious. No wonder she and Louise had thought him beneath contempt. How could he have done that? Of course Joanna would have felt betrayed. He knew what it felt like to be betrayed. Could she ever forgive him? He feared she might never forgive him for his betrayal, and for this illness, yet more suffering she didn't deserve, and that would be his punishment, which he did deserve. All his fault. But now how to convince her he loved her, not Grace; how to make it up to her?

And the third night Thomas sat by Joanna's bedside and held her hand. She was beginning to respond now. And so he talked to her about how he'd been privileged to be part of the company of women these last few days, that he understood that love and friendship were both important. That he'd been sustained by his love for her, the friendship of Louise and Freer, and the community of women who had helped them all get through. And when she had mended he'd talk more with her about his love for her and how he hoped she'd be able to forgive him for what had happened. He understood, of course he did, that she was right to be angry with him, but he hoped that the anger would leave her over time. He hoped she could love him again as she had when they'd declared their love in France. And ever since, until …

'Remember how the bluebells shimmered in the sun, and how I told you that you have the most beautiful blue eyes in the whole wide world, and that you are the loveliest person I know.'

He stroked her hair. 'I love you, Joanna. I've never been so terrified as when I thought I might lose you. I couldn't bear to lose you and Annie, and all that you are to me.'

All through that third night Thomas watched over both Joanna and Annie from his chair, sleeping fitfully, dreaming of his own mother, wishing she hadn't been cursed with seeing things that weren't there. The dreams, the absences, the visions. Then seeing Michael rise from his grave and scorn him for doing women's work. Thomas woke with a start, Michael's laughter ringing in his ears.

Annie was crying. She was pulling up her legs in pain and was only comfortable held high against Thomas's shoulder. After she had quietened, as Thomas put her down to lie her in her crib, she smiled, her mouth widening in a great toothless grin of recognition. Her tears forgotten, she seemed to demand that Thomas smile back, and when he did he was rewarded with yet another grin, her eyes firmly fixed on his. He swaddled her as tight as he could and tucked aside the wisps of hair and stroked her head till she yawned and, at last, shut her eyes. His daughter, his responsibility.

Thomas walked over to the window and looked down at the streets below at the women of the night, and at the men caring nothing for them, coupled in the alleyways and courts. He turned away.

He wondered how it was that anger and joy were doled out to us when we were born, but then what happened? He looked at Annie, now so peaceful and sleeping, and knew her hunger and pain would return and then, once again, she would become an inconsolable, raging creature. Freer believed that grown men and women might, one day, be able to extinguish anger and folly. Thomas wasn't so sure. He had seen the darkness.

Thomas paced around the floor for some time before he could finally settle himself. He flung himself back in the one decent chair in the room and looked across at the sleeping Joanna and Annie. He listened to their breathing. Both peaceful. He gazed out of the window and watched the moon slowly losing itself in clouds.

Could he ever make amends to Joanna for the hurt he had caused her? Would she ever forgive him?

54

Better Than A Ghost

24 December 1818, Wych Street, London

It was the first day that Joanna felt she might survive, no longer hanging on to life moment to moment, her strength fading, Louise's and Thomas's voices floating above her, whilst hearing her mother's voice quite clearly, 'Now, my little one, you have a child of your own. You must fight, fight as hard as you can.' She wanted her father. She wanted to see her father. And then there was Thomas. She didn't want to leave Thomas either. No, she didn't want to leave this world at all.

~

Her father and aunt Rowley came back from Bristol on the fifth day of her illness, or so Thomas informed her. By now she was sitting up, feeding Annie and could get out of bed with help to use a chamber pot. She was weak but on the mend. Still, on seeing the relief on the faces of her father and aunt, she burst into tears. They had come. Thomas had sent for them but, he explained as he came to tell her, 'I didn't dare say in case I couldn't reach them before they'd already left for Ireland.'

'You thought I was going to die too,' Joanna said.

Thomas held her close. 'I was never going to let that happen, Joanna. Never.'

She hugged him and asked him to pass her hairbrush. 'I must try and look my best,' she joked.

But she found she was too weak to pull the brush through her hair, so Thomas took it from her and brushed it, gently teasing out the knots.

'I've had sisters, remember. And a mother who couldn't look after them.'

Joanna tried to imagine it, Thomas helping his mother as a daughter might. No wonder he was good with Annie, and with her, too … if only he hadn't found Grace again. She put these thoughts to the back of her mind as her father and Aunt Rowley walked in. Her father was almost in tears as he hugged her. He had been given permission to stay as long as was necessary to ensure that Joanna was out of danger, and that was exactly what they intended to do, he told her.

Aunt Rowley too seemed to have lost some of her stiffness. Soon she was talking to Thomas as though he were a proper relative, one due some respect, though she was astonished to hear that he'd assisted in nursing Joanna. 'But surely that is woman's work,' she exclaimed.

Joanna smiled weakly. 'But he was the best nurse I had, Aunt Rowley, and he helped look after Annie as well.' Aunt Rowley said she wasn't sure that this was a husband's duty but, as if deciding to let the matter pass, turned round to look at Thomas.

'I must thank you, then, for the care you have shown to my dear Joanna.'

Thomas smiled and inclined his head, 'She is very dear to us both,' he replied.

Joanna was pleased to see this new warmth between her family and Thomas but could see that Aunt Rowley felt a little uncomfortable in these cramped rooms; decent, but not of the quality that she was used to. 'You look a little tired, Aunt Rowley. Perhaps you should return to your lodgings and I will promise to visit you there, if I am well enough, tomorrow or the next day. Thomas, like you, Father, has permission to be absent from his duties, and I'm sure he will escort me as far as the Strand.'

Joanna was beginning to feel mended, recovered from this strange dark time, when she had believed herself to be worthless, unable to find the strength to do anything other than look after Annie. She was weak in body, but somehow stronger in her mind than she had been for what seemed a long time. Now she could look forward once again. She felt like the old Joanna. Almost.

~

Joanna carefully made no mention of Grace. But as they lay in bed that night, Thomas knew he must. He stared into the half-light. 'I'm sorry for my foolishness in going to the theatre.'

'On two separate occasions, as I understand it.' He heard the edge in her voice.

Louise must have told her this, but he could see now that she'd been right to do so.

'Yes. Once to see the play, and once, in the hope I might speak to her, after the play.'

'So did you?'

'No. She was with … someone.'

'Another man?'

'The Squire's younger son from Burton, the one who first introduced her to acting.'

'I see. Is she a good actress then? Good at deceiving people?'

Trust Joanna to think of that. Thomas hadn't really considered this before.

He'd always thought of Grace as someone he could trust, her Ophelia more truthful in grief than he could ever have imagined possible. No, that was not deceit.

'Yes, I think she's a good actress, but I'm not sure that acting is just a matter of one person deceiving another … More like an agreement to deceive each other, perhaps? I don't know. But I don't think she ever intended to deceive me.'

'So, do you still love her?'

Only the memories, he wanted to shout out. Just my memories. Not the real flesh and blood of her.

'Not any more,' was what he did manage to say. 'I love you. I love you far, far better than a ghost.'

55

The Conquering Hero

February 1819, Wych Street, London

Mary Booth was about to go to bed by the time they got home. 'Wait a minute,' she said, 'I've got a letter for you.'

She passed it over. 'Your wives went to bed some time ago, so you'd be best reading it down here, and then you won't be disturbing them.' She glanced at the timepiece behind the shop counter. 'For sure, Enoch won't be back just yet.'

Thomas detected a disapproving note in her voice, but wasn't clear if it was directed at them, or Booth, or men in general. Thomas sat down by the dying embers of the fire, beckoned Freer to join him and proceeded to read Ashby's letter aloud.

German's Cottages, Heaviley, Stockport, January 31st, 1819

Dear Cowper,

I apologise for my delay before writing again, leaving you with our tale of despair at the collapse of all our hopes. But we are fortunate that Parson Harrison is still at liberty to lead our efforts to obtain justice. Whilst Harrison too was on the platform at Sandy Brow, fortunately his address most likely came too early in the proceedings for the spies to record. This undoubtedly saved him from incarceration, alongside the other three, who still languish in Chester. We have recently heard that the prisoners now wish to use some of the funds raised for their defence to have their trial heard in London. They rightly fear there would be considerable prejudice against them in these parts. Indeed, we have already seen how much ill-will there is towards working men, expressed in so many ways by the principal manufacturers.

After suffering such a blow to their hopes this summer, many workers are now turning their thoughts to obtaining proper representation in Parliament, rather than let the borough mongers and manufacturers have it all their own way.

So those of us who have always favoured political action have been much encouraged by Harrison's Stockport Union, whose members seek to take an active role in such events. We are fortunate, too, in that many prominent reformers give lectures at Harrison's Windmill Rooms on Sunday nights, which both inspire us and raise much-needed funds. We have also entertained speakers such as Dr James Watson, a supporter of the late Thomas Spence from London, who was lately here, collecting money for his petition and national convention schemes.

Thomas turned to Freer. 'Spence's Plan and Full Bellies?'

Freer grinned. 'And his People's Farm. Go on, carry on reading.'

We have also received a most gracious letter from Mr William Cobbett, to our nation's shame still in exile in America. He thanked us most sincerely for the public praise of his works through our meetings, though cautioning us to avoid in particular all attacks upon the King and his family.

Earlier this month, Harrison was able to re-open prisoner Bagguley's day and evening school, where Bonnie has now resumed her attendance and is becoming much interested in political affairs.

But the event which has most lifted our spirits was a visit by the well-known reformer, Mr Henry Hunt. He arrived here on January 17th and, after taking tea at a friend's house, visited the Union Rooms. Entering to the stirring song,' See, the Conquering Hero Comes', Mr Hunt then spent a good part of the evening discussing with us how best to secure a fair trial for our three speakers imprisoned in Chester. Supper and a bed were then provided at The Red Lion prior to the public meeting in Manchester at St Peter's Fields arranged for the following day.

The meeting was a well-attended affair where, amongst other business, a draft remonstrance to the Prince Regent was drawn up. Spirits were high and we were all much encouraged in our efforts, in spite of the collapse of the stage part way through the proceedings. Though thankfully, nobody was much hurt.

There are, of course, many differences of opinion regarding the details of how we might proceed, but Hunt's visit demonstrated that both local and national reformers are able to work together to secure our aims in a peaceable fashion.

Boy is well and growing fast. Although we can only guess at his age, Bonnie insists we celebrate his birthday this March, the anniversary of our finding him at Badajoz, as his eleventh. He is a steady worker and attends both Mass and Sunday school, and Harrison's classes three nights a week. He still keeps his own counsel, but we are used to that, as is everybody who has come to know him. Nobody seems to think the less of him for it. Bonnie thinks matters may change when he finds a sweetheart. Let us hope so, for all we want for him is a full belly, good health, and a family of his own, one day.

As always, my friends, may you live in peace.

Samuel Ashby

Freer was beginning to look sleepy. Thomas carefully refolded Ashby's letter. He would show it to Joanna later. He thought of Boy growing up fast, and wondered if they would ever get a chance to visit him.

Suddenly Freer came to life and sat bolt upright. 'Does Ashby say who this Henry Hunt is, then?'

56

A Falling Out

Thomas heard raised voices from the back parlour, and after a while a tall man flung open the door and marched out into the main room, quickly followed by Daniel Owens. The tall fellow sat down heavily on a stool and called for a drink, while Owens retreated to his usual corner by the door. Thomas was fairly sure he hadn't seen the tall man before. With his dark flowing locks, loosely tied behind in the old-fashioned way, olive skin and a multitude of freckles, he wasn't a fellow you'd easily forget. He now addressed the rest of the tap-room.

'I just spoke the truth. Owens's pal, Evans, is the dullest speaker I have had ever had to listen to in my entire life.'

'No need for insults, Wilde,' said Owens from his corner. He picked up Crowe's copy of *Sherwin's Political Register* and began to leaf through it, but without attempting to read it. He seemed more interested in listening to what was being said.

Crowe, surprisingly, now pitched into the argument. 'You and your pal, Wedderburn, would have got nowhere without Evans and Owens here organising your Archer Street debates.'

The dark-haired fellow held his ground. 'You can organise as much as you like, but it's no use slapping up handbills all over, and then, the first time people pay their money, they swear they'll never come again because it's all been so bloody dreary.'

Thomas leant over and whispered to Booth, 'Who's the tall fellow? Wilde, I think Owens called him.'

'Alexander Wilde …Wilde by name and wild by nature.'

'But what's he talking about?'

'The Archer Street chapel, Soho. It was set up last year by Owens's pal, Evans, along with one of Wilde's friends. Registered themselves as dissenting ministers. Used to meet three times a week. Sundays were free. Evans lectured in the morning and Wilde's pal, Wedderburn, in the afternoon. The other debates, on Wednesday evenings, cost you sixpence or so, every couple of months.'

'Used to? What happened?'

'There was a falling out. Wedderburn's just gone off to open his own chapel, somewhere down Hopkins Street, Brewer Street way.'

Freer lowered his voice. 'What kind of dissenting ministers?'

'Unitarian, I think,' muttered Booth.

Freer looked surprised. 'Unitarian? I was brought up a Unitarian but I never came across anyone like these fellows.'

Booth whispered, 'Only way you can do it, nowadays.'

'Do what?' asked Thomas.

'Hold meetings, have political debates. You get a licence as a non-conformist minister, and then you're away.'

Freer grinned. 'Is that just a London contrivance?'

Booth shook his head. 'I don't think so.'

Thomas bent closer. 'Maybe a bit like Ashby's Parson Harrison?'

'Sounds like it,' agreed Freer.

Booth shuffled in his chair. 'Though they say Wedderburn's taken the business of being a preacher a bit too far.'

'Too far?' asked Thomas.

'Fire and brimstone, hell and damnation, that kind of thing.'

Thomas saw Owens give up his pretence of studying the *Register*. He stood up again.

'Let me remind you that none of you would have got anywhere without Thomas Evans, making sure we all conduct ourselves in such a way that we cannot be prosecuted.'

'So how come Evans and his son have just spent the last year in gaol?' Wilde retorted.

'You damned well know why. You and your hot-headed friends, thinking they could storm the Tower of London with a drunken mob. They were damned lucky. If the jury hadn't smelt a rat with that government spy, then the Watsons, Thistlewood, the whole lot of them would have ended up in the Tower all right, …and then their heads cut off, rather than getting off scot-free whilst sensible folk like Evans were clapped in gaol.'

Wilde was undeterred. 'Evans might or might not be sensible. That could be a matter for debate in itself, but what's the use of having so-called sensible debates following rules and regulations, if nobody bloody comes to them.'

Thomas began to wonder who might land the first punch. He looked across at Freer, who grinned. He seemed to be enjoying the heated exchange.

But Owens now assumed a bit of a preacher's stance himself. 'Let me remind you also that we have no need to attract followers with threats or trickery, once they hear

Spence's message that "The profit of the Earth is for all, yet how deplorably destitute is the great mass of people." '

Apothecary Griffin looked up from his columns of figures.

'Can we not agree that we should find a way to work together? You know that my good friend, Dr Watson, is meticulous in the organisation of the Society's affairs, but I don't think any of you could possibly accuse him of dullness, or of betraying the cause. And he will be joining us here, making use of our kind landlady's hospitality in the back parlour. We must work together to organise ourselves in the coming months. After all, the rest of the country has now taken up the fight, but unless London takes the lead, how can we act as one and harness each other's strengths? Gentlemen, a truce is called for.'

Wilde sneered, 'If they're looking to us in London, then they'll be waiting for a long time for those mail coaches to go missing.'

Booth whispered, 'It's the agreed signal to let the provinces know that London has risen.'

Thomas wasn't sure he wanted to hear any of this, when all he'd come for was a companionable evening with Freer by someone else's fire.

Griffin rose to his feet. 'You may be correct, Wilde. Nevertheless I will advise Dr Watson that you and Wedderburn are looking to widen our membership further through your new chapel. And that Evans, together with Owens, will continue to help organise matters as they arise within the Society. Our other good friend, Arthur Thistlewood, is, of course, unavailable, owing to his present detention in Horsham gaol.'

'As if any of you cared how he's had to suffer.' Wilde spat his contempt through the small gap in his front teeth, walked to the door and turned to address the company. 'Don't think you've seen the last of me.'

Freer whispered, 'I thought you said they dropped the charges against Thistlewood and these others.'

Booth whispered back, 'Oh, they did. But Thistlewood went and challenged Lord Sidmouth to a duel.'

Freer exclaimed, 'What? The Home Secretary?'

Booth nodded. 'The very same. Thistlewood reckoned Sidmouth owed him money for debts he accrued over the treason trial. But when no reply was forthcoming from Sidmouth, Thistlewood, as an former officer in the militia, considered his honour to have been impugned.'

'Is he mad?' Freer asked.

'Possibly, but definitely desperate. They're all as poor as church mice. Believe me, money, or the lack of it, is behind much of this.'

'They're all owed money, then?' asked Thomas.

'That's what Thistlewood and Watson and their hangers-on seem to think.' Booth called for another drink and, keeping his voice well below the general hubbub, beckoned Freer and Thomas to move closer.

'Right, so come this so–called storming of the Tower nonsense, all black flags and tri-coloured cockades, December 1816, folk were duly brought to trial for high treason in the March, starting with Griffin's pal, Dr Watson. But, in the meantime, in the February, Evans and his son, who had nothing to do with any of the rioting, apart from organising the subscription to pay for their defence, had been arrested for high treason also.

'So what do the government do next? Suspend Habeas Corpus and restrict public meetings and publications. And for their troubles, Evans and his son are both locked up in Cold Bath Fields for more or less the whole of that year. Without any charges ever being brought to court.

'You can imagine the difficulties this placed on Mrs Evans, who, I might add, is a good friend of Ma's. But Janet Evans is made of strong stuff and kept their business going, and in the process made some friends in high places. The Westminster reformers were very much on the Evans's side and awarded them a fair bit of cash from their special relief fund, which was more than the Watsons and their followers ever saw.

'Well, that was the end of a long friendship. Susan Thistlewood and Janet Evans used to help each other out and minded each other's children for years, as well as looking after Watson's two after his wife ran off.'

As Booth spoke, Thomas found himself imagining how money worries and the sense of betrayal might ruin lives. 'So they are no longer friends?'

Booth shook his head. 'You can't ever take back what's been said, can you? Not once it's been said.'

Freer expressed his disappointment. 'And they can't find a way to co-operate, for the greater good?'

'Oh, I expect they'll rub along when they need to, though it's true enough what Wilde said about Owens's friend Evans. He's not what you'd call a good speaker. But he is an excellent organiser. He set the Society up on a proper footing and improved the organisation of our 'free and easys.''

Thomas scratched his head. 'Free and easys?'

'Our meetings in the taverns. After all, isn't it every Englishman's right to carouse in an ale-house? Even this government would struggle to shut all the ale-houses down.'

Booth drained his tankard and signalled for another porter.

'And Evans is strongly committed to Spence, both the man and the plan. And full of the best intentions, urging us all to become more respectable, trying to ban smoking, letting in women for free and so forth, but when it was his turn to speak at Archer Street, hardly anybody turned up. I mean … speeches delivered from a pulpit, with the 'congregation' sitting on benches.'

Booth paused to pay for his drink.

'Not like Wedderburn and Wilde, who can pack them in for any debate, on any topic you can think of, and keep everyone glued to their seats. They can make you laugh, cry, feel happy or angry, all in the space of five minutes.'

Booth leant back in his chair and smiled. ' Songs, comic turns, diatribes against the government, you won't find anything more entertaining. You should go and listen to them at their new place. I can't. It's in a hayloft, up a ladder.

Booth pulled a ragged handbill out of his pocket. 'See.'

57

Pamphlets

14 April 1819, The Strand, London

They left The White Lion early, leaving the quarrelling friends far behind. Thomas suggested they walk towards the river before heading home. So they crossed over the road and cut down the narrow passage off the Strand, leading to the Essex Street steps. But as they began to turn into the wider court they spotted Bear, leaning unsteadily against its far wall, his lines of script almost complete, but his hands trembling and scarcely able to grasp the chalk.

He swung round. 'Will, Thomas.' He gestured towards what he'd written so far. "WHAT PERSON CAN SAY THAT THEY DO NOT HOLD THEIR POSSESSIONS AS TENANTS OF THE PUBLIC?" JOHN LOCKE. THE LAND IS THE PEOPLE'S FA ...

'How are you?' Bear tried to smile; then collapsed onto the flagstones.

Thomas rushed over to him. 'Fainted.'

Freer smelt his breath. 'Hungry.'

Bear stirred.

'When did you last eat?' Freer asked.

'Don't know,' Bear slurred.

Freer began to head up the alleyway to the Strand. 'I'll get something from the pie shop.'

Thomas propped Bear against his barrow and tried to keep him awake, talking to him about anything he could think of, how he had a wife with the most beautiful blue eyes, and a baby daughter, called Annie, who was also the love of his life, and how he and Freer had fought at Waterloo, with medals to prove it, not that he expected Bear to approve of that, being a man of peace …

Bear was grunting, now. Almost smiling. Crookedly. Like an old man. But how old? About his father's age, perhaps? If he was still alive. He had been when Grace left the village. But four years ago might as well be a lifetime away. Thomas gently ran his fingers through Bear's great mane of hair, much as he used to when, as a child, he would sit on his father's lap and play with his hair, before … before everything went wrong. If only he could have explained. If only his father could have understood what had really happened. But that would have destroyed him. Thomas started to gabble to Bear about his mother, Michael, Hannah, but managed to stop himself before the memories overcame him.

Bear was getting cold. Thomas covered him with his jacket. He told Bear how he admired him for trying to do what he did, not that Thomas could see how anybody was ever going to change the world, but it was good that he kept trying, and that he hadn't given up. Keeping going, regardless, rather like his father, who'd had to spend his entire life working in the fields … And most likely who he'd never see again.

Bear stirred. Thomas patted his arm. 'Will has gone to get you something to eat.'

Bear found his hand. 'You're a good man, Thomas, eh.'

'Not really, Bear.'

'Good enough for me, anyway.'

By now Freer had appeared and knelt beside them.

'Got some beer, as well.'

As he drank and ate up Freer's offerings, Bear gradually began to revive.

Thomas was still bothered, though. 'But where are you living?'

'Decent enough lodgings,' he managed to say, 'though rather a drain upon my purse.'

He heaved himself up and bent over his barrow, rearranging his pamphlets.

Freer picked one up.

'How much are they?'

'A penny to you.'

'I'll take two.'

'Thank you,' Bear mumbled and picked up his piece of chalk again. 'I'll just finish this now.' He turned back to his chalkings.

As they hurried away, Thomas looked at Freer. Much as he liked Bear, he was fairly sure the Government didn't. 'Is that wise?'

'He wouldn't have accepted charity, and they'll keep my Rights of Man company in the bottom of my campaign box. I might even read them.'

Thomas sighed. One of these days, Freer was going to get himself into serious trouble reading these kinds of books.

58

St James's Park

May 1819, St James's Park London

It was Mary Booth who first suggested the walk to the park. 'It will do you good to get some fresh air and see some proper trees.'

Mary Booth had been brought up in Hoxton, practically in the country, she said, and swore there was nothing like country air and greenery for restoring the spirits. 'I always go in the spring,' she added, 'for it is the time of year when everyone is promenading, and I can see all the latest styles.' After which, she laughed, she would come home and give her stock of clothes some trifling, but, she could be sure the very latest, touches of fashion.

Joanna, inspired by this notion said that Thomas and she should take Annie to St James's Park. Thomas, though, hesistated. This was precisely where he and Grace had last met each other, when she'd been in London with Squire Rearsby's family and he'd been on royal escort duty. Something that Joanna didn't need to know.

'Perhaps we could go to another park?' he suggested. But Joanna had her mind set on St James's. When invited to join them, Freer thought that he and Louise might inspect the progress of the buildings on New Street over towards Carlton House, and possibly examine the very first gas lamps to be erected in London on Pall Mall. But on the morning of the proposed expedition, Louise was emphatic. They would come to the park.

It was a beautiful but frosty cold day, with no sign of rain, for once. Hard to believe it was May. As they crossed behind Horse Guards, Thomas could see once again the trees fringing the canal, framing the prospect of the Queen's House in the distance. But this time, instead of spying an elegantly dressed woman, her auburn curls poking out from beneath a straw hat, waiting for him, he felt the weight of his young daughter in his arms and the warmth and the curve of Joanna's breast pressed against him. If only he could lay Grace's ghost to rest.

59

The Stockport Fray

May 1819, Pimlico, London

German's Cottages, Heaviley, Stockport, April 1819

Dear Cowper,

Matters are still no more settled here. During another reform meeting at Sandy Brow, February just gone, a most furious fight broke out when the local yeomanry cavalry took it into their heads to attempt to seize the Cap of Liberty from the stage.

The cap, a very handsome affair, emblazoned with the words Hunt and Liberty, was the very same one Hunt had displayed in January at our Manchester meeting. But why the yeomanry should make such an objection to it, and risk provoking the angry response they met with is quite beyond my understanding. Their commanders are clearly men of no sense, with a poor understanding of prudent military behaviour. If Wellington could refrain from throwing his men into unnecessary battle, then why cannot lesser commanders follow his example?

I can only think that they have decided to declare war, and that we are the enemy, so they now regard our banners in the same way as we used to regard our enemy's colours.

They therefore wish to capture them, not only to destroy the enemy's morale but also to increase their own. But, just as we soldiers will defend our colours to the end, so the crowd offered the most sturdy defence of our cap of liberty. Bonnie in particular, incurred the wrath of one of the yeomanry, who threatened her most severely.

The crowd protected itself with stones. The yeomanry retreated. The Riot Act was read. The crowd dispersed to the marketplace, where it was read again. Tempers were roused all round. It was a sorry day for those of us who try to preach peace and moderation in all our affairs.

But I am glad to say that none of us are any the worse for this affray. Boy and Bonnie, as usual, send their best wishes. Bonnie has now learnt to write her name with great confidence and is reading simple chapbooks. Boy can read and write as well as ever, but keeps his own thoughts. I trust that you will not be called upon to perform similar duties in London, but I know, of course, that our old commanders would have more sense than to provoke a perfectly peaceful crowd to violence.

As ever, may you live in peace.

Samuel Ashby

~

Fallowfield snapped shut his writing case. He was getting tired of Ashby's tales from the North. Why couldn't Cowper tell him what kind of sedition he and Freer were committing, instead of pages devoted to the wretched Joanna and the exploits of a small child, all written for the benefit of the brat, he assumed from their cheerful tone. He had never had Cowper down as a naturally cheerful man.

But at least he knew that Cowper and Freer were definitely mixing with the kind of men they should be avoiding, if they were truly loyal subjects of His Majesty. Or reporting them to the authorities. They were a disgrace to the uniform. And sooner or later he'd have them both.

60

Pigs' Meat

May 1819, St Martin's Lane, London

Thomas was walking back along St Martin's Lane when he spotted Bear's handcart further up the alleyway past the church; and there was Littlethorpe, apparently looking over the books on it. Thomas was intrigued. Littlethorpe might be able to write his name, but he still struggled to read any document that he might have to put his name to.

Thomas moved closer. They weren't books that Littlethorpe was fingering, but some kind of coins or tokens, and by the time Thomas caught up with him, Littlethorpe had already bought a couple.

Thomas quickly greeted Bear, who, thankfully, seemed less frail, and slipped another couple of coins in his direction as though making a purchase, then hurried Littlethorpe away far enough that he could speak to him without Bear overhearing.

'Can I have a look at what you've just bought?'

'These two?'

He handed Thomas a small coin engraved with a pig trampling what appeared to be a bishop's mitre and a crown into the ground, encircled with an inscription, saying Pigs' Meat, published by T Spencer London, and something else he couldn't read.

Littlethorpe smiled. 'Reminds me of the time my dad nearly met his end in an argument with a boar. Clever things, pigs, but you can't turn your back on them. The big fellow over there said it used to be for advertising a penny paper called Pigs' Meat but there's not much call for these things nowadays as the man that wrote the paper's long dead. That's why it was going cheap.'

'And the other one?'

'Some folk dancing round a maypole.' Thomas peered closer. It did look like a maypole, but with what seemed to be a head stuck on the top.

Thomas's blood chilled. He didn't want Littlethorpe showing these round the barracks.

' Have you ever heard of a group calling themselves the Society of Spencean Philanthropists? '

Littlethorpe pulled a face. 'What a mouthful. Na. Should I have?'

'Littlethorpe, get rid of them. I'm serious. Do not keep them.'

Littlethorpe didn't look happy.

'I'll give you what you paid for them.' Thomas said.

'That don't matter. I just like them, that's all.'

'You have to throw them away, I'm telling you. For your own good. Right now. You've no idea how dangerous those little things are.'

Thomas hoped his tone of voice was urgent and serious enough to make Littlethorpe do as he was told. There was no knowing when there might be a sudden inspection of the soldiers' property. He still blanched when he thought about Freer's copy of Paine's *Rights of Man*, never mind Bear's two pamphlets hidden in the bottom of his travelling trunk, 'in a false compartment', he'd once cheerfully confessed. A sensible man would have ditched Paine's book in the

306

Thames, by now. Still, with any luck, nobody would suspect that a troop serjeant-major might be hiding away a book condemned as seditious.

He glared at Littlethorpe, who shrugged and dropped the little tokens into the mire.

'Good riddance, eh,' said Thomas, hoping that Littlethorpe was the only soldier who'd been tempted to buy some of Bear's tokens.

~

But when Littlethorpe came to him clutching a pamphlet which he had acquired on one of his nightly visits to The Cock up the road, Thomas feared that his efforts to keep his friend out of mischief might still come to nothing.

Littlethorpe told him they'd been a bunch of fine fellows, talking of sharing things out, who'd given him this to look at, but, of course, he couldn't make head nor tail of it, so he'd brought it for Thomas to read.

Thomas was busy inspecting a lame horse at the time and without thinking much further about it, put the already ragged pamphlet aside to pick up when he'd finished. When the farrier arrived to take care of the horse, Thomas took the pamphlet outside and began to leaf though it. The first words he caught sight of were 'the end of aristocracy and landlords, all land to be owned by parishes, with rents to be shared equally amongst the parishioners; universal suffrage, including women; elections to a national Senate; money for those unable to work, infants to be free from abuse and poverty.' He recognised echoes of Thomas Paine and other preachers of dangerous, unattainable dreams. He knew that anything like this found in Littlethorpe's possession would get him into serious trouble. Had he been given more than one pamphlet to read? He'd better find him. Right now.

~

Littlethorpe had already left the King's Mews by the time Thomas got there. Taking directions, Thomas went straight on up St Martin's Lane, looking to bear left at Litchfield Street. And then, as he turned, he heard distant, but raucous singing, and among the voices, yes, he was sure, was Littlethorpe's high tenor spilling into the night. It led him directly to The Cock on a far corner with Grafton Street.

He stepped straight into another world. A dimly lit room, frequent toasts booming over the sound of thumping tankards. Thomas recognised the tune, *Maid of the Mill*, but strained to hear the words till he picked up a spare song sheet that had wafted to the floor.

'As for me, though in Prison I oft have been cast
Because I would dare to be free,
And though in black Newgate I did pen this Song
My Theme I've not alter'd you see.
In jail or abroad whatever betide
My struggles for Freedom shall be
Whatever Fate bring I will think, speak and sing,
The Rights of Man, Boys for me.'

Much as he too liked to sing, and much as he treasured memories of similar evenings spent among friends, he wasn't tempted to join in, though it was clear to him that these songs of defiance bound the entire company together in heartfelt fellow feeling. He was far too preoccupied, peering through the fug of pipe smoke, looking for Littlethorpe.

But gradually the singing stopped as all eyes turned on him. He drew himself up, as tall as he could make himself, and announced calmly and with all the authority he could muster that he'd come to escort one of his soldiers back to the barracks. Straight away. It was not permissible to come this far from the barracks; not now, not in the future. As Thomas was speaking, he caught sight of Littlethorpe. He smiled, walked up to Littlethorpe and clapped him on the shoulders. He made as if to be severe with him, but bent down to whisper, 'Just bloody come with me, right.'

Littlethorpe, spinning a little on his feet, his face flushed but not totally glazed, stared back, uncomprehending. And, indeed, Thomas sensed no hostility. The company did seem good-natured enough, slapping Littlethorpe on the back, all apparently wishing him well, not that Thomas could pick out many single voices from the murmur. And there were even a few who were clearly gentlemen, though down on their luck, amongst the crowd, their shabby but once well-cut clothes and confident bearing distinguishing them from the rest.

Littlethorpe had fortunately not reached a belligerent stage and Thomas was able to man-handle him out of the door in the general direction of the better lit streets, exaggerating the difficulty, but also finding he needed to hold Littlethorpe up as they walked.

When they reached the main streets Thomas let go of him and Littlethorpe leaned against the wall. Thomas faced him and spoke very sternly. 'Littlethorpe, I read the pamphlet. All right, some might say it takes a common-sense approach to matters we all think are very important. It's not wrong to care about the state of the nation and the well-being of the people. But if you're found in possession of it ... Don't you understand? It would only take one man in your company to tell someone in authority and you'd be severely flogged, or worse.'

Littlethorpe still looked uncomprehending. And still very drunk. Thomas repeated his words even more slowly. 'Do you understand what I'm saying? Having such a pamphlet is a flogging matter at the very least. You'd be charged with spreading disaffection and undermining army discipline, and you know that's a serious offence. And if the civil authorities got hold of you, and thought that you were spreading disaffection, then it could mean transportation to Botany Bay or worse.'

'All over that bit of paper?'

'Yes. All on account of that bit of paper.'

He touched Littlethorpe gently on the arm. 'You understand now why I had to make so much of this being a breach of military discipline, and that you wouldn't be able to go back to The Cock?'

Littlethorpe slumped against the wall. ' I reckon.'

Thomas sighed. 'You see, the pamphleteer's writing in a way some would see as dangerous … the land to be shared out, men and women to vote, money for those unable to work, infants free from poverty.'

Littlethorpe stared at his feet. 'When you've only got to go ten yards behind all these fine streets to find people not even scraping a living, that doesn't sound so bad to me.'

'I know, Littlethorpe, I know.'

Thomas had felt almost the self-same thing, but his soldier's caution worried away at him. How could it work? His experience of human kind so far had led him to believe such ideas would likely prove a recipe for disorder. But, as for the sentiments driving them, he was beginning to see what Freer was talking about. What his hero, Thomas Paine, meant. And maybe this Thomas Spence too.

~

He remembered when he and Freer had been walking along the narrow passage towards Clare market last winter. They'd come across a bundle of rags, a drunk or so they'd thought at first. But when they tried to move him, as not to step over him, they'd realised he was dead. And when Thomas had tried to find some indication of name or address, all he'd been able to feel were his ribs. It had reminded him of the horses who'd slowly starved to death as the Regiment struggled across the Pyrenees in that bitter winter of 1813. And now this man too, but on the streets of a great city, not a desolate mountain range.

He closed his eyes, trying to blot out the memory. He was beginning to see everywhere he looked corpses, resurrected, pretending they were alive, pretending they were living well enough on this great field of battle between rich and poor.

Yet he had seen what anarchy could do. What it had done at Badajoz. How it had killed Boy's mother, how the Prussians had exacted their revenge on the French, how the French officer had horsewhipped that elderly bewigged man on the Neuilly Bridge. Because he was angry. Because Napoleon had lost the war.

He wondered at the nature of human kind, that it could come to this. This so-called peace. But it would be dangerous to encourage Littlethorpe. In more ways than one.

'Be that as it may, Littlethorpe. Laws have been passed so anyone reckoned to be breaking them is going to be made an example of.'

'So, like that bloody lancer that killed Dog. They will do it because they can.'

Thomas nodded, 'Yes, just like the Polish lancer.'

Littlethorpe turned and began to totter back, without support, towards the barracks, with Thomas walking alongside to shield him from the crush of carriages. Suddenly the thought struck Thomas that Littlethorpe had been alone at The Cock. No Byrne or his usual cronies.

'Were none of your pals with you at The Cock?'

'Didn't want anybody else to get into trouble. Till I knew more about it.'

'It?'

'What those gentlemen types were talking to me about. 'That it was time to consider physical force rather than moral force.' That's why I think they welcomed a soldier, who knows what it's all about.'

'Littlethorpe, I may not be your keeper but I am your troop serjeant-major. If you know of any plan that will lead to violence, then it's your duty to tell me. And it will be my duty to tell Captain Haywood.'

Littlethorpe, looking a little more sober, nodded. 'I know. I told them. I told them that's how all that business with the French began. I told them. I used to enjoy fighting but I've had enough. Any of us who've been through Waterloo have had enough, eh?'

Thomas had never thought to hear the belligerent Littlethorpe declare himself as battle-weary as the rest of them. He hardly knew what to say.

'Still, if we have to, we'll have to, won't we?'

Littlethorpe tottered a little closer to the familiar smells of piss and beef stew. 'But on whose side, eh, Troop Serjeant-Major?'

Thomas didn't answer for some time. 'Let's pray it never comes to that.'

Depositing Littlethorpe by the guard house, Thomas saluted the guards and made his way home to Joanna and Annie. What was he to do? He too would have everything to lose if even a word of this came out. He reached home, made his way down into the cellar, took out the pamphlet Littlethorpe had given him, and placed it sheet by sheet into the dying flames of the kitchen fire.

61

The Anniversary Dinner

June 1819, The Strand, London

'You can't. It would be madness.'

Thomas and Freer were standing outside the side entrance of The Crown and Anchor. But Thomas was standing in front of the door, barring the way.

'It's only a dinner to mark Thomas Spence's birthday. I'm sure Owens wouldn't have asked me if it was anything more.'

Thomas raised his eyebrows. 'But it won't be just a dinner, will it? There'll be speeches and toasts, and before you know it, you'll be drinking to the death of the Prince Regent.'

'That might not be such a bad thing.' Freer laughed.

'Be serious. Believe me, I know what kind of things can go on in these places.'

'It's The Crown and Anchor, not some low-life alehouse.'

'Disloyal toasts are disloyal toasts, wherever they are.'

'So, how come you know so much?'

'I had to fetch Littlethorpe back from one of those places once.'

'Right.'

'And I could see how easy it would be to get caught up in everything, the songs, the toasts, the drinking. And then …' Thomas trailed off. He'd said quite enough.

'Owens said I could make a positive contribution to the debate.'

'Freer, you could talk a horse's hind leg off if you wanted to, but that doesn't mean you should.'

Freer pulled a face. 'It would be interesting.'

'No, it wouldn't. You'd get very drunk and start throwing things at each other when you couldn't agree.'

Thomas yanked Freer out of the path of a dangerously overloaded cart. 'If you weren't killed by one of these bloody things first.'

Thomas now grasped the already rather drunk Freer by the elbow. 'So, am I taking you home to Louise and Billy or not?'

'Did Louise send you?'

'Now that would be telling, wouldn't it? Shall we go then?'

The last time Thomas had seen Freer this drunk was at Thomas's wedding, when the bridegroom had also been less than coherent, but that was with sheer happiness. This was different. He guessed that Freer was now regretting his acceptance of Owens's invitation, as his friend was no longer offering any resistance to being guided home.

'You know what, Cowper?'

'No. What?'

'You have a dangerously low opinion of the power of argument for doing good in the world.'

'In my experience,' Thomas muttered, 'words can cause just as much harm as good.'

62

On A War Footing

July 1819, Wych Street, London

German's Cottages, Heaviley, Stockport, July 1819

Dear Cowper,

I trust you are well in these troubled times, for we have just heard that both squadrons of your old cricketing adversaries, the 15th Hussars, are being sent to Lancashire to keep the peace. As I feared, the local magistrates and yeomanry are getting ready to put themselves on a war footing.

Any provocation, I might add, now seems to be largely arising from the actions of the authorities, for we have also just heard that indictments have been drawn up against Parson Harrison and Sir Charles Wolseley, directly as a result of their attending our June meeting at Sandy Brow. They both gave animated and lively addresses, as you would expect, but to regard their words as seditious is beyond belief.

Held only the day before these indictments were drawn up, a meeting in Birmingham may also have inflamed the authorities. It made a bold gesture to secure some representation for a city without any, by electing Wolseley as its legislatorial attorney, charging him to speak on behalf of its people. Doubtless, in the mind of a clerical magistrate, this would smack of sedition, nay, even the threat of revolution.

Fortunately, although Wolseley was arrested by one of our sheriff's officers at his home in Staffordshire, he has now been bailed. Harrison, though, has, so far, managed to evade arrest.

Parson Harrison has many supporters here, and indeed Bonnie has just returned from a meeting of the Stockport Female Reformers held this very day. She tells me that all with one voice shouted out 'Harrison and Liberty for ever. Harrison and Liberty for ever.' Bonnie has heard too that Parson Harrison is still determined to attend the London meeting, planned for July 21st at Smithfield.

Indeed, by the time you receive this letter, the Smithfield meeting may be over and done, but I am confident that, so long as my old regiment has had any part in it, all will have been conducted in a peaceable enough manner.

But, if you receive this letter before then, you may wish to look out for our Parson Harrison, who is a vigorous and fine speaker, though even the most eloquent of men pale by comparison with Mr Henry Hunt, whose great power of speech and mastery of language inspire all those who have, like us, been fortunate enough to hear him speak. You may remember that I have spoken of him before, when he came to Manchester in January.

I am told that he has already promised to return this August to address a meeting, not unlike the one in Birmingham, when we too were hoping to elect our own legislatorial attorney of the people. But, given the circumstances of Sir Charles Wolseley's arrest, we may have to seek further advice. It would be foolish to risk the imprisonment of this Wiltshire gentleman, who has thrown in his lot with us reformers.

For, as you may rightly judge, with the many personal recriminations now being traded between the yeomanry and the townspeople, we might be said to be in a state of civil war. Furthermore, each side knows the faces of the other too well now to hide ourselves away.

In peace as ever,

Samuel Ashby

~

Jack Fallowfield stretched back in his chair. War footing, eh? And the man talks about peace. Shouldn't be long now before Freer and Cowper show their true colours. And when they do, he'll be waiting for them.

63

Smithfield

21 July 1819. London

Captain Haywood seemed hot under the collar, Thomas thought. *It looks like he's got something important to say.* Although his long nights of gossiping with Thomas had been severely curtailed by both their marriages, Haywood had not lost his talent for indiscretion ... and exaggeration.

'We may be about to have a riot on our hands,' he announced, as he rode into the stable yard at Somerset House at five-thirty that morning. 'Captain Webster's already on his way to Horse Guards.' He nodded in Thomas's direction. As was his habit Thomas had been getting his own horse ready for the day, leaving his serjeants to oversee the men and horses at the King's Mews. 'Thought I might still catch you here, as well, Cowper. Saves me going through everything twice.'

Haywood signalled to Thomas and Freer, who was just behind, to follow, delegating three of the men to take care of their horses. Thomas would rather have stayed and attended to Mam'selle. With these light mornings, he felt glad to be alive, and grooming his horse settled him perfectly for the day ahead. He still missed Fearless enormously, but his steady mare was a sweet creature and he hoped would not be tested in battle as Fearless had been. Thomas tried to pay attention to Haywood, who was talking almost as fast as he was walking away from the stable block.

'Over at Smithfield Market, don't you know, where the cattle are forever running loose. One of those meetings where working men lay down their tools to go and listen to so-called gentlemen, who should know better, about their so-called rights. I hope we shan't have a riot on our hands to deal with but the City authorities have decided they need reinforcements. And who are we to argue?'

Thomas tried to halt the flow just a little, so they wouldn't miss anything important that might slip away in the rush across the yard.

'I'm told, sir, there have been a number of meetings like this across the country.'

Haywood stopped and turned round.' So, you've heard of this Henry Hunt, have you?'

Freer and Thomas nodded.

'Well, this is the very fellow who seems determined to cause us trouble.'

Freer, clearly relieved not to be still limping at such a fast pace after Haywood, now joined in. 'Sir, have the authorities received information that we are to expect trouble-makers?'

Haywood coughed. 'Not exactly. But this gentleman, and indeed he is a gentleman, chooses to use his education in ways that stir up the crowds to indulge in rioting and dissension. You have perhaps heard tell of the Spa Fields riots, of December '16? We were in France then, of course.'

Thomas and Freer nodded. Thomas hoped Haywood wouldn't ask how they knew.

'He was never convicted of anything, but they say that at the first meeting he was responsible for enraging a vast crowd, in such a fashion that at the second meeting a number of his supporters came early, intent on causing mischief by encouraging some foolish men to attempt to storm the Tower. If it hadn't been that some dragoons had happened by, and given chase, who knows what would have happened? And damn me if the man hasn't returned, no doubt intent on whipping up more ill feeling'

Having heard Owens explain the sequence of events at the two Spa Fields meetings in rather more detail only the other week, Thomas knew Haywood's version of events was incomplete, though it was widely accepted. He was now surprised to find himself believing more of Owens's account than Haywood's entirely second-hand version, even though Owens was hardly impartial.

Haywood suddenly seemed to remember himself. He coughed again and returned to his orders.

'Lieutenant-Colonel Pennington has instructed me that we are to be alert, and ready in case of disturbances. But he emphasises that we are not to challenge the man directly. However, there will be crowds and, as we know, where there are crowds, trouble is likely to be brewing.'

'So, now firstly, I want you both to draw up a contingent of your calmest men. They will be nearest the edge of the crowd. You will keep in reserve, at the far back, those whom you consider to be hot-headed. Remember that we expect from all your men the kind of discipline that wins wars, not causes them.' Haywood looked genuinely concerned. 'After all, it would be a sorry business were we to quarrel with our countrymen.'

Then Haywood sniffed with clear disapproval. 'I should add that some people say this Hunt's an admirer of Napoleon. Maybe he is, but keep that quiet, will you. We don't want any Waterloo men hearing that. Of course, I have complete trust in your discretion and good judgement. So, if anyone asks, you are to deny all knowledge of such a rumour.'

Thomas and Freer exchanged glances, shaking their heads to indicate that neither of them had heard of this before. There was really no point, Thomas thought, in telling them about it. Typical of Haywood, though. Still, if any man repeated it to anger his comrades against Hunt, at least he and Freer would be prepared.

~

Thomas, contrary to his instructions not to have anyone hot-headed close to the crowd, had decided to have Littlethorpe by his side; although the man was belligerent and had a history of dissent and disobedience, he was useful in difficult situations. Just as long as he controlled his resentments. After all, his grandfather's farm had been taken from him, and friends in Nottingham had died trying to stop machines putting them out of work. But the risk was worth taking.

They rode slowly up from the King's Mews, down the Strand, past St Clement Danes and then up Fetter Lane, heading up towards Charterhouse, behind which the Smithfield cattle and sheep markets sheltered.

~

Thomas looked around him at the crowds. Many he imagined would be struggling to eke out a living, others fearful that they, like the Nottingham craftsmen, would soon have no employment. Smithfield, measuring scarcely three acres or so, was really too small to house a live meat market, never mind a gathering of this size. There must have been thousands there, marooned in the mire left by the animals, all crammed into this tiny space, patiently waiting. He saw a tall man wearing a white top hat. Hunt, he presumed. The man was perching on a cart, alongside a couple of other men. They must be speakers too, Thomas thought.

Any further and Thomas and his men would be completely caught up in the crowd. Thomas ordered the men to stand back while he and Littlethorpe edged their horses just a little closer. None of them must break rank.

Hunt began to speak. It was hard to hear, but the crowds in front of them passed on what they could to their fellows behind, as Hunt's message rippled steadily through the crowd And Littlethorpe had a sharp and attentive ear and was particularly adept at relaying Hunt's words.

'Please be aware of the presence of troops,' he passed on to Thomas, grinning.

'Something about Parliament meeting once a year and all men of settled abode getting the vote.' Littlethorpe grinned again. 'So that rules us out then.'

Littlethorpe continued to strain his ears. 'And something about moral force peaceful enough for all people to support the cause. No need for physical violence or something or other.'

So how would it work? Thomas puzzled. How would they know that a candidate was a good man or not? If you couldn't talk directly to the men you voted for, how could you know if they were decent people who would do what was best? Suppose a man had the gifts that Hunt had in rousing a crowd, but only had ambition for his own advantage and despised the people?

Thomas scanned the expressions of the people in the crowd. He could tell that many of those who could hear the orator's words clearly were hanging on to every sentiment, ready and willing to do his bidding. On the other hand, those who couldn't hear fully but caught just the odd word like Littlethorpe, seemed to be showing signs of restlessness and a readiness to move. If only they hadn't been pressed so tight. Thomas sensed a lack of attention that might only be relieved by movement, and looked at Littlethorpe for confirmation.

'What do you think about the back rows?'

Littlethorpe scrutinised the crowd.

'Maybe just a few lads who've come looking for a scrap. But look at the rest of them. This crowd isn't going to go marching on the Tower, is it?'

Thomas looked again at the women and children, mostly in their best frocks and bonnets. There might be the odd scuffle or argument, but surely nothing they couldn't deal with quite easily and with no fuss. He turned round in the saddle to see Captain Haywood moving towards them.

'A lot of people, Cowper. And not much room to move. What's your judgement?'

Thomas spoke as clearly as he could. Haywood didn't like too many details all at once.

'Littlethorpe and I have been observing the crowd closely, sir, listening to what's being said and watching for troublemakers. In a crowd this size, of course, there will be pickpockets, footpads and no doubt some troublemakers. But there are enough good citizens, who haven't come looking for arguments and fights, to deal with any miscreants themselves. My judgement is that if we do not provoke or rush them, the crowd will remain peaceful.'

Haywood seemed rather surprised by Thomas's long report but then he too turned to the crowd and studied the faces.

'As Pennington's orders explicitly state, we are to do nothing to provoke them.'

Thomas focused once again on the speaker, who, although speaking out strongly, had no weapons and carried himself like a honest man with fiery passions but no apparent ill intent. He smiled. This Hunt fellow reminded him of Freer, his ideas and his passions and with as good a heart. No, their job was only to prevent such disorder as would threaten life and limb of subjects, government or monarch. And at the moment, the worst he could imagine would be that some of His Majesty's subjects might suffer a cracked head and the loss of their purse.

Haywood turned back from surveying the crowd, murmuring quietly so those not meant to, wouldn't hear.

'Let's take a leaf out of Wellington's book and shelter on the lee side of the slope on the battlefield.'

Thomas grinned. 'I think that would be a good tactic, sir.'

But then, suddenly, they heard a great commotion. Thirty or so men were making their way towards the carts, shouting for the crowd to stand aside, and waving official looking documents in the direction of one of the speakers.

Haywood looked anxiously around him and then at Thomas.

Thomas remembered the women in Nottingham shouting abuse at them when they'd been raw recruits, and thought of how Freer had once remarked that their very presence had served to remind the women of their past grievances. Would that happen now?

They would have to stay visible but unthreatening. That would be his judgement. He turned again to Haywood.

'If we just keep out of their way, sir, watch what they do next. As long as we are in a good position to move, should we have to, then we will do our duty according to our orders and not provoke.'

Thomas heard the words of Henry Hunt mediated through Littlethorpe ringing in his ears '... moral force ... peaceful ... enough people to support the cause. No need for physical violence.'

Thomas tried to assess the crowd's reaction as one of the speakers was bundled away. He now realised the man was probably Ashby's missing Parson Harrison. He expected roars of outrage, and then, who knew what might happen, once the crowd's blood was up. But instead he witnessed attentiveness, and caught snatches of Hunt's words, soothing and calming, promising the redress of righteousness.

'… Respect our prince, and venerate the family and title. … obtain our rights and privileges without bloodshed. The horrible scenes of revolutionary France will never desolate our beautiful island … Jehovah will bless you, and assist your exertions. Your cause is his …'

Haywood tightened his reins, ready to leave, gesturing towards Hunt. 'I confess I'm surprised, Cowper. Not such a bad fellow, after all, as far as I can see, urging peace, and not kicking up a fuss when they came to arrest that other fellow. So let's all keep on the lee side, if we can.'

64

A Vindictive Personal Affair

August 1819, London

German's Cottages, Heaviley, Stockport, August 10ᵗʰ,1819

Dear Cowper and Freer,

Thank you for your letter commending the behaviour of our two speakers, Hunt and Parson Harrison, at the Smithfield meeting and the constraint displayed by both of these parties after Harrison's arrest. Sadly, no such constraint has been exercised here by any of the parties. We are beginning to feel the pursuit of Harrison to be a vindictive, nay personal affair, and that he'd been dragged away from Smithfield to make a particular example of him. As a consequence, having sneaked Harrison back to his home by the indirect route from London, the sheriff's officer was set upon and badly injured by one of Harrison's frustrated supporters. Help was immediately requested from the barracks at Manchester, and a troop of your friends from the 15ᵗʰ Hussar soon arrived, and were able to restore the peace without any further harm being done.

I fear, though, we are to be punished for this business. The papers have already reported that two six pounder artillery guns together with two troops of the 6th carbineers, are being sent to the vicinity of Stockport and Manchester, as well as the second divisions of the 31ˢᵗ Regiment of Foot. We hear, too, that considerable quantities of arms and ammunition have been conveyed from Chester to Manchester; in readiness for what purpose, we do not know.

They have already spiked the few remaining cannon from Lyme Park, in case they fall into the reformers' hands. As if we would have men in the area, who would know how to fire them to any effect. And all for what?

The Patriotic Union's next reform meeting, on August 9th in St Peter's Fields, Manchester, was to be addressed by Mr Hunt, who is well known for his peaceable and conciliatory manner in the face of extreme provocation, as you yourselves witnessed at Smithfield so recently.

We are now, though, somewhat embarrassed because, even as late as August 5ᵗʰ, the magistrates contrived to declare our meeting illegal. However, we were quickly able to obtain legal advice and were able to rephrase the purpose of the meeting in such a way that it can now go ahead.

But none of this could be conveyed in time to alert Mr Hunt before he had arrived at Bullock Smithy on August 8ᵗʰ. He was not much pleased at this, but, after many apologies, a good supper with some supporters at the Union rooms and a night's rest, he has agreed to remain in Manchester so that he might address the meeting now to be held on the 16ᵗʰ.

In the meantime, we have warned him against accepting any presents or parcels, as we hear there may well be attempts to entrap him with the possession of forbidden publications.

We have already put out our best clothes. Bonnie, like the other female reformers, is to wear a white dress, though she complains a great deal about its impracticality in a hot dusty summer. We have also been busy preparing our banners. I have had to modify Bonnie's banner on account of its passionate language. I am to share mine with a fellow handloom weaver whilst Boy is to play a drum alongside us. This will help us all keep in step as we march to Manchester. Bonnie is very happy to see him take up the drum again and tells him that Dermot would be so proud. Boy just smiles and does not say anything but I am glad that Dermot's lessons are now to be employed in the spirit of peace and good will, rather than in war.

I will write to you with a full report after the 16th. I know your thoughts will be with us.

Yours in peace,

Samuel Ashby, Bonnie and Boy.

~

Jack Fallowfield assumed that the Home Department would be pleased to receive confirmation of all the details of the coming meeting in Manchester, but they were forever grumbling that what they really needed people like him to do was to smoke out the conspirators and their plots long before they happened. And the only way to do that was, in their opinion, to join them, encourage them to reveal themselves. As if he could …

65

Armed resistance?

August 1819, London

It was early August and everything seemed quiet, for once, in the city, though not at The White Lion. Thomas began to realise just how much fund raising and organisation these meetings needed. Thomas could see too that Freer was particularly enjoying all the comings and goings, including seeing Hunt at close quarters when he'd called in to collect his Smithfield expenses. 'He has lodgings nearby,' Booth whispered. 'But he's really more of a Crown and Anchor man.'

Thomas was sitting in his usual corner with Freer and Booth when Apothecary Griffin and his friend Dr Watson rushed in, but rather than Griffin then retiring to his usual corner with his columns of figures, the apothecary briefly nodded at Thomas and then the landlady and both men made their way to the back parlour. Shortly afterwards Wilde and his pal, Wedderburn came in, followed by a thin fellow with a scrawny fringe, in a coat that had seen better days. He was accompanied by another man with sharp features and side-whiskers, who Thomas recognised as one of the speakers at Smithfield.

Booth whispered, 'Arthur Thistlewood, you know, the one jailed for challenging Sidmouth to a duel.'

'Oh, him,' Thomas exclaimed.

'He got out of prison a few weeks ago but seems to be even less cheerful than before.'

Freer butted in, 'So what are they doing now? Organising another big meeting?'

Booth shook his head. 'I doubt it. Now Thistlewood's back, it'll just be another one of their damned committees.'

Thomas and Freer returned to their porter, but it became difficult to ignore the increasing level of noise spilling out from the back parlour. Thomas recognised Wilde's voice and that of his friend Wedderburn, who seemed to have adopted the booming tones of an outdoor preacher.

'We need to set an example to the younger fellows. I for one would put myself at the forefront and at the very head of any campaign of armed resistance.'

Booth sighed. 'Not another Spa Fields. That's all we bloody need.'

Thomas and Freer looked at each other. Freer shrugged. 'Probably just a lot of hot air.'

Thomas nodded. 'I can't see Watson and Griffin agreeing to something like that again.'

Booth ordered another porter. 'Let's drink to peace and harmony and all that, shall we?'

Freer laughed. 'What? Are you trying to put us out of a job?'

Thomas retorted, 'Unlikely.'

Thomas leant back against the wall and listened to the arguments in the back rooms rise and fall. With the Government arresting reformers like Parson Harrison if they so much as addressed a meeting to demand change, he couldn't see how the Government was ever going to be persuaded to accept reform. He supposed they felt much like an embattled army, surrounded on three sides by the enemy except for a forest at the back of them. But even Wellington, when he had placed his troops in that position, had been mindful of his lines of retreat. Even Wellington might have had to dash through the forest whilst pretending to the rest of the world that he was merely falling back to retrench.

But this Wedderburn, in particular, sounded as though he was ready to fight all and everyone who stood in his way, whatever the chances of winning.

~

'Well, it seems that was one too many speeches rallying the troops at Hopkins Street,' Booth announced. 'Wedderburn was arrested last night.'

'What for?' Freer asked.

'As you might expect from the fiery preacher man, blasphemous and seditious libel.'

Booth shook his head. 'I can't see this lot and Hunt agreeing for much longer that the only way forward is legal redress through the courts and constitutional means, can you?'

Freer grunted, 'Not really.'

Thomas began to wonder if he and Freer shouldn't find somewhere else to spend their evenings.

66

St Peter's Fields

16 August 1819, Manchester

The warmth of the sun on his back reminded Boy of Spain, or what he could remember of it: that first summer after his mother died, when Thomas was in hospital in Lisbon, when he'd played on his own in the dust, the sun beating down until Bonnie came looking for him to drag him back into the shade of the bell tents.

He missed the sun. But not as much as he missed Thomas. And Joanna and their quiet afternoons teaching him his lessons, even the things he'd never need to know, like the angle of fire for guns. No, he didn't need to know anything about guns and sabres any more, though Bonnie seemed set on making a drummer boy of him …

'Now you're eleven,' she'd announced a few months ago, 'you can play Dermot's drum.' So she'd sent him off to a neighbour everyone called Joshua, on account of his playing the trumpet, to learn how to put a beat to a tune. And the pair of them had been playing together ever since to aid the men's drills and marching on the Great Moor.

But now everyone was all of a bustle, in their best clothes, getting ready for the great procession into Manchester.

'We shall march like Roman soldiers down their old road,' Ashby told him as he bent over him to straighten his jacket, whilst Bonnie spat on the corner of a handkerchief and wiped his face clean. Boy couldn't see why Ashby should be so bothered about the Roman soldiers, because Ashby had sworn never to go soldiering again. But Ashby said he liked to think that the marchers too were part of history, that 'we deserve to have the vote the same as any man of privilege.'

'It's important,' Ashby said, after he'd taken him on that freezing January day to first hear Orator Hunt, 'never to give up.' And now they were to hear him again in St Peter's Fields on a summer's day that couldn't have been more beautiful.

Bonnie had already left, hurrying down Hillgate to the market place with her banner, whilst Ashby, Boy and the group from Heaviley waited for Joshua and his well–drilled reformers to arrive from Bullock Smithy. Boy quietly took his place alongside the rows of men, women and children three or four abreast, and they set off at a steady walk to cover the next seven or eight miles. Joshua the trumpeter, a corporal like Ashby, who had also seen action at Waterloo, was in charge of setting the pace.

'Mind, I were four years younger then,' he declared every so often, as their bones jarred over the stone setts on Hillgate. But they all seemed to fall into step easily enough with a good stride as Boy felt the steady thrum of his beat clear his mind of everything but the marching.

With a great burst on his trumpet, Joshua now led the way to the market place, up the steep lane winding past the Court Leet and on to The Bull, where they found some other groups, together with the band of female reformers all in white. Bonnie waved to him. Looking as pleased as could be, she was holding her very own banner amidst all the others for *Annual Parliaments and Universal Suffrage, Vote by Ballot, No Corn Laws and Success to the Female Reformers of Stockport*, and in pride of place a crimson Cap of Liberty.

They set off to the tune of *God Save the King* but with words of their own.

O sacred Liberty
We will thy vot'ries be
Espouse thy cause

Boy thought the solemn music just right to begin their walk, but when they came to cross the bridge over the Mersey at the bottom of the valley and the drumbeat seemed to be taking care of itself, Boy's thoughts began to wander and he noticed the steepness of the valley sides, their bare sandstone like a open wound, left to fester in the shadow of the red-brick mills with their chimneys higher than any trees.

Inspire us with thy love
That we may Patriots prove

The hill into Lancashire was steep enough to slow them all up, but Joshua, like the experienced infantryman he was, reset the pace so none of them felt too winded to keep in step. The women twitched their skirts a bit higher; the men adjusted their grip on their flags and bent their heads ready for the climb.

And fearless rise above
Corruption's laws

'We're now approaching the Heatons,' Ashby announced as soon as he saw the windmill's sails high on the hill.

The sun was getting hotter. And now back more or less on the level, the men and women began to take up a tune that Joshua played on his trumpet. 'Another wretched regimental trophy, like Dermot's drum,' Boy heard Ashby mutter.

Why give to your tyrants the laurel of fame
For honest Wat Tyler more glory can claim,
When villains presum'd honest maidens to vex

The female reformers adjusted their bonnets and roared their approval.

Wat felt like a man, and defended the sex
Ça Ira, ah ah, Defenders of women for me

Boy looked around him again and could see stooks of wheat already stacked in the distant meadows. In others the hay lay loose on the ground waiting to dry. Sometimes he saw a great house, an old black-and-white hall, overlooking grazing cows, and quivering fields of oats not yet harvested. They might have been in a different country.

Let the sons of Oppression eternally sing
The praise of nobility and prelates and king

They had picked up pace again on the now broad toll road leading to Levenshulme village and beyond, and there was plenty of room for the marchers as well as the heavily laden carts trundling in both directions.

We despise the distinction that monarchs create
But respect worthy fellows whatever their state
Ça-ira, ah, ah, All worthy good fellows for me

It reminded him of the regiment's great march up the entire length of France, the first time they beat Napoleon. By Bonnie's reckonings he would have been scarcely six but he still remembered it well, everyone managing to stagger on, even though they were exhausted.

Tom Paine, a true Englishman, high in renown
Shews that plunder's the system of mitre and crown
They strive by degrading the people's degree

Boy remembered the baggage wagons, the horses, their sweaty, piss-sweet skin, the rattle of their harness, the rhythm of their bodies.

And here he was on quite a different march.
But we know that mankind has a right to be free
Ça-ira, ah, ah, The rights of the people for me

Boy remembered the way from last time. Once they'd passed the church and big houses at Ardwick Green they would be nearly there, dipping down across the canal, until they reached the tightly packed streets of Manchester itself. Everyone was getting excited. Most of them hadn't heard Orator Hunt speak before. Boy knew they wouldn't be disappointed. This was a man who knew how to make his words dance straight into your heart. He could still remember some of Orator Hunt's words. Boy loved words. He loved words so much he didn't dare speak them.

He remembered too the large red flag on the platform with the words, *Hunt and Liberty* underneath a Cap of Liberty. He remembered too Hunt's last words to the meeting: '… when men are actuated by honest principles, no persecution can put them down. And if I desert the principles which I have hitherto professed,' he pointed to the blood-red flag, 'may that colour be my winding sheet.'

How could anyone ever forget those words? He, for one, never would.

~

They had passed the Infirmary now and were parading so all could see them down the narrow streets down towards Deansgate, at the back of St Peter's Fields. 'It's another Roman road,' Ashby whispered. 'That's why it's so straight.'

Then let honest Britons adhere to the plan

Boy beat his drum to the words and then the words found him and he found the words and he sang loud and clear:

Of reason and Truth, and the just rights of man;
Let us join heart and hand, to support that free nation,
That fights for the world and the world's reformation
Ça-ira, ah, ah, Truth justice and freedom for me.

~

Still on Deansgate. They turned left up yet another straight street and then sharp right in to St Peter's Fields.

Ça-ira, ah, ah, Truth justice and freedom for me.

Still bare of grass, no more a field in the summer than it had been in the winter. The new brick houses on the opposite side looked less raw in the sunshine, but the houses they had just squeezed past were as grim as Boy remembered them, with their deep cellars where, Ashby told him last January, 'Entire families are obliged to live in the one room below ground, the walls running with water.'

Boy felt lucky to be living on the high ridge of Heaviley, above the smoke stacks and within sight of the fields.The Stockport groups were early, in time to watch the men in charge of the meeting setting out a couple of carts to make a speakers' platform, propping their ladders against the sides. Their supporters began to gather around the wagons, positioning the many banners alongside them, 'ready to protect the perimeter,' Ashby said.

Bonnie was close by, still holding high her flag supporting the female reformers, her broad back and sturdy arms perfect for the task. How many times had Boy seen her show the visiting tourists how she'd carried Dermot from the battlefield on that back of hers.

Boy now noticed a group of stern-looking gentlemen making their way in to one of the tall houses overlooking the field. Just like crows, Boy thought.

'Reckon they'll be the magistrates,' Ashby said, 'come to see we behave ourselves.' Boy understood. He'd heard plenty of grumbles about the magistrates in Stockport and how they had the sheriff's men in their pockets and cared nothing for the plight of working men and women.

Everything was now in place and Boy could see that even the ever-calm Ashby was getting excited, and as the other groups were beginning to drift in and look for a place to hear what Orator Hunt had to say, Ashby urged them move closer to the carts.

'We mustn't go too near, as there will be others more important than us who require access to the platform. But, as we have arrived so early, it would be foolish not to go as close as we can.'

Boy felt the sun warm again on his back and looked at the dust rising gently as the crowds began to assemble and find a place to stand. He heard music and cheering and the faint sounds of songs to the beat of marching feet, which eased up as column after column poured into the square. Boy remembered Hunt's last words in January: *let this be my winding sheet*. He wished he could speak like that. He understood the power of words. He knew what words could do. And if this man could hold the whole of this crowd in the palm of his hand when he spoke to them, what else could words do?

Ashby and Bonnie signalled him to come closer and produced a kerchief of food. 'Let's have these now. Hunt'll be here any minute.' Bonnie passed him a barm cake. In the background they could hear Orator Hunt's supporters as they drifted in and took up their positions, but still no sign of the man himself. Everybody seemed to accept that he would be most likely to be late, that his way would have been blocked by well-wishers and he would have taken the longest route possible to show himself to those who weren't in the Fields. Though many of those might not be his supporters; Boy had heard women shouting and booing at Bonnie and her female reformers as they made their way down the cramped streets between Ardwick Green and the Infirmary.

At last cheers rang out as Hunt arrived in his carriage, which was also full of well-wishers, including a woman who

Boy decided must be a female reformer because of her white dress and because she was carrying a banner like Bonnie's, as proud as could be. She then climbed on to the platform alongside the men. Boy knew that Bonnie would have liked to have been as bold but she had often said to him, 'I have yet to learn how to speak in public.' What she most likely meant was remembering not to swear like a trooper every second word.

Gradually the crowds became denser as they shuffled themselves even tighter to allow the special constables with their heavy black truncheons to make a passageway between the platform and the house where the stern gentlemen had entered an hour or so before.

Orator Hunt, with his white hat and the well-cut clothes of a gentleman, looked much the same as he had in January but now glistened with sweat in the August heat. Like them all he was dressed in his best but not for the warmth of this August day. Boy waited, waited for the words to come, but instead he heard the sound of horses in the distance; at a trot, then a canter, then a gallop, pulling to a halt at the edge of the field.

Boy saw they were stopping in front of the house the stern gentlemen had entered. What could they want? Boy tensed his muscles. He felt something was wrong. Orator Hunt paused, raised his hat and urged the crowd to give three cheers time three for the noble cavalry. Boy took another look. They weren't regular cavalrymen. More like yeomanry. He knew about yeomanry. They were men who liked playing at war. The Cheshire Yeomanry had already declared war on the Stockport reformers. These men weren't from Cheshire, though. So what were they doing here?

Boy stayed silent, listening, listening in case something happened. He wasn't sure what but he didn't like the way the horses pawed the ground, snorted and tossed their heads. Suddenly the horses moved forward, fast, faster, and faster into the crowd. Ashby pressed back, Boy pressed back, Bonnie too. Now Ashby was lost somewhere behind the horses, the soldiers yelling, pulling down the speakers from the carts, dragging them away to the house where the stern gentlemen were. Then the yeomanry began to seize the flags, knocking down every colour from its place to claim it as booty. The dust rose higher; Boy couldn't see more than a few yards ahead; but he heard the horses whinnying and then closer, spinning and round and round in a frenzy, their bits half yanked out of their mouths, their hooves flying in people's faces. And now the yeomanry were upon them, raising their sabres, steel glinting in the sun. Everywhere upon them. Especially the women. Picking out the figures in white. Boy saw one coming for Bonnie. He was after her flag, he was after Bonnie, there was no escape, she'd be struck down. He lunged in front of her, to protect her, as if his own mother. Words. Have to be spoken. Words. Have to be spoken.

'Let him take the flag, Bonnie. Don't let them kill you. They're just words on cloth.'

He sees the soldier try to yank the flag out of Bonnie's grasp and raise his sword. This isn't battle. This is slaughter. This is rage.

Boy looked closer and recognised the man who'd been at that affray in Stockport, the man who'd threatened Bonnie with revenge. Boy cried out as he thrust himself between the soldier and Bonnie. It was Bonnie the soldier wanted to hurt. But he felt his back exploding with pain, blow after blow slicing at his arms, his head, his back as he tried to push Bonnie out of the way. They fell down together, Boy lying on top of Bonnie, waiting for the death blow. It didn't fall. The soldier tucked the banner under his arm and rode off leaving them sprawled in the dirt.

Boy was hurting everywhere. Bonnie was winded, but she heaved him up and screamed curses at the retreating soldier. Before they could think clearly about escape they heard another thundering … the horses of the hussars, their riders with red plumes in their hats like blood streaming in the air came down upon them, some with flat sabres, some with the edge, pressing them, driving them back through the passageways out of the field, but too narrow to allow escape. Boy could hardly breathe. Everywhere people on the ground, people falling through railings collapsing into the cellars, people screaming, crying, cursing, dying, dead.

~

Ashby found them, tugged them close to him, pulled them away from the crush. But hardly able to move. Ashby yelling at an officer of the hussars, his Waterloo medal glinting in the sun.

'For Heaven's sake, let us all go. We are trying to escape. We are not the enemy. We are not the French.'

Boy heard the officer shout and turn upon the yeomanry.

'Desist, will you. Can't you see they can go no faster? Let them be. Do not come any closer.' The officer tossed his red plume, pulled his pelisse across his arm and raised his sword to stop the men behind him.

He managed to hold the yeomanry back long enough to let Ashby, Boy and Bonnie leave the way they had come, in threads and tatters but alive. Boy knew what it was to be allowed to live. But the pain; the pain; he felt the slashed arm, which Bonnie had now wrapped in a petticoat.

Bonnie was picking him up and carrying him on her back just as she had Dermot. But even Bonnie could not carry Boy all the way home, all those miles.

Ashby was talking to her. 'We must find a cart. I don't care if we have to steal one. We have to get him away from here.'

Words. Words. Words have to be spoken. 'Thomas … Fetch Thomas.'

67

The News

19 August, Early Evening, 1819, London

Thomas had just finished his duties when Haywood came into the courtyard, a large newspaper folded under his arm. Thomas stopped to pay his compliments, but Haywood seemed distracted, not at all his usual cheerful self.

'Dreadful business in Manchester with that Hunt fellow.' He brandished the paper.

Thomas was puzzled. What on Earth could have happened to get Haywood so agitated about Hunt again? Then Thomas remembered Ashby's last letter. Hunt was in Manchester to address another of his *monster meetings*. Thomas tried to keep his voice steady.

'What business is that, sir?'

Haywood pointed to the columns of print. 'Even The Times thinks it's a sorry affair. It casts a shadow upon all our reputations. And to think the fine fellows of the 15th Hussars were involved.'

Thomas remembered Smithfield, how easily matters could have got out of hand under the wrong leadership, and immediately thought of Ashby, Bonnie – and Boy. He hardly dared speak.

'Something has happened, at one of Hunt's meetings?'

'It most certainly has. Scores of people killed and injured. It's not known how many. And quite unnecessarily, according to the report. I can scarcely believe it.'

'Did the crowd riot, sir?'

'It seems they did not, and according to this, Hunt did nothing to inflame the situation … indeed, the very opposite. But it appears that the gentlemen yeomanry took it upon themselves to play at soldiers. Chasing after flags.'

Thomas was desperate to know more and asked Haywood something he would never have asked ordinarily. 'Would you mind, sir, if I had a look?'

Haywood handed Thomas the paper. 'Keep it if you like. I have read quite enough. Quite enough.' He turned and made his way towards the officers' mess.

Thomas sat down and studied the tiny print.

The Yeomanry cavalry was seen advancing at a rapid trot to the area: their ranks were in disorder, and on arriving within it, they halted to breathe their horses, and recover their ranks …

Horsemen readying themselves to charge into a crowd? And yes, no mention of disorder or riot. He could hardly bring himself to read further.

Manchester Yeomanry cavalry rode into the mob, which gave way before them, and directed their course to the cart from which Hunt was speaking. Not a brickbat was thrown at them – not a pistol was fired during this period … Hunt, after exhorting people to tranquillity in a few words, turned to the officer and said "I willingly surrender myself to any civil officer who will show me his warrant."… and Hunt and Johnson then leaped from off the waggon and surrendered themselves to the civil power.…

So they were trying to make an arrest of the speakers on the platform as had been done, without horsemen and quite peacefully, at Smithfield?

As soon as Hunt and Johnson had jumped from the waggon, a cry was made by the cavalry, "Have at their flags." In consequence, they immediately dashed not only at the flags which were in the waggon, but those which were posted among the crowd, cutting most indiscriminately to the right and to the left in order to get at them. This set the people running in all directions, and it was not till this act had been committed that any brickbats were hurled at the military. From that moment, the Manchester Yeomanry cavalry lost all command of temper.

Thomas could hardly believe what he was reading. But he could see the scene depicted by the newspaper reporter only too well. He remembered too, how Ashby had said that the local yeomanry seemed driven to seize the reformers' banners as though they were regimental colours, as if the Stockport Fray were the battle of Waterloo.

A man within five yards of us in another direction had his nose completely taken off by a blow of a sabre; while another was laid prostrate, but whether he was dead or had merely thrown himself down to obtain protection we cannot say... Just as we came to the house, the constables were conducting Hunt into it, and were treating him in a manner in which they were neither justified by law nor humanity, striking him with their staves on the head.

'Cowper ... Cowper.' He heard Freer shout. 'Have you seen the posters put up by the *Political Register*? Horrid Massacres at Manchester. For God's sake, Cowper, what the hell's happening?'

~

21 August 1819, The White Lion, London

Freer sat down and signalled Thomas to join him. Thomas placed their tankards down on the table, taking care to avoid spilling them, as if this might restore order to their lives. Thomas had written to Ashby and was awaiting news, but Freer had just managed to get hold of a copy of *Sherwin's Political Register*, published that day.

Freer began leafing through the pages. 'Crowe's friend, Richard Carlile, was there. He was an eyewitness too.'

'Still no names of the dead and injured?'

'Carlile wouldn't know, would he? He was lucky to get away. Or else he'd be locked up with Hunt and the rest of them.'

'It's just … I've had no letter from Ashby.'

'It's early days yet.'

'But does Carlile support *The Times's* account?'

'It rather looks like it.' Freer skimmed over the opening page. 'So are you wanting to check its account against his?'

'Not really.'

Freer grunted. ' But seeing as no-one likes to admit a man with Carlile's reputation might be right, you thought you should?'

'I just want to be clear about what happened.'

'Like everybody agrees on Waterloo.'

'We can but try to find the truth of it.' Thomas folded *The Times* to the right page, wishing none of it were true … that it was another one of his bad dreams; that he'd wake up and could go back to being a loyal servant of the Crown instead of this growing certainty that this had been a deliberate attack upon men, women and children. Suddenly he was back at Badajoz, amidst the carnage of revenge. He forced himself to concentrate on the newspaper.

Freer waited for Thomas to find his page and then began reading aloud, darting about Carlile's account, trying to pick out the most important points.

'HORRID MASSACRE AT MANCHESTER

It is impossible to find words to express the horror which every man must feel at the proceedings of the agents of the Borough-mongers on Monday last, at Manchester...

Had the agents of the Borough-mongers suffered the meeting to proceed, there is no doubt but it would have terminated peaceably: the people shewed no disposition to fight, ...'

Freer stopped. 'The rest of the article is an open letter to Sidmouth, though not, thank God, inviting him to a duel.'

Thomas tried but failed to smile. These were desperate times and bred desperate men. He was beginning to sympathise with Thistlewood's challenging Sidmouth to his preposterous duel; his frustration, his determination to make someone pay, somehow.

Freer began again.

'A LETTER TO LORD SIDMOUTH,

Secretary of State for the Home Department,

On the conduct of the magisterial and Yeomanry assassins of Manchester, on 16th August 1819

London, August 18th, 1819

MY LORD,

As a spectator of the horrid proceedings of Monday last at Manchester, I feel it is my duty to give the public a narrative of those proceedings, through the medium of a letter addressed to you, who ought to be the conservator of the public peace. My motives for doing this are two-fold; the first is to call on you, as Secretary of State for the Home Department, to cause the magistrates of Manchester and Yeomanry Cavalry acting under their direction, to be brought to the bar of public justice, for the unprovoked slaughter of the peaceable and distressed inhabitants of that place and neighbourhood, whilst legally exercising their rights...'

Thomas interrupted. 'That's what Ashby said, that they'd taken legal advice and they were entirely in their rights to hold the meeting, as long as they changed the original wording as to its purpose.'

Freer took a sip of ale. 'Exactly.'

'And secondly, in case of the default of the existing government to give satisfaction, to the full extent of their means and power, to the mangled and suffering, and the friends of the MURDERED INHABITANTS of Manchester; the people, not only of Manchester, but of the whole country are in duty bound and by the laws of nature imperatively called upon to provide themselves with arms and hold their public meetings with arms in their hands, to defend themselves against the attacks of similar assassins acting in the true Castlereaghan character....'

Freer stopped. 'A point well made, but I don't imagine anyone is intending to bring the magistrates or the Yeomanry to account, do you?'

Thomas was more worried about the casualties. 'And they're still saying there could be more than a dozen dead and hundreds injured?'

Freer nodded. 'Nothing would surprise me with a group of untrained cavalry clods let loose.' He picked up the paper again.

'I shall now proceed to give your Lordship a narrative of the proceedings at the meeting...

About 11 o'clock the People began to assemble around the house of Mr Johnson, at Smedley Cottage, where Mr Hunter had taken up his residence; about 12, Mr Hunt, and his friends entered the barouche: they had not proceeded far when they were met by the Committee of the Female Reform Society, one of whom, an interesting looking woman, bore a standard on which was painted a female holding in her hand a flag surmounted with the cap of liberty, whilst she trod underfoot an emblem of Corruption, on which was inscribed that word....

The remainder of the committee followed the carriage in procession and mounted the hustings when they reached them....

On leaving Smedley Cottage, bodies of men were seen at a distance, marching in regular and military order, with music and colours. Different flags were fallen in with on the road with various mottoes ... The scene of cheering was never before equalled. Females from the age of twelve to eighty were seen cheering with their caps in their hand, and their hair in consequence dishevelled ...'

Thomas almost smiled. 'You can just imagine Bonnie, can't you?'

'I certainly can, shouting to the rooftops, bonnet off and all.'

'Information was brought to Mr Hunt that St Peter's field was already filled, and that no less than 300,000 People were assembled in and about the intended spot of meeting ...'

Thomas thought back to July. ' That's a huge number. More than Smithfield, I reckon.'

Freer put the paper down and closed his eyes as if trying to imagine that number. 'Sounds like it to me too.'

'The procession arrived at ... about one o'clock ... Mr Hunt began his discourse by thanking them for the favour conferred on him .... when a cart, which evidently took its direction from that part of the field where the Police and Magistrates were assembled in a house, was moved through the middle of the field to the great annoyance and danger of the assembled people, who quietly endeavoured to make way for its procedure.

The cart had no sooner made its way through, when the Yeomanry cavalry made their appearance from the same quarter as the cart had gone out. They galloped furiously around the field, going over every person who could not get out of their way, to the spot where the Police were fixed, and after a moment's pause, they received the cheers of the Police as a signal for attack.

The meeting at the entrance of the cavalry, and from the commencement of business was one of the most calm and orderly that I ever witnessed....

The Yeomanry cavalry made their charge with the most infuriate frenzy; – they cut down men, women, and children, indiscriminately, and appeared to have commenced a premeditated attack with the most insatiable thirst for blood and destruction .... One woman, who was near the spot where I stood and who held an infant in her arms, was sabred over the head, and her tender offspring DRENCHED IN ITS MOTHER'S BLOOD....

The brutality of the Police equalled in ferociousness the massacre of the Yeomanry cavalry. A better character has been given of the Regular Troops for their endeavours to disperse the people without wounding or otherwise injuring them. The women appear to have been the particular objects of the fury of the Cavalry Assassins ...'

'Freer, Bonnie's all right, do you think?' Thomas broke in.

Freer patted his arm. 'Bonnie's as tough as they come.'

'No one is that tough if you're being hounded by soldiers with sabres, on horses trained for war.'

'But like they say, no news is most likely good news. Shall I go on?'

Thomas sighed and nodded.

'It will be in vain, my Lord, to attempt to palliate this circumstance by exaggerated statements and falsehoods; the many thousand witnesses ... will proclaim it as it happened. Those who have hitherto opposed the demand for Reform, are now heard to condemn this act ...The present is an important crisis for England. A reform, or despotism, must immediately follow...'

Freer stopped reading for a moment. 'Perhaps some good will come of it, after all, if enough right-thinking people are angered by what has happened.'

Thomas wasn't so sure. 'But, if it cannot be settled in peace, we may end up with more bloodshed?'

Freer picked up the paper again. 'Then we have to hope that reason will prevail rather than violence.'

'After these Yeomanry cavalry (which belonged to Cheshire and Manchester) ...'

'The Cheshire Yeomanry were there too. The ones Ashby's always complaining about.'

Freer nodded. 'So it would seem. Do you want to hear more?'

'... After these Yeomanry cavalry (which belonged to Cheshire and Manchester) had performed this grand achievement of attacking by surprize an unarmed assemblage of People, and dispersing them, they were not content, but persisted in riding after, and cutting down, those who were flying from them ...'

Freer shook his head. 'What the hell were the magistrates thinking of, sending in the bloody yeomanry when they had trained soldiers to call on? Not that they needed to send in anyone at all. Just look at Smithfield.'

He resumed reading.

'In either case, my Lord, as an individual, living in a country where the laws will not protect the subject, I shall feel it my duty to make the best preparation for the defence of myself, family, and property, against the attack of a Magistrate, Police-Officer, or a troop of Yeomanry Cavalry, who begin to shew a contempt for those laws which they are commissioned to respect and enforce.

Your Lordship's Fellow Citizen,

R. CARLILE'

Thomas shuddered. 'Well, Carlile and *The Times* are agreed. Totally unprovoked.'

Freer threw the *Register* onto the table. 'One thing's certain, though. We're going to be confined to our barracks, going nowhere for the next few weeks. Till the government decides whether we're staring revolution in the face. Or not. Mind you, I wager that Richard Carlile will be staring Cold Bath Fields prison in the face, by the end of today, once they've read this.'

Both now sat in silence, broken minutes later by Booth walking in.

'Thought I'd find you here.' He waved a letter. 'Just been delivered.'

It was from Ashby. Thomas wasn't sure if he wanted to open it.

~

Ashby's letter was short and to the point.

German's Cottages, Heaviley, Stockport, August 17th 1819

I write in great haste with terrible news. They say even people in London will have now heard of what happened on St Peter's Field yesterday, when those of us at the great meeting to hear Orator Hunt were cut down in our hundreds. Bonnie escaped with nothing worse than bruises but Boy, whilst protecting Bonnie, was cut about by the yeomanry's sabres. At first we thought he had escaped serious injury, and he was able to ride home with us on a cart, all of us in deep sorrow but relieved to be alive. But during the night he began to develop a fever. I now fear his sickness may prove to be unstoppable.

So, I write on two accounts; one is to ask you to send immediately some of those medicinal herbs which have been so efficacious in the past. My second request may, however, prove to be more difficult. Boy has made it clear he wants to see you. And, much as I have tried to comfort him, and explain that you are two hundred miles away, and under the orders of the military, he has refused to accept this, crying and sobbing. Otherwise he is being very brave and appears resigned. Bonnie says, why don't you ask Captain Webster or Haywood for some leave of absence? They were always fond of Boy.

Thomas closed his eyes. He couldn't bear to read any more. Haywood had already announced that none of them could have any time away from their duties. They were expecting trouble.

So any request for absence was bound to be refused. It was not a risk he could take.

He handed over the letter to Freer to read. 'It's Boy. He's been badly hurt. '

Freer swore, 'So our bloody troops got him after all.'

Thomas leapt up. 'Not yet, they haven't. I'll get the rest of the mixture Griffin and I made up for Joanna.'

He turned to Booth. 'Where does the mail coach for the North go from?'

Booth leant back and thought. 'Now that depends on which bit of the North you're going to.'

Thomas pulled back.' Oh, I'm not going, I just want make sure a parcel gets tonight's mail.'

'Then don't wait for the soldiers' post, use the receiving house on the Strand.'

Thomas nodded at Booth, 'I'll do that,' and then turned to Freer. 'I'd better go home and make up my parcel.'

68

The Journey

21 August 1819, London to Manchester

Of course, he was bloody going. He strode out of the door with his sabretache, packed for the journey, leaving behind a letter and money for Joanna and a letter, with a request to make of Freer.

Booth's eyes followed him. Suppose Booth told someone that he hadn't come back after his supposed trip to the receiving house?

The receiving house advised The White Horse at Fetter Lane. A short walk away. But the mail would be going any minute. Thomas hurried straight under Temple Bar onto Fleet Street before turning off. He was right to rush. The horses were already being readied, the coach, standing by, dazzling red and black with gold lettering.

All he needed now was his ticket. Only one left, outside. He counted out his money and checked his sabretache, yet again, for the packets of herbs that had helped Joanna, but with which he was less familiar. Perhaps, as Ashby said, if they were near fields, it would be possible to find more. Given time. But he wasn't sure if he had time. Fevers like the one Ashby described might linger for days, but with no better outcome than those that came on quickly. He comforted himself. Boy was young and strong and… He didn't like to think further than that.

He climbed up next to the coachman, who was dressed, as if for winter, in his full-length coat. The guard was already climbing aboard his box, with his blunderbusses, pistols and timepiece. A respectably dressed man and woman placed themselves inside, whilst another couple of fellows climbed up behind him and the coachman on the double bench seat. They were young gentlemen, as far as he could tell, who were choosing to ride outside for the thrill of it, rather than through necessity.

Thomas tried to block out their laughing and joking but it was not to be. And they were soon off, the coachman shouting out to them to watch their heads under the archway. Thomas pulled his cape tightly over his shoulders and grasped the guardrail. The journey would take all night and he told himself he must rest, apply the skills he had learnt over so many years, to sleep in the saddle while his horse found his own way. But he got little rest that night. He dozed; he worried; he bounced; he rocked himself into a rhythm of expectation and exasperation. To begin with, he watched intently, fascinated by the skill of the coachman driving the four horses, the wheelers providing the strength, the leaders the direction and the coachman the knowledge as to when to apply the drag to hold the coach back going down the hills, and when to order his passengers to get out and walk up them. But it was a brief distraction. Thomas found himself suspended between hope and grief on a journey where he could neither look at the scenery nor focus on anything else, existing in this netherworld of not knowing whether Boy might still alive or dead. And so the mail rode into the night, with only the briefest, albeit regular stops, to change the horses.

By sunrise they were riding over open moors, the sun's rays illuminating hills cut out against the sky and stunted trees scattered among cottages of sturdy stone. Yet within these sweeping barren lands, they came upon the town of Buxton, where the owners of these empty landscapes must come to visit its elegant assembly rooms and take the waters. Another country entirely from the scattered valleys, studded with smoke-filled chimneys, which now announced the outlying hamlets outside Stockport.

Thomas had already asked if he might be dropped at Heaviley, which he understood to be at the junction on the main London Road, just before the coach had to slow up to turn down the hill. And so Thomas, cast off as speedily as a sack of mail, found his way to Ashby's cottage, took a deep breath and tapped on the door.

Bonnie opened it and almost knocked him over with a great hug. He had last seen her at Dermot's grave at Mont St Jean, before she had marched off with Boy to Brussels.

She swore several times over. ' If he dies I'll kill the bastards, all of them.' And then she wailed. 'It was me, they were after. If he hadn't thrown himself in front of me it …it should have been me. I've lived my life.'

Thomas touched Bonnie's arm. 'But that would have been the last thing he would have wanted. For you to die.'

'In front of him, an all, just like his mother?' Bonnie sobbed.

By now Ashby had rushed in, abandoning his loom and shook his hand. 'I thought you'd never be able to come.'

'How is he?'

'Not well. I'll show you up.'

Thomas emptied his packets on the table, asking Bonnie, 'If you could warm a large pan of water, I'll be back down as soon as I can.'

Thomas hurried past the workshop, and up into the attic where Boy lay.

Thomas sat down by his bed and held his hand.

'It's Thomas,' he said, 'Thomas.'

Boy stirred.

69

Absent Without Leave

22 August 1819, London

For once in his life, Will Freer felt lost for words. Haywood had asked him a direct question to which there were only two answers: a lie, which would be immediately discovered, or the truth, which would probably result in Cowper being court-martialled. If only he could throw in some mitigating circumstances, before Haywood was obliged to begin quoting regulations. Fortunately, Haywood was still talking.

'Might I see this letter, sir?'

Haywood looked puzzled but handed it over. 'How that's going to help, I don't know... Cowper is either absent without leave, or not.'

Freer recognised the hand immediately, using the same tricks to disguise itself, employed in the fraudulent accounts that had ensnared Webster in Hythe. But how the hell did Fallowfield even know about this business in the first place?

Freer handed it back. 'It might be useful if you showed this to Captain Webster as well, sir. I think he might recognise the malicious intent behind the letter which renders it both correct and incorrect, sir.'

'You've lost me there, Troop Serjeant-Major.'

Freer took a deep breath. 'Troop Serjeant-Major Cowper's absence is not only to perform of an errand of mercy, but also an attempt to mitigate some of the consequences of the dreadful business in Manchester this last week. Like ourselves, sir, he is most concerned to make sure this affair doesn't stoke the fires of rebellion and discontent either in Manchester or in London.'

'So is he or is he not available for duty in London?'

Freer was sweating now. How the hell had Cowper thought he might get away with claiming to be ill for more than a few days at a time? He imagined Cowper'd assumed Boy's condition would become clearer, one way or another, before then. Or maybe he really just didn't care.

'It's Boy, sir. He's been grievously injured by the local yeomanry. Cowper fears for the lad's life and for the wider consequences of yet another innocent life being lost. He took with him, sir, some of his herbs, and hopes they will save him.'

Freer took another deep breath. Lady Catherine had not so long ago given birth to Haywood's first son, but the child had been sickly for weeks until Cowper found some healing herbs his Grandmother used to employ, over Islington way.

'As you know, sir, Boy is much like a son to him.'

Haywood looked genuinely upset. 'But why didn't he say? '

'He didn't want to put you in a difficult position, sir.'

Haywood nodded. 'So, as the letter indicates, it is true he has gone to Manchester?'

'So I understand, sir.'

Haywood now looked perplexed. 'But you told me the note was incorrect.'

'In intent, sir. I recognised the writing of someone who I know wishes harm to Troop Serjeant-Major Cowper.'

'So, would you recommend I show this to Captain Webster?'

'He may be able to advise further, sir.'

Haywood tucked the letter away, indicating he had finished their conversation. 'I might well do that. Thank you, Troop Serjeant-Major.'

Freer paid his compliments and left. Would Haywood's obvious sympathy for Cowper's dilemma be enough to save him from being court-martialled?

70

'You tyrants of England'

22 Aug 1819, Heaviley. Stockport

Thomas is pressing his hand. He's come. Thomas will look after him. He'll find a way. But if he can't, then … as long as Thomas lives, he will be loved. By Joanna and Bonnie too. That is all he needs to know. That he is loved.

~

Thomas is raising him up now, trying to get him to drink one of his concoctions. He must drink it. He must try. He must try and live. If only he can live; doesn't want Thomas to leave him again.

He's drifting, floating. Now his mother is shouting for him. The priests say his mother will be waiting for him. He remembers her smell, her skirts he's hidden underneath. Bleeding though. She's bleeding. She is dying. He knows about dying.

Not yet. Not yet, though.

He's marching, banners flying. Bonnie, in her white dress. With the others. Four abreast, step by step.

He's drumming. Dermot Murphy wanted him to be a drummer.

He can hear the words breaking through. He can hear himself singing.

He's following the tune; he's singing the words. He's shouting the words from the rooftops.

You gentlemen and tradesmen that ride about at will,

Look down on these poor people. It's enough to make you crill.

Ashby's holding a banner. Got it into their heads that destroying our banners will stop us being heard. Stop us complaining we only exist to put money into their coffers.

Look down on these poor people, as you ride up and down

I think there is a God above will bring your pride quite down

We're marching, keeping time, keeping order, singing.

You tyrants of England. Your race will soon be run.

You may be brought to account for what you have sorely done.

Thousands of us, thousands come for miles to hear Orator Hunt. Dressed in our best.

You tyrants of England. Your race will soon be run.

You may be brought to account for what you have sorely done.

Cheering ... three times three cheering ... Screaming. Horses. Trampling. Horses everywhere. Yeomanry. Sabres. Slashing. At Bonnie, at me. At me.

~

My mother hiding me; she's hiding me from the soldiers. Yelling angry mouths, twisted horrible faces. My mother's hiding me, hiding me from the British soldier pulling her to the ground. But now I see his face. With those grey eyes. Staring ... Shooting the drummer boy ... Chasing me into the school. Words. Have to be spoken ... Words ... Have to tell Thomas ... I love you ...

71

'Your race will soon be run'

25 April 1819, Heaviley, Stockport

He was losing him. The comfrey poultices on Boy's wounds didn't seem to be working, and Boy was scarcely conscious enough to drink the infusions.

Thomas took his hand and squeezed it. Boy squeezed it back.

'I'm still here.'

He stroked his head. 'I love you. Joanna too. We love you. Always.'

And so they remained hand in hand till the darkness finally fell.

~

Thomas couldn't bear to let him go. But Bonnie, though in tears, was as practical as ever. 'It's too hot. We'll have to lay him out now. Ashby will have to go and see the Parson, to get him buried.'

Thomas emptied out the rest of his savings from his boot and laid them on the table. Boy deserved better than a pauper's grave.

And so they laid him out together, Bonnie, at first, refusing his help. It's women's work, she'd insisted; until she saw he could be as tender as any woman in these, his last offices, for Boy.

~

Thomas could see that Ashby was astonished. So many men had come to carry Boy's coffin down to the church or join the funeral procession. But Ashby dabbed at his eye and spoke firmly and clearly.

'Remember how we marched that day, side by side, with Boy playing his drum? And so,' Ashby faltered, ' we shall march side by side again to take him on his last journey.'

They took it in turns to carry Boy's coffin on their shoulders, one man at each corner though Thomas insisted he could manage the mile and a half or so to the town. And so they trudged slowly down Hillgate towards the parish church, then pausing under the grand stone arch into the churchyard whilst the funeral knell tolled. And Boy was finally laid to rest in the cold earth by a hesitant curate who seemed just as disturbed by the lack of any record of baptism as by the circumstances of Boy's death.

Thomas knew he had to stay strong, not even shed a tear. He was in his soldier's uniform. He couldn't let people see that soldiers cried too, though some of the men were weeping. But as he walked slowly away to take the mail back to London he knew he'd left for ever a part of himself in that graveyard overlooking the distant hills.

It was only after Boy's funeral that he dared to open the letter from Freer. *'You're a fool, Cowper, but thank God for Haywood and Webster too, who've granted you leave of absence until September 1st. They decided that they could treat you as if you were an officer, who has merely overstayed his furlough. Don't ask me why this makes any difference, but apparently it does, so, whatever happens, get your arse back here for then.*

PS Joanna tells Louise she is pregnant but hadn't wanted to say anything to you until she was quite sure. The baby is due sometime in December. She said I might as well tell you in my letter, so you'll have both pieces of good news at once. We have, of course, all been worried about the possible consequences of the letter that was sent to Haywood. We are, also, all still hoping to hear better news of Boy.

Will

~

Thomas returned from Stockport a broken man. It was the only way he could describe how he felt. And now he had to tell Joanna, who he knew loved Boy almost as much, maybe as much, as he did. He hadn't dared send any news, so his return that morning wasn't expected. He dashed past Booth colouring his prints and rushed upstairs. Joanna must have heard him coming and came to their door. She smiled in welcome and then looked into his eyes, and turned pale.

'He's dead, isn't he?' she said.

'I tried everything but … it was no use.'

'Oh, Thomas.'

Thomas pulled her into his arms.

'If we have a son I shall call him Boy,' said Joanna through her tears.

Thomas tried to smile. 'Plenty of time to think about that, but, yes, I'm sure you're right. We have to commemorate him in some way, don't we?'

'And he'll always be in our hearts.' With that Joanna clung to him, sobbing.

Thomas had never been more glad to have her in his arms.

72

The Golden Cross

1 September 1819, London

Jack Fallowfield hurried up Whitehall. Yes, The Golden Cross was as good as anywhere to meet. Four storeys high, four bays wide, opposite the statue of Charles I, and hard to miss from the street, its large sign visible from way off even in a winter fog.

Even more importantly, one customer among the many passing through its rooms would scarcely be noticed. And a back entrance which made it difficult to keep track of the comings and goings, and so busy inside even a cavalry serjeant sitting in a dark corner would attract no attention.

Rooms full of travellers waiting to depart, taking their refreshments, checking the times of their coaches, impatient to get on their way, and the serving maids too busy to flirt or pass the time of day, too busy to bother with niceties, too busy to notice that a soldier was receiving a fair number of visitors, paying for their drinks, then passing them money. Yes, the place was ideal.

Besides, Jack liked The Golden Cross. Or rather, it suited his purpose. But still he had to admit he liked the tavern's to-ing and fro-ing. These days he missed the constant moving around, from barracks to barracks, from town to town and country to country. He preferred to gather no moss. He

366

missed that sense of expectation, that readiness to uproot. Yes, he missed that, though the only place he wouldn't want to go to was Ireland. Never again, please God. But for the moment he was content to stay in London doing his duty. Serving His Majesty. And London could be as dark and dangerous as any forest.

Jack passed through the entrance and chose his corner. He had come for information. He felt at home. And he waited.

~

So the brat is dead. His informant had been quite definite. Absolutely no doubt. Cowper went to the funeral up Manchester way, though how he managed that when every man has to be accounted for... Still, he always was the favourite. But thanks to God's justice one of his enemies has been dealt with. There's only Cowper left now.

He leant back, smiling to himself. This business of Peterloo has set everyone's nerves jangling. It would be a good time to lead an unwary man astray.

73

Hunt's Procession

September 1819, The White Lion, London

Thomas shook his head. He wasn't in the mood for all this. No one here was blaming Hunt, not even Thomas, but it was hard not to feel that, if only Hunt hadn't agreed to speak, if only Hunt hadn't been such a target for the authorities, and if only Hunt hadn't drawn such large crowds, Boy would still be alive.

But Thomas knew it was important to keep the memory of Peterloo, as everyone now called it, alive and kicking. To keep prodding away at the authorities, who had still not brought anyone to justice.

'You can't prosecute soldiers for doing their duty,' some newspapers grumbled.

'But you can prosecute those whose actions are so provocative and extreme they cause the death of innocent people,' argued others. Instead of which, Hunt and his fellow speakers had been the ones arrested, bailed now, but under threat of imprisonment, at the very least. Much as Thomas wished that the meeting had never taken place, he could see no justice in that.

Freer was furious. ' It's what we've come to expect, after all.' He rattled off his disappointments: no Parliamentary enquiry, no examination, never mind prosecution, regarding the legality of the magistrates' actions … publicly thanked by the Regent himself for the preservation of the peace. But the speakers are to be charged with treason …

Booth interrupted, 'Lesser charges, now, we think. Learnt their lesson after Spa Fields, I reckon.'

So Thomas agreed Hunt must be honoured, his very existence celebrated as a thorn in the flesh of all those who abused their authority. Like the Manchester magistrates.

But agreeing how this might be done caused yet more arguments to erupt between the various supporters. So Dr Watson and Griffin had set themselves up with others at The White Lion to form a special committee, whilst Owens and Evans and his supporters convened at The Crown and Anchor.

Owens proposed that Hunt's procession into London should end at The Crown and Anchor, where a substantial dinner could be provided for him and his many supporters. Owens and his friend Evans liked their food and were comfortable enough to afford to sell tickets at seven and sixpence. But what about those who can't afford such a fine meal, queried The White Lion organising committee. So the matter went back and forth between the two committees until a compromise was finally found.

The following day Thomas and Freer entered to find Apothecary Griffin undeterred and sitting in his usual corner, making lists.

Booth whispered, pointing to the many sheets of paper piling up on his table, 'Just have a look at Griffin's lists, will you?'

Thomas walked across to Griffin and sat down beside him. Griffin smiled, a rare thing. 'Your committee has taken on a considerable task,' Thomas said.

'Oh yes.' Griffin waved a sheet of paper at him. 'Fortunately the committee members do have some experience of organising such events, though they are not usually on this scale. Watson and I have just been drawing up the orders of the day. Look.' He showed Thomas the order of the procession, its route, the favours and slogans to be displayed, as well as banners and bands.

It seemed to be just as complicated as any ceremonial review organised by one of Wellington's staff officers. The orders of the day occupied a whole column.

~

The day of Hunt's entry into London. Dawn had broken by the time Thomas had readied his troops and ridden back with them to their appointed places along the route. There were already crowds of people streaming up towards the open fields of Islington, on their way to join the procession. Others were struggling to get themselves a good place at the front of the crowd.

Soon Thomas heard that there were thousands lining the streets all the way from The Angel to The Crown and Anchor. And so Thomas and his troop waited outside The Crown and Anchor. At first there were men walking slowly, bearing huge branches of trees, mostly oak; then the men waving sticks stuck on pitchforks, and others carrying white flags with red ribbons, green ribbons, white ribbons and with laurel in their hat bands. There was a green silk flag emblazoned with gold letters, bands and horses. Then a white flag bordered with crêpe, commemorating the victims of Peterloo. Then a faded red flag, supporting universal suffrage, and then more bands, more horses, and even a dog with a favour in its collar, demanding no dog tax. It was as if a travelling fair was coming to town and Orator

Hunt was the prize fighter. Hunt himself was sitting in a barouche with Watson and Thistlewood, and some others Thomas didn't recognise, but Thomas still wondered why a gentleman would risk all for this brief moment of glory, when the fight was still to be won.

They had only a moment or two of concern, when good humour got lost in the press of the crowd as people jostled to see their hero. Then, as the soldiers kept the pathway open and let the carriage stop to turn into the main Arundel Street entrance of The Crown and Anchor, Thomas found himself craning forward to catch another glimpse of the man, but saw Boy sitting there instead, waving at him, shouting, telling him over and over again, he had to stop them killing the women and children. He told himself Boy wasn't there, that he couldn't be telling him these things, but he could scarcely concentrate on his orders to maintain a proper space between the carriage and the entrance to the tavern. At last he managed to pull himself together and saw that his men, at least, had followed their orders. But Thomas wasn't sure he could follow his any more.

74

The Cock

November 1819, The Cock, Litchfield Street/
Grafton Street, London

Thomas could just make out, through the thick fog of smoke, the slightly shabby fellow with the scrawny fringe who had accompanied Thistlewood to the committee meeting at The White Lion. He nodded and walked over to Thomas. 'We are greatly in need of soldiers like you, my friend; men who have known the hardships of battle and who are now prepared to fight yet again, not only for their own lives, but for their children's and grandchildren's futures; men who can teach us how to drill, and how to defend ourselves and our families, even if to the death.'

Thomas said nothing. His head was already spinning. He wasn't sure whether it was the effect of the porter or the stirring songs and music, but his blood was already thumping through his veins.

But, of course, he knew exactly why. Much as he had tried to calm himself, he was still angry. All the time. About what had happened to Boy and the others ... Just so the yeomanry could boast they had captured the 'enemy's' colours.

He wanted to be a man of peace. But maybe he wasn't born to be one. He remembered his father's tirades and frustrations; his mother's fury; his own anger, when he pushed his mother into Michael's open grave. Thomas had never wanted to feel that angry again. But he only had to think of what had happened to Boy and all the others and he found himself catching his breath, trying to control his breathing. The shabby gentleman was clearly waiting for an answer. But he wasn't ready to give one just yet. He gazed around the room: ardent reformers all, but disciplined would-be soldiers, or defenders of their families, he very much doubted. And, turning back to the shabby gentleman, he could have sworn he saw Fallowfield in the shadows, on the turning of the stair, going upstairs. He looked again. Nobody there.

'I fear you have the wrong soldier, my friend.'

'In case you change your mind, you will find me here, most evenings.'

He gave Thomas a handbill giving notice of a forthcoming meeting at Hopkins Street Chapel. 'You may nevertheless find this of some interest.'

Thomas nodded and took the handbill, but left as rapidly as he could through Long Acre Lane, before cutting across the Garden to home. Joanna might even have waited up to see him, Annie lying on her shoulder sleeping.

~

Tickets cost one shilling and admitted the bearer to the twice weekly evening debates and lectures, with one on Sunday afternoons, for a period of one month. Thomas took out his shilling and followed the crowd slowly making their way up a ladder to the next floor.

It was an old hayloft, in such a poor state that Thomas would have forbidden his men to store any forage in it. But it was a vast, cavernous space and could hold, he estimated, several troops of soldiers within its walls, perhaps three hundred or even more.

There were no seats, and with just a simple desk for the lecturer, it couldn't have been plainer, but Thomas felt the great anticipation and excitement ripple through the audience as Robert Wedderburn, a giant of a man, came up the ladder, followed by Alexander Wilde, and readied himself to speak.

Wedderburn roared, declared himself to be a self-taught West Indian, son of a Scottish plantation owner and an enslaved mother, revelling in how he'd been cast out by his wealthy family, then forced to make his living as a sailor, then as a criminal and pauper. But now he knew 'like Spence, the earth is given to the children of men, making no difference for colour or character, just or unjust.'

He now pretended to be drunk. 'Times were bad then and Christ became a Radical Reformer... but this much I know ... he was born of very poor parents ... who like us felt with him the same as we now feel, and he says I'll turn Mr Hunt ... and then he had that exalted ride upon the Jackass to Jerusalem the people run before him crying out HUNT FOREVER for that was the same as crying out Hosanna to the son of David.'

He now took up the posture of a prize fighter for 'Christ's jubilee will be upon us ... then shall the worthless kings who thirst for human blood to support their tottering thrones turn their swords and spears into ploughshares and pruning hooks, then will it be said, and not before, as the apple tree among the trees of the wood, so is my beloved sovereign amongst the sons. I sat down under its shadow and its fruit was pleasant to my taste. The Jubilee will soon be upon us.'

Now Wedderburn turned his attention to the Bible itself. 'When I go to sleep at night, I am visited by visions, voices telling me to beware of false prophets, so I have to ask this question of myself and all of you in this room.'

Visions, as Thomas knew only too well, had to be listened to.

Wedderburn continued, 'So is the Bible really the word of God? For surely God is a Moloch, and Joshua is a liar and a fool for commanding the sun to stand still, and is not the author of the Bible a murderer because he had John the Baptist's head struck off to gratify the desire of a whore? After all even God's representatives on earth are hardly on the side of the Angels?'

He then regaled his audience with ribald jokes about the local clergymen, none of whom Thomas had heard of, but who were clearly well known to his listeners, who laughed appreciatively at each and every one so named, till, apparently exhausted, Wedderburn perched on the edge of the desk, to pause and look round the room, into the eyes of as many people as he could.

'So remember my friends, we should think none greater than ourselves.'

The audience of more than two hundred or so cheered, and resolutely put their hats back on, to demonstrate their defiance to a world which they knew considered them to be worthless.

Thomas felt his anger growing formlessly over the last few months slowly take shape and distil itself into a determination to put his grief and his disgust with the Government to good use.

He clattered down the ladder into a foggy autumn night and made his way through the darkness back to The Cock.

75

The Six Acts

December 1819, The White Lion, London

'So they're all bloody passed, now. All six of them.'

Freer, who had taken it upon himself to keep The White Lion's tap-room informed of every possible twist and turn in the Government's policies, was practically shaking as he stood up to discuss the implications of the Six Acts for the reformers.

'From now onwards, even discussing radical reform could be, in our revered Home Secretary's words, 'an overt act of treasonable conspiracy against the King and his Government.'

Wilde suddenly thumped the table. 'I suppose they think the present arrangements are so satisfactory who could possibly want to change them?'

Griffin agreed. 'If they would only allow us the opportunity, we could bring about reforms that support decent laws and good order. That is in our interest just as much as it is in theirs.'

Thomas looked up, surprised. There had been a decisive falling-out with Hunt among many of the tap-room regulars, including Wilde, Griffin and Dr Watson over his strategy of following only constitutional channels.

Freer continued. 'Hence, we are forbidden to train in the use of weapons…'

'As if that's going to stop those of us that can see no alternative but to defend ourselves,' Wilde grumbled again.

'And any of our houses can now be searched for weapons which can be seized. Well, that could get someone like Owens into trouble straight away with his tools, knives and hammers.'

'Probably thinking of them pike heads for sale in Finsbury market last month.'

'Ah, you couldn't have killed anyone with those damn things.'

'But they say there's more where they came from.'

Thomas hadn't heard any further from the shabby gentleman at The Cock. Maybe Thomas hadn't sounded quite enthusiastic enough, or maybe this new act really had deterred them.

Freer, consulting his piece of paper, ploughed on. 'And we'll never be able to hold another meeting like Smithfield again. The only public meetings allowed from now can only be held at parish level, with all sorts of other restrictions thrown in for good measure.'

Griffin shook his head. ' Parish meeting numbers are hardly going to persuade anyone we're serious.'

'Exactly. Now, blasphemous and seditious libels … however you might define them, will attract harsher penalties. Anyone fancy fourteen years transportation?'

Owens looked indignant. 'And I reckon with all these clerical magistrates around, you're going to be hard pushed to avoid falling out with them, one way or another.'

Wilde smacked his lips with derision. 'I've heard, and, all that the magistrate, the Reverend Hay, late of Peterloo, is about to be awarded one of the richest livings in the country.'

Thomas heard the intake of breath as they all digested this.

Freer consulted his paper again. 'They say trials, too, will be brought to court faster, but whether that is a bad or a good thing, I don't know.'

Griffin looked up from his figures. 'It'll certainly give us less time to organise a subscription to pay for the defence.'

'And gather witnesses.' Thomas spoke up. ' Like they're having to do now for Hunt's trial.'

Freer sighed, but moved on. 'But, crucially, the last act in particularly is why we are gathered today. If it wasn't for Carlile and the like, no one would know what was going on in this country, which is precisely why they want to add fourpence tax to the papers to stop us reading them.'

'What, on everything?' Owens exclaimed.

'On anything printed at least once a month and costing less than sixpence.'

Booth interrupted, 'But if all publications were put up to at least sevenpence that would avoid the tax …'

Griffin sighed.'If the customary price of a publication is twopence, then a rise to sixpence with the tax, or sevenpence without the tax is still not affordable for a ordinary worker.'

Freer laughed. 'Well, at least the Government wouldn't get the money.'

Crowe smiled. 'And The Republican's still outselling The Times. Mind you, it's Jane Carlile who's keeping everything going. Still, there can't be many men who'd have kept on writing after being fined £1500, losing all their stock, and then sent to prison for three years.'

Freer was still indignant. ' This tax is nothing but a gag on free speech.'

Owens butted in. 'And I'm telling you these blasphemous libel and sedition charges are only going to get more common, the way things are going on.'

But what was to be done? Thomas wished he knew.

76

St Clement Danes

December 1819

With its spiralling tower and steeple and vast, galleried interior, intricate plasterwork and mighty pulpit, it didn't seem like a church meant for the likes of them.

Thomas was used to leading his men on their church parades to St Martin in the Fields, just as vast an edifice but a good deal less fancy than this place. He smiled. He realised that after all he did know one of those clerics who'd been ridiculed by Wedderburn. The vicar at St Martin's had been scorned for his loyalist address throwing in his lot with the magistrates in their fight against sedition.

Thomas looked at the vast windows, scarcely illuminated by the feeble light in this bitterest of winters, bent his head and closed his eyes. He could, at least, give thanks for Joanna's safe delivery of another healthy daughter, Eleanor. Joanna hadn't liked the name at first, but Thomas had convinced her. 'It's the name of a queen who was much loved by her husband. She died in the village my father came from, near where my mother and grandmother used to live.'

'I expect she'll get called Ellie, though,' Joanna whispered, carrying her forward to the font to be welcomed into God's Kingdom, in a church that still didn't seem meant for the likes of them.

As the vicar splashed his daughter with holy water, Thomas wished her instead a more secure future in this earthly Kingdom.

~

Joanna clutched Eleanor to her. Even now she half-wished the baby had been a boy, so she could have honoured Boy. But maybe that was foolishness. Best that Eleanor shouldn't have to live in Boy's shadow. Look at Annie. All blonde curls and determination, she was already a little person. Eleanor. Thomas had chosen the name. He'd said it was about love, the love of a king for his wife. She was glad her child had been given such a name. Thomas had been so troubled since Boy had died. Even Ellie's birth had hardly stirred him from his low spirits. Though recently he'd begun to take more interest in what was going on around them, even getting angry sometimes. Not that he was like that. That wasn't her Thomas. He'd said when they'd first married that soldiers should never get angry. Will said it was a good sign that he'd stopped moping about, that he was drilling his troops hard, and when he came with them to The White Lion he joined in the conversations instead of standing back. So Will reckoned he was recovering. 'We are all recovering from the shock of Boy's death. But that doesn't make us any less angry, and it's right that we should be angry,' he told Louise and Joanna.

Joanna looked round the grand church and remembered what Louise had told her. Bonnie had said that the boy would probably have been baptised a Catholic so maybe he should have been buried a Catholic. But Bonnie had also asked Ashby to write asking them to light a candle for him. If there are any candles to light, he'd written, light one for him. Joanna noticed there were some small candles near the altar. Yes, she promised herself. She would come back and light a candle for Boy.

77

A New King

Midnight, 29 January 1820, London

Joanna was woken by a great booming sound. She jumped out of bed. Thomas was already up. It was midnight. What could be happening? Thomas was out on the landing. She could hear Will's and Louise's voices too, and Mrs Booth's on the landing below. It seemed the whole house was awake. Mrs Booth shouted, 'It's Great Tom at St Paul's. Somebody has died.'

'Well, it's not the sound of war or the sound of joy, is it?' Booth said.

'Most likely the the old King,' Will said.

So the bell tolled on with a pause after every sounding.

'Three time three. It's a man,' Mary Booth declared. 'It must be the King.'

All downstairs by now, Thomas and Will looked at each other. Mrs Booth sat down heavily on the nearest chair.

'So now we'll be cursed with the Regent turned King,' she exclaimed. 'To be sure, he'll change neither his manners nor his mistresses. What does that say about us, that we tolerate such a man? That fat wastrel treats women as worthless trifles, to be cast off at his whim. To the devil with him.' And with that, Mrs Booth rose from the chair and made her way back upstairs.

~

The King's death was confirmed and the Regent declared King two days later, 'to avoid the anniversary of Charles I's execution, I expect,' said Mrs Booth, who had no liking for the monarchy, as she had made clear many times. And now Joanna, Louise and Mrs Booth were sewing together under the great window in her room. Joanna, though still no lover of sewing, enjoyed these times together with the two women. Mrs Booth was a born storyteller and a woman of strong views, who never hesitated to voice them. She and Louise sometimes had differences of opinion but they were always amicable and well argued, and often ended in laughter. But, on the subject of the new King, Mrs Booth spoke with some anger.

'We Londoners had hopes for Princess Charlotte, and when she and her child died it was a blow to those of us who'd been looking forward to some decency returning to the conduct of affairs. Of course, all the fat prince's brothers immediately abandoned their mistresses and acquired wives in the hope of fathering legitimate children. So what became of all the illegitimate children and discarded women? They'd have to fend for themselves. All right, they'd have more money that you and I could dream of. But too many of us know what it's like to be rejected in this way. Fallen women they called us. And all because of those, those …'

'Fallen men, you mean,' said Joanna, teasing.

'Exactly. And as for our dear prince, he abandoned his own wife years ago. You'll have heard of Princess Caroline, of course. Not to his taste he said. Fathering a daughter was as much as he could manage, and after that the princess was obliged to travel abroad, after the war, whilst he went back to his mistresses. That's his idea of duty. For sure, the women won't come out well from this.'

She put her sewing aside. 'I wonder what he'll do with Princess Caroline? After all, she's the man's lawful wife, but will she ever become Queen? I don't expect the Prince Regent, sorry, His Majesty King George IV, is going to be keen, but you know how appearances have to be kept up'.

~

'But what's going to change for us?' Thomas said. Freer looked gloomy. 'I dunno, but could it get much worse? Remember him reviewing us at Hounslow on our return from France? It was not a pretty sight.'

But as Haywood and all their other officers reminded them, when the arguments between the supporters of new king and those of his exiled wife became a matter of public debate, 'The troops' loyalty to their commander in chief must be without question.'

But everyone seemed unsettled, even the troops, now that the old King was dead. All seemed worried that any loyalties to the old King would not be enough to protect the new one.

78

The Call

23 February 1820, London

The call came sooner than he expected. Booth put his head round the door of The White Lion and signalled to Thomas. 'Urgent letter for you.'

Thomas prised open the seal. *7 o'clock tonight, confirmed at the Cato Street hayloft. Be there.*

Thank God, he's not on patrol duty tonight. So where the hell's Cato Street? Somewhere in Soho, like Hopkins Street? Better not ask Booth. Maybe check with the fellow at The Cock.

Booth tilted his head. 'Everything all right, Cowper?'

'Yes, fine, thank you, Booth. Just tell Joanna, will you, I've had to go out.'

Not much time. It was already five o'clock. He turned and headed straight out, up Drury Lane, and into Covent Garden, sidestepping the crowds still gathered under the arcades, before cutting across towards Seven Dials. Cato Street must be the new hayloft they've been renting since Hopkins Street had to close. Though Thistlewood said it belonged to one of his friends and would be left at their disposal, even if Wedderburn was still in gaol. He hesitated. Should he or shouldn't he turn into Litchfield Street and call in at The Cock, check if Thistlewood's friend might be there? Get proper directions.

Thomas sighed. To have left instructions as vague as this seemed careless, if not downright foolish. He began to sweat, in spite of the cold, which, though easing up, was still bone-chilling, and there was even talk of ice floes on the Thames estuary downstream. Decision made. It wouldn't harm to put his head through the door. He turned back and, cutting through Lumber Court, its streets still littered with remains of the morning's fish market, he noticed Bear's barrow lying on its side, its publications scattered everywhere, but with no sign of Bear himself. Thomas walked over to the barrow and saw Bear hidden behind it, curled up and talking to himself quite wildly, trying to strip off his clothes.

Thomas had seen this before. When they'd been climbing through the high Pyrenees in the winter they'd come across some deserters behaving in exactly the same way. An old serjeant who'd served with Moore at Corunna took charge. 'They've gone crazy with the cold,' he'd said. 'They think they're warm. Too warm. They're dying from the cold and when they begin to strip off their clothes the end's in sight. But there is one way we might be able to warm them quickly enough to save their lives …'

Thomas could see that Bear would be dead before he knew it, if he didn't get him warmed up. He stopped, flung his arms round Bear's middle and hauled him, protesting all the way, to The Cock. By now Bear spoke no sense and acted as though Thomas was his bitter enemy, struggling, even trying to bite his arms, until Thomas pulled him, still protesting, into the warmth of The Cock tap-room.

'Please,' he said, 'I need blankets and warming pans, anything to stop him freezing.' The landlady of The Cock looked at Bear's half-naked figure, streaked with dirt and stinking of piss and fish, and began to object.

Thomas searched for some money, handed it over, and then yet more until the landlady finally fetched a couple of old ragged blankets. Thomas braced himself. They had managed to save all but one of the deserters, following the old serjeant's instructions to lie side by side next to the freezing men, wrapped together in as many blankets as they could find. He would have to try and warm Bear that way. He looked around. People were studiously avoiding them, both now stinking after Bear's hours amongst the fish. Thomas wondered what o'clock it was. He looked around. There was clearly nobody else to be persuaded or to be relied upon to do this. Bear, thrashing restlessly about under the blankets, was looking at him, still confused. Thomas would have to make a choice.

He fingered the note in his pocket, hopped from foot to foot with indecision then climbed under the blankets and hugged Bear to him, stopping his thrashing about, but also transferring his own body heat to Bear's almost certainly dying body.

Eventually, exhausted by holding Bear down, he offered some more money to the most ragged of The Cock's customers to take it in turns to revive Bear, but all he received in return were ribald comments. Thomas had never felt quite so ridiculous, but this was the only way he knew to revive the old pamphleteer.

He heard six o'clock chime on the landlady's clock, kept safe in her back parlour. He looked at Bear, who had stopped struggling and seemed to be reviving, but not enough to be left alone, his face flushed pink, and still rambling but less incoherently. And now the landlady's clock was chiming seven. Already too late. Thomas felt the anger of the last months gradually seeping away. He sat up, felt Bear's hands and face and chest, before tucking the blanket firmly around him. He leant his back against a nearby stool, and contemplated the one life he had managed to save. But what to do with him now? Where to take him? Doubtless all his pamphlets would be lost to curious passers-by by now. Probably the barrow itself would have been taken. His life saved but his living lost. Thomas tugged the blanket more closely around him and thought about another time he'd saved a life, when he had clutched, a kicking and screaming, terrified boy about four years old. And the tears finally came.

By eight o'clock he had organised a warm bath for himself and Bear in the landlady's kitchen. But what about clean clothes? Freer was on a late patrol, but his own men would only be standing by in the barracks. He called the pot-boy over and tore a page out of his notebook and gave him careful instructions, payment to follow.

~

Byrne read out Cowper's note. Byrne was to go to Wych Street, then to The Cock, with two sets of clothes, one set for Cowper and one set for a stout man but about the same height, called Bear; and Littlewood was to go straight to the fish market in Lumber Court to salvage what he could of this Bear's belongings.

~

Bear and Thomas, no longer stinking of fish and dressed in clean clothes, were sitting in the landlady's back parlour, Bear still wrapped in blankets but shivering and complaining of being cold. That was a good sign, Thomas remembered, thinking of the freezing deserters.

'You're quite sure Mrs Booth said she'd have him?'

Byrne nodded. ' I told her the clothes were for a man you called Bear that you'd found half-dead on the streets, and she just said,' Isaiah. Isaiah Brown? Best bring him back

389

here. I'll find him somewhere.' Used to be a good friend of her husband's, she said, but then there was some sort of falling-out. So we can take him back there.'

'Not sure he's well enough to go anywhere at the moment.'

Byrne surveyed the kitchen with a critical eye. 'That Mrs Booth keeps a better fire. Come on, let's just get him there. We don't want to be trailing back here again in a hurry. You and me, and Littlethorpe. He must have finished finding the books and things by now.'

Thomas threw more blankets over Bear and guided him to the door, Byrne carrying their dirty clothes wrapped in one of the ragged blankets, and so to Lumber Court, where a triumphant Littlethorpe stood guard over Bear's handcart and stock.

'I was bigger than the skinny bugger who'd claimed it.'

And so the three of them took it in turn to hold on to the still grumbling Bear as they pushed him on the cart back to Wych Street.

Thomas clattered through the door, waking Booth up.

'Sorry, Booth,' Thomas muttered. 'Is your mother still up?'

But Booth just sat on the edge of his bed, seemingly unable to say a word. 'Possibly.' he finally said.

Then Byrne came with Bear, dropping him on the nearest chair, before rushing up to Booth and slapping him on the back.

'Well damn me, if it isn't Enoch bloody Booth.'

'Damn me an' all, Byrne,' was all Booth managed to say.

Byrne smiled at Thomas. 'Sacred Heart Convent.'

79

Cato Street

24 February, 1820, London

Haywood bustled forward. 'The Bow Street runners have apprehended a whole viper's nest of conspirators calling themselves the Spencean Philanthropists. In a hayloft on Cato Street, Marylebone way. Planning to blow up the entire cabinet at dinner. Killed a man.'

Thomas felt his stomach turn over. So this is what the note had meant. So this had been why they wanted his help ... the assassination of the Government ministers? Not drilling peaceful reformers in the skills of self defence.

'There's your so-called reformers for you. Probably friends of that Hunt fellow.'

Who else was involved? Not Griffin and Watson, still in prison for debts incurred after Hunt's grand procession. Carlile, too, in prison for blasphemy. And Wedderburn and Wilde, also for blasphemy. Not Owens, surely. But Thistlewood? And Thistlewood's friend?

Haywood was still talking. 'Damned Coldstream Guards. Arrived too late to help.' He stuck out his chest. 'They should have asked us. We would have been more reliable.'

Captain Haywood was not a happy man. Thomas imagined that his frown expressed disbelief that any right-thinking loyal subject should behave like the French. All of them had heard enough tales about the Terror, how Napoleon had had to restore order. But then he'd made himself Emperor and gone on to conquer the rest of Europe. Until Waterloo.

Thomas tried to look calm. 'I don't expect, sir, they would have wanted soldiers on horseback clattering up the street, sending the conspirators scurrying out the back windows.'

'You're right, of course, Cowper. Leave us to deal with the riots. After all, that might be our next task, if this news gets out and people decide to finish the job. So we are to patrol the streets day and night and to keep the main arteries leading into Westminster free of trouble.'

Thomas quickly decided how best to deploy his men. He wondered how long it would be before the news got out, and whether this would be some kind of signal for other groups to take violent action.

80

Thirty Pieces Of Silver

24 February 1820, The Golden Cross, London

Fallowfield was furious. 'What the hell happened? '

Booth shrugged his shoulders. 'All I know is that he came across this old man, Bear, who was half-dead on the street. And he stopped to help him. That's why he never got to this damn hayloft of yours.'

Fallowfield cursed. 'I was that bloody close to getting him arrested for treason.'

Booth sat back with a quizzical look. 'I know it's a serious enough offence, but drilling reformers isn't treasonable yet, is it?'

Fallowfield thumped the table. 'If he'd only been there in time, he'd have been arrested. Caught up in the plot ...'

'Thistlewood's? Thought you said it was all in his imagination.'

'But enough to get the man and his friends arrested.'

'If they manage to find him. Good man, eh, leading them a fine chase.' Booth grinned and winked.

'Don't you believe in anything, Booth?'

'No point. My father was a believer. And look what happened to him. Why should I lose sleep over ideas, sacrifice myself for ideals and principles that change in passing from one man to another? Give me something solid, like a comfortable bed, a good fire and a pint of strong porter at the end of an evening watching all the believers talk themselves into early graves.'

Fallowfield summoned the serving girl. 'Small ale for me, porter for him.'

'So what do you believe in, Serjeant?' Booth queried.

'Nothing you'd understand, Booth,' Fallowfield replied. 'I place myself in the hands of the Lord and he directs me as he chooses.'

'But who is it that hates Cowper? You, or God?'

'Men like him, weak and insubordinate, aren't fit to be in the army. Not like us born soldiers. We understand the necessity of discipline and sacrifice in the ranks.'

'If you say so.'

The girl brought their drinks. Fallowfield paid and then passed the rest of the money over to Booth. Booth drank rather more than his print colouring occupation allowed for. Fallowfield knew how it was to drink too much. Besides, they'd known each other since the Sacred Heart Convent, that sanctuary full of broken men that the nuns felt bound to try and mend.

Fallowfield tapped his sabretache. He wished he knew for certain that Freer and Cowper would be doomed in this world as well as the next. But on that point God was silent.

81

The Trial

April 1820, London

German's Cottages, Heaviley, Stockport, April 2nd 1820

Dear Cowper,

I write to report upon the trial of Henry Hunt and our other friends who were arrested after Peterloo. It was held in York during the Lent Assizes. We witnesses had a hard time of it but were determined to give every support to Mr Hunt and our friends.

Some of us walked as directly as we could over the Pennines, passing over the great Blackstone Edge, full of peat and tricks and bogs, much as the trial proved to be.

We had arrived in York with great hopes, approaching the walled citadel through the great gate at Micklegate, marching down the hill until we found lodgings in an alehouse next to the river. Mr Hunt was to join us the next day, but to lodge in a coaching inn near the Assembly Rooms. We arrived in the midst of elections and the hustings outside the courthouse gave us much hope that the jury within would be supportive of extending the vote to honest working men.

Mr Hunt conducted his own defence and was very nimble in doing so. Although many witnesses were called who testified that there had been no provocation from the crowd, the jury were much swayed by the accounts of the 'respectable' magistrates, who, with great solemnity, swore that they had saved the nation from untold dangers and harm. We, however, told our story with great regard for truth, and we expected that the jury would be swayed by our honest accounts. It was not to be, as five of the ten accused, Henry Hunt himself, Samuel Bamford, Joseph Healey, Joseph Johnson and John Knight, were found guilty and have been sentenced to prison, their sentences as yet to be decided. Thankfully, the original charge of high treason was commuted to that of seditious conspiracy.

But as I have said, there were many tricks and sleights of hand that made it difficult to put our case simply. This is why lawyers are paid such great amounts of money, it seems.

We are downcast, but not defeated.

Yours, as ever, Samuel Ashby

~

Thomas folded the letter away. He was grateful that he was not to be tried along with Thistlewood and his fellow conspirators at the end of the month. There would be no reprieve this time for the hotheaded men, whose wild dreams led them to imagine they could bring a government down. But they certainly could have brought Thomas down, if he'd hadn't stopped to help Bear. No doubt about it, saving Bear had saved his life.

82

Brought To Account

1 May 1820, Newgate, London

The troops had a long night ahead of them, keeping the crowds behind the barriers, thirty yards or so from the gallows, lest any attempt be made to rescue the prisoners. Haywood had already told them that the Home Secretary had had to dispense with the tradition of drawing the conspirators to the scaffold on hurdles in case they were seized by the crowd. The workmen, too, were busy all night, erecting the scaffolds in front of the windowless brick fortress of Newgate, before raising the great beam that held the nooses across the entire structure, now festooned with black fabric. Then, at last, the execution blocks were put into place, with sacks of sawdust sprinkled all around.

It had been a swift trial, so Captain Haywood said. Ten men found guilty and sentenced to a traitor's death, 'head severed from your body and your body divided into four quarters to be disposed of as His Majesty shall think fit.' Five of them were to be transported for life, the others were to be hanged and beheaded.

As dawn broke Thomas heard birds singing, and Saint Sepulchre tolling its death knell, its tower and churchyard packed to overflowing. He surveyed the scene. Like a throng at a bear baiting, the crowd seethed with anticipation, pushing and shoving to try and get a better view, now the places in the taverns and houses overlooking the scaffold were long gone. The coffee stalls were set up and a great number of other stallholders were noisily plying their wares as though it was St Bartholomew's Fair.

At seven o'clock, Haywood ordered them to stand in reserve. The magistrates read the Riot Act, instructing all present to behave in an orderly fashion. If not, the army would be sent in. Thomas steadied his men and watched for a signal. But the crowd gradually quietened, and when the men were brought out, Thomas noticed that they fell completely silent.

The executioner spent what seemed to Thomas to be an unnecessarily long time tying up the prisoners, the crowd sighing and groaning as each man's noose was tightened in turn, then again falling completely silent as each trapdoor opened. But one drop failed, didn't break the man's neck, and the executioner's assistant was obliged to pull hard on the man's legs.

After half an hour or so, the bodies were cut down and placed in coffins. The time had come to carry out the next part of the sentence. A masked figure burst through the trapdoor, carrying a butcher's knife.

He dragged Thistlewood's body out of its coffin and up to the block. Thomas felt his neck flinch as the executioner brought down the butcher's knife and cut off the head. The executioner held up Thistlewood's head, dripping with blood; he cried three times, 'This is the head of Arthur Thistlewood, a traitor,' the crowd hissing and roaring.

The masked butcher repeated this dramatic performance four more times, but his fingers grown slippery with so much blood, he let slip the last head, dropping it upon the scaffold, which now looked more like a slaughterhouse than a scene of judicial punishment.

As Thomas saw those heads raised, he felt himself gag, saw Quilley's face, the young French officer's, his own, anyone's but the conspirators of Cato Street. And as the people turned away in silence, Thomas wondered if they were seeing their own heads, their own bodies writhing, dragged down by the executioner to ensure their final gasp.

And so, Thomas pondered, the crowd had been treated to the spectacle of misguided men, of whom he had almost been one, paying the price for rage. A rage that could become channelled into unreasonable action. A rage that had gripped Thomas after Boy died.

He suspected too that it had been rage that had driven the yeomanry; to realise that their workers, and those who had nothing, had had the boldness to demand anything at all. Surely one day, he thought, we will be able to see that we have more in common than what divides us.

Even the men that had died today were not so very different from their fellows. He looked round and wondered how many in the crowd sympathised with the men on the scaffold. And what it would take for the crowd to erupt into the shapeless, helpless kind of rage he had witnessed at Badajoz?

Thomas checked his horse. They would be expected to respond. If things got out of hand, it would be up to them to keep the peace, to hold back the rage of others, whilst curbing their own. But how do you do that without destroying these men and women, who now have nothing to lose? How do you demand peace and good behaviour from those who you regard as the enemy?

Thomas looked down to the end of the street, and saw Fallowfield, stern and unyielding, at the head of his small section of men. He remembered the time Fallowfield had taught them to fire their carbines, when Thomas had realised that Fallowfield respected neither his men nor his officers, only himself. He was the only one worthy to dispense justice, the only one able to channel the rage; and now, now he was a God-fearing soldier, Thomas feared him more than ever before. There would be no end to his righteousness.

They said the conspiracy was riddled with spies. Well, at least one of them, Thistlewood's friend, George Edwards with the scrawny fringe. At the very heart of the conspiracy, urging the men on. But how far did these spies go to arrange the entire plot? Far enough to drag an unknown, unimportant soldier into the net, just because they could? Just because it would make a fine example to the rest of the troops? Or was it just someone who really hated him?

Thomas suddenly understood. All Fallowfield needed was a willing messenger. All he needed was someone prepared to accept the pieces of silver. All he needed was a fellow patient recovering from his wounds in the Convent of the Sacred Heart.

List of historical figures mentioned in the book

National reformers
Major John Cartwright
William Cobbett,
Orator Henry Hunt
Sir Charles Wolseley

Writers and theorists
Thomas Paine
Thomas Spence

London based radicals
Richard Carlile and Janet Carlile
Thomas Evans and Janet Evans
Arthur Thistlewood and Susan Thistlewood
Dr James Watson
Robert Wedderburn

Manchester/Stockport based radicals
John Bagguley
Samuel Drummond
'Parson' Joseph Harrison
John Saxton

Peterloo trial defendants found guilty
Henry Hunt
Samuel Bamford

Joseph Healey
Joseph Johnson
John Knight

Military men/politicians
Duke of Wellington
Viscount Combermere

Government/Royalty
Lord Liverpool, Prime Minister
Lord Sidmouth, Home Secretary
Queen Charlotte, wife of George III
George III
The Prince Regent, later George IV
'Queen' Caroline, The Prince Regent's estranged wife

One of the many spies
George Edwards

Acknowledgements

I prefer to use original archive material and a range of secondary sources and not rely on just a few. However, I would like to acknowledge, in particular, those books (and the one website), which I have used more extensively.

https://revjosephharrison.wordpress.com/ for much of the material on Joseph Harrison and his circle.
McCalman, Iain, Radical Underworld, Clarendon Paperbacks, Oxford University Press, 2002.
Marlow, Joyce, The Peterloo Massacre, Ebury Press 2018.
Riding, Jacqueline, The Story of the Manchester Massacre, Peterloo, Head of Zeus Ltd, 2018.

I wish to thank the Centre for Eighteenth Century Studies at the University of York, which hosted a conference on Peterloo in March 2019. Thanks are due to all the participants for their talks and insights and, in particular, to Alison Morgan, Jon Mee and Robert Poole for sharing their many years of experience and knowledge about Peterloo.

The book was completed before the publication of Robert Poole's The English Uprising, Peterloo, Oxford University Press, due in July 2019.

I would also like to thank fellow writers who have read extracts and made helpful comments along the way: Doreen Gurrey, Ged Hemblade, Will Kemp and in particular, Martin Riley for his suggestions at a crucial stage in the book's development; and Carole Bromley, as ever, for her valuable feedback and ongoing support. Also to Peter Coleman, a special thank you for his formidable editing and proof reading skills. Thanks also to Lesley McDowell from Jericho Writers for her helpful report and Janet Senior and Alex Gordon for their generous hospitality during my various research trips to London.

Many thanks also to my cousin, Jill Peters, for her shared interest in our great-great-great grandfather and to Jill and David for their 'research' pictures of the villages in France and Penny Davies, Jane Kasam and other friends who have contributed their knowledge and support during the writing of the book.

Thanks above all to my family, who have had to live patiently with this book for as long as I have.

I am grateful also to the staff at York Publishing Services for their help, advice and skill.